To Mark Weir, It's my pleasure to
offer you a touch of Alternative
History! Hope you like it!

A
Southern Yarn

by

R. W. RICHARDS

"⟨ ⟩" *R. Richards*
11-6-53

Library of Congress Cataloging-in-Publication Data

Richards, Ronald, 1947
    A Southern Yarn/by Ronald Richards
    ISBN 0-9625502-0-5

A SOUTHERN YARN is published *in the United States* by
ROKARN PUBLICATIONS, P.O. Box 195, Nokesville, Virginia, 22123.

First Printing, June 1990
Second Printing, October 1991

PRINTED IN THE UNITED STATES OF AMERICA

Recall now the spring of 1864. The much heralded Ulysses S. Grant has been given complete control of the Union war effort against a weakening Southern Confederacy. He crosses the Rapidan, only to be rebuffed in the Wilderness. Undeterred, he tests Lee's mettle once again at Spotsylvania, and finds the legendary Gray Fox unyielding. Again he swings south, this time finding the rebels solidly entrenched along the North Anna river at an obscure bend called Ox Ford . . .

History records the face-off at Ox Ford as little more than a footnote in the saga of America's Civil War, but to R.W. Richards it becomes the springboard upon which to launch a historical fantasy which Civil War buffs will want to devour. Can you picture Grant surrendering to Lee? Lincoln captured by Mosby? Give your imagination free rein and enjoy this one!

My sincerest thanks to the following individuals who provided invaluable assistance in the preparation of this manuscript:

Meg Tomarchio,
of the Business Support Center
Manassas, Virginia

Sheryl Richards

Donald Lutes

Susan Paddeau

Nancy Willard-Chang,
of Willard Press
Manassas, Virginia

Jeffry Bogart,
Chief Editor
RoKarn Publications

Special Thanks to Nancy Willard-Chang who designed and illustrated the cover.

The author would like to extend his gratitude to Shelby Foote and Douglas Southall Freeman. Their books, *The Civil War* and *R.E. Lee*, a biography, supplied the actual history which this Southerner wove into his yarn.

I would like to dedicate this book to
Robert E. Lee and the brave men who served
in the Army of Northern Virginia.

For Kimberly, Tara and Justin.
No better children could a man ask for.

As we enter the second edition
special thanks are due
to my lady, Lacey,
who stood by me every step of the way
and who did so much
to make this printing possible.

Up until the eleventh of May, 1864, the Battle of Spotsylvania had been going decidedly in favor of the Army of Northern Virginia. Lee's gray-clad veterans were solidly entrenched in the most formidable system of defenses ever seen on the American continent. Time and again had General Grant hurled his own troops against these lines only to see them turned back with terrible losses. The Army of the Potomac had been losing men at three times the rate of their Southern counterparts.

All that changed quickly. R.E. Lee was a brilliant general not many would argue that point. As a tactician and a leader of men there were few who would claim his equal. Yet even the best of men are mortal, and as mortals they are prone to make mistakes from time to time.

On this date, General Lee made such a mistake. For a solid week his men had been in contact with the enemy. The two armies grappled first in the Wilderness where the old Gray Fox managed to teach the cigar-chomping Grant a lesson or two in warfare. When the Union commander disengaged, Lee was a step ahead of him, correctly anticipating both the sidle to his right and its ultimate destination. Thus the Army of the Potomac arrived at Spotsylvania only to find Lee solidly entrenched in its path. Thus began the next round.

In trying to stay ahead of his foe, Lee committed a tactical blunder. He sensed a movement afoot, but he was unsure as to its direction. In his mind Grant was either going to retreat toward Fredericksburg or slide to his right again. In either event he was determined to move his own forces with all possible speed, either to pursue the retreating Federals or to block the next southward thrust.

To the soldiers who manned its systems of trenches and traverses the Salient was known as the "Mule Shoe". The apex of this position, the toe of the shoe as it were, was held by General Edward "Old Clubby" Johnson's division, whose units included the famed Stonewall Brigade, the same men who had won such renown at the First Battle of Manassas.

A SOUTHERN YARN

Supporting these troops were several batteries of artillery, twenty-two guns in all. So that he could gain the fastest possible start, Lee had ordered all the guns removed. Johnson's infantry were capable men, veterans all of them, and as stout as any commander could expect. Unfortunately, from their point of view, they were about to be struck by a full corps of Union infantry. They would be outnumbered at least five to one. They no longer had the support of artillery and in the final analysis, they were only human . . .

Thick, rolling mist clung to the ground in the pre-dawn hours of darkness. Above the occasional cry of a whippoorwill there could be heard a steady drone, at first barely audible, but gradually increasing in volume. Gray-clad soldiers crowded in their trenches, anxious ears tuned to the steadily growing noise at their front. Younger ones among them cast inquisitive glances at their older comrades.

Among the veterans was a sergeant, Seth Reilly by name, known affectionately to his men as the "Professor" — a reference to his pre-war occupation as an instructor of English and Latin at The College of William and Mary. He was a dark-haired, stoutly built man of thirty-five who had served in the Army of Northern Virginia since Lincoln called for volunteers to put down the southern rebellion. Though he had been wounded several times in the course of the war, his only visible scar was a saber slash which started on the left side of his forehead and dropped straight down his face until it disappeared in the thick curls of his beard. He sat on the floor of the trench with his back to the earthen wall, his head cocked slightly as he listened intently to the steadily growing drone in the distance.

Across from Reilly stood Jonas Willem, a young lad who had barely reached his eighteenth birthday. He had only been with the army for six months, and had seen no action at all until the Wilderness. There was trepidation in his eyes as he gazed nervously northward.

"What's that noise, Professor?" he asked finally.

"Boots, boy," returned Reilly. "Thousands of 'em. That's an army on the march."

"I thought as much," said Willem. "You think Lee was right? Are they pullin' out?"

1

"Nope."

"They're not?" Willem stooped low to stare directly into Reilly's face.

"Your ears need a little more trainin', boy. The noise has been growin' for the last half-hour. The Yanks aren't leaving. They're coming this way."

Willem didn't say anything, but Reilly could almost see the lump of fear growing in the boy's throat.

"Stay calm, boy. You're part of the Stonewall Brigade. Never in the course of this war have we failed to hold a position. I don't imagine that'll change today. Now go to your post and wait for orders."

Willem rose and stepped away, but Reilly detected the approach of their company commander, one Captain Kyle Robertson. He quickly climbed to his feet to meet him. A somber expression masked Robertson's face as he stopped just shy of the sergeant, "Howdy, Seth," he nodded.

"Captain," returned Reilly.

"You been listenin'?"

"Hard not to."

"What kind of strength you think they'll throw at us?"

"I make it a corps, maybe a little better."

"That's what I think. We've got our work cut out for us, old friend."

"Nothing we haven't faced before," mused Reilly. "What about the guns? Did Johnson ask for our guns to be sent back?"

"Yeah. The last I heard they were on the way, but I gotta wonder if they'll get here in time. I don't think we have but ten or fifteen more minutes. The Yanks picked a perfect morning to do this. This fog makes a nice smokescreen. I can't see a damn thing."

"Neither can they."

"It'll work far more to their advantage than ours."

Then the captain looked Reilly straight in the eye, "We've been together a long time, Professor."

"So we have."

"This could be it for the both of us."

"If God so wills it," agreed Reilly in his usual stoic fashion.

"Good luck to you," said Robertson as the two clasped arms.

"Same to you, Captain."

"Get your men ready."

Robertson moved off to check on the next platoon. All the while the ominous drone to their front continued to grow in volume.

"All right, fellas!" barked Reilly, "Stand to arms! If you know any prayers, now would be a good time to say 'em! While you're talking to the Almighty, you might put in a little request for our artillery to get back in time."

There was a flurry of activity as his riflemen took their positions on the firing step. Shoulder to shoulder they stood, grimly awaiting the inevitable.

"This dampness has probably ruined your powder charges," explained Reilly. "Change 'em and be quick about it!" He watched patiently as each of his men recharged his musket.

"They're getting closer!" stammered Willem with more than a little fear in his voice.

"No talking!" snapped Reilly. "Fix bayonets and keep your eyes to the front!"

Suddenly, they heard commotion to their rear, horses and caissons, gun crews leaping into action.

"The cannons!" shouted Willem gleefully.

"Not in time!" cursed Reilly. "Look to your front! Stand ready!"

Through the mist they came, tens of thousands, the men of Hancock's corps, the best of Grant's army. The air filled with the deep-chested roar of Union soldiers as they charged pell mell through the dissipating mist.

Those who defended the apex of the "mule-shoe" had time for one quick volley. Effective though it was, it came far too late to stop or even slow the vast wave of blue which engulfed their trenches. Some sections of the line held briefly, but most caved in with the first contact. The sun rose and with the new dawn came a scene of carnage and mass confusion.

Using his bayonet and the butt of his musket, Reilly fought off his attackers with savage fury, but the situation was obviously hopeless. Hole after hole was punched through the Confederate lines, and through these gaps poured a veritable flood of Union infantry. In a brief moment of respite, Reilly stole a glimpse to the rear, wondering what had become of their desperately needed artillery. To his dismay he saw the guns in Union hands. They had arrived just in time to be captured.

From that point, their situation deteriorated rapidly. Union forces gained the Rebel rear in strength, cutting the entire Stonewall Brigade off en masse.

The divisional commander, Edward Johnson, known to his men as "Old Clubby" because of the hickory cane he used, was stumbling about trying to bring order to the confusion, waving his cane wildly, exhorting his men to greater efforts until he suddenly found himself facing dozens of enemy rifles, leaving him no recourse but to surrender.

All around, the story was the same. The Stonewall Brigade was fast passing from existence as one company after another gave up the hopeless fight and surrendered. Reilly was about to order his own men to give it up when Robertson intervened.

"I see a gap!" cried the captain, "This way! Quick!"

"Follow the captain!" echoed Reilly, "Move!"

They ran east some twenty yards then bolted over the rear wall of the trench, joining hordes of other refugees in a desperate dash for the rear. Reilly stopped for a moment and peered back toward the trenches in time to see throngs of bluecoats overwhelm the last defenders and close the gap through which he had just escaped. The Stonewall Brigade had passed into history. In point of fact, thirty minutes of fighting had seen the loss of no fewer than half of Edward

Johnson's division, most of them like their commander, captured. Reilly turned and resumed his flight.

His legs spanned no more than a hundred yards when he came across Robertson. The captain was seated on the ground with his back to a tall maple. A thin trickle of blood oozed from one corner of his mouth and his eyes held the drifting expression which often signals impending death. Reilly knelt by his captain's side and gently touched the dying man's shoulder, "Sir?" he beckoned.

"That you, Seth?" the reply came as a struggling whisper.

"Yessir."

"Get out of here! Get the boys out and keep 'em together!"

"But, Captain . . ."

"Go on, Seth! I'm done for! Go on!" he tried to raise a hand to emphasize his intent, but the effort was too much. His arm dropped limply to the ground and his head lolled over his chest.

Reilly stole a glance at the trenches and saw Union troops forming to continue their advance into the salient. He gripped the dead captain's shoulder for a second, said a brief good-bye and rose to rejoin his comrades.

He found them waiting for him about sixty yards further south. In all there appeared to be over a hundred men clustered together in a stand of cedars and pines. He recognized perhaps fifty from the Stonewall Brigade. The others were stragglers from other units. He saw no officers. Everyone seemed to be looking to him for leadership. With Robertson's last words still fresh on his mind, he fully intended to take charge.

"We can't stay here," he declared firmly. "The Yanks will be here any minute. We'll fall back until we find a sizeable organized resistance to link up with. Let's go!"

Silently they turned south, the bitter taste of defeat fresh in their mouths. Their's was not a fast-paced retreat at first, but soon the Federals closed upon them and Union bullets began nipping at their heels. Quickly they accelerated their pace, and before long they were part of the rout.

Another patch of trees lay ahead of them and into these woods they ran. Although the trees afforded them some degree of shelter, not a man among them was of a mind to stop or even slow his pace.

And still the enemy came, though not so close as they had been when Reilly left the side of his dead captain.

At last it seemed as though they might out-distance their pursuit, but even this possibility was dampened by a final outburst of Federal rifles. Two men convulsed in pain before toppling dead to the ground. A third cried out as a bullet tore through his thigh.

"Professor! I'm hit!" he called as he slumped to the ground with his back to a tall poplar.

Sergeant Seth Reilly wheeled about as those words reached his ears, and saw young Jonas Willem clutching his right leg with both hands. A deep crimson stain was already spreading across his gray uniform. His facial features were locked in fear and pain as he struggled to endure the wound, and his frenzied eyes flashed a desperate message: Don't leave me!

Reilly reacted at once, stepping sideways into the path of another retreating soldier, a mountain of a man from Front Royal, Virginia, known affectionately to his comrades as "Ox". Reilly drove one hand to his chest and stopped the huge fellow in his tracks.

"Give me a hand with Jonas," he growled.

"Professor?" Ox cast an anxious glance back over his shoulder

"I said give me a hand!" snapped the sergeant, and the expression in his steel-gray eyes left no room for argument.

Ox nodded silently and the two men moved at once to the aid of the stricken Willem.

"Grab his musket," instructed Reilly.

"You get it, Professor. Jonas don't weigh nothin'. I'll carry him by myself, you bring the guns."

6

With seemingly effortless motions Ox hoisted the wounded man over his shoulders and started away.

"You hold on boy," he urged, "I'll get ya out of here."

With three muskets cradled in his arms, Reilly fell in behind them. They soon caught up with the others and within a few minutes they appeared to have left the Federals well behind them.

"I don't understand this," huffed Ox as he passed quickly through a broad meadow alive with daisies and bright orange tiger lilies. "Where are they? By all rights they should have overwhelmed us by this time. We ain't movin' that fast."

"You complainin'?" chided Reilly

"Nope, just curious."

"Well, whatever the reason, you best be thankin' your lucky stars. If the Yanks keep takin' their sweet time, we might make it out of here alive!"

*　　　*　　　*　　　*

Robert E. Lee had been downing a sparse breakfast by the dim light of a lantern when the first clamor of battle reached his ears. He knew at once what had taken place. The only question centered on the severity of the blow. Seeking an answer to this query he mounted Traveller and rode north toward the salient. A thousand thoughts raced through his head as he spurred his horse toward the fighting. He knew from the noise that the very center of his line had been struck, but what strength? Had his men held? One factor consistently tugged at his conscience. He had stripped that sector of the line of its guns during the night. Had it been a mistake? The guns had been sent back up, but did they arrive in time?

He found answers to some of these questions when he encountered the first of many fugitives who were still fleeing rearward. He called upon them to stop, trying to impress upon them how badly they were needed by their comrades, but his efforts were largely fruitless. Some rallied by his side,

7

but most kept running, a crazed look of fear seemingly frozen on their faces.

Nearing the base of the salient he came across one of Johnson's staff officers riding to bring him news of the morning's disastrous turn of events.

"What has happened, man?" demanded Lee.

"Bad tidings, General!" stammered the fellow with a hasty salute.

"Save the extra verbiage, sir. What news?"

"They've broken through."

"Where?"

"At the apex. A pre-dawn attack with overwhelming numbers, the entire center of the line is gone."

"Our losses?"

"Heavy, General. 'Old Clubby' and George Stewart were captured. Half the division was taken or shot. They captured the Stonewall Brigade almost to the man."

"Grievous indeed," sighed Lee, momentarily averting his eyes. Each word from the other man's mouth had been like a tiny knife piercing his heart. "The Stonewall Brigade," he repeated softly as memories of the not-so-distant past flooded his mind. Was this the end? Was the Army of Northern Virginia unraveling? If so, the Confederacy was surely doomed.

Determined not to yield to any shred of defeatism, he took a deep breath and regathered his shaken composure: "Come with me," he said to the staff officer. "We will find General Gordon."

They urged their horses very nearly to a full gallop and before long located General John B. Gordon, whose division Lee had posted at the mouth of the mule shoe for the very purpose of forestalling a disaster such as the one which had apparently taken place. Gordon was mounted, and at first did not notice Lee, as he was heavily preoccupied with subordinates and runners.

"General Gordon!" called Lee, beckoning with one hand.

The Georgian spied his commander and immediately

guided his horse to Lee's side, saluting smartly as he reined in.

"What word from the front?" asked Lee. "I've already learned of their initial successes. What are the latest developments?"

We aren't in as bad a shape as it first appeared," explained Gordon. "They overran the apex, but Rodes and Wilcox were both able to refuse their flanks. We're still holding both faces of the salient."

"Good news," nodded Lee. "What about the enemy? In what strength was their attack?"

"Four corps as I understand it. Three directed at the salient. Every assault was repulsed save the one at the apex."

"Who broke through?"

"Hancock . . . from all appearances."

"I thought as much. He's a fine soldier, that one. Stopping him won't be easy, but stop him we must. If your information is correct, his attack has been laterally contained. Well and good, but if he breaks through here he will have cut this army effectively in two. Need I explain the implications any further?"

"No, General. I understand the situation."

"Hancock must be stopped and driven back."

"I've already deployed a brigade as a skirmish line to slow their advance while we ready a counterblow."

"Well done," nodded Lee. "It occurs to me, General Gordon, that for the second time in a week I am laying a great responsibility on your shoulders."

"I've merely had the good fortune to be in the right place at the right time, General. But I'm honored to know you place such faith in me. I'll not fail you."

"I know you won't. Go now, we must chase those people from the salient."

At about this time Sergeant Reilly and his group of survivors, swollen now to more than two hundred, emerged from the woods, having passed through the thin skirmish line established earlier by Gordon. That same line was fast

9

giving ground to the Union advance, which was now nearing the point of its deepest penetration. Upon leaving the woods, Reilly glanced up and spied the two generals in conference not fifty yards away. "Take heart, boys!" he called. "There's Lee with Gordon! They'll find a way to plug this gap."

A murmur of approval rose from the ranks, and the men quickened their pace, not with further retreat in mind, but to link themselves with the counterattack Gordon obviously intended to deliver. They watched as Gordon moved away from Lee, taking up a position near the center of the line between his two brigades.

Gordon rose in his stirrups and glanced up and down the line, making sure that all was ready. He was about to give the signal to charge when he noticed Reilly's group, "Whose men are you?" he called.

"Johnson's," came the reply from Reilly.

"Virginians?"

"Most of us!"

"Attach yourselves to Pegram's brigade, Virginians like yourselves! Prepare to go forward! I'm told we have a little ground to recover!"

"A little," replied Reilly with a chuckle. He turned to his fellow fugitives, "C'mon fellas!" he gestured. "We're back in business!"

As Reilly's men blended into the ranks, Gordon prepared once again to signal the charge. He raised his arm, but hesitated a moment, sensing the presence of someone just behind him. The fury of the battle was drawing even closer. A stray bullet from the woods tore through his coat grazing his skin. He turned and to his horror found General Lee just behind him and to the side. Lee obviously planned to lead the charge himself.

Closer came the fighting, bullets were kicking up little plumes of mud and dirt all around them. Gordon wheeled his mount and confronted the gray-haired Confederate commander.

"General Lee!" he huffed, "This is no place for you! Go

back, General! We will drive them back!"

From Lee there came no reply. He stared resolutely to the front, his jaw firmly set, ready to charge with his soldiers.

Troops from both brigades began to gather around the two horsemen, curious as to the outcome of their confrontation.

Seeking the support of his men, Gordon raised his voice and renewed the challenge, "These men are Virginians and Georgians! They have never failed you! They never will, will you boys?"

"No! No!" the reply sang out from dozens of throats, "General Lee to the rear!" they cried. "Lee to the rear!"

Still there was no response from their commander. Lee sat straight in the saddle, almost as if in a trance, his eyes riveted on the front, apparently determined to take part in their desperate effort to stave off defeat.

Several tense moments slipped by, precious moments, for the enemy was very nearly upon them. Finally, Sergeant Reilly took matters into his own hands. Pushing his way through the crowd he grabbed hold of Traveller's reins, jerked the animal's head around and led him toward the rear through throngs of cheering graybacks.

Gordon wasted not another second. He wheeled about and gave the order to charge, sending his two brigades into the woods to join the third which was already heavily engaged.

Satisfied that he had removed General Lee from harm's way, Reilly stopped and turned to gaze up at the legendary figure who commanded the Army of Northern Virginia. The two men regarded each other in respectful silence. It was Lee who spoke first.

"What is your name, son?" he inquired.

"Reilly, General. Seth Reilly."

"Where are you from?"

"Williamsburg."

"Ah, a most pleasant town, Williamsburg. Did you live near the college?"

"I taught there . . . before the war."

"I see."

Lee turned away, a flicker of sadness appearing in his eyes.

"General?" posed Reilly. "You and I have vastly different roles to play in this affair. Will you return to yours so I can return to mine?"

Lee nodded and dismissed the younger man with a formal salute. As Reilly started back toward the fighting, the General called out to him, "Sergeant, earlier I heard you say you were part of Johnson's division. Which unit?"

"The Stonewall Brigade, General. A few of us escaped after the breakthrough this morning."

"Ah! Jackson's men!" a faint smile crept across the General's face. "You've a proud tradition to uphold!"

"We intend to, General."

"How many of you remain?"

"About fifty, I think."

"God bless you . . . all of you."

"Thank-you, General. Let's hope He does."

Gordon's charge was the turning point of that day's fighting. By all rights, however, it shouldn't have been. He threw three brigades against four divisions. The southern attackers were outnumbered more than three to one. Logically, they should have been decimated. Perhaps in another war in another time they would have been, but this was the Civil War, and these soldiers belonged to the Army of Northern Virginia . . . Lee's men.

The press in the North was forever fond of mocking these soldiers: "half-starved scarecrows" they were frequently called. True, they rarely had enough to eat, and yes, their attire often left a great deal to be desired, but oh could they fight. On this day in particular they left no doubt as to their abilities on the battlefield. Inspired by Lee, led by Gordon, those three brigades hurled themselves into the oncoming ranks of bluecoats and fought with demonic fury. With the first contact they blunted the Union drive, and with unparalleled determination they began to drive it back.

In point of fact, Hancock's initial success was fast waning. The point of advance had lost its sense of direction in the maze of trenches and traverses, and found the terrain confusing. Many of the Federals simply milled about, unsure as to what to do next. More of them continued to pour through the original gap until at last they numbered more than twenty thousand. Unfortunately, from the northern point of view at least, they had lost all sense of military cohesion. They had simply degenerated into a huge mob, packed closely into an area no more than a half mile square. In the face of Gordon's counterattack they fell back in hopeless confusion.

The next stage of the battle was brutally one-sided. So many Union soldiers crammed into such a small area presented a host of irresistible targets. It was almost impossible to miss. Gordon's men drove them like a herd of cattle. The Rebel counterattack was soon reinforced by the remnants of Johnson's division as well as surplus troops from either face of the salient. With this additional strength they were able to drive the Federals all the way back to the original line.

Union resistance stiffened at this point and here began an ordeal which few of its survivors would ever forget. The two sides fought each other at scarcely an arm's length, with only the logs of a single parapet between them. Lee's army had been able to maintain the integrity of its position all along the salient except the apex — the toe of the mule shoe. The Confederate general well knew the danger of allowing an enemy to remain in possession of even a sector of his line. He ordered Gordon to continue his efforts until all the Federal forces had been driven from the rebel position.

This proved impossible. The Union troops were far too numerous and had the extra advantage of a fortified position. Acknowledging the possibility of failure in this task, Lee ordered his engineers to construct a new line of entrenchments across the base of the salient, one-half mile to the rear of the apex.

A SOUTHERN YARN

By noon, an exhausting bloody stalemate had ensued, with neither side able to claim an advantage. In this case, the word stalemate should not be construed as a lull in the fighting. There was no lull. All the day long did the terror and carnage continue. Bayonets and sabers were thrust between logs. Rifle barrels were wedged into tiny slits and gaps then fired. A day-long drizzle had turned the floor of the trenches into a muddy quagmire. A generous effusion of both northern and southern blood was added to the mud throughout the day, creating a thick, slippery scarlet ooze into which the men sank ankle deep.

Over the course of the war, the veterans had lived through many horrifying experiences, but nothing could compare with the "Bloody Angle" at Spotsylvania. As the day wore on, men on both sides would simply give into despair, scrambling to the top of the parapet to fire down upon the enemy, remaining there until they were shot down themselves. Some were driven to insanity by fear or rage. Fatigue reduced the vast majority of the troops to mindless creatures who fought mechanically, with no other purpose but to survive the ordeal.

The coming of the darkness brought little in the way of relief. The intensity of the fighting slackened somewhat, but it did not end.

About an hour after sunset, Seth Reilly slumped to a sitting position in the mud, his back against the rear wall of the trench. His arms and legs were numbed by fatigue. His eyes held a vacant stare, and he found it difficult to keep his mouth closed, as though he no longer had control of his facial muscles. Beside him lay Al Watkins face down in the scarlet mud. The two of them had fought together — and survived every action since First Manassas. Watkins would never fight again.

Reilly took a deep breath, trying desperately to find some vestige of life and strength inside himself. He glanced absently around at those of his men who still remained. All were in the same shape as he . . . utterly exhausted. Time and again he had alerted his superiors to the possibility of total collapse. "The men are spent!" he had argued, but the reply was always the same: "Hold on. Just a little longer. Hold on."

Suddenly he heard a noise, and his survival instincts took control. He rose on shaky feet and readied his Enfield. Someone was approaching from the rear. Moments later, a head and two arms appeared at the edge of the trench. Before the man could make another move he was grabbed by several pairs of hands, hauled over the logs and deposited none too gingerly into the mud. He rolled over cursing, only to find himself face to face with a half-dozen bayonets.

"Easy, fellas," he offered sheepishly. "I'm on your side."

"What unit?" growled Reilly.

"Headquarters. I'm a courier."

One by one the bayonets were pulled away. Reilly helped the soldier to his feet.

"Jesus, God!" hissed the runner as his eyes quickly took in the grisly scene of death and carnage.

"It ain't pretty," muttered Reilly in a voice barely over a whisper. "What's the word from Lee? Keep your voice down. The Yanks are just on the other side of that wall, and they tend to have big ears."

The soldier gulped nervously, and nodded his understanding.

"What word?" repeated Reilly impatiently.

"They say you have to hold on a bit longer. The new fortifications aren't quite ready."

"Hold on?" This came from one of the riflemen, a private by the name of Saunders, "Are they crazy?" He spoke loudly, not caring who might hear. "Do they know what we're goin' through up here? Hell couldn't possibly be any worse than this!"

"Get a grip on it, boy!" snapped Reilly. "And keep your Goddamn voice down!"

"We've been fighting since four-thirty this morning, Professor! How can we hold on any longer? You've seen what's on the other side of that wall! The Yanks are lined up twenty deep in some places! Lee can't ask us to hold out any longer! We've done enough!"

Reilly reached out with one hand, grabbed Saunders by the collar and pulled him close, until the two of them stood nose to nose. "That'll be about enough out of you!" he snarled in a half whisper. "If Lee says we gotta hold on, then we're gonna hold on! Do you hear me?"

Saunders nodded meekly.

"Get back to your post and get a grip on yourself! We need every man!" He released the rifleman and watched carefully as Saunders trudged wearily through the slime to his place at the wall.

"Sergeant," voiced the messenger. "Would you know where I can find Colonel Hammond? I'm supposed to deliver him orders."

"That way," gestured Reilly. "You should find him about thirty or forty yards down the line."

"Thanks," acknowledged the fellow as he turned away.

Moments later gunfire erupted again. One man was killed instantly. Another was wounded, and in his pain leaned against the forward wall for support. A Union bayonet was immediately thrust through a gap between the logs and into his back. He howled out in painful despair, then toppled in a heap to the mud.

"Return their fire!" shouted Reilly, stepping forward wedging the barrel of his rifle into a narrow slit in the logs. He pulled the trigger and heard a scream from the opposite side of the wall. Quickly, he danced away and reloaded. So it went.

The night passed in agonizingly slow fashion. As the hour neared midnight, the level of fighting tapered off all along the line. There were still some exchanges of gunfire now and again, but they were brief and spaced well apart. Both sides appeared content to wait until morning before resuming the slaughter on a grand scale.

Midnight passed. Not long after that, Reilly glanced

around to see Colonel Hammond. "What's up?" he asked, momentarily forgetting all thoughts of military protocol.

"We're pulling out," whispered Hammond. "I just got word from Lee. The new line is ready. Get your men together and move off to the left. Stay together, and for God's sake, stay quiet. If the Yankees get wind of this, we could have serious problems."

"Yessir," nodded Reilly.

"Good luck, Sergeant," said the colonel in parting.

Dawn found the Confederate side of the trenches deserted. The evacuation had been carried out without a hitch. Slowly and quietly the gray-clad soldiers left the front and fell back to the new line at the base of the salient. Here they found newly dug entrenchments strongly fortified with log parapets. A wide band of abatis covered the approach to the line all along its length. Moreover, all of the firepower which had been spread throughout the wings and apex of the salient was firmly packed into this single line. The new position fairly bristled with artillery.

"They'd be crazy to attack this," observed Ox after a cursory appraisal of their new entrenchments.

"They've done crazy things before," replied Reilly. "You remember Fredericksburg?"

"Vividly," grinned Ox as he sat down to catch a few minutes of well-earned sleep.

*   *   *   *

With the first hint of dawn, Union troops poured over the parapets only to find their enemy gone. Only the bloated corpses of the dead remained to greet them. Word was immediately dispatched to the rear and the weary bluecoats advanced no further, preferring to wait and see what might develop.

Ulysses Grant was of no mind to break off contact with the Rebels. The previous day's attack had achieved a spectacular breakthrough, which if followed through would have

17

divided Lee's ragged army cleanly in two. As he listened to the latest reports from the front, one bitter thought kept running through his head: "The war could have been over by this afternoon."

"Runner!" he called.

"Sir?" a fresh faced boy of eighteen quickly presented himself.

"Inform Generals Meade, Hancock, Wright, Burnside and Warren that I wish to meet with them at once."

"Very well, General!" he saluted and quickly departed.

Within thirty minutes his comrades had arrived, and a brief but spirited council of war was underway.

"I understand the Rebels pulled out of the salient last night," said Grant.

"That's right," nodded Hancock.

"Where are they?"

"They've entrenched themselves rather solidly across the base of the salient.

"I see."

Grant stepped to the front of the tent and stared through the open flap. He reached casually inside of his tunic and withdrew a cigar. "What about the rest of their lines?" he asked as he struck a match on the heel of his boot.

"Intact," said Meade. "Lee's not pulling out. He did nothing more than give up the salient."

"Are we going to attack again?" advanced Wright, a little too eagerly.

"Maybe," replied Grant, who then turned to Hancock. "What happened yesterday? You broke through, just as we planned. We had a splendid opportunity to bring the whole affair to a swift conclusion. What happened?"

Hancock sighed audibly and averted his eyes. His tunic was unbuttoned at the neck and he was covered in grime from head to foot. "We broke through," he said. "But things didn't go quite as planned."

"I'm no idiot, General!" stormed Grant. "I know it didn't go as planned! I want to know why!"

"The rebels in the trenches recovered quickly and refused their flanks. They stopped us from sweeping the wings of the salient."

"I can understand that!" fumed Grant, puffing madly on the cigar, chewing the end as though it were some sort of bone. "What I don't understand is why you stopped? You had a clear shot to the Confederate rear! For God's sake! This damn war could be over right now! What happened?"

"We were stopped," sighed Hancock somewhat petulantly.

"By what?"

"Lee had some people in reserve. They counterattacked."

"In what strength?"

At this Hancock hesitated, glancing down at the ground as though he were groping for words.

"In what strength, General?" pressed Grant.

Hancock took a deep breath, raised his eyes and offered the following answer: "I'm not entirely sure. I can only offer a guess based on the information which was brought back to me."

"Let's hear it."

"Three brigades."

"Three brigades?"

"As near as we can determine."

"You were stopped by three brigades?"

"What their counterattack lacked in numbers, they made up for in ferocity."

"I shouldn't wonder!" huffed Grant. "You had twenty thousand men! Three understaffed Rebel brigades would have been outnumbered four or five to one! They are the ones who should have been overrun!"

"It didn't work that way, General Grant. No one is more sorry than I."

"I'm not blaming you, Hancock," offered Grant quickly. "You're a damn good soldier. I just can't help being frustrated, that's all."

19

A SOUTHERN YARN

"Now you see what we've been up against for the last couple of years," remarked Meade. "Lee's no easy nut to crack."

"Never mind Lee!" snapped Grant. "He's no superman! He puts his pants on every morning one leg at a time, the same as you and I! He's a good one, no question of that, but there's no point in deifying him. He's no God! He can be beaten! You proved that yourself at Gettysburg, George, or have you forgotten?"

"No," demurred Meade, "I haven't forgotten."

"Good! See that you don't."

Grant began to pace back and forth across the width of the tent. "Frustrating," he muttered to himself more than anyone else. "I'm trying to figure out what we have to show for ten days of constant fighting."

"A lot of casualties," noted Warren in a wry tone of voice.

"I know what our losses are, thank you!" snarled Grant. "I also know that the Rebs are taking a beating, and they can't replace their losses! We can!"

"All of us understand the arithmetic," argued Meade. "What about today? Do you plan to attack again?"

Grant shifted his cigar from one corner of his mouth to the other and peered out into the dull gray drizzle which had been falling for more than twenty-four hours, "This has the look of an all day rain," he grunted.

"So it does," concurred Meade.

"So close," muttered the Union commander. "We came so close to breaking that army in half."

"What are your orders?"

"They're whipped. I know they are. I can feel it. No one's ever pounded them like we have in the last week. Did you notice how Lee stays behind his fortifications? He hasn't the strength to take the offensive against us and he knows it!" He clenched his right hand into a fist and swung it as if directing it toward the chin of an imaginary foe.

"Your orders, General?"

"I want one more crack at them," he declared, calming

20

himself by puffing stoically on the cigar. "One more, but not today, not in this muck. We'll stand in place for a couple of days, if the weather improves we'll attack. In the meantime we can decide where to deliver the next blow. That's all I have to say at the moment, gentlemen. If you'll excuse me, I must communicate with Washington." He stepped out into the rain and within moments he was gone.

One by one his generals followed suit, until only Meade and Hancock remained. For long moments the latter studied the face of the man who had defeated Lee at Gettysburg. "You're looking rather pensive, George," he advanced.

"Am I?" Meade cleared his throat and turned away, glancing uneasily into the rain.

"I can always tell when you're worried. Those furrows above your eyes start resembling valleys. What's troubling you?"

Meade sighed audibly and dropped his gaze to the rain-spattered mud. "I guess I don't entirely share his optimistic view of the situation. Lee doesn't seem beaten to me, nor does his army. What do you think?"

For several moments Hancock pondered his reply, carefully weighing his words, "That counterattack in the salient was boldly led and fiercely delivered. He's right about one thing; the Rebs have taken a pounding, but I think I may have to agree with what you're saying. Lee and his soldiers are a lot more resilient than Grant realizes."

"That's what worries me."

"Don't let it weigh you down too much, George. Grant's a fighter. I think Abe's finally found a match for Bobby Lee."

"That seems to be the consensus of opinion," nodded Meade. "But I wonder if anyone bothered to tell Lee. I'm inclined to believe he has other plans, and our new commander would do well not to take him lightly."

"Relax, George."

Hancock clasped the other man's shoulder with a firm hand and stepped past him out into the rain, "He'll learn soon enough." He moved off several paces before Meade's final words reached his ears.

"At what cost?"

Hancock stopped, slowly turning his head until his eyes met those of Meade. The two stared at one another for a short spell, but not another word passed between them.

*   *   *   *

The thirteenth of May passed without incident, the armies content to rest in place, both somewhat numbed by the previous day's carnage. Union forces didn't even bother to occupy the abandoned perimeter trenches of the mule-shoe. On the southern side, the shock of battle was compounded by the reception of sobering news. Jeb Stuart, the legendary hero of the Confederate cavalry had been mortally wounded in battle at an obscure place called Yellow Tavern, not far from Richmond. He died in the capital several hours later. Lee wept when word of Stuart's death reached him.

By noon of the thirteenth, it was apparent there would be no Union thrust. Weary Rebel soldiers were permitted to stand down for the first time in days. Seth Reilly sat on the floor of the newly dug trench, his head slumped forward, arms wrapped about his raised knees.

"Sergeant?"

He raised his head and gazed wearily toward the source of the voice. He didn't recognize the face, but he saw the bars of a captain on his shoulders. Slowly, he climbed to his feet and offered a meek excuse for a salute.

"You're Sergeant Reilly?"

"Yessir."

"Captain Hennessy, Division Headquarters."

"Pleased, I'm sure."

"We've just received a dispatch from General Lee. He wanted to know if you were still alive and how many of your men remain."

"I'm still kickin', Captain. A little mortified I think, but alive nonetheless."

"Your men?"

"Twenty, there's twenty of us left. Would you tell General Lee we were honored that he asked about us?"

"You may get that chance yourself. He sent a furlough for you and your boys. Ya'll can move to the rear for a while. God knows you've earned it."

"Thank you, Captain."

Reilly took the written orders from the officer's hand.

A short time later, Reilly and his orphaned infantrymen found themselves a secluded stand of willows and cedars in which to recline and hide momentarily from the horrors of war. A narrow creek of clean fresh water meandered through the trees, and to the man they drank greedily. Having taken their fill, they lounged on the damp ground, some to fall asleep, others to occupy themselves swapping tales.

"Whitt?" Reilly called, addressing himself to Corporal Simmons.

"Yo, Professor?"

"Take care of the boys will ya? I want to check on Jonas."

"Go ahead, Professor. We ain't goin' no place."

"I'll be back before long."

"Take your time. Give Jonas my best, hear?"

The surgeon's tents were only a twenty minute walk, but Reilly took his time, arriving at the field hospital some thirty-five minutes after leaving the other survivors of Jackson's old brigade. The sergeant was a veteran. Three years of war had done much to harden his senses to carnage and death. Yet despite his years of experience, the sight of the crude southern medical facilities turned his stomach. Several tattered canvas tents provided shelter for the wounded and those who toiled in their behalf. Reilly stopped outside the main tent, took a deep breath to control the contents of his stomach, and started his search.

If nothing else, Spotsylvania had generated more than its share of business for the medical practitioners. Beside one tent, several dozen wounded men lay in the open waiting for treatment, among them a number of Union prisoners. Just beyond another shelter lay rows of neatly arranged corpses awaiting the burial teams. Perhaps most disturbing of all were the bushel baskets brimming with freshly amputated arms and legs. Reilly shuddered and averted his eyes. He said a quiet prayer in hopes that Willem's leg was not in one of those baskets. He spied two stretcher bearers carrying a wounded soldier toward the surgeon's tent.

"Pard' me," he called.

The two men stopped, "Be quick, Sergeant," snapped the first impatiently. "We haven't got all day."

"I understand. One of my men was brought here yesterday morning with a leg wound. You know where I could find him?"

"Yesterday mornin'? If he's still alive, you might find him in one of the recovery tents. Those three over there on the left."

"Much obliged," replied Reilly.

The stretcher bearer nodded, glanced back at his companion, and they resumed their brief trek.

Reilly walked to the recovery tents, stealing a glance inside one, but not entering. Men were moaning in pain, and there seemed to be a lot of confusion in one tent; doctors and nurses shouting at one another and darting here and there with no apparent rhyme or reason. He stepped away, moving to the entrance of the third tent. Things appeared more calm here, although several wounded soldiers were vocally venting their anguish. Reilly stood quietly at the entrance of the tent for several minutes until finally he was approached by a nurse whose clothing was heavily stained in crimson.

"Are you hurt, Sergeant?" she asked wearily, wiping sweat from her forehead with one sleeve.

"Me? No ma'am," stammered Reilly. "Actually, I came here to find someone. One of my men."

"When was he brought in?"

"Yesterday morning . . . leg wound . . . thigh . . . left thigh."

"I've seen more than I care to remember."

"I imagine so."

He glanced away uneasily, "He's a young fella . . . seventeen, maybe eighteen. Sort of blond hair, kinda long."

"Does he have a name, Sergeant?"

"Name? Oh yeah, Willem . . . Jonas Willem. He's a private with the Stonewall Brigade."

"I see. Will you wait here? I'll check our log."

"Yes, ma'am. I appreciate your help."

She returned several minutes later, and Reilly could read only positive news on her expression.

"He's fine, Sergeant," she smiled. "You should find him all the way in the corner, down there on the right side. I can't give you an exact cot number, the men get moved so often, but he's down in that corner. The doctor says he should have a complete recovery."

"Great! beamed Reilly with a broad grin. "That's definitely good news. I'm much obliged."

"Think nothing of it, Sergeant."

She started to pat his arm, but resisted the impulse, not wanting to touch his uniform, caked as it was in scarlet mud. "Go ahead, Sergeant," she urged, "But don't stay too long. These men need their rest badly."

"Thank you again," said Reilly, tipping his ragged cap in salute.

He found Willem on the fourth cot from the end of the row, "Howdy, boy!" he greeted. "Good to see you've still got two legs."

"Professor! You're still breathin'!" Willem's face came alive with smiles.

"Either that or you're talkin' to one hell of a ghost! How ya doin'?" He clasped the lad's right hand.

"Pretty fair. My leg ain't hurt as bad as I first thought. At least they didn't have to cut it off."

"You best be thankin' your lucky stars! How long are you going to be laid up?"

"They tell me three or four weeks. I'm supposed to be

headin' for Richmond with some of the others later this afternoon."

"Do tell? Reckon I got here just in time, eh?"

"I reckon. I heard we knocked 'em out of the mule-shoe. That so?"

"Yep. Kept 'em out too, but it was the worst fight I've ever been in. I pray to God we never see anything like it again."

"How'd you get leave?"

"We pulled back to a new line across the base of the salient last night. Lee, himself, wrote a furlough for the whole unit."

"No kiddin'? Lee did that? How'd we rate?"

"Long story, Jonas. Let's just say we earned it."

"Professor?" Some of the enthusiasm faded from Willem's young face, "How many of us are left?"

Reilly glanced away and hesitated several moments before he could reply, "Countin' you . . . twenty-one."

"Good lord!" whispered Jonas. "The whole brigade!"

"Try to look at the bright side, Jonas. Most of the boys were taken prisoner in that first rush. If they can endure Yankee prison camps at least they'll have a shot at livin' through this war. That's more than I can say for the rest of us."

"Could be, Professor. Could well be."

"Listen, young fella, I've got to get back to the boys. You take good care of yourself, hear? Take five or six weeks if you need it. Understand?"

"Whatever you say, Professor."

The two shook hands one last time but as Reilly turned to leave, the wounded soldier called after him.

"Professor?"

"Yes, Jonas?" The sergeant quickly turned back around.

"You know, I never did learn to read or write or nothin' like that."

"Nothing to be ashamed of Jonas. The land has been your education, and not a bad one at all."

"I know that. I got no regrets. It's just that . . . well . . . I'd sort of like to let my folks know what happened and that I'm not dead or nothin'. I want 'em to know what happened."

"Are you trying to ask me to write them a letter?"

"Would you?"

"My pleasure. Can you give me the address?"

"Just send it to Caleb Willem, New Oak Farm, Galax, Virginia."

"Gotcha."

"One more thing, Professor."

"What's that?"

"When you tell 'em about me gettin' wounded, do you think you could fudge a little, maybe make it sound like I got hit when we were attackin', instead of runnin'?"

"I suppose I could arrange something along those lines," grinned Reilly.

"I'd be much obliged."

"Think nothin' of it. Get well boy, and go easy on the girls down in Richmond. I don't think they're quite ready for the likes of you."

Outside the tent, Reilly paused momentarily. He took a quick look at the row of bodies lying uncovered in the early afternoon rain, "Thank God you're not one of them, Jonas," he muttered, then he started back to rejoin those who remained of the Stonewall Brigade.

He was lost in his own thoughts when he entered the stand of woods which sheltered his men. Several greetings were passed his way, but he seemed not to hear them. A small fire was burning and there was a pile of wood stacked nearby drying in the heat of the flames. A pot with a crude concoction passing for coffee was brewing, and he was drawn to the odd blend of aromas which drifted through the misty air. He sat down next to the fire and proceeded to pour himself a cup.

"Jonas OK, Professor?"

"Yep. He didn't lose the leg. Looks like he'll be fine.

27

He'll be on his way to Richmond before the day is out."

"That's good, Sarge. That's real good."

"Yep. He wants me to write his folks, let 'em know what happened."

"You're the man to do it."

"I suppose. I'll take care of it later."

"You weren't payin' much attention when you came in, Professor. You didn't see our new recruit."

Reilly gave his corporal a puzzled look, "Recruit?"

"Over there," gestured Simmons.

The sergeant turned until he spied a young boy sitting among the veterans near the bank of the creek. "We don't need another drummer boy," he growled. "We don't even have a drum."

"He wants to be a soldier."

Reilly whirled about and glared angrily at the corporal, "Are you joking? He's a kid! He should be home milking cows with his mother!"

"His ma's dead, Professor. He's an orphan. He wandered in here shortly after you left. Says he's ready to fight Yankees."

"Be serious, Whitt! He can't be more than twelve years old."

"Claims he's fourteen."

"In a pig's eye! What'd you tell him?"

"Told him to sit tight till you got back."

"Damn!" hissed Reilly. "You probably encouraged him. You should have just sent him packing."

"Where? He's got nowhere to go. He's an orphan. Besides, I've heard rumors they'll soon be drafting fifteen year olds. So I told him to hang around."

"He's nowhere near fifteen!"

"The guys have already grown kind of fond of him, and you should see how well he can shoot a rifle."

"Are you trying to put me on, Whitt? You can't be serious! Are you really trying to talk me into this?"

"He's got nowhere to go, Seth," demurred Simmons in

28

an apologetic tone. "Why don't you just talk to him?"

"I don't believe this." Reilly turned away and stared angrily at the swift flowing waters of the creek. "What's his name?" he asked several moments later.

"Cody Wilder."

"Call him over here."

"Right."

Simmons rose to his feet, "Hey, Cody! C'mon over here, boy!"

The lad quickly presented himself, flanked on all sides by battle-hardened veterans.

"This here's our sergeant," said Whitt. "He goes by the name of Seth Reilly, but we call him Professor."

Young Wilder offered an awkward salute, "Pleased to meetcha, Perfessor," he said in his deepest voice.

"That's Professor," corrected Reilly.

"Yessuh, Professor," repeated the newcomer.

"Stand easy, boy," chuckled Reilly. "You're not in this man's army just yet."

As he spoke he conducted a cursory appraisal of the lad. He saw a typical farm boy, tall for his age, several inches over five feet, and lean. His reddish-blond hair was a mass of unmanageable curls which all but covered his forehead.

"How old are you, Cody?"

The boy cleared his throat, doing his best to maintain a deep voice, "Fifteen, suh."

"You don't need to call me sir, I'm only a sergeant, and if you're fifteen, I'm sixty. How old are you, boy? And don't you lie to me again!"

"Uh . . . fourteen," stammered Cody.

"You're lying again."

"Um . . . I'll be fourteen pretty soon."

"How soon?"

"Next fall . . . in October."

"Jesus, God!" hissed Reilly, turning away. "He's a child!"

"I'm not either!" snapped Cody boldly. "I wanna fight! I can shoot better 'n anybody here!"

29

Reilly glared at the boy, who refused to flinch.

"I got nowhere to go," declared the lad.

"He's got grit," noted Simmons.

"He's too damn young," growled Reilly, thinking of his oldest son, William, who had just turned twelve.

"Tell the sergeant why you're here, Cody."

Wilder nodded, then looked Reilly square in the eye. "My pa was killed up in Maryland at Sharpsburg," he explained. "Fever took my little brother about a year ago. Me and ma worked the farm together as best we could till a few weeks ago. Yankee cavalry showed up and burned everything. Ma tried to stop 'em from torchin' our house. One of 'em kicked her down. She hit her head on a fence rail. She never woke up. I got her into Staunton, but there wasn't nothin' anybody could do. She died. I buried her and started east. I'm gonna join Lee's army."

"You came here from the Shenandoah?"

"Yep."

"Alone? On foot?"

"Yessuh . . . I mean, Sergeant."

"I told you, Seth," smiled Simmons. "He's got grit."

"I should say!" chuckled Reilly.

"What do you say, Professor?" called one of the men. "Can we keep him?"

"How about it, Sarge?"

"Quiet!" snapped Reilly. "Listen to yourselves! You act like we're talkin' about a lost puppy or somethin'! He's only a boy!"

"Well," offered one. "He's sort of like a lost pup. He's got no kin and no home."

"That's right!" argued Cody. "I got no family left and no place to go! I got a score to settle with the Yankees and I plan to settle it!"

"You must have some family somewhere," insisted Reilly. "Aunts . . . Uncles?"

"A few. They're down south of Danville, but I ain't goin' there. I'm gonna fight. If you fellers don't want me, I'll find another bunch!"

"C'mon, Seth," urged Simmons. "Think about it. We can probably take better care of him than anybody else. Give him a chance."

Reilly sighed in exasperation, taking off his cap and scratching his head.

"These fellers tell me you're part of the Stonewall Brigade," advanced the lad. "That true?"

"Part of it?" returned Reilly as his eyes wandered over the small band of survivors. "I'm afraid we are the Stonewall Brigade . . . all that's left of it. Look at us, boy! Were all that's left of a damn fine group of men. Look at our uniforms! Blood and mud! We haven't had a chance to clean ourselves yet! It's a good thing you didn't get here two days ago, kid. You missed a big one! Dear Lord, you don't even know what war is!"

"I've seen what war is," replied Wilder calmly.

Reilly stared quietly at him for several moments before making any reply. "I guess you have," he breathed at last. "Listen, they tell me you can shoot."

"Better 'n anybody back home."

"Let's go out in that field and see what you can do."

They moved out into the open, Reilly, Simmons, the boy and the remnants of the Stonewall Brigade.

"What'll we use for a target?" Simmons wondered aloud.

"I see one," said Wilder, pointing to a thin sapling off in the distance.

"Are you kidding?" joked Reilly. "You don't really think you can hit that do you?"

"Yep."

"Give him a musket, Whitt. Let's see what he can do."

Simmons handed over his Enfield and ammo pouch. "You'll have to load it."

Wilder placed the butt of the rifle on the ground and went to work.

"This is ridiculous!" laughed Reilly. "The damn rifle's bigger than he is!"

31

"Just watch," urged Simmons.

Having loaded the gun, Cody took his stance, gauged the range and wind factor, then took aim. He took one deep breath and kept it. He held the rifle perfectly still, not quivering the slightest. Then he pulled the trigger, not reacting at all to the noise or the kick.

Reilly quickly turned his eyes from Cody to the sapling, and his jaw dropped as he watched the bullet cut clean through the upper part of the trunk, severing the top three or four feet.

"Good Lord," gasped the sergeant.

"Can you imagine what he could do with a Whitworth?" probed Simmons.

"Unbelieveable," muttered Reilly.

"Can I stay?" pressed Wilder.

"I reckon so," relented Reilly. "If you're bound and determined to do this, you may as well do it with us."

"Thank you, Perfessor!" grinned the boy.

"That's Professor! If you're going to hang around you better learn to say it right!"

"Yessuh, Professor!"

"Whitt, take him on up to the quartermaster. Get him outfitted and take care of whatever paperwork they want done."

"Will do, Sergeant. C'mon, Cody. Let's turn you into a soldier, eh?"

"Sounds good," laughed Wilder. "Sounds real good."

Reilly watched them as they disappeared in the direction of the supply depots. Once again, the image of his own boys came to mind and he swallowed heavily to subdue the lump forming in his throat. "God forbid this war lasts long enough to draw them into it," he whispered.

*　　*　　*　　*

Rain continued into the fourteenth, but Grant opted for a shift of troops from his extreme right to his left, in effect doubling the weight which could be thrown at Lee's right. The march bogged down in a morass of mud and was so badly delayed he had no choice but to abort it.

The fifteenth brought no relief from the rain, but Grant decided to shift those who had been moved left back to the right, reasoning that Lee would have weakened his own left to respond to the movements of the fourteenth. However, even in this decision he hedged, choosing instead to concentrate two full corps on the Confederate center. As soon as the weather allowed, Wright and Hancock together would storm straight down the mule-shoe in the hopes of breaking Lee's newly constructed line and dividing his army in two.

There was no rain on the sixteenth, nor any noticeable contact between the two armies. The seventeenth was virtually cloudless. Dazzling blue skies blanketed most of central Virginia, and the glaring heat of the sun reminded many of July and early August.

*　　*　　*　　*

"Hey, Professor!" cried Ox. "Come on out of those woods! It's a beautiful day! It's like summer out here!"

Reilly yawned sleepily and stretched his arms overhead. The brilliant light of the mid-morning sun filtered lazily through the fresh green foliage of the trees, casting an aura of warmth and life all along both banks of the creek. A pair of cardinals squawked noisily at one another as they cavorted playfully through the trees, proudly displaying their bright red plumage for any who cared to see.

"It's spring, Professor," remarked Buck Randall, a private from Rockingham County, Virginia.

"Sure is, Buck," smiled the sergeant in reply, "I gotta admit, it feels good."

"You know what this means, don't you?" posed Simmons.

Reilly nodded somewhat solemnly. "If it stays like this all day, the ground will dry. That means the Yanks will probably

33

have another go at us, probably tomorrow. I guess this means the end of our furlough. They'll expect us back on the line by nightfall."

"We could all be dead by tomorrow afternoon," noted Randall.

"Possibly," admitted Reilly. "But I don't think I want to look quite that far ahead. Whatever happens tomorrow is going to happen. We still have today, and we're still on furlough. I don't know about you guys, but I intend to enjoy this day to the fullest. For starters, I'm going to wash the mud and blood off of me and this uniform." He began to unbutton his tunic, "Anyone care to join me?"

"Sounds pretty reasonable to me," nodded Simmons.

Before long all of them were stark naked, frolicking like a bunch of school boys in the cold, clean waters of the creek. The war seemed a thousand miles away as they hooted and howled, splashing one another mercilessly. By late afternoon, they were played out, and they lounged easily in the weeds and wildflowers along the creekbank, drying themselves and their ragged but slightly cleaner uniforms. After downing their evening rations they broke camp, packed their gear and started back to the front lines.

The sun had set by the time they reached the trenches and the whole region was bathed in the faint glow of twilight. Young Wilder was fascinated by everything he saw, the soldiers, trenches, parapets, and especially the guns.

"What's all that stuff out there?" he asked eagerly as he gazed through a firing slit in the parapet.
"It's called abatis," explained Reilly. "We put it there to impede the momentum of a charge."

"What?"

"It slows the Yankees down a bit. They have to pause to knock it all out of the way. It gives us time to shoot a few more of 'em before they reach our lines."

"I get it," nodded Wilder.

"Hey, fellers!" cried a burly loudmouth from one of Gordon's brigades. "Since when did you take to robbin' the cradle? What nursery did you find him in?"

Actually the sight of the young lad in the ranks of the infantry wasn't too unusual, but some of the older men couldn't resist getting their jibes in from time to time.

"Shut up, Watson!" barked Randall.

"Hey, Watson!" taunted Ox. "I got three Yankee dollars in my pocket says this boy can outshoot anybody in your outfit!"

"Yankee dollars, eh?" came the reply.

"Yep! Three of 'em! You game?"

"Anybody? Even Hennessy?"

"In a heartbeat! You on?"

"I don't know, Ox. I ain't got any Yankee money!"

"Well, if you come across any, let me know, hear? In the meantime, shut the hell up!"

*   *   *   *

The skies remained clear throughout the night and there wasn't much of a moon to speak of so the men of both armies had an open view of countless dazzling stars. Conversation on both sides centered mostly on the attack everybody anticipated in the morning. On the Confederate side the main question was where the blow would land. Reilly's group argued for two hours over this before sleep brought an end to it. Some believed the Federals would charge straight down the salient just as they had done before, but most disagreed. These men argued that Grant would be foolish to attempt the salient a second time. He would storm the left, or possibly the right, but surely not the center.

The same questions were going through the mind of Robert E. Lee that night, but he was not forced to stab in the dark for answers. The reason for this was very simple, he still had the bulk of his cavalry. When Stuart left to keep his appointment with destiny at Yellow Tavern, he took but a third of the cavalry. This left the Confederate commander with plenty of troopers to serve as eyes and ears. As a result, he was able to detect and analyze each of Grant's movements almost as soon as they were underway. Grant, on the other hand, had dispatched almost all of his cavalry on Sheridan's raid, leaving himself to grope in virtual blindness about the Virginia countryside.

Having studied all of his scouting reports, Lee couldn't help but come to one conclusion: Grant would strike his center again. Two full corps of Union infantry were poised to make the attack. Accordingly, he made his preparations and strengthened his newly constructed fortifications. His infantry on this sector of the line were further braced by twenty-nine pieces of artillery commanded by General Ewell's ordnance officer.

On the opposite side of the affair preparations were every bit as intensive. It couldn't be said that morale was at an all time high, but on the other hand it certainly wasn't bad. From the general staff meetings all the way down to platoon size pep talks, one theme dominated: Lee's line can be broken, his army can be torn in two, and the respective pieces readily gobbled up by Union troops who were hungry for victory. If sufficiently pressed, one healthy charge could conceivably bring the long war to its final conclusion. As the first tentative hint of dawn peeked over the eastern horizon, thousands of bluecoats moved into jump-off positions, convinced that victory might finally be at hand.

Not long after sunrise, lookouts posted in a church tower confirmed what Lee's mounted reconnaissance had already told him. The Federals were coming straight down his center. Tens of thousands of Union bayonets were gleaming in the early morning sun. Close to thirty-thousand men would be pouring over the mouth of the salient.

The order was quickly passed to the men who held the center: "Stand ready! They're on their way!"

The gray-clad riflemen could hardly believe their good fortune. Incredibly, their antagonists in blue were about to hurl themselves into the strongest segment of the Confederate line.

"This'll be easier than Fredericksburg," remarked one.

"It'll be more like Gettysburg," said another. "Cemetery Ridge in reverse."

"Well, boy," said Corporal Simmons to Cody Wilder. "You're about to get your first taste of soldierin'."

"I can handle it," he boasted in reply, and in truth he didn't appear at all nervous.

Sergeant Reilly stopped briefly as he made his rounds among the men. "Whitt," he directed. "You take care of this kid, hear? Don't let him do anything stupid, okay?"

"No problem, Professor. I'll watch over him."

"Good. Cody, you stick close to the corporal, understand? He's been around a long time. He can teach you a lot. Pay attention to him."

"Yessuh, Perfessor."

"What's that?"

"Professor . . . Professor," he pronounced.

"Keep workin' on it," chuckled Reilly. "You'll get it right sooner or later."

The lad quickly returned his smile, then focused his attention back on the front.

"By the way, boy," said Whitt. "The Enfield has an effective range of about eight hundred yards, but there's no need to waste ammo trying to prove it. Don't fire till we do, hear?"

"Yessuh."

*   *   *   *

The original timetable called for the Union thrust to begin at eight o'clock in the morning. However, the whole affair started off badly from the outset. Despite the fact that the rebel trenches along the face of the salient had been abandoned for days, Grant's men did not seize them, preferring to remain just to their north. These abandoned fortifications proved to be far more of an obstacle than anybody realized. Essentially, they were a complex maze of trenches, counter-trenches, traverses and parapets. Two hours were

37

lost before the assault force was able to pass through these lines and reform for the charge. By that time, the hope of achieving surprise was totally lost.

Once clear of the trenches, the two corps of Union infantry formed their battle lines and started forward. With their many flags flying boldly in the morning breeze, and their bands filling the air with martial music, these brave men made for a grand spectacle. Line after line of blue, stretching as far as the eye could see, bore down through the very mouth of the salient intent on breaking the Rebel line.

In that line every grayback stood ready, watching in solemn silence as the many waves of blue drew closer.

*   *   *   *

"My, but them Yankees always make for a pretty sight," remarked Ox, "Almost like they was on parade."

"Lookin' pretty don't win battles," said Hal Saunders.

No matter how smart they looked, General Ewell fully intended to wreck these advancing lines of Federals before they ever reached his own infantry. With twenty-nine pieces of artillery at his disposal he certainly had the firepower to realize these intentions, and he wasted no time in doing just that. No sooner did the attack get underway in earnest than he opened fire with long range shots.

The impact of this barrage was immediate. Shell after shell crashed into the Union ranks and exploded with devastating fury. Widening gaps were soon apparent in the first two lines. The Rebel gunners continued their work at a frenzied pace, giving the Federals no respite whatsoever. Quickly a wispy cloud of blue smoke took shape and drifted lazily across the field of battle, stinging the nostrils of Yank and Reb alike.

As the attack drew closer, Ewell gave the order to switch from shot to canister; deadly ammunition specifically designed to shred flesh from bone. The Federal infantry suffered horribly with the first volley, and their wounds grew more terrible with each succeeding round.

"Get ready, kid!" ordered Simmons. "It's our turn!"

"Volley fire . . . present!" from a hundred throats the order rang out.

"Fire!"

The entire Confederate line exploded in a wall of musket fire every bit as effective as the canister which spewed forth from the cannons. The first two lines of Union infantry were utterly decimated. The next two were not in much better condition, but at last they reached that abatis. They tried feverishly to dismantle these obstacles, but the Rebel fire was far too intense. No one could long endure it.

For several minutes they continued the effort, but soon their officers realized the utter hopelessness of achieving any success against such a defense. The order to retreat was quickly given and gladly received. Leaving nearly a third of their comrades dead or wounded on the field, the two Federal corps bid a hasty retreat.

Nowhere along the lines had a single Union soldier actually reached the Confederate fortifications. In no instance was there a need for a soldier on either side to use his bayonet.

"Cease fire!" came the command from the rebel line, and their guns fell mercifully silent.

"Why are we stoppin'?" wondered Cody. "They're still in range, we can knock off a bunch of 'em!"

Simmons looked patiently at the boy before making his reply, "Number one, there's no honor in shooting somebody in the back. Number two, this army can't afford to squander ammo. We'll need it if they try us again."

They didn't. In point of fact, they had just suffered the absolute worst wounds of the campaign. More than eight thousand Federal soldiers fell in that charge without a single one reaching the Rebel parapet. Grant had wanted one more crack at Lee. He got it. His men paid the price.

"Everybody okay?" quizzed Reilly, moving up and down the line to check his troops. As it was, there wasn't a serious wound among them. In truth, the last day of the battle took very few Confederate lives. Lee's victory was about as lop-sided as anyone might hope for.

*   *   *   *

So ended the battle of Spotsylvania, an ordeal for both sides which lasted more than a week. Grant lost more than eighteen thousand men, while inflicting just over ten thousand casualties on his southern counterpart. Moreover, to put the entire situation in perspective, since Grant had crossed the Rapidan, the two armies had clashed twice, at the Wilderness and again at Spotsylvania. Both times Grant failed to drive Lee from the field, and in the process he had suffered more than thirty-six thousand casualties — a number greater than all those who were even in the army of the Potomac at the time of First Manassas.

For his part Lee had suffered the loss of seventeen thousand men in the two battles. Since the outset of the campaign he had been able to sustain a kill ratio of two-to-one over his opponent. Yet he could take little solace either in these figures or his twin victories. He too knew the arithmetic. His losses may have been numerically smaller than Grant's, but they constituted a far bigger percentage of his army. He realized as well as anyone else that the South was fast exhausting its manpower reserves, while those of the North had been barely dented.

If the South were to prevail in this struggle, it would have to do so soon and in spectacular fashion. To continue the present war of attrition would be to face inevitable defeat. With these sobering thoughts in mind, he began to study his maps, anticipating Grant's next move.

For his own part Grant was admittedly discouraged by twin failures, but surely not to the point of despair. The thought of retreat never entered his mind. No sooner had the guns fallen silent than he began to devise another plan for the destruction of his southern counterpart. He was beginning to see the futility in assaulting an army entrenched in fortified earthworks. Lee would have to be drawn into the open where he could be exposed to total defeat.

Accordingly, he proposed to detach Hancock's corps from the army, sending it on a march six miles east of Spotsylvania to the Richmond, Fredericksburg and Potomac Railroad. Here they would turn directly south to Milford station, well to the rear of Lee's right flank. He expected Lee to leave his fortified position and lunge after Hancock to prevent a rearward thrust, whereupon he would fall upon the Army of Northern Virginia with all his remaining strength. Lee and his beleaguered army would pass into history. The war would be over.

Unfortunately for Grant, things would not go quite as planned. Though he himself was in the process of receiving some thirty thousand reinforcements, and would soon have an additional eleven thousand with the return of Sheridan's cavalry, Lee also was fast making good his own losses.

Two factors in widely spaced areas of Virginia contributed to this development. Grant's campaign had begun as a three-pronged effort, his own forces comprising the center. To the west, Franz Sigel had been assigned the duty of conquering the Shenandoah Valley. To the east, Ben Butler had sailed up the James and landed with a sizeable force south of Richmond. Both of these men had come to grief. General Breckinridge, with the help of the cadets of Virginia's Military Institute, dealt Sigel a decisive blow at the Battle of New Market and sent him reeling down the valley toward Maryland. Butler was stopped by Beauregard and effectively bottled up on a tiny peninsula known as the Bermuda Hundred. With these two Federal incursions neutralized, Lee was able to draw reinforcements from both regions to assist in the next confrontation with Grant.

A minor skirmish at Spotsylvania involving Grant's extreme right also contributed to the derailing of his design. The action itself was largely inconclusive from a tactical standpoint, but the contact produced intelligence which Lee was able to put to immediate use. He discovered that Grant's right flank had been largely denuded, which to him meant but one thing, another sidle to his own right. He prepared to meet it.

Grant too drew knowledge from the brief encounter on his right. It showed that Lee was not adverse to taking a swipe at him if the opportunity could be found. Accordingly, he decided not to dangle Hancock too far away, lest that able officer be lost. Instead, all four corps of the army would march toward Milford station at close intervals, Hancock leading the way.

All day long on the twentieth of May the signs of an imminent Federal march were unmistakable. Lee therefore kept his own forces ready to move at a moment's notice. Under cover of darkness on the night of May 20, Grant slipped away and marched east. It was not until six hours later that the lead elements ofthe Rebel army moved out to intercept them.

Whether by intuition or superior use of existing intelligence, Lee once again correctly guessed his opponent's intentions and was able to choose the ground on which they would meet. Though it pained him to yield another twenty miles of his homeland to the northern invaders, he chose the North Anna as the next line of defense. Given the added advantage of an interior line of march, he could easily afford to allow his adversary a six hour head start and still beat him to the

North Anna.

By dawn on the twenty-first, both armies were well into their respective marches. Robert E. Lee and his staff officer, Colonel Taylor, were astride their horses atop a small rise watching as the men of Anderson's corps passed toward the southeast. The men of each unit cheered their commander as they passed and he invariably replied with a tip of his hat or a wave of his right arm.

"Well, General," remarked Taylor. "Two battles so far, what do you think of this man Grant?"

"Are you asking me if I agree with the general sentiment that he is butchering his own men to no good end?"

"I'm curious as to your estimation of his abilities."

"Then let me say Mr. Lincoln has never sent me a tougher opponent. General Grant knows full and well what he is doing, and what the ultimate result will be if we continue fighting at this pace. I've heard him called a butcher, but I'm afraid I don't agree. He appears to be a man of purpose, and he seems to allow no interference with that purpose. General Longstreet made a comment to me before he was wounded in the Wilderness. Apparently he knows General Grant very well. They were friends before the war. He compared Grant to a bulldog. He said that once he latches on to an opponent, he simply doesn't let go. I've come to the conclusion that old Peter was right. General Grant has no intention of letting go of us until we perish or yield."

"Is there yet hope for us?" pressed Taylor.

"Strange we should be discussing such a prospect, Walter. We've just dealt those people two rather emphatic setbacks, yet we find ourselves wondering if we still have any hope for victory."

"Do we?"

"I think so, my friend, but if we are to win at all we have to do so in the open field. Even now we are yielding ground, far too much of it to suit me. We cannot allow ourselves to be pushed back much further. If Grant reaches the James, this whole affair will settle into a siege. There can be only

one result of such a turn of events. The superiority of northern manpower and resources will literally strangle us. We'd
have no choice but to . . ." He stopped in mid-sentence, unable to say the obvious word, "We must defeat them, Walter!"
he continued. "We must do so decisively and soon!"

*   *   *   *

General Grant was in high spirits that same morning,
sure that he had managed to steal a march on old man Lee
and confident that the end was near. Even as Lee was com-
menting on Grant's singleness of purpose, a regiment of
Massachusetts infantry had an opportunity to witness that
aspect of Grant's character at work. They were marching
south along the railroad when they spied their commander
seated atop a flatcar gnawing on a hambone. He seemed
oblivious to all else as though nothing else existed save the
remaining meat on that bone. They cheered him wildly and
waved their hats in salute. Grant acknowledged their greeting
with a wave of his arm, then quickly returned to the business
at hand, savoring every bite as if it might be his last. To those
infantrymen one thing was obvious. Ulysses S. Grant rarely
allowed himself to be distracted. Once he had established a
goal, he pursued it relentlessly allowing nothing to interfere.

"You see that?" one soldier called to his companions.
"That's what he's doing to Bobby Lee! He'll just keep chewing till nothing's left!"

His comrades agreed in a rather boisterous fashion, most
of them convinced that a match had at last been found for
the fabled Rebel General. Despite their recent setback, their
spirits remained high.

True, they had twice been bested, but it was not toward
the Potomac they marched, but the James. They were not
retreating as they had after so many previous defeats, they
were moving forward, it was the Rebels who were giving
ground.

Away they marched and not too much later Grant

polished off the remaining meat of the hambone. He leaned back against the front wall of the flatcar and savored the feeling of being full. He was on the verge of dozing when sounds of several approaching horses brought him to full attention. He opened his eyes to find Meade along with several staff officers and a small escort. "Good afternoon, George," he grunted. "How goes the march?"

"On schedule for a change. Everything seems to be going well so far."

"Good. That's the kind of news I like to hear. Any word on Lee?"

"Only that he's marched from Spotsylvania. Hancock hasn't reported any contact as yet."

"Have you studied the maps?"

"Sure have, General."

"Where do you think he'll try to stop us?"

"The next natural line of defense is the North Anna river. I think he'll try to head us off before we reach it."

"I agree, but I think we'll get there first. His men must be close to starvation, don't you think? They can't possibly march as fast as these fellows."

"Don't take him lightly," cautioned Meade.

"I'm not. Believe me, I wouldn't, especially after what I've seen in the last two weeks. By the same token, I refuse to overestimate him. We have a head start of several hours. Our men are in fine shape, both physically and mentally. The physical condition of Lee's troops has got to be deplorable. I think we can reach the North Anna before he does, and if we do we can wrap this thing up once and for all."

"We'll know soon enough," replied Meade, who had long since learned not to question the fighting qualities of Lee's ragged Confederates. Far too many times he had watched in despair as they baffled the so-called experts. Looking for an excuse to change the subject, he spied the neatly cleaned hambone lying next to Grant on the car, "Was it good?" he asked, gesturing toward the bone.

"Huh? Oh, that. I've had better, but it wasn't all that

bad. Anyway, whatever it may have lacked in taste, it made up for in quantity. I'm stuffed."

"Good. You've earned it. Don't let yourself fall asleep. You may wake up alone out here."

"Wouldn't dream of it, George. You go on ahead. I'll be along shortly."

"As you wish, General."

Meade saluted and nudged the flanks of his horse with his boots, leaving Grant to ponder the digestion of his copious meal.

*   *   *   *

Lee was following a parallel line of march at that point and wasn't especially distant from the long column of blue-clad infantry. He rode toward the North Anna in the company of Colonel Taylor and two guides, Eustis Moncure and W. G. Jesse. These two young cavalrymen had grown up in the general vicinity of the North Anna and were well-acquainted with the region. Through the black of night they rode south toward a tiny hamlet known as Traveller's Rest. Here they turned onto the Telegraph Road and soon reached Mud Tavern.

"General," called Moncure. "The enemy is but a mile to our east."

Lee reined Traveller to a halt and gazed eastward as he stroked the broad neck of the horse. "How do you know?" he asked.

"My cavalry unit was here around noon, sir. We ran into Yankees in substantial numbers on the road to Guiney's station. We were forced to retire in the face of superior numbers."

"I see," mused the General. Turning toward Taylor, he voice his response to the potential Union threat. "Walter, find General Anderson and have him dispatch a regiment toward Guiney's to cover the passing column."

With Moncure and Jesse, Lee continued south, and soon

they overtook Ewell's artillery. Much of it was stuck in the mud and weary drivers cursed heavily as they urged their exhausted animals to pull it through. Lee and his party passed the guns and were rejoined by Taylor at Jericho's Mill on the Ta River. They crossed here, but within a half mile, they came across yet another log jam of broken wagons, guns and cursing soldiers. Lee wound his way through the darkness, giving instructions to the officers and offering words of encouragement to the men. Though they couldn't see him in the darkness, his voice had an immediate effect. Tempers were calmed. Wheels began to move again.

Before long, Lee and his companions reached a crossroads, the junction of the Bethany, Welch's and Bowling Green Roads. Here again Moncure spoke up, warning Lee that Union forces were no more than a mile east of their position.

"Walter," instructed Lee. "Have a courier remain here to convey this information to General Anderson."

"Very well, sir," came the reply.

"Advise him to protect his left flank at all times along this road."

"I will, General."

"Good. Come, gentlemen, we still have a ways to go."

*　　*　　*　　*

Seth Reilly and his men were exhausted. They had been marching all day and well into the night, having covered at least fifteen miles. Their pitiful rations left their stomachs empty and to the man they were bone weary. Along with other stragglers from Ewell's infantry they had fallen out by the side of the road. Some slept. Others merely sat upon the damp grass and rested their aching feet.

Reilly himself was awake. He sat near the road with his arms clasped about his knees while he puffed stoically on his pipe. Tired though he was, he was too keyed up to sleep. Though his body craved rest, his mind refused to consider it. He was wrapped up in his thoughts, his mind filled with images of home and family, of war and the prospects of peace. He wondered whether he would survive, or if any of his men would live through the ordeals which yet lay ahead. He agonized over the possibility of his sons being dragged into a war which was beginning to seem interminable. He glanced over at young Cody who was snoozing peacefully just a few feet away. "Just a child," he whispered to himself.

Cody Wilder had been warmly welcomed into the ranks of Stonewall's survivors. It pleased Reilly to see how protective of this orphaned waif his men had become. Yet the boy himself was something of a puzzle. There was an innocence about him. He seemed to possess the same childlike qualities Reilly remembered seeing in his own boys. Yet during the last charge at Spotsylvania those qualities were nowhere to be seen, submerged beneath bitterness and a raging hatred toward anyone wearing blue. He seemed almost savage in his desire to kill Federals, and he truly was a dead shot. Could so strong a hatred ever be sated?

"God forgive us all," he muttered, averting his eyes from the sleeping lad. He sighed heavily, exhaling a cloud of tobacco smoke, then leaned back, reclining on one elbow. Before too much longer he had closed his eyes and was on the verge of dozing off himself.

The sound of hooves brought him back to awareness, but he didn't bother reaching for his Enfield, assuming the riders to be friendly. He sat up as they approached, spying several men, at least two of them officers. They reined to a halt, obviously studying the crowd of stragglers on both sides of the road.

Several moments passed and then one of them spoke, addressing himself to the throng of soldiers, "I know you do not want to be taken prisoner, and I know you are tired and sleepy, but the enemy will be along before or by daybreak and if you do not move on you will be taken."

Something about the officer's voice and demeanor was familiar to Reilly, but in his sleepy state he could not quite place it. As he struggled to remember, others among his number shot tart replies toward the man, knowing they were shielded from identification by the darkness.

"Well!" one of them cried. "You may order us to move on, move on, when you are mounted on a horse and have all the rations that the country can afford!"

The officer made no reply and several moments passed in silence before Reilly came fully awake and realized who had come upon them: "Marse Robert," he said in a half-whisper using the affectionate nickname by which Lee was known to the foot soldiers of the Army of Northern Virginia.

Others who were nearer to the rider stood and peered into his face, and they quickly echoed Reilly's words, "Marse Robert!" The name spread like wildfire through their ranks, and within seconds they were all on their feet as if they had never known fatigue.

Ox stood boldly forward and spoke out, "Marse Robert, we'll move on and we'll go anywhere you say, even to Hell if that's your will!"

"Thank you, soldier!" chuckled Lee. "I think I should be quite content if you merely reach the North Anna before our friend, General Grant."

"Count on us, Marse Robert!"

"I am. God speed to you!"

Reilly shouldered his musket and haversack, then stepped to the road, moving past Ox until he stood beneath the General himself.

"Ah, Sergeant!" he beamed. "We meet again."

"Yes, sir," nodded Reilly.

"Are these your men?"

"Mine are among them."

"They're fine soldiers, Sergeant Reilly. Fine indeed. Take good care of them."

"I will, General. I'd like to thank you for the furlough. It did us all a world of good."

"You're quite welcome, Sergeant. I wish I could have done more."

"We appreciated it, General, and none of us expected more."

Lee nodded and smiled his understanding, "Forgive me, Sergeant, but I'm afraid I really must move on. I must reach the North Anna in time to arrange a reception for our northern visitors. Perhaps when there is more time we can speak again."

"I'd like that, General."

"Then I'll look forward to it." He tipped his hat and gently tapped his boots to Traveller's flanks.

Moments later the riders disappeared into the darkness. Several dozen men were gathered by the roadside, all of them still watching in awed silence.

"All right!" ordered Reilly. "We've got a river to reach! Move on!"

They fell in together, a hodgepodge mixture of soldiers from a number of different regiments. With all possible haste they resumed their trek for the North Anna.

At about 2 a.m. on the 22nd of May, Lee and his entourage came across a little house near the side of the road. The pale glow of a lamp could be seen in the front room. The owner of the house was awake; sleep being impossible when an army is marching past one's doorstep. Hearing the horses pull up outside, he rose from his chair and stepped out to the porch.

"Good morning, sir," Colonel Taylor extended a greeting. "Might we stay here a spell to rest our animals?"

"Certainly," came the reply. "Please come in and sit down a few minutes."

They thanked him and dismounted, but only Lee and Taylor went inside.

"Dear me," said the fellow, an elderly gentleman, when he recognized General Lee. "I never thought I'd ever get to meet you. Please sit down, I'm honored to share my house with you."

"Thank you," smiled Lee as he took off his hat. "But I'm afraid you have me at a disadvantage. You apparently know my name, but I've never had the good fortune to make your acquaintance."

"My name is Flippo, Doctor Joseph Flippo," he offered his hand which Lee took with a firm grip.

In short order they were seated in the front room. "Would you care for refreshments? I haven't much, but you're certainly welcome to it."

"No, my good man," declined Lee. "We really can't stay that long."

Flippo stole a glance through the window at the long lines of gray-clad infantry trudging wearily past his home. "Is the enemy far behind you?" he wondered.

"Not especially," said Taylor. "You'll be seeing Federals on the heels of our last units."

"Dear me," muttered the doctor. "I don't think I ever imagined the war reaching my doorstep."

"General Grant has proved himself a most worthy opponent, Doctor. Thus far we've been able to withstand his attacks, but in the process we've been forced to yield substantial amounts of land."

"I see," mused Flippo. "Will there be another battle soon?"

"In all probability, yes. I envision the North Anna as an ideal line upon which to make a stand."

"You can stop him, General," said the doctor. "If anyone in this Confederacy can stop him, it's you."

"Thank you for the vote of confidence," chuckled Lee. "I hope I can prove worthy of it."

Not too much later they resumed their journey and reached Mt. Carmel Church, about three miles above the North Anna, well before dawn. He found his headquarters tent already set up and the lead elements of Ewell's corps resting nearby. As he prepared to retire for an hour or two of badly needed sleep, he inquired as to whether Moncure and Jesse had any rations. Seeing that they had none, he instructed them to report to his own tent for provisions. The two young men may have had visions of an ample meal waiting for them, but they were quickly disappointed. The General's cook could offer them nothing more than a couple of cold, stale biscuits and a little coffee which was hardly palatable.

"This is all the General eats?" wondered Jesse aloud.

"Is your belly empty?" demanded Moncure.

"Yep."

"Then shove those biscuits into it and stop complainin'!"

"I wasn't complainin'! I'm worried about the General!"

"Just eat."

The sun was just beginning to grope for the eastern horizon when Lee arose from his cot and prepared to resume the march with Ewell's corps. One of the first decisions of the 22nd was to dispatch Moncure back up the same route they had just covered. The young cavalryman was to find General Wade Hampton and instruct him to use his mounted forces to harass and retard the advance of the enemy while falling back toward Hanover Junction.

As he prepared to depart he received welcome news. Three of Pickett's brigades, those of Course, Kemper, and Bartow, had arrived that night along with Hoke's brigade; all of them from the Bermuda Hundred line below Richmond. Furthermore, the arrival by rail of Breckinridge with two brigades from the Shenandoah Valley replaced well over a third of his losses from the Wilderness and Spotsylvania. In the company of Major Jed Hotchkiss, the second corps topographical engineer, he started forward to study the approach to the North Anna.

The race to the North Anna had been won by the men in gray. Lee instructed Ewell and Anderson to cross to the south bank, but not to destroy the two wooden bridges. His study of the terrain told him not to contest a Union crossing of the river itself, since the northern bank was substantially higher than the southern through most of the river's course. Better it would be to make a stand somewhere to the south of the river itself. The 22nd passed with no sign of the enemy, though word of his advance toward Hanover Junction continued to arrive by way of General Hampton.

On the morning of the 23rd Lee rose early and mounted Traveller so that he might conduct a personal reconnaissance of the ground along the North Anna's right bank. By noon the last of his army, including the cavalry, had crossed the river, all save two tiny commands assigned to guard the bridges lest they be needed for a thrust to the left bank. At about the same time, the first elements of Federal forces began to appear along the North bank, and before long it appeared that they were massing in considerable strength. Once again, Lee had correctly gauged Grant's intentions. Once more the Army of the Potomac found Lee's grizzled veterans waiting squarely in its path.

When the first action opened Lee was in the yard of a home called Ellington which overlooked the river some distance away. The owner of the house, one W. E. Fox, approached the General and invited him to share his hospitality. Lee accepted, but paused at the sound of artillery. Union batteries were hammering the tiny commands which had been left behind to guard the bridges. Southern cannons opened up immediately in their support.

"I will only be able to stay for a few minutes," said Lee apologetically.

"As you wish, General," said Fox, glancing nervously in the direction of the gunfire. "Would you like some refreshment?"

"No, but you are most kind to offer."

"Please, General, I'd be most honored."

"Thinking that he had perhaps offended the gentleman, Lee promptly reconsidered. "Do you have any buttermilk?" he asked. "If so, a glass would be much appreciated."

After seating the General on the porch Fox scurried off to fetch the milk, returning soon with a pitcher, a glass and plate with some stale bread. Just as Lee was pouring his milk, a Federal battery commander must have spotted the uniform on Ellington's porch. One gun loaded with round shot was aimed at the house and fired. The projectile passed within a few feet of R. E. Lee and embedded itself in the thick oak of the door frame. Fox jumped as though he had just seen a ghost, startled quite nearly out of his wits. Moreover, he was amazed that Lee had hardly reacted at all. The General finished pouring his milk and drank it casually, as if nothing had happened.

"Mr. Fox," he said as he stood to leave. "I fear my presence here has drawn some unfriendly attention from those people across the river. I think I should leave lest they reduce your fine home to rubble."

"Yes . . . of course," stammered Fox with a fearful glance toward the river.

For a second or two Lee allowed his eyes to study the shell in the door frame, then he turned once more to his host. "Thank you for the milk, good friend. I pray God will keep you and your family safe during the next few days."

"You're welcome, General. May He keep you as well."

Away he rode and was soon back at headquarters; however there was little time to rest as the sound of artillery fire upriver indicated Federal activity in that direction. He felt compelled to conduct a personal investigation but found himself feeling suddenly unwell, as though he were on the verge of succumbing to exhaustion. In any event, he felt quite unable to ride and chose to be transported upriver in a carriage. Well to the west of his main positions, he found a skirmish underway between southern horse artillery supported by light cavalry and a force of Federals on the opposite bank. Using his spy-glass he conducted a quick study of the enemy's strength and came to an even quicker conclusion. He turned to his courier and issued the following instructions: "Go back and tell General A. P. Hill to leave his men in camp. This is nothing but a feint; the enemy is preparing to cross below."

He returned at once to Hanover Junction and before long he received news from Hill. Lee had guessed correctly again. Union troops were crossing at Jericho Mills, about two miles above Ox Ford.

Hill himself had not gone forward to ascertain the facts. He still was not completely recovered from an illness which had kept him prone during the battle of Spotsylvania. He dispatched one of his divisional commanders, General Wilcox, to conduct the reconnaissance. During the latter part of the afternoon Wilcox discovered sizeable numbers of Federal troops pushing through the woods on the south side of the river. Hill ordered Wilcox to attack with his division, not realizing that one division would in fact be attacking an entire corps of the Union army.

The action lasted until darkness forced a halt. Over six hundred men were lost to no real purpose, since they failed to force the Federals back across the river. Perhaps if Hill had used his entire corps things may have been different, but such was not the case. The only positive aspect was the intelligence which came from this costly skirmish; Grant was obviously intent on crossing the river and forcing a major confrontation.

On the extreme right that evening another conflict gave the same indication. The small garrisons at the two bridge heads were attacked and overwhelmed. Some of the men escaped across the river, but close to two hundred were captured.

Two possibilities existed in Lee's mind. First the whole affair might constitute a rather heavy-handed ruse designed to mask another sidle to the southeast. The second possibility, that of a major battle on the present ground seemed more likely. To prepare for the former prospect, Lee ordered General Anderson to pack his wagons and prepare to march if such a move became necessary. Preparing for the second option required substantially more thought. Grant had already crossed the river on the left flank and could easily do so on the right. If Lee chose to fight close to the river he would place himself at a disadvantage since the ground on the north bank of the river was considerably higher than that of the south. What then was he to do?

It wasn't long before a plan began to take form in his

mind. He had previously ridden the entire length of his line and had virtually committed the topographical maps to memory. Upon this foundation he began to devise a trap for the Army of the Potomac. Along the river's course there was only one place where the ground on the southern bank dominated that of the north: Ox Ford. This was the center of the Confederate line and only here could he stop a Federal thrust across the river itself. Ox Ford therefore would become the apex of a new line. Anderson held this ground with Ewell's corps stretched to his right. Lee ordered both men to abandon their positions on the river, save for that at Ox Ford itself and to form a new line stretching southeast from the ford, away from the river, all the way to Hanover Junction. A. P. Hill was also shifted to a new line from the ford southwest to a northward loop of the little river. When these dispositions were completed under the cover of darkness, his new line was essentially an inverted "V". One wing would have its flank anchored by the little river. The flank of the other was secured by the swampy ground to the east of Hanover Junction. Should either line falter under the weight of a Union assault he could readily draw from the other for support. It has been said that he virtually closed his line as one might close an umbrella. All of his commanders were instructed to entrench as they had done at Spotsylvania. The orders having been dispatched, he retired for the night, though he found it difficult to sleep. The same problem which had forced him to use a carriage that afternoon was creating havoc in his stomach. Under these circumstances sleep was all but impossible.

Seth Reilly received his orders just after 9:30 p.m. on the 23rd: Pull back to a new line and dig in again. The movement itself required no more than an hour, but the work which followed continued throughout the night. Trenches had to be dug and trees felled by the hundreds.

"Here, boy," said Reilly as he handed a shovel to young Wilder.

"What am I supposed to do with this?" queried the lad.

"Dig. I'm afraid there's more to being a soldier than fighting and marching. We have to be solidly entrenched by morning. Get started. We'll rotate shifts through the night. Make sure you throw the dirt to the outside of the trench so as to build an earthen wall. We'll need all the protection we can get tomorrow.

For several moments Wilder just stood there, shovel in hand.

"You got a problem, boy?" pressed Reilly.

"I guess I never thought much about diggin' no holes. I joined up to kill the people who killed my Ma and Pa."

Reilly stood in silence for several moments while all around soldiers dug feverishly to prepare for the storm they knew would come. "Listen, Cody," he said at last. "I've been in this army since the beginning. I've seen everything there is to see and I've done everything a man can do. I've long since put aside thoughts of glory and honor. There's no damn glory in war, just death. And after that, more death."

"I ain't lookin' for no glory."

"Yeah, I know. You're lookin' for revenge. I reckon you've got cause, but I assume you're not lookin' to die real soon, eh?"

"Ain't thought too much along that score."

"Then get to work. This trench could mean the difference between livin' or dyin' for a whole lot of us. From your perspective it might mean another day that you get to kill bluecoats. Lemme tell you a little story. When Lee first took over this army some of his ideas didn't exactly set us on fire. The first time he ordered us to dig trenches a lot of us flat-out refused. We fussed and fumed like a flock of schoolboys, said diggin' wasn't fit work for a white man. We coined some unkind names for Marse Robert. We called him 'Granny Lee,' 'Spades Lee,' and things of the like. We learned though. We learned real fast. Bobby Lee's a smart cookie. Every time we fortify ourselves like this we add the equivalent of ten thousand muskets to our strength. Maybe fifteen. Do you understand? We've been losin' this war, boy. We win battle

57

after battle, but we're losin' this war. There ain't too many able-bodied men left in the South anymore. They're all dead or maimed. That's why they're talkin' about draftin' fifteen year olds. That's why nobody's objectin' to a youngster like you learnin' how to use a bayonet. We need these trenches, boy. They save our lives, and that's crucial. Without us the South will fall. Our land and our people will be at the mercy of conquerors. Do you understand?"

"I reckon."

"Start diggin', boy. You're already fifteen minutes behind everybody else."

"If you weren't so long-winded, Perfessor, I'd probably have this trench half dug by now!" Cody flashed an impudent grin.

Reilly could only shake his shaggy head in exasperation. "You ever gonna learn how to say my nickname right?" he demanded playfully.

"One day . . . maybe!" laughed the boy as he let fly a spadeful of central Virginia's rich brown earth.

All the night long they worked. Throughout the length of the five-mile line they dug trenches and traverses, felled trees and built parapets. They had long since become experts at this sort of work. They were finished well before dawn and the results of their labors included a wide belt of abatis to retard the momentum of any Union charge.

Lee arose about 3:00 a.m. after two hours of fitful sleep. Just as he stood from his cot a sharp pain ripped through his stomach nearly doubling him over and forcing him back to a sitting position. He remained there for several minutes until the spasm passed. Cautiously he regained his feet, standing momentarily in place to be sure of his balance. He took a step toward the tent flap, then stopped, hesitating, wondering if the pain would recur. It didn't. He took a deep breath and moved out into the warm night air.

Taylor was waiting outside. "I'm sorry, General." he said. "I'm a little late. I guess I dozed off."

"No apology necessary, Walter. I'm not entirely punctual

myself. Are the horses ready?"

"Yes, sir . . . over there." Something about Lee's tone of voice spawned an uneasy feeling inside Taylor's breast. He reached to pick up the lantern which sat just outside the commander's tent. "Are you okay, sir? You look a little pale."

"It's nothing, Colonel. I'll be fine. Come, we've a lot to do before daybreak."

The two men mounted and proceeded to ride toward Ewell's positions where the General intended to study the fortifications which would serve his army on the morrow. They found the front lines alive with activity as his battle-hardened veterans worked feverishly to prepare for the next clash of arms. For an hour the review continued without incident. Lee and his soldiers exchanged warm greetings and words of encouragement as the General passed along the rear of their positions. At about 4:30 a.m., Lee and Taylor topped a ridge from which they could survey the trenches of Anderson's position beneath the bright light of the moon. Several soldiers who had paused in their labors glanced up and spied Lee's familiar profile. "Marse Robert!" they cried, "We'll be ready for 'em!"

The General doffed his hat and waved to them in acknowledgement.

"The men appear in fine spirits, General," remarked Taylor.

"Indeed so, Walter," agreed Lee. "I'm truly blessed to lead men such as these. They may not look like much, but I firmly believe they are the finest fighting men on this planet."

"A point I'd never argue, General," smiled Taylor.

Suddenly the old General stiffened as if in severe pain. Unwilling to reveal his obvious discomfort to the troops who passed below, he did his utmost to retain his composure, though his facial expression was one of utter agony.

"General?" called Taylor in obvious alarm. "Are you all right?"

"My stomach!" muttered Lee through clenched teeth. "Pain . . ." he whispered.

Taylor's alarm grew quickly as he watched the color drain from Lee's face and a thin sheen of perspiration pop up along his temples. "We're going to have to get you to a doctor, General. Can you sit your horse for a while longer?"

Lee nodded stiffly.

"Come then."

Quickly he led the General down the far side of the ridge out of sight of the infantry.

Once they passed from view, Lee could hold on no longer. He toppled forward, collapsing on Traveller's sturdy neck, his fingers clutching at the horse's mane.

"Hold on, General!" urged Taylor. "Gwathmey's wagon isn't far!"

Before long they found Gwathmey, Lee's personal physician, and with the help of orderlies they assisted the General down from his mount and laid him gingerly on the stretcher. Once prone, Lee appeared visibly relieved of the spasm which had literally doubled him over.

"Can you describe the pain to me?" asked Gwathmey.

"Cramping," pointed Lee. "More serious than anything I've ever experienced."

"This is all we need," groaned Taylor.

"Quiet!" snapped the doctor.

"Gwathmey," said Lee. "It doesn't feel nearly as bad when lying down, but I can hardly lead this army from my back. Have you nothing I can take?"

"I have a few things in my wagon, General, but I can't prescribe an effective treatment if I don't know the source of the ailment. I may have to conduct an examination and perhaps some tests."

"Proceed, Doctor," ordered Lee. "We haven't time to discuss the matter. I seriously doubt if General Grant will postpone whatever he has in mind pending the recovery of my stomach."

"Very well, General. I'm afraid you'll have to ride with me in the wagon."

"I'm in no shape to ride a horse, Gwathmey. I accept

your kind invitation, but do let's get moving, shall we?"

They loaded him into the wagon, making him as comfortable as possible for the bumpy southward journey to follow.

"What is it, Gwathmey?" groaned Lee, clutching his stomach with both hands, rolling onto his side, curling into a fetal position. "What could possibly cause such pain? Dear God, it burns!"

"You must lie flat, General," instructed the doctor calmly. "The cramp should pass soon enough."

"Pass it may," stammered Lee through clenched teeth. "But it certainly won't be soon enough. What caused this? Can't you at least tell me that?"

"I could only wager a guess."

"A guess? Gwathmey, you're a physician. You have to know! What am I to do?"

"A physician I may be, but that title doesn't bestow upon me the wisdom of Solomon. A host of causes could have brought on this condition. For two weeks I've been warning you to guard your own health. You are not a young man anymore — a fact which you seem to ignore more often than not! You've slept rarely over the last two weeks and your diet has been something less than deplorable!"

Lee reclined on his back as the pain in his entrails eased once again. "You needn't berate me, old friend," he sighed. "One could hardly describe these last two weeks as idle time."

"I can't help but feel responsible. I should've berated you sooner. It was negligent of me to do otherwise. You've allowed your resistance to deteriorate badly, and I stood by like a passive observer."

"Nonsense! In any event, this argument does little in the way of healing. What can be done? The Confederacy is facing its most severe crisis to date, and I find myself confined to this cot, betrayed by my bowels . . . of all things! What can you do?"

"I'm not sure, General, allow me to dwell on it for a moment or two; I should be able to come up with something."

"Be quick, dear friend. There's an opportunity taking shape here and the Confederacy can ill afford to let it slip away. Grant isn't like the others. He doesn't accept defeat easily and he won't limp back to Washington like his predecessors. If he is to be stopped he must be crushed, not merely repulsed . . . crushed."

Suddenly Lee groaned aloud as a wave of cramps constricted his entrails. Once more he rolled to his side, his hands groping at his stomach as if he could somehow massage the pain away. "If I can get one more pull at him, I will defeat him!" he asserted. At that moment, Lee's eyes were elsewhere, transfixed on the battle he was planning, but he was seized by yet another spasm of pain. He moaned, "Help me, Gwathmey! You must help me!"

"I'll do what I can, General," sighed the physician. "I have a friend in Richmond, a chemist of considerable skill. Perhaps between the two of us we can come up with a concoction to purge this malady."

"Then do so," Lee drew a breath through clenched teeth, "Please do so."

"I'll leave for the Capital at once. I imagine it will be late tonight before I return. However, General, I will go nowhere unless I have your word that you won't leave Hanover Junction. Whatever business you had in mind for today must be conducted from this tent."

"Would that I could give you such an assurance, Doctor," groaned Lee. "Unfortunately, there's a war going on and it's my responsibility to hold up our end of it."

"Will you at least try to remain here as much as possible?"

"If Grant will allow it . . . yes. Now go, Doctor, and please hurry!"

Gwathmey departed quickly, and before long he was carriage-bound for Richmond. He felt as if the weight of the whole world was on his shoulders, knowing full well that the fate of the Confederacy rested on the success of his mission.

General Lee reclined on his back, having endured the latest bout of abdominal pain. "Ah, Doctor," he whispered, though no one was close enough to hear. "How can I lead this army from my back?"

When asked to describe Robert E. Lee, friends and foes alike would oft reply with a single word: "Steel." This aspect of his character refused to desert him. Despite the unwillingness of his body to cooperate, his mind continued to plan. He knew the strengths of his position, and was keenly aware of how deadly a trap he had devised for the Army of the Potomac. Only two questions remained. Would Grant walk into the trap, and if so, could it be closed? Only Providence would decide the first, so Lee gave it little thought. Instead, he directed his efforts toward compiling a strategy for springing the trap should the opportunity present itself.

"Orderly!" he called.

The sentry quickly presented himself. "Sir?"

"I should like to speak with Colonel Taylor at his earliest convenience."

Within ten minutes, Taylor was at his General's side. "You asked for me, sir?"

"Yes, Walter. I've been thinking about how we should receive our friend, General Grant."

"What do you have in mind?"

"Several possibilities arise, but all of them depend on how he chooses to deploy once he finds us. In any event, the right course of action will require accurate knowledge of the enemy's disposition as well as the right personnel to carry out our plans."

"Nothing new in that, General. It's been that way from the beginning."

"True."

Lee winced suddenly as a flash of pain sliced through his intestines.

"General?" The fear in Taylor's voice was readily apparent on Taylor's face.

"It's okay, Walter," sighed Lee. "It will pass, or so claims our dear Doctor Gwathmey."

Moments later it did pass, and Lee's facial muscles relaxed visibly.

"I need to see Generals' Hampton and Gordon as soon as it can be arranged," he muttered, trying to appear calm, though the effort was obviously forced.

"I'll take care of it, sir. Why don't you try to rest for a spell, okay? I believe Doctor Gwathmey left specific orders to that effect, did he not?"

"I'll rest, Colonel. There isn't much else I can do under the present circumstances. Send Hampton and Gordon to me. I need to speak to each of them."

*   *   *   *

All that day as Lee grappled with fiery pain in his entrails, Ulysses Grant's army of Federals continued to arrive along the banks of the North Anna. One corps had crossed at Jericho Mills, but they chose to entrench after Hill's half-hearted attempt to drive them back across the river. Near the center of the position Burnside's corps came face to face with fortified Confederate positions on the south bluff at Ox Ford. Below the ford Hancock approached the river, but reported no contact with the Rebels. Grant paused momentarily to ponder the situation, but his orders weren't long in forthcoming. He instructed Warren to advance from Jericho Mills and Wright to follow his heels. Burnside was instructed to study the possibility of an assault against those Rebels who held the south bank of the ford and Hancock was ordered across the river with instructions to find the enemy.

Burnside was first to report and his observations were brief and to the point: any attempt to cross at the ford would simply bloody the water.

Time passed and Grant began to grow impatient at the lack of information. From Wright, Warren and Hancock there was no word. Where was Lee's army? Had the land simply swallowed them up? Was the force at Ox Ford merely a rearguard to slow him down? Why hadn't Lee made a stand? Surely there was no better place than the North Anna.

Soon word arrived from both wings . . . no contact, the Rebels were nowhere to be seen.

"Keep moving," ordered Grant. "They're out there someplace." He glanced up from his maps and turned to Meade. "Lee would not have fortified Ox Ford as a delaying tactic," he declared. "He's out there. I know he is."

"I have no doubt of it," concurred Meade. "He means to give us battle."

"Wright and Warren are sweeping down from one direction, Hancock from the other. Lee must be between them. We'll have him caught in a vise, and if such is the case, he'll be hard pressed to worm his way out."

"Don't jump to assumptions. If Lee's out there it's because he wants it that way. They beat us to the North Anna, and they had time to occupy ground of their own choosing."

Grant cast Meade a sideways glance then turned to gaze out across the river. "We'll know soon enough," he growled as he stuffed the cigar back into his mouth.

Just then a courier approached on horseback. The young man dismounted quickly and presented himself to Grant with a hasty salute.

"Message from General Sheridan, sir!" he proclaimed.

"Let's have it," nodded Grant casually.

The rider reached inside his tunic and produced a small white envelope. He paused to straighten out the wrinkles, then handed it to Grant.

"What's he say?" asked Meade.

"He'll rejoin us before the day's out," replied Grant without taking the cigar from his mouth.

"What strength?"

"About eleven thousand."

"Good. They'll come in handy."

"Handy indeed. They should be enough to round-up whatever's left of Lee's army when we're finished with it."

Meade made no verbal reply, but those near him were

65

able to read the expression on his face. They found it dis-
quieting. The victor of Gettysburg apparently had serious
reservations about the approaching clash of blue and gray.
Whatever these thoughts were he didn't say, but one thing
was obvious: he did not share Grant's optimistic assumptions
about the outcome.

*   *   *   *

Robert E. Lee rose from his cot and stood on legs which
were shaky at best. He stepped slowly to the table which
served as his field desk and leaned on it for support. It was
still relatively early on the 24th, though Doctor Gwathmey
had already been gone for over two hours. For at least half
of that time there had been no pain ripping through the
General's belly, and he had begun to think the malady had
passed. He took several deep breaths to clear the cobwebs
from his mind.

"Orderly!" he called.

The soldier poked his head inside the tent. "General?"

"I'm going out to confer with General Hill. I believe I
may require a carriage. Would you be kind enough to inform
Colonel Taylor?"

"Straight away, General."

The orderly saluted and then quickly departed to locate
Taylor.

The Colonel arrived about ten minutes later, stepping
into the tent to find his commander fully dressed and ready
to depart. "What's this I hear about you're wanting to leave?"
he challenged.

"You heard correctly. Have you obtained a carriage?"

"Yessir, but I must protest. Doctor Gwathmey left strict
instructions with you, General. You were not supposed to
leave your cot."

"Doctor Gwathmey is a splendid physician," admitted
Lee. "But he does not have the responsibility of repelling this
invasion. I do. My instincts tell me Hill will face the greatest

numbers. I simply wish to insure myself as to the integrity of his position."

"You've no cause to doubt Little Powell, General," argued Taylor, using A. P. Hill's nickname. "Moreover you are not well. Look at yourself. You're trembling. I've never seen you so pale. For you to travel, even by carriage, would be a mistake. I think you should return at once to your cot, General . . . in all due respect."

"I appreciate your concern, Walter. Believe me I do. Nevertheless, I must be the judge of my own condition. I haven't experienced any significant pain in well over an hour. We are going to Anderson Station. Shall we proceed? I should like to get there and be able to return before any relapse occurs."

"Very well," sighed Taylor reluctantly. "You are one stubborn old man, do you know that?"

"So I've been told, old friend," Lee managed a weak smile. "Come . . . help me to the carriage."

Within thirty minutes they arrived at A. P. Hill's headquarters. The weather was relatively pleasant that morning, and the fresh air had done much to revive both the General's spirits and his physical vigor. As a result, he was able to mask his true condition and carry on a rather detailed exchange with General Hill and his staff.

Toward the end of this meeting, however, things began to sour. Just as Lee was inquiring about the previous day's action at Jericho Mills, his intestines began to send twinges of pain through his stomach. He listened patiently as Hill explained the failure to hurl Warren back across the river. The reason for that failure soon became obvious. The attack had been delivered piecemeal, utilizing only a portion of Hill's available strength. An opportunity to wreck a quarter of Grant's army had been irrevocably lost. Hill finished speaking and fell silent.

The pain in Lee's stomach grew sharper and he struggled to resist the urge to double over. His facial muscles began to contort and he could no longer mask what was happening inside his body. To those present, it was readily apparent how truly ill he had become. The rumors they had been hearing were true. Suddenly, in a rare display of temper, Lee turned toward Hill and shouted angrily, "Why did you not do as Jackson would have done, throw your whole force upon those people and driven them back?"

Suddenly, it would not have been difficult to hear a pin drop inside that tent. Every man there was frozen in a uneasy silence. They were shocked by Lee's anger, but they could see he wasn't well. For his part, Hill showed admirable restraint in holding his tongue. A. P. was well known for his fiery temperament, and if such a rebuke had come from any other man, an argument would no doubt have ensued. Before Lee, however, Hill kept his emotions under control and endured the humiliation which had been delivered in the presence of his staff.

Lee himself was locked in a struggle to hold on to his composure, but he was rapidly losing the battle.

"Colonel," his voice barely exceeded a whisper as he turned to Taylor, "I think we should be getting back to headquarters."

"Of course, General."

Taylor gingerly placed one arm about the ailing general's shoulder and guided him toward the exit and the waiting carriage. He helped Lee into the vehicle and did his best to make him comfortable. He turned then to the driver. "One moment," he said, "I'll be back in no time at all."

Quickly, the colonel disappeared into the tent where he found General Hill and his officers standing like a collection of statues as though all of them were still in a state of shock. "It was not his intention to embarrass any of you," he explained quickly. "He's not himself at the moment."

A. P. Hill himself was still recovering from a protracted illness which had idled him through most of the last two weeks. "You needn't explain," he said softly. "We understand. Tell the General we'll not fail him again."

Taylor nodded and returned to the carriage without saying another word.

For Lee, the ride back was much like a pendulum swinging from gut-wrenching agony to moments of relative calm. In the midst of painful seizures the General would say nothing, but the contortions of his body and face were ample indications of his discomfort. When the spasms passed and he regained his composure, he would attempt conversation.

"Walter, did you speak to Hampton and Gordon as I requested?"

"Yessir. Both men will be in to see you before the afternoon is out."

"Good. Do you remember that sergeant we encountered on the roadside during the march?"

"Reilly. I believe you told me his name is Reilly."

"Yes, that's him."

"You said that he and his men were all that remained of the Stonewall Brigade."

"So they are. I've been thinking about him. I've been considering the possibility of a field promotion. In any event I'd like to speak with him again. Could you send for him? You should find him in Gordon's division."

"I'll take care of it."

"Thank you, Walter."

He seemed about to say something else, but the words died in his throat as he braced for another spasm of abdominal pain. "Dear Lord . .," he whispered several moments later, doing his utmost to endure the agony in silence.

By early afternoon he was back in his tent lying prone on the cot. Though he was not actually feverish he began to show symptoms of delirium. He tossed and turned fitfully on the cot both unwilling and unable to get the rest he so desperately needed. His soldiers were now in excellent position to throttle the Army of the Potomac. Lee knew this better than anybody, but he raged against the debilitation which he saw robbing him of that opportunity. "We must strike them a blow!" he would say time and again as he lay prostrate in his tent. "We must never let them pass us again. We must strike them a blow!"

On the other side of the river, couriers were arriving at Grant's headquarters with puzzling but welcome news. Wright and Warren were reporting limited contact with the Rebels. They were only pickets and they gave ground at the slightest pressure, but at least they provided evidence that Lee hadn't disappeared altogether. From Hancock came similar word. Grant gave them all a simple reply: "Keep pushing."

When the couriers had departed, he returned to his map alongside General Meade, "If things go according to plan we could wrap this affair up before the day's out," he declared.

Meade glanced up and his eyes met those of his commander. "All due respect, General," he replied. "But you've said that before. Bear this in mind, things rarely go according to plan."

"You're too cautious, George," argued Grant. "If Lee has deployed as I think he has then we'll have him snared in a vise. Wright will extend Warren's line and completely overlap the Rebel flank. From such a vantage it shouldn't be too terribly difficult to overwhelm them. We ought to be able to roll them right up like an old rug."

"I think you're underestimating Lee," retorted Meade, but in a tone which was hardly convincing.

"I think you've overestimated him. You people have lionized that man for too long. He's no God! He's every bit as vulnerable as you or I, in fact, a bit more so if I'm any judge of strategy. I tell you, George, there's no more bite in the Army of Northern Virginia. They're too weak to take the offensive against us. That business yesterday at Jericho Mills should be ample proof of that. They will only fight from behind entrenchments, and if Wright overlaps their line they're done for."

Meade knew better than to argue with him. He shrugged his shoulders in resignation and backed away from the table. "You offer a compelling argument," he sighed reluctantly. "I suppose we'll know before too much longer whether you're right or not."

Their wait was soon to end. Early in the afternoon, the lead units of Warren's corps stumbled out of the woods into a meticulously cleared field of fire. No more than a half mile away was Hill's corps of Confederate infantry. They were heavily entrenched. Most of the bluecoats agreed that these fortifications were even more formidable than those they had stormed unsuccessfully at Spotsylvania. Their orders were to attack as soon as the enemy could be found, but Warren and Wright were quick to see how profitless such an enterprise would be. Scouts were dispatched to probe the Rebel left, pursuing Grant's intentions to overlap their line. They returned with sobering news. The enemy flank was securely anchored. No flanking movement appeared possible from that quarter. Grant's design for Lee's destruction had been foiled before it even got off the ground.

On the opposite end of the field, Hancock's infantry found a similar spectacle waiting for them, a solid line of foreboding entrenchments bristling with Rebel guns. Attacking them was out of the question.

"Dig in," ordered Hancock, sensing the offensive possibilities offered by the Rebel position.

Wright and Warren issued similar orders, and after a detailed study of the ground they forwarded their reports to headquarters.

Grant was pacing impatiently outside his tent when the couriers from both wings arrived at roughly the same time. He didn't even wait for the soldiers to dismount before launching a tirade of questions in their direction: "Have you found the Rebels? Where are they positioned? Why hasn't the attack begun yet?"

Both men climbed down from their sweating horses and presented themselves to their commander with a smart salute.

"Everything's in writing, sir," said the first, handing his dispatch over to Grant.

"The same from General Hancock," added the second as he pulled forth a worn brown envelope.

"Very well," nodded Grant, taking both messages. "Stand by for orders."

He stepped into his tent with Meade and a number of staff officers close on his heels. Several moments passed as he carefully perused the written reports. Finally he tossed the papers aside and let his eyes drift aimlessly toward the roof of the tent.

"So what's going on out there?" probed Meade.

"Lee's dug in along an inverted "V" with the apex at the ford. Solidly entrenched on both wings. Fortifications stronger than those we stormed at Spotsylvania. Both flanks securely anchored, no chance of overlapping his lines. They've asked me to cancel the orders to attack. Even as we speak they're all out there digging trenches opposite the Rebels."

"Are we agreeing to their request?"

"How's that?" For a moment Grant's mind seemed to be elsewhere.

"Are you going to cancel the attack?"

"I don't know yet. It seems to me we have him right where we want him."

"That can work two ways. He may have us as well."

"Then why hasn't he gone on the offensive? I'm not blind to the strengths of his position, but if it makes for so fine a springboard why hasn't he attacked? I tell you, George, the Rebels are beaten. They won't fight us unless they're solidly entrenched."

"You may be right, General," admitted Meade. "But shouldn't we continue our focus to this particular situation? Whether he's beaten or not, Lee reached the North Anna before we did. He got his army entrenched before we could scarcely lay a finger on him. If we storm those earthworks now, we may easily wind up with another Spotsylvania on our hands." Meade paused for a moment, carefully gathering his thoughts. Then, lowering his voice, he continued, "General, please bear this in mind, in the last twenty days this army has suffered over thirty-five thousand casualties. We shouldn't squander our men to no good purpose. Cancel the attack, at least until after we've had time to think this thing out."

For several moments a tense silence hung over the tent as Grant pondered his alternatives. No one spoke. Men could hear their own hearts beating like the pounding of regimental drums. Thousands of lives hung in the balance. How would Grant respond?

"Cancel it," he asserted at last.

One could almost hear the collective sigh of relief which took place among his officers.

"At least for the time being. Have them continue digging in. We'll hang around another day or two. There's bound to be a weak link somewhere along Lee's front. We'll find it."

Word of the cancelled attack came as welcome news to the Union soldiers who were still heavily engaged in the process of digging in. None of them were looking forward to the prospect of charging a position such as the one they faced at Ox Ford. Although they admired Grant for his tenacity, many were beginning to openly question his tactical abilities.

Among the rank-and-file there was the inescapable feeling they had been outgeneraled once again. Twenty days had passed since they had crossed the Rapidan and entered that tangled maze known as the Wilderness. There they had been mauled, though they had certainly fought with steadfast determination. Then came Spotsylvania, a battle which had held much promise, but produced results little better than those of the Wilderness. Now they were across the North Anna, but they found themselves once more facing a fortified enemy. They were coming to accept Robert E. Lee as a mere mortal, but they frankly wondered how he consistently outfoxed his northern counterparts.

Their coming up on the short end of the tactical contest was but one debilitating factor at work among the Federal soldiers at Ox Ford. The last twenty days had been grueling

73

at best. The troops had been constantly fighting or marching. Thirty-five thousand of their comrades had been shot down or captured. Those who remained had changed considerably. All of them had lost weight. Many of their uniforms were torn and tattered. In short, the Army of the Potomac, though numerically strong, was not in the best of shape. The strength of its morale was tenuous. There was more than a little grumbling going on among the common soldiers. Some were even bold enough to raise the prospect of mutiny if the order came down to charge the Rebel trenches. Officers of rank were rightly concerned. Too many negative elements were at work. The army was ripe for disaster.

*   *   *   *

Hanover Junction was also the scene of frantic activity. Numerous messengers arrived at Lee's headquarters with word of the enemy's dispositions. When he learned that the enemy was entrenching opposite his lines, Lee gave into frustration.

"Why, Walter, why?" he cried angrily. "Why did this have to happen now? Sometimes I feel as though the fates are against us!"

"I honestly don't know what to say, General," returned Taylor somewhat sheepishly.

"The opportunity is passing. We should be attacking them right now! And here I lie, betrayed by my own stomach!"

"This isn't something you can help, General," soothed Taylor. "Perhaps you should just relax until you recover."

"Relax? Dear Lord, Walter!" Lee was sweating rather heavily, his face painfully contorted, one arm propping him up, the other clasping his lower abdomen. "How can I relax? What I should do is relinquish command, but to whom? Tell me! Who can I turn this army over to? Beauregard? It's too late. Grant will see the danger and pull away before Beauregard could get here. Hill? He's still recovering from his own sickness. Jericho Mills was enough to show he's not truly ready for active duty. Anderson? He's been in command of a corps for less than a month. Nor is Ewell an option. What am I to do?"

"Rest," urged Taylor, "General Hampton will be here within the hour. Conserve your energy for that meeting."

"Hampton," repeated Lee with a weak nod. "Bring me the maps of our positions, Walter. If those people are digging in out there, then Grant must be planning to stay for a while. Perhaps we can still get a pull at him before he sees the danger and withdraws.

Within forty minutes, General Wade Hampton was climbing down from his lathered mount to meet with his commander. From head to toe he was covered in dust, having been all day in the saddle. He was a big man with a thick brown beard which flowed down across his upper chest. He wiped the grime from his hands and turned the reins over to an orderly.

"Would you wipe him down for me?" he asked.

"Yessuh."

"Thanks. Is the old man inside?"

"Yes, but he's feelin' kinda poorly."

"I've heard the rumors. How sick is he?"

"It's kept him on his back for the last couple of hours."

Hampton grunted something and moved inside the tent. At once his nostrils were assailed by a foul odor, a most unpleasant by-product of Lee's intestinal malady. He held his composure, pretending not to notice anything out of the ordinary.

"Good afternoon, General," he announced softly. "I understand you wished to speak with me."

"Ah! General Hampton!" Lee turned his head, but made no attempt to rise from his cot. "Do come in please!" he gestured toward a stool next to the cot.

Hampton nodded and proceeded to lower his bulky frame to a three-legged stool.

"Do you realize the opportunity we have here?" quizzed

Lee.

"I've got a fair idea," nodded Hampton.

"We're losing it. We should have gone on the offensive at the first sight of their forces. Now the Federals are digging in. Every hour which passes reduces the chances of a successful frontal attack on our part."

"I realize that, General," agreed Hampton.

"Nonetheless, I've given this matter more than a little thought, and I'm not ready to give it up just yet."

"What do you have in mind?"

"A flanking movement. Over the last few weeks I've made it a point to get to know General Grant in the fullest possible detail," Lee paused and his facial muscles tightened considerably as another spasm of pain rippled through his entrails. After it passed he took a deep breath and resumed speaking as though nothing had happened. "I've read all the field reports from Grant's western campaigns, particularly those of Shiloh. Did you know that Johnston and Beauregard were able to move their entire army to within striking distance of Grant's without being detected?"

"I'd heard something to that effect."

"It seems General Grant does not always think to take a sure defensive posture. His mind is ever on the attack."

"A lot of us have noticed that tendency, sir, but you have to admit it hasn't failed him yet."

"Perhaps because no one has been able to take full advantage of it."

"What exactly are you scheming?" posed Hampton with a curious smile.

"A flanking movement, as I said earlier. Moving from this wing is probably out of the question. The swampy ground outside of Hanover Junction would work against us just as much as it hinders those people. I want to know what his dispositions are on the opposite wing. Would you conduct a forced reconnaissance along the Little River?"

"I'd be happy to, General."

Lee smiled weakly, "I thought as much. Probe for weaknesses. See if you can find a spot where a sizable force of infantry can cross without being seen. If you locate such a place, we may yet deal General Grant a blow from which he won't easily recover."

"I'll certainly give it my best effort, sir."

"I have no doubt of that," nodded Lee. "On the assumption you'll succeed, I'm going to put together an assault force. We'll be waiting to hear from you."

"I'll try not to keep you waiting too long," said Hampton as he rose to leave. "By the way, I think you should know, Sheridan is rejoining Grant today."

"I see." Lee averted his eyes for the moment as the image of Jeb Stuart flashed briefly before his mind. "What sort of strength does he bring back with him?"

"Something over ten thousand by our estimates."

"Keep tabs on them. I'll want to know exactly how they are deployed."

"Very well, sir."

"Leave at once, General. Every available minute of daylight is precious to us."

"I understand," nodded Hampton, and with a quick salute he was gone.

Lee collapsed weakly against the unyielding canvas of his cot. Taylor was quickly at his side.

"Are you okay, sir?" He applied a cool, wet cloth to the General's forehead and temples.

"I've been better," Lee muttered softly.

"This idea of yours, it's a long shot at best."

The General's reply was barely audible. "I've taken long shots before, Walter."

"I know agreed Taylor. "But this one . . . I think this one ranks with the most desperate."

"Are these not desperate times?"

"I suppose," murmured Taylor with a grim smile on his lean face.

"Will General Gordon be coming soon?"

"Not until late afternoon, but that young sergeant you

77

were asking about should be here before too much longer."

"Ah yes . . . Reilly."

"Are you sure you'll have the strength to speak with him?"

"I'll manage," replied Lee, closing his eyes and taking a deep stabilizing breath.

At about the same time, Seth Reilly was walking alone along the narrow dirt lane which wound into Hanover Junction from the north. He had received his invitation from Lee and found it rather puzzling. Why would the General want to see him? Still he managed to keep his curiosity under control and remained with his men until their fortifications were complete. Leaving Whitt in charge, he set out on foot towards Lee's headquarters, some ten miles down the lane. Other than the usual traffic of couriers he saw no one until a troop of cavalry coming from the direction of the Junction thundered past him. He recognized the lead rider, Wade Hampton, Stuart's successor. He gazed after them when they had passed, wondering what they were up to, then he turned south and resumed his solitary trek.

About a half mile from headquarters he heard the sound of hoofbeats behind him. He stopped and moved to the side of the lane, watching as a single rider came into view. Moments later the horse drew abreast of Reilly and came to an abrupt halt. Reilly had to stare at the face for a moment, but quickly recognized Evander Law, a brigadier general from Alabama. He stood to attention and gave the general a salute.

Law returned the salute, "Afternoon, Sergeant."

"General."

"Where might you be headed?"

"Headquarters. I received a summons earlier this afternoon but I couldn't break free right away."

"That a fact? What's your name, boy?"

"Seth Reilly. I'm with the Stonewall Brigade."

"You fellas took one hell of a pounding at Spotsylvania. I heard the brigade was captured pretty much intact."

"A few of us escaped," said Reilly, hoping he would not

be required to relive that nightmare for the sake of another curious general.

"Would you like a ride, Sergeant?"

"Sir?" Reilly was surprised at the offer and wasn't quite sure how to respond.

"Do you want a ride? Don't just stand there, climb up here behind me. This horse may be old, but he's plenty strong enough for the two of us." Law extended one hand to assist Reilly up.

"Thank you, General."

He took one hand and hoisted himself onto the horse, "I'm much obliged."

"No problem, boy. We're both goin' in the same direction."

They rode quietly for sometime. Evander Law offered little in the way of conversation, but he kept a constant cheerful whistling. Considering the circumstances, Reilly found this somewhat curious and at last found it impossible to contain himself.

"General," he advanced. "If you'll pardon my saying so, you seem in uncommonly good humor."

"Indeed I am, Sergeant! And why shouldn't I be? General Lee has just devised one of the most ingenious traps I've ever seen, and Grant walked straight into it with his eyes wide open."

"Trap?" posed Reilly. "I'm not sure I follow you. After all, you have the advantage of rank on me. You get to view this affair from a different perspective than I. All I know is, we march, we dig trenches, we fight, then we march again."

Law pulled his horse to a stop. "Climb down, Sergeant," he said. "I'll explain it to you, give you a glimpse of the larger picture, so to speak."

"Fine by me," grunted Reilly as he slid to the ground.

Law soon joined him. He handed the reins to Reilly and drew forth his sword. With the tip of the polished blade he drew a long arching line in the soft ground.

"The North Anna," he said, gesturing toward the line.

Reilly nodded.

"Ox Ford," continued Law, jabbing the sword in the ground adjacent to the river line. He then proceeded to draw the two wings of Lee's army with their apex at the Ford.

"Still clear," said Reilly. "But where's the trap?"

"General Grant now finds himself skewered on the horns of a military dilemma. By accepting Marse Robert's kind invitation to cross the North Anna, he has divided his army essentially into three sections — the weakest being here at the Ford itself. The problem from Grant's point of view is fairly simple. If he storms our lines he exposes his men to the same sort of punishment they suffered during the last charge at Spotsylvania. Moreover, even if they were to score a breakthrough, Lee can readily draw from the other wing to seal the breach."

"True."

"The best is yet to come," said Law. "If we find an opportunity to take the offensive, Grant could find himself facing serious difficulties. No matter which of his wings we strike, Grant could be forced to draw reinforcements from the other. The problem is, those reinforcements would have to cross the river twice, here and here, before they could do any good. By the time help could be brought from one side to the other it could easily be too late for the Federals."

Reilly's face broke out in a wide grin. "I'll admit my knowledge of strategy is limited," he said. "But this sure looks good, General. It surely does. Do you think Marse Robert can pull it off?"

"I've known Lee for a long time," sighed Law. "If there's a man alive who can create an opportunity where none exists, he's that man. In any event, we'll just have to wait and see. I hear tell he's been sick the last couple of days. Maybe that's why he hasn't already gone over to the offensive. Let's hope he recovers soon. It would be truly a shame if such an opportunity as this were to be lost because of an illness."

"A shame indeed," nodded Reilly.

"Well," Law sheathed his sword and remounted. "Climb

up behind me, Sergeant. Lee's headquarters is only ten or fifteen minutes ahead."

Reilly was somewhat hesitant about approaching R. E. Lee's tent. True, he had been summoned. He had written authorization from Taylor to prove it. Still, he was somewhat awed at the prospect of presenting himself at the General's quarters. At last he worked up his nerve and walked up to the soldier who stood guard at the tent flap. "Sergeant Seth Reilly to see General Lee," he announced, handing his authorization to the sentry.

"Let him in!" Taylor's voice sounded from inside.

The sentry stepped aside and pulled the tent flap open for Reilly.

The sergeant removed the tattered kepi from his head and stepped inside. At once, his nose was assaulted by the foul odor of excrement, but steeling himself to the odors, he stood to attention and saluted Taylor. Looking past the Colonel, he spied General Lee lying on a cot at the far corner of the tent.

"Sergeant," said Taylor with a touch of weariness in his voice. "The General still wants to speak to you, but you must understand, he's not been himself of late."

"The rumors are true?"

"He's sick . . . yes."

"Is it serious?"

"If you mean life-threatening, no. At least, we don't think so, but it's certainly debilitating. Let me caution you on one thing, Sergeant. Rumors are flying, and you well know the power they carry. When you get back to your men, don't speak of the General's condition. Don't fuel the fire which rumor has already sparked. Do you understand?"

"Perfectly, Colonel."

"The General will see you now, but please don't tax his strength." Taylor stepped away.

Reilly approached Lee's cot and looked down at the General. Lee was lying prone on his back, a thin gray blanket tucked in around his chest. His eyes were closed and he appeared to be sleeping. Reilly was disheartened by the pallor evident on Lee's face. The General was sweating heavily, his white hair literally soaked and plastered against the sides of his head. The veteran sergeant wasn't sure whether to wake him or not. He looked back at Taylor for advice, but the Colonel merely nodded his head. Finally, the sergeant decided to clear his throat, doing so rather loudly.

Lee's eyes opened at once. At first he appeared startled, perhaps even disoriented, but this quickly passed. His eyes found Reilly but several moments passed before he recognized him.

"Ah, Sergeant Reilly!" He smiled weakly. "Forgive me if I don't sit up. I'm afraid I've been somewhat incapacitated."

"I understand, General. You just rest easy, maybe I can come back another time."

"Nonsense," Lee gestured with one hand. "I've been looking forward to seeing you. There should be a stool or something over there. Pull it close and seat yourself."

Reilly nodded and glanced around until he saw a three-legged stool nearby. He moved it to the side of the cot and sat down gingerly, testing its strength before allowing his full weight to descend.

"This was a most inopportune time for me to fall ill, Sergeant. There's an opportunity here, but I fear it may be slipping through my fingers."

"There will be other opportunities, General."

"I wonder about that. I fear Grant may be able to maneuver us back to the James. If so, this affair will become a siege. From that point it would be only a matter of time . . ." His voice trailed off.

"We won't let that happen, General. The men of this army would march into Hell for you."

"They have many times," mused Lee in a voice barely stronger than a whisper. "In any event," his voice grew stronger, "I haven't given up on this particular situation. We may yet find a weakness in Grant's disposition. If we do, we'll move at once to exploit it."

"That's the spirit, General," smiled Reilly.

There was a cool, wet cloth hanging near the cot. Reilly picked it up and proceeded to dab away the sweat from Lee's temples and forehead.

"Thank you, Sergeant. That feels much better."

"Is there anything else I can do?"

"No . . . not at the moment. Actually, I didn't summon you here to be my nurse. I've decided to offer you a field promotion to the rank of second lieutenant. You've certainly earned it. Do you accept?"

"Lieutenant? Why, sir . . . I'm honored. In truth, I've never really thought of myself as an officer."

"Do you accept?"

"Yessir, most definitely. My sons will be excited when they hear of this."

"You have sons?"

"Two, sir. The oldest is twelve."

"Blessings they are. Believe me, I know. I have a couple of my own. Do you remember when I met you, Lieutenant?"

"Yessir, just after the Union assault on the mule shoe at Spotsylvania. I don't think I'll ever forget."

"You pulled me away from the fighting."

"It seemed the wisest thing to do."

"Sometimes I forget my place," said Lee. "I lose track of the total picture while focusing on one aspect alone."

"That's surely understandable, General. A great deal rides on your shoulders."

"Yes," mused Lee softly. "Didn't you tell me you were once a teacher?"

"Yessir, I was . . . before the war. I was an instructor at The College of William and Mary."

"That's right, I remember now. Do you plan to return to the field of education? I mean when all this is over, of course."

"I hope to. If I live to see the war end."

"An admirable calling — education. I've been giving the matter a great deal of thought lately. I may enter the educational field myself someday, when this wretched war comes at last to an end."

"I should think you'd be a welcome addition to the faculty of any institution, General."

"Thank you,"

Lee paused momentarily and rolled to his left side to cough. "I've been thinking about Washington College out in Lexington," he continued when the spell passed. "Do you know anything about it?"

"It's a very good school, General, but then again, so is William and Mary."

"Is that a sales pitch, Lieutenant?"

"Let's just say I threw it out for you to ponder."

"If I'm ever able to ponder anything of a peaceful nature."

"That day will come, General. One way or another, this war can't last forever."

"True."

Lee nodded, and for several moments his eyes closed again as he braced for another bout of stomach spasms. "You've lost no more men since Spotsylvania?" he asked when the pain eased.

"None. There's still twenty of us. Twenty-one actually. We added a recruit during the lull in the fighting."

"A recruit? We could probably use a few thousand more. Tell me, do you still refer to yourselves as the Stonewall Brigade?"

"Yessir, although we've been laughed at from time to time. I suppose it's a bit ludicrous for twenty-one men to be called a brigade."

"Nonsense. You have my blessing to continue just as you've been. It's important to this army that the Stonewall Brigade lives on. General Jackson was a dear friend and a superb soldier. In honor of his memory, I will keep the Stonewall Brigade as an active unit on the rosters of this army."

"That means a great deal to us, sir. We'll not shame

General Jackson's memory."

"You certainly haven't so far. Tell me, you've only been under the command of General Gordon for a short time, how would you assess his abilities?"

"He's a fine officer. He understands tactics and strategy and he knows men. He's a very good leader."

"I thought as much. I've had much the same opinion of him since he exemplified himself in the Wilderness."

Just then, almost as if by design, they heard the approach of a horse and the voice of a man who identified himself as General Gordon. Taylor stepped to the tent flap and backoned him in.

Gordon and Taylor conferred briefly at the tent entrance before the latter stepped to one side. The divisional commander from Georgia then approached Lee's cot, pausing only to return Reilly's salute. The newly promoted second lieutenant had risen from the stool and moved out of the way.

"You asked to see me, sir?" queried Gordon.

"I did indeed."

Lee gestured for the younger man to take Reilly's place on the stool. "You're no doubt aware of the opportunity we have here?"

"I am, sir, but if you'll pardon my saying so, time is fast passing us by. The Federals are digging in and the opportunity you speak of could well be lost."

"My feelings exactly," said Lee, grimacing as his stomach contorted again. "In point of fact, we have already lost whatever chance we had to engage those people in a frontal attack."

"That's a shame, General," sighed Gordon with a look of utter resignation on his face.

"Don't despair, General Gordon. All is not yet lost. We may yet find a way to deliver Grant a hefty blow. General Hampton has the cavalry out searching for any weakness or opening on the enemy flanks."

"That's good news, General. Specifically, it's good to

know you're not ready to discard the idea."

"Quite to the contrary. Despite this blasted illness, I'm determined to follow it through if a way can be found."

"You have my complete support. I think you know that."

"I think I may require more of you. If General Hampton is able to detect an opening, we must swiftly exploit it. Any delay could prove fatal to our hopes. In any event, General Gordon, I would have to be blind not to see the contribution you've made to our cause over the last several weeks. In the Wilderness and again at Spotsylvania, you demonstrated the qualities of a very fine officer."

"Thank you, sir."

"I'll be frank, General. I need you again. If a weakness can be found, the task of exploiting it will fall on your shoulders."

"I'm prepared to do anything you ask, sir."

Lee reached down and picked up an envelope from the ground next to his cot. "These are formal instructions. Along with your own division, I'm assigning you three additional brigades. When you leave here you can inform Generals Breckinridge, Hoke and Bartow. I realize all these units are under strength, but if my calculations are reasonably accurate, you should have an assault force of perhaps ten thousand men."

Gordon opened the envelope and quickly perused the orders and troop dispositions. "You want me to gather these troops in a central location after dark?"

"That's correct. I've designated the place there on your map. Wait there for further orders as I won't have an exact plan devised until I hear from Hampton."

"Very well," nodded Gordon.

"Should nothing develop by daybreak I'll send word. In that event, you will return to the lines and we'll try again tomorrow night, assuming General Grant remains in place for another day."

"That could be a big assumption, General. Grant would have to be blind not to see what's right in front of his face."

"I realize that."

Lee gripped both sides of the cot as another tremor of pain rippled through his belly. "From this point everything rests with General Hampton. If he can find an opening, we'll make our move."

"Then I best be getting back to my men. The afternoon wanes and I've got a lot to take care of."

Lee managed a weak smile, "God speed, General Gordon."

"Thank you, sir. Let's hope he's smiling on us tonight. Is there anything I can do?" He gestured towards Lee's stomach.

"Regretfully, no," replied Lee. "I'm afraid I'm as comfortable as the circumstances will allow. The good doctor Gwathmey has journeyed to Richmond on my behalf. Perhaps he'll be able to find a remedy. The best thing you can do for me, General, is to be ready to march tonight at the tap of a drum."

"We'll be ready." declared Gordon calmly.

"I'm counting on that."

*   *   *   *

The afternoon was passing altogether too slowly at Grant's headquarters on the northern bank of the river. Outside of his tent the Union commander paced impatiently back and forth, wearing a deep rut in the soft, green Virginia grass. All the day long his army had been divided on the point of a wedge, and as the afternoon wore on he began to share the apprehensions of his subordinates. He refused to admit to these fears, just as he refused to admit he had been outfoxed again by the elusive Lee. This was not surprising to the officers on his staff. His behavior was consistent with his recent past. After all, he didn't acknowledge his defeat in the Wilderness nor the setback at Spotsylvania. He may not have expressed his concerns verbally, but his agitated behavior spoke for itself. Ulysses S. Grant had the appearance

87

of a very worried man. Finally, he moved off of his newly created footpath and joined Meade beneath the boughs of sprawling maple alive with the fresh green of spring.

"George," he said, taking the cigar from his mouth. "It seems to me if Lee had any cards up his sleeve he'd have played 'em by now. Don't you think? We've been here all day and there hasn't been hardly a peep out of them. I think we've been worried over nothing. Do you agree?"

"Perhaps," mused the victor of Gettysburg. "I can't explain this inactivity on the part of the Rebels, but I wouldn't be too quick to let my guard down."

"I agree," nodded Grant. "And along those lines I can think of one move we can make which will go a long way toward defusing this situation."

"That being?"

"Break the wedge. Storm the bluffs over Ox Ford. If we take them, we can reunite the entire army in a single line south of the river."

"Did not General Burnside argue against such a move? The ford is heavily defended."

"Ambrose may have been stricken with a slight case of timidity. I can straighten that out quick enough. Orderly! Fetch my horse!"

"General, are you sure about this?" pressed Meade, anticipating but one result in such a move.

"Don't be going soft on me, George. I'm inclined to think we can clear the Rebs out of there by sunset. The picture will look altogether different by morning. In addition to Burnside's attack, I want everybody else to be alert for an opening or a weak spot. They can attack on their own initiative."

General Meade started to resume his argument but thought better of it. Grant was obviously not in good humor and for Meade to press his objections would only risk incurring the General's ire and a charge of insubordination. He turned to one of his own staff officers.

"Fetch our horses," he ordered stiffly.

A short time later Meade stood to one side as Grant expressed his wishes to a rather astonished Ambrose Burnside.

"Let me get this straight," demanded the commander of the ninth corps incredulously. "You want me to storm those heights?"

"That's correct. Soften them up for a spell with artillery. Then attack. I want you established on top of those bluffs by dark."

"General," hesitated Burnside as he looked to Meade for support. "Are you sure about this?"

"Don't be an idiot, Ambrose. If I wasn't sure I wouldn't give the order."

"Sir, have you studied those heights? They're up there in considerable strength."

"I'm aware of that," huffed Grant. "But I also remember a place called Missionary Ridge down in Georgia. We stormed a fortified ridge several times higher than those bluffs and we sent the Rebels scurrying for their lives."

"Yessir, but that was in Georgia. Those guys were led by Braxton Bragg, and as I read the papers they had real bad morale problems. These Rebs fight for Bobby Lee. Believe me, sir, they're a different breed than the ones you scattered in Georgia."

"The Hell with the papers, General!" stormed Grant. "They don't interest me! Are you questioning my orders?"

"No, Sir!" stammered a very flustered Burnside.

"Get your guns into action now! Pound on 'em for an hour, then take the ford! Am I clear?"

"Perfectly."

"I'll be waiting for your reports at my headquarters."

"Of course."

"What's that suppose to mean?"

"Nothing General. I'll forward my reports to you as soon as the situation develops."

"See that you do, Ambrose. Good luck to you. I expect to see your standards on the ridge by dark."

"We'll do our best, sir. But General, my corps is divided all over the place. I've got only one division on hand."

Grant paused a moment and peered up at the bluffs on the opposite side of the river. "One division should do the trick," he growled while chewing on his cigar. "Once you're across I'll have troops from both wings link up with you to form a continuous line. Now get busy, General. The afternoon won't last forever."

Grant and Meade departed and the latter seemed none too happy about the assault which was to take place.

Burnside set about preparing at once for the attack. Ten batteries of guns were wheeled into position and trained on the opposite heights. Moments later, they opened fire and the air was filled with the roar of cannons and screaming shells.

Lee's gunners wasted no time in returning this fire, and though their guns lacked the range of the superior Federal ordnance, the higher elevation of their position allowed them to reach the Union pieces. The exchange which was supposed to have lasted for an hour was over in just forty minutes. The result was hopelessly one-sided. The Union firepower, though considerable in weight, either sailed over the Rebel lines or slammed into the earthen walls of the entrenchments. There was a great deal of smoke and noise, a lot of dirt flying, but very little in the way of damage.

As for Burnside's losses, they were hardly negligible. Six guns were destroyed, several more damaged. Numerous caissons were blasted into shreds and over a hundred men were killed or wounded. Little was accomplished except to provide ample testimony to the advantage of elevation in an artillery duel.

Sensing the futility in continuing the barrage, Burnside ordered his guns to cease-fire and withdraw out of range. At the same time he ordered two brigades of infantry forward and called a courier to his side.

"Tell General Grant that we've softened them all we can from this vantage point," he explained. "Advise him that we're moving ahead with the assault."

"Yessir!" The soldier saluted smartly and wheeled his mount around.

Two brigades moved swiftly into position within a hundred yards of the river. The order to advance was given and four thousand brave men started forward. Their flags snapped smartly in the afternoon breeze, and their drums sounded an increasingly rapid beat.

Up on the bluff, the prospect of a charge by Union infantry was greeted in joy by some, utter disbelief by others.

"I can't believe they'd actually try to take this position!" said one Rebel rifleman shaking his head.

"I can see the logic in making the attempt," commented a major nearby. "Grant's in a pickle. Taking the ford would be an avenue out of it."

"It ain't gonna happen!" growled the rifleman.

"Not anytime soon," concurred the officer.

Orders were quickly issued. Guns were brought forward and positioned at the very edge of the bluff. Soon, they were loaded with grapeshot and waited only for their prey to draw closer.

"Let 'em get to the river," came their instructions.

Moments later, the Federals broke into a run and the first of them charged into the river.

"Fire!" Came the cry from the bluff.

The cannons opened up first. At once, huge gaps were torn in the northern ranks. Then came volley fire from massed numbers of riflemen. The attackers fell by the hundreds, but those behind them pressed on, oblivious to the screams of the wounded. Another round of canister followed at once by a second and third volley of musket fire. In a matter of minutes, the attack was over. A few Union soldiers actually reached the south bank of the river. Not one made any serious attempt to climb the bluff. The river itself was choked with bodies of dead and wounded northern soldiers. The survivors, their spirits broken by the onslaught of southern lead, turned and fled for the safety of their lines.

Burnside's earlier prediction had been fulfilled. The North Anna at Ox Ford was running red with Union blood.

Burnside himself rode disconsolately back to Grant's headquarters to deliver the news. Grant was waiting for him outside the tent, having been alerted by the sudden collapse of gunfire from the direction of the ford. As soon as he saw the corps commander, he knew what had happened. Burnside's shoulders were slumping badly. His face was the very epitome of gloom.

"Well?" probed Grant.

"I think you may have to devise another scheme to re-unite this army," muttered Burnside in a tone barely audible. "Ox Ford can't be taken."

"Did you press your full weight?"

"I committed two brigades to the initial thrust. They were slaughtered in the river. Not a man reached the bluffs themselves."

Without a word, Grant turned about and disappeared into his tent.

Meade was there, and though he and Burnside were not necessarily the best of friends, he at least took time to inquire after Burnside's troops.

"How severe were your losses?"

"I can't give you an exact number. Perhaps as many as a thousand. Many were washed downstream. I've sent parties to search for bodies and survivors."

"I see."

Meade looked away. "You did your best. Get back to your command and keep everyone dug in tight."

"Very well, General."

Burnside saluted in a somewhat haphazard fashion and turned away.

Meade took several steps toward Grant's tent, but stopped short of entering. He could see the General's silhouette inside. He was sitting on a chair, stooped forward, hands clasped tightly. He had all the appearance of a man deep in thought. Meade could smell the heavy odor of

Grant's cigar. "He must be puffing like a madman," he thought. "Ah well, I suppose he's best left alone right now." He turned and walked off toward his own tent.

*   *   *   *

At Hanover Junction, the first hint of a Union attack came in the low rumble of gunfire which echoed across the sky. Lee's headquarters was roughly two miles from the apex of his line, but certainly close enough to hear the tumult of battle. Sick though he was, Lee attempted to leave his cot when the first faint rumble drifted past his ears.

"Where do you think you're going?" demanded Taylor, placing one hand on Lee's chest to discourage the General's attempt.

"Are you deaf, Walter? That's the sound of gunfire, and unless my instincts betray me, it's coming from the ford. We have to get up there!"

"We have to do no such thing," argued Taylor hotly. "You're a sick man, General. You're not leaving your cot!"

"That's preposterous! I need to know what's going on!"

"We'll know soon enough. They'll send word. Stop worrying and lie back down. You talked me into taking you out earlier this morning and that proved a mistake. You're staying put till Gwathmey gets back."

"You're worse than a mother hen!" complained Lee, who collapsed backwards, contorting in abdominal pain.

"Just try to relax," urged Taylor. "I'll find out what's going on."

"Do so quickly!" groaned Lee, rolling to his side.

Within thirty minutes Lee had received word from the ford. A Union attempt to storm the bluffs had been easily repelled. Casualties were minimal and both sides had resumed a stand-off.

The rest of the afternoon and evening passed without incident and before long, darkness had settled over Central Virginia. Newly promoted Lieutenant Reilly began to gather the survivors of the Stonewall Brigade.

"All right you guys," he whispered. "Pack it up, we're movin' out."

"Where we goin?" quizzed Evan Peterson.

Keep your voice down, Evan," scolded Reilly. "No need to let the whole world know."

"Where we goin?" The question was repeated in a whisper.

"Don't worry about it right now. I'm not entirely sure myself. We're gonna meet a few other units midway between our two wings. Then we're gonna wait and see what develops."

"Are we gonna attack?" posed Cody.

"Hush," said Reilly. "Let's just get out there."

Back at Lee's headquarters, matters couldn't have been much worse. Lee's intestines were on fire and the General's normal composure was fast disintegrating under the pressure of constant unbearable pain. In delirious anger, he railed about the need to strike Grant a decisive blow. It was to this atmosphere that Dr. Gwathmey returned that night.

The doctor pulled his buggy to a halt about fifty yards from Lee's tent. He could hear a heated argument taking place inside. Three voices were readily discernable. Lee and Colonel Venable, a veteran member of the headquarters staff, were engaged in a boisterous shouting match. Taylor's voice could be heard trying to calm the two men. Shaking his head sadly, the doctor handed the reins to an orderly, picked up his leather bag and stepped down out of the buggy. He was nearing the tent when Venable stormed out in a huff and nearly knocked him over.

"Oh . . . Doctor . . . I'm sorry!" stammered Venable as he grabbed hold of Gwathmey's shoulders to prevent him from falling.

"It's quite all right," came the reply, "No harm done."

Venable released the doctor and stood back. For a moment, the two men regarded each other in silence. Finally Venable could contain his frustration no longer.

"I have just told the old man he'd better send for Beauregard!" he exclaimed. "He's not fit to command this army!" With this he gave the doctor a curt nod and stomped off into the night.

Gwathmey shrugged and stepped into the tent, and his expression soured quickly as his nostrils were assailed by the foul stench which accompanied Lee's malady. He saw Taylor sitting alone to one side, his face mostly covered by his hands. Lee was in a sitting position on his cot, his arms wrapped around his stomach. He was rocking to and fro, groaning softly. The tent itself appeared to be in a state of disarray. Furniture had been overturned. Papers were strewn about carelessly, along with various pieces of Lee's uniforms and personal belongings.

The general glanced up as Gwathmey entered. "Doctor!" he gasped. "Did you hear what that man just said to me?"

"I imagine half of Virginia heard it. No one around here seems to be making any effort to control his volume."

"He told me I wasn't fit to command this army!"

"He may be right! Have you stopped to think about that? Look at this place! Look at yourself!" He reached down and righted a small table on which he placed his bag.

"I'm a sick man, Doctor! Dear God! I've never experienced such pain!"

"I understand, General. That's why I'm here."

"Your friend . . . the chemist . . . did you find him?"

"I did."

"Can he help?"

"We'll know soon enough."

He opened his bag and began removing its contents. In a matter of moments, the little table supported a collection of beakers and vials containing a strange assortment of powders and liquids.

Lee stiffened a little, and one eyebrow arched curiously as he eyed the odd collection on the table, "What's all that?"

"You might call it one chemist's contribution to the war effort," remarked Gwathmey as he carefully unfolded a piece of tattered paper.

"And that?"

"The recipe for your cure, or at least durable relief. You'll have to be patient for a few minutes. I need to mix all the ingredients, and the proportions must be exact or the concoction won't work. By the way, in the event this fails I want you to move your headquarters several miles to the southeast, away from any possible combat. Furthermore, if this fails, I think you should give serious consideration to Venable's suggestion. You really aren't in any condition to lead this army."

"Mix your ingredients," whispered Lee. "and please hurry."

No less than twenty pain-wracked minutes passed before the doctor completed the first batch. He had filled a quart-sized beaker with the mixture which he then held to the lantern in order to examine it more closely. In color and consistency the concoction had an unpleasant resemblance to loose mud. Gwathmey poured several ounces into a glass.

"Here," he handed the glass to Lee. "Drink it all."

"You're joking," objected the General. "That's the most disgusting stuff I've ever seen." He held the beaker to his nose and his face literally recoiled at the aroma. "Good Lord!" he huffed. "You can't honestly expect me to ingest anything like this!"

"I most certainly do. Drain the glass, and within thirty minutes you should notice a definite improvement in your condition."

"Thirty minutes?"

"Drink it."

"The pain will abate within thirty minutes?"

"I said you would notice an improvement. The degree is still a matter of speculation. Drink it."

Lee sat as straight as his abdomen would allow and held the glass to his lips. Summoning his discipline for the effort, he opened his mouth and drank quickly, swallowing the contents of the glass in four deep gulps. Coughing and gagging, he handed the empty glass back to the doctor. "In all my days, Gwathmey," he sputtered, "I have never tasted anything so vile."

"It wasn't designed to titillate your taste buds, General. Now, please lie down on you back and remain there until the concoction starts to work."

Lee promptly obeyed.

Every minute seemed to consume an eternity in passing. Lee remained prone while Taylor and Gwathmey sat close by nervously checking their time-pieces. All of them knew how much rested on the success or failure of the doctor's efforts.

"A half-hour has passed," whispered Taylor at last.

"So it has," nodded Gwathmey, who then turned to the General. "Do you feel any change in the level of discomfort?"

"I'm not sure," stammered Lee. "There's been no spasm for several minutes. The feeling of constriction inside of me seems to have lessened."

"Try sitting up," suggested Gwathmey.

Lee complied, although there appeared to be some hesitation in his movements. He gripped the edge of the cot, bracing himself for the spasm he thought would surely come. Several minutes passed. Nothing happened.

"Well?" pressed Gwathmey a little impatiently.

"There's no pain," whispered Lee, not fully believing his own words.

"Try standing."

Lee rose slowly to a standing position.

"Any change?"

"None, Doctor. I don't feel the pain. There seems to be no cramping."

"Walk about the tent."

Lee obeyed, though each step appeared to be very tentative.

"I can move around," he declared confidently. "The discomfort is minimal. Doctor, I think your witches' brew may be working!"

"Of course it is!" chuckled Gwathmey. "After all, look who put it together!"

"Modesty aside," interrupted Taylor. "Is the General cured?"

"No," Gwathmey shook his head. "Let me explain what's happening here."

"Please do," urged Lee. "You'll have my undying attention."

"This remedy was designed to control only the symptoms of your illness, the pain and constriction. There is a malady of some sort at work inside your system. All we can do is control the symptoms until it runs its course."

"How often must I drink this stuff?"

"Several ounces an hour, every hour until you've shaken the virus itself."

"As you wish," concurred Lee with a look of revulsion on his face.

"There's more," continued Gwathmey. "And you must listen to me carefully. A full recovery from this illness depends on you changing your habits. You must get sufficient rest and it's imperative that you correct your eating habits. You have to eat proper foods. I've brought back some rice, onions and vegetables from Richmond. These are the types of things you must eat."

"You know how I feel about eating better food than my soldiers."

"Doctor's orders. Besides, those soldiers need for you to be healthy. You do them precious little good writhing all over this cot. Do you understand?"

"You've made your point painfully clear, Doctor."

"Good. Hereafter you must drink a glass of this every hour. I'll be back in a little while to mix up another batch."

"Where are you going?"

"To prepare you a decent meal. I'll be back."

Before he could leave however, they heard the sound of hoofbeats and several excited voices. Moments later General Wade Hampton burst into the tent. His uniform was layered in dust. His bearded face was a picture of sweat and grime. He paused just inside the tent, his eyes taking in every detail of his surroundings. His gaze settling finally on Lee.

"General," he nodded. "It's good to see you on your feet."

"Thank you. I'm feeling better. Weak of course, but the pain has eased considerably. The good doctor here may have worked a miracle."

"That's good news," smiled Hampton.

"You've something to report?"

"Yessir. I think we may have found what you were hoping for."

"Where?"

"Have you a map?"

Lee turned to Taylor, "Walter?"

"Straight away, General," replied the Colonel, who quickly dug through a pile of topographical maps until he found the right one. "This should do," he announced as he pulled it from the pile.

"I think I should sit back down, Walter. Spread the map out on the table by my cot, will you?"

The old General sat down gingerly on the cot while the others gathered around. Taylor placed the map on the small table and stood to one side. All eyes were on Hampton as he approached. Everyone fell silent. Lee was sure the others could hear his heart pounding. So much rode on the report Hampton was about to deliver.

Stuart's successor stepped to the map and peered down studying it for several moments before speaking. "The extreme left of A. P. Hill's position is here," he said as he tapped the map with one finger. "He's anchored against this loop of the Little River. General Wright's entire corps of Federals is positioned just to the west. He's overlapped Hill by several hundred yards, but the river itself combined with Hill's flank positions have stopped him from moving forward."

"General," mused Lee patiently. "We know all that."

Hampton smiled and continued his discourse. "The extreme right of Wright's position is about a third of a mile from the river. He has about two regiments dug in along the river to ward off any flanking movement on our part. Save for these units his flank is in the air."

"I knew it!" exclaimed Lee as he clenched his right fist. "Can those two regiments be circumvented?"

"I believe so. We found a place to cross the river up here, nearly a mile west of the Federals. The water is barely waist deep and the entire area is thickly wooded."

"Excellent!" beamed Lee. "Well done, General!"

"Ah, but there's more!" Hampton's smile had grown into a full-fledged grin. "We located a narrow path through the woods — too narrow for anyone on horseback. I sent my scouts across on foot. The path leaves the woods directly behind Wright's position. If the reports I heard are accurate, we could conceal thirty thousand men in there with no problem."

"We need hide only ten thousand," declared Lee, his excitement growing by the minute.

"I have scouts waiting for them at intervals along the way."

"Splendid! We haven't a moment to lose!" Lee bent lower over the map, his eyes intently studying every detail. "General," he glanced up at Hampton. "There's no time to write out detailed orders. I'll explain my plan to you, and you pass the instructions on to General Gordon verbatim. Am I clear?"

"Perfectly," nodded Hampton.

"Listen carefully . . ."

Twenty minutes later, Wade Hampton strode briskly from Lee's headquarters and mounted his horse. With every passing minute, he was becoming more enthusiastic about the prospects of a major victory. As he rode through the darkness of the night toward Gordon's assault force he found himself continually trying to quell his optimism, less it blind him to the many factors which could easily go wrong.

General Gordon's group had been assembled three full

hours before the Georgian had an opportunity to seek out General Breckinridge.

"Ho, there!" he called, spying the brigade commander in conference with several officers. "I haven't had the chance to congratulate you on your victory at New Market."

"Why, thank you, John!" replied Breckinridge. "However, I think it's prudent to give credit where credit is due. The heroism of VMI's cadets played a major role in our success at New Market."

"So I've heard," said Gordon. "One day I'll have to journey out to Lexington and pay my respects to those young men."

"They'd be honored, I'm sure," returned Breckinridge. "Listen, I don't mean to sound presumptuous, but the orders I received were somewhat vague. Can you give me a better idea of what we're doing out here?"

"I don't know the details just yet myself. We're supposed to wait on the cavalry. Hampton's been out trying to find an opening on one of Grant's flanks. If he finds it, Lee wants us to exploit it."

"You think such a move possible?"

"I do indeed. All we need is the opportunity, and I think it will be soon forthcoming. I can't explain why, but I have this feeling inside of me tonight. It's unlike anything I've ever felt before. Look around you. Look at the faces of the men we lead. We couldn't ask for better soldiers. I feel as though we're on the verge of making history!"

"Don't let yourself get carried away," continued the other.

"Believe me, I won't, but it's a heady feeling, isn't it? Lee's got himself a card up his sleeve, and we're the card."

"It strikes me as something of a heavy responsibility."

"That indeed, but if the opportunity arises, this group of soldiers can set a tremendous chain of events in motion."

"It all depends on whether providence decides to smile on us or not. In any event, we'd be wise not to count our chickens before they hatch."

A SOUTHERN YARN

"Believe me, I'm trying to remain calm, but I guess I am finding it a bit hard to restrain myself."

Their conversation continued along these lines for another hour until the sound of hoofbeats drew their attention southward. Moments later, Wade Hampton was standing in their midst.

"Greetings, my friends," he intoned. "Are your men ready for a march?"

"As ready as they'll ever be," replied Gordon. "What news?"

"If we leave right now I can have you hidden in the woods behind Federal lines well before dawn."

"Are we authorized by headquarters to march?"

"Authorized is the wrong word. I bring orders from Lee. We move at once. I'll explain everything to you on the march."

Orders were quickly issued, and within minutes a column of Rebel infantry ten thousand strong was making its way south toward the Little River. They took no artillery nor any heavy supplies. Lightly equipped and their spirits buoyed by the prospect of pulling a surprise on their northern counterparts, they made excellent time. There was heavy cloud cover that night, blocking the pale light of the moon and stars, and masking their movements from unfriendly eyes.

Hampton and Gordon walked side-by-side leading their horses near the head of the column. During the course of the march, the cavalry commander explained Lee's instructions in meticulous detail. Essentially, they would move straight south and cross the Little River. Once across they would swing west, describing a broad arc around the Union flank, moving back up to the river behind Wright's positions. Here they must of necessity take great care. Silence would be imperative as Union cavalry patrols had been active during the daylight hours. They would recross the Little River and enter a thick copse of mixed hardwoods, cedar and pine. The region was almost jungle-like in character, heavy with briars, brambles and vines. The path which awaited them was narrow, only one man at a time could pass. They would march to the very edge of the woods, but they were to remain secluded until the first hint of dawn. To their right, deployed along the river, were several hundred Union infantrymen.

Directly to their front, barely a hundred yards away, was the extreme right of the Union line. All in all, Gordon's men would cover roughly ten miles before they came to rest in the woods behind the Federals.

From here, the plan of attack was fairly simple. Just before dawn they would burst out of the woods. Several hundred would charge back toward the river to neutralize the Federal infantry dug in along the banks. The rest would storm the main Union line, taking the very end of it, then swing left, sweeping the Federals back toward the North Anna.

As soon as the Union line was unhinged, A. P. Hill would join the fray, releasing the extreme left of his line, one brigade at a time, to join in the assault. Hill's troops were to move behind Gordon, extending the new Confederate line with the idea of preventing any Union escape upriver in the direction of Quarles Mill. Lee preferred to see the Federals herded straight down their line where they would have to cross the river under the shadow of his guns at Ox Ford.

By the third hour past midnight, the van of their column reached the Little River. Quietly, the lead elements waded in up to their waist and moved across. Several of Hampton's scouts were waiting on the north bank to lead the infantry deep into the woods. No one spoke. Every precaution was taken to prevent any noise from sabers, bayonets or metal buckles.

Gordon and Hampton stood off to one side as they watched the former's troops file silently past.

"I won't be far away," whispered Hampton. "I've got close to six thousand troopers waiting about a mile from here."

"You'll be joining in the attack?"

"Not straight away. Sheridan is back. If Grant finds himself in a pickle because of you, he'll be desperate for rein-forcements to throw in your face. Hancock's too far away, but Sheridan is a definite possibility. He's got over ten thousand cavalry with him. If he shows up, we'll be around to lend a hand."

"Good. I'll count on that."

There, the two parted company. They shook hands and wished each other well, then Gordon waded across the Little River and disappeared into the woods.

Once across the river they had perhaps a mile and a half to cover, but this last leg proved to be the most arduous of the march. There was no visibility to speak of. Men stumbled and fell. Briars bristling with thorns whipped at their faces in the dark and tore at their arms and legs. All of this they endured in silence. Not a cry was uttered. From those woods came no sounds whatsoever.

At last they reached their goal, coming to a halt some twenty yards from the open field on which the Union army was dug in. Gordon and his officers directed traffic, routing different units to their jump-off positions using only hand signals and facial expressions. All was ready. Dawn was but an hour distant. Ten thousand Confederate infantry lay on their bellies in the woods directly behind the Union lines. They were quick to take advantage of the little rest they could snatch before daybreak brought the onset of battle.

*   *   *   *

Ulysses Grant slept fitfully that night, and with good reasons. Burnside's failure to break the point of Lee's wedge left him facing the same dilemma when the sun rose on the twenty-fifth of May. His army was still divided and still re-mained in defensive positions. This was hardly cause for op-timism, and Grant knew it. He consoled himself with one thought. All his corps' commanders were under orders to take the offense if they spied any weak point along the Rebel lines. He resolved to stay at Ox Ford one more day in the hopes such a weakness could be found.

*　　　*　　　*　　　*

R. E. Lee didn't sleep much either, but for entirely different reasons. Several doses of Gwathmey's concoction had completely freed him of pain. Moreover, the good doctor had filled him with fresh vegetables and rice. He hadn't regained his strength yet, but some of his vigor returned. All night long, he went over his plans, continuing to make preparations for the approaching battle and for what he hoped would be a victorious aftermath.

Seth Reilly was another of those whose eyes didn't close that night. He moved quietly, weaving through the trees and undergrowth, checking on his men. He found Cody Wilder awake and staring wide-eyed into the night.

"Nervous, boy?" he whispered.

"Some . . . I reckon," came the muted reply.

"You'll be okay, just don't do anything stupid. Don't try to be a hero, just stay close to the rest of us."

"Okay," nodded the boy.

"Ever heard the Rebel Yell?"

"Heard of it. Never heard it though."

"You will when the sun comes up. I've had Yankee prisoners tell me it freezes the blood in their veins. I've heard generals say the Yell gives them the advantage of another thousand muskets. Anyway, when we charge I want you to scream like a banshee has hold of your soul, you hear?"

"Yessuh."

"Good. Rest easy,"

He gave the boy a fatherly pat on the shoulder. "I'll check back on you later."

He moved off, slithering over the cool damp earth on his elbows and knees. He sought out and found Ox, whose cumbersome bulk was lying prone in a bed of bright green ferns. "The weeds will never recover from this," Reilly chuckled beneath his breath.

"Give me a break, Professor. That was a long walk."

"Believe me, I know. Listen, I want you to do me a favor."

"Name it."

"Stay close to the kid when we rush the Yanks. Don't let him do anything foolish, okay? Just kind of watch over him."

"You got it, Sarge."

"I'm a lieutenant now."

"Oops . . . sorry about that."

"See that it doesn't happen again," chided Reilly with a grin and a generous poke in the big man's ribs.

As the blackness of night gradually loosened its grip on the sky, General Gordon conferred briefly with his officers, assuring himself that every man understood what was expected of him. Day would soon be breaking. Quietly, they crept into the positions from which they would soon burst out of the woods and into history.

Across the way Union troops were beginning to stir. A squad of Union cavalry passed by on its way to the Little River. Off in the distance, a bobwhite began to sing out a greeting to the new day. He was soon answered by a second, and to their chatter was quickly added the song of a whippoorwill. A knee-deep mist clung to the open ground which separated the two forces. To the eye of an artist it would have been difficult to find a picture more serene than the environs of the North Anna River that morning. This calm belied the savagery which was about to burst forth all across that peaceful landscape. Before the sun was to set on the twenty-fifth of May, 1864, the aspirations of Ulysses S. Grant would lay in ruins along with much of the Army of the Potomac.

General Lee was already on the way to join Hill on the western wing. During the night, as his strength returned, he had bathed and donned his field uniform. He requested that Traveller be brought to him, but this led to an argument with Dr. Gwathmey.

"I'll not have you riding!" insisted the physician.

"Why not?" returned Lee. "I'm feeling much better and

I've always accompanied my men into battle."

"Riding a horse could undo everything the remedy has done. I insist you travel by carriage. What will you accomplish by landing yourself on the cot again?"

Lee hesitated a moment, pondering his next words. "Might we compromise, Doctor?" he asked. "I'll ride the carriage to the front, but when the battle starts I'll sit my horse. Is that acceptable?"

Gwathmey knew how futile it would be to continue the argument and quickly decided to accept the compromise. "Only if you take a copious amount of the treatment with you," he said, adding a condition of his own. "The physical stress you're about to expose yourself to may require more frequent and heavier doses."

"Very well."

Lee then addressed himself to a waiting orderly. "Young man, would you be kind enough to fetch my carriage and see to it that Traveller is properly saddled?"

"Certainly, General."

The private saluted and quickly departed.

A short time later Lee's party was moving briskly across a narrow, bumpy dirt road toward A. P. Hill. Both Colonel Taylor and Doctor Gwathmey rode in the carriage with their General. Behind them the first pale hints of dawn were becoming evident on the horizon. After a quick glance in that direction, Lee turned to Taylor, "Well, Walter, we'll soon know whether these efforts bear fruit."

"I feel very good about this, General. The Wilderness and Spotsylvania reduced our numbers to be sure, but the quality of our soldiers hasn't been adversely affected. I think we might be a match for this fellow Grant."

"I think so, too," mused Lee, allowing himself the luxury of a faint smile.

Not too much later they arrived at Hill's headquarters where they were greeted by the corps' commander himself. He saluted Lee, who returned the courtesy.

"Good morning, General. It's good to see you again! I

assume you've prepared your men?"

"They're ready, General. Gordon should be commencing his attack any minute. I have units entrenched inside the loop of the Little River and others just to their east. They will be the first to join Gordon."

"Good. Do all of your officers understand their instructions?"

"I believe so."

"I surely hope so. It's important to extend Gordon's left once he starts the sweep. We must overlap the retreating Federals so they cannot slip away to the west. They must be herded toward the ford itself."

"My officers know what's expected of them," returned Hill, who appeared somewhat miffed at Lee's expression of doubt as to his abilities. The bungled affair at Jericho Mills was still very much on the minds of both men. Sensing the other man's discomfort Lee quickly shifted to a more positive tone.

"You've a fine corps, General," he said. "I have great faith in you and your men. I have the feeling you will all distinguish yourselves before the day is out."

"Thank you, sir. We'll make every effort. If you'll come with me, there's a small rise over yonder from which we can watch the battle progress."

In the woods behind the Union trenches, all was ready. The first wave crept to the very edge of the woods and waited for the jump-off signal. Seth Reilly was among his men. Thoughts of home and family were put aside, overshadowed by the irresistible instinct to survive. His throat was dry and the palms of his hands were sweating heavily. His body always reacted in this fashion when he was about to take part in a major attack. He cleared his throat and pulled the brim of his weatherbeaten kepi down over his forehead.

"You fellas figure you've got one more yell left?" he addressed the question to no one in particular.

"Sure enough," came the reply from Ox.

"No problem there," chimed in Evan Peterson.

"Don't be too quick with it," suggested Reilly. "The Yanks aren't expecting us. Let's see if we can't cross a little of this open ground before we announce our presence."

From Gordon came another order which was passed quickly from one man to the next: "Fix bayonets."

It was done quietly. No one standing farther than ten feet away could have heard anything out of the ordinary. Most of Lee's veterans could have performed this task blindfolded without the slightest fumble.

The sun was only minutes away from making its first appearance of the day when Gordon rose to his feet. He glanced to his left and right, asssuring himself that his officers were ready. Then he calmly removed his hat and upon this signal was launched the attack which would reverse the tide of history.

"Let's go!" urged Reilly as he climbed to his feet.

Within seconds they were in the open moving at a dead run through the pre-dawn darkness toward the Union lines. Their battle flags were unfurled and flapped sharply in the early morning breeze. Two thousand were in the first wave moving east against the main Union works. Eight hundred infantrymen from Hoke's brigade comprised the force which struck south against the Little River entrenchments. Five seconds elapsed before the first alarm sounded from the Federal positions.

"Rebels!" Came the cry which echoed quickly up and down the line. Sleepy northerners jumped to their feet and groped for their muskets.

Then came the yell, the wild, blood curdling Rebel Yell which was screamed simultaneously from ten thousand Confederate throats, striking fear and panic into a thoroughly surprised enemy.

Within seven seconds of their jump-off, the men in the first wave overran Union gun emplacements, capturing six batteries of guns undamaged. Up to that point, Gordon's men had yet to fire a shot, saving their ammunition for the moment they reached the trenches.

Wright's defenders had time for one largely ineffective volley before Gordon's infantry reached their lines. In a matter of moments they were overwhelmed in much the same fashion as the Stonewall Brigade at Spotsylvania. The opening phase of the battle was over almost as soon as it had started. The Stars and Bars flew triumphantly over the extreme right of the Union position. More than three thousand Federal soldiers became prisoners in the space of a heartbeat. For a time there was confusion among the Rebel victors, but Gordon would not allow such a state of affairs to continue long enough to interfere with their ultimate purpose. Quickly, he reorganized his forces, detailing some to mobilize the captured artillery, others to escort the mob of prisoners rearward, while the main body began sweeping the Federal line.

From his vantage point atop the knoll behind Hill's position, Lee watched calmly as all of this unfolded before his eyes. He saw the Confederate battle flags flying over the Union positions. He saw the prisoners, hands held high, being marched toward Rebel lines. He shifted his glass toward the little river and saw much the same thing. The Union forces along the river capitulated quickly. They were disarmed and led away at once so Hoke's men could rejoin the main force. Lee lowered the glass, and for a fleeting moment he responded with a smile.

"So far so good," he said softly.

*   *   *   *

Three miles to the north the rumble of distant gunfire brought Ulysses Grant to his feet. Quickly, he pulled on his boots and stepped outside to the cool pleasant air of early morning. His headquarters had come alive, buzzing with activity as the sounds of battle grew steadily in the distance. He spied Meade listening intently with one foot propped on a rotting log.

"What do you make of it?" Grant asked.

110

"Hard to say," came the reply, "There's a number of possibilities."

"I'll bet it's good news," said Grant, ever the optimist. "Wright or Warren is involved. One of them must have found a weakness in the Rebel lines. They're moving forward on their own initiative. That's good! It's what I've wanted all along!"

Meade made no attempt at a reply for several moments as he continued to listen to the increasing volume of gunfire erupting to the south. "I don't think so," he said at last, turning to face Grant. "For one thing, Bobby Lee is not particularly prone to making serious mistakes. I don't think he's left us any opening. You'd best consider the possibility that he's attacking us."

Grant growled something unintelligible and turned away. "Courier!" he called to a nearby soldier.

"Sir!" The fellow came to attention and saluted.

"Get out there and find out what's going on! And be quick! I want information and I want it fast!"

"Yessir! Straight away!" The rider fairly hurled himself into the saddle and within a space of a heartbeat or two he was racing toward the river at full gallop.

Meade followed Grant back into his tent, then waited patiently while his commander lit his customary cigar. "Assuming we're under attack," he said at last, "How do you plan to respond?"

"I'll have to think on it for a spell. As you've taken pains to point out over the last twenty-four hours, our present position doesn't leave us a whole lot of options." He puffed vigorously on the cigar and stared at something outside the tent.

"Nevertheless, we'd best come up with some ideas."

"I don't think exaggerating the danger will serve any purpose. Wright and Warren are both competent men. They've got two full corps plus one of Burnside's divisions out there. Their numbers are considerable. I have confidence in them."

"What if they need help?"

Grant said nothing.

"There's Sheridan," suggested Meade.

"I'll keep him in mind," nodded Grant. "If it'll make you feel better, go ahead and send for him. He could be here by the time our courier returns."

Meade turned away to seek another dispatch rider.

As Grant and Meade were concluding their brief conversation the fury of Gordon's charge continued to grow in intensity. More than twenty minutes had passed since the Rebels charged out of the woods. In that time, they had cleared close to a half-mile of Union trenches. In the process they had captured forty Federal artillery pieces, and these they quick put to good use. Having already cleared a considerable length of enemy breastworks, Gordon had opened a wide avenue through which reinforcements could safely cross from Hill's trenches. Two brigades from Hill's corps had already crossed. A third was enroute. With his strength continuing to grow in this fashion, Gordon pressed the offensive without a moment's hesitation.

For his part, Lee was elated, "This is the moment we've been waiting for since those people crossed the Rapidan!" He cried aloud making no effort to mask his excitement. A twinge of pain rippled through his stomach, but he paid it no mind. "Little Powell!" he called to Hill, "You must continue feeding your men into the attack! Gordon needs every available man!"

"He'll have them!" concurred Hill with a broad smile.

"Have we couriers?"

"Here, Sir!" cried one of several dispatch riders who stood nearby.

"One of you ride at once to General Anderson on the bluffs over Ox Ford! Tell him there may soon be thousands of Federals trying to cross to the north bank under his guns. He must do all he can to impede their efforts!"

"Yessuh!" replied one who quickly pulled his mount away.

"Word of this must go at once to General Ewell!" continued Lee. "Advise him to stand ready! When Grant hears of this action he will probably attempt to relieve the pressure on this front by storming the other wing. We cannot allow such an attack to succeed."

"Very well, General!"

A second rider broke away from the group and raced down the knoll.

Wright's corps was in danger of total collapse. His officers tried valiantly to quell the panic which had taken a vise grip on their foot soldiers, but to no avail. They fled like rabbits.

Gordon's infantry was fast on their heels, sweeping the trenches, gathering prisoners in droves. Deploying the additional brigades sent across by Hill, he extended his left some hundred-fifty yards from the Federal trenches. Since the bulk of the enemy were either in flight or still in the trenches, most of his infantry faced no opposition. These he urged forward at a furious pace, so they quickly outdistanced their compatriots on the extreme right. As a result, his line soon described an oblique angle to the Federal position. Having established such a formation, he was then in a position to effectively block any attempt by the Northerners to bolt in the direction of Jericho Mills.

Seth Reilly and the remnants of the Stonewall Brigade were in position on the line about twenty yards west of the Federal trenches. They and their comrades were pushing relentlessly northward against mediocre resistance. Less than an hour had passed since the attack was launched. Close to a mile of Union trenches had been cleared. At this point resistance began to stiffen. A thick pall of blue smoke covered the battleground, in some places hovering close to the ground, in other places drifting lazily with the mild currents of early morning air. The acrid smell of gunpowder clung to the soldiers' nostrils, but this they paid no mind. More than anything else they smelled victory . . . devastating victory . . . a triumph more complete than anything they had ever hoped to experience.

"Press 'em!" shouted Reilly. "Push ahead! Push ahead! Keep moving!"

They maintained their pace with a steadfastness of purpose, and they refused to allow any organized resistance to develop until a mile of trenches had been cleared.

Here they encountered their first real challenge of the day. General Warren had withdrawn a full division from his own trenches and dispatched them at once to General Wright. They were deployed in a line of battle perpendicular to the earthworks extending about eighty yards west. Their numbers were bolstered by a division of Wright's own infantry along with a considerable horde of refugees who had finally brought their fear under control. In all, they managed to muster some fourteen thousand muskets. Quickly, they braced themselves to receive the Rebel assault.

However, this effort was doomed from the start, regardless of how bold its intentions may have been. By this time, Gordon's strength had grown to eighteen thousand men. Moreover, the extreme left of his line had already overlapped the new Federal position. To this could be added the weight of fifty captured Federal guns and nearly thirty Rebel guns which had come across from Hill. Against these, Wright could only field twenty-eight pieces. Warren still faced the possibility of an attack across his front. He had already detached a full division of infantry. He could not risk weakening himself further by sending artillery as well.

Gordon's response to the challenge was little short of perfect. Three terrifying volleys of cannon fire, a deadly mixture of grape and shot, were unleashed on the hastily organized Union ranks. He conformed his line so that much of his infantry could strike the Union flank while the rest stormed their front. As the echoes of the third volley of artillery died on the wind, the infantry stormed forward, their bayonets gleaming brightly in the early morning sun. The Rebel Yell rose from thousands of throats, curdling the blood of Union defenders.

Despite the tactical hopelessness of their situation, the Federal riflemen stood their ground during the first few moments. They were able to deliver four quick volleys, inflicting the worst losses suffered by the Rebels at Ox Ford. Better than four thousand Confederates fell at this stage of the battle. Among these were Hal Saunders and Buck Randall, both of the Stonewall Brigade.

Struck simultaneously on the flank and from the front, the Federals tried desperately to maintain the integrity of their line, but to no avail. Under the weight of fourteen thousand Rebel bayonets their lines gave way and collapsed. Many fell dead or wounded. Some chose to simply throw down their weapons and give up the fight. Most simply turned and ran.

It was here that Cody Wilder's young life very nearly came to an abrupt end. Like his comrades in the Stonewall Brigade, he was locked in hand-to-hand combat in the moments just before the Union resistance collapsed. Unfortunately, he found himself facing a burly northerner at least twice his age who outweighed the boy by a good eighty pounds. In short order, the Yankee knocked Cody's musket from his hands, and with the butt of his rifle he drove the boy into the ground. For a moment, he stood over the lad, leering down with an indifferent grin on his face. Then he raised his musket high, centering the bayonet on Wilder's heart. Just as he was about to drive the blade home, he jerked upright, yelping in pain. He dropped his weapon, the bayonet barely missing young Wilder. Behind him stood Ox, who slowly withdrew his own bayonet from the man's back. The fellow sprawled dead across Wilder.

"Get him off me!" Cody's muffled voice was barely audible beneath the bulky form of the dead soldier, "I can't breathe!"

With one foot Ox rolled the body off of the boy, "Reckon you oughta pick on Yanks yer own size from now on," he quipped with a sly grin. "C'mon," he beckoned, "You ain't got time to be takin' no naps! We gotta keep movin'!"

115

A SOUTHERN YARN

"Thanks, Ox," Cody jumped to his feet. "I owe ya one."

"Don't mention it. You'll probably owe me a couple 'fore the day's out. Pick up your musket and let's get back into it."

*   *   *   *

Sheridan was on hand when the dust-covered courier arrived at Union headquarters. He and Grant were conferring in the latter's tent as the rider slipped hastily from his saddle. General Meade was there, anxious strain etched on his battle-worn face, "What word?" he demanded harshly.

"Not good, sir," replied the soldier. "Lee's attacked. He struck Wright's flank at first light. The Rebs are rolling up our line. I've got a brief written report here from General Warren."

"Let's have it!" beckoned Meade.

Moments later, having read the hastily scribbled report from Warren, Meade presented himself at the entrance to Grant's tent. His eyes had sunk low in their sockets, his face ashen.

"What's wrong, George?" queried Grant. "You look as though you've seen a ghost."

With a sideways glance in Sheridan's direction, Meade responded at once, "Lee's taken the offensive. As we speak, the Rebels are driving Wright back upon Warren. Here's the written summary."

Grant quickly scanned through its contents and turned his attention to a hand-drawn map of his positions. "How much ground has been lost?" he asked Meade.

"I believe two miles remain between the Rebels and the river."

"That gives us a little time to knock some of the wind out of Lee's sails."

"Too little," argued Meade. "Whatever response you have in mind had better be delivered fast. As things now stand we're on the verge of losing half this army."

"Don't be so gloomy, George!" snapped Grant. "This is

Lee's last gasp. He hasn't the resources to remain long on the offense."

"Tell him that!" spat Meade, his exasperation becoming ever more apparent. "Did you read the dispatch? They've overlapped our lines! His intentions are obvious. He's trying to herd two corps of our infantry into the ford itself! Don't you see?"

"Let's not be impudent, General," barked Grant angrily, squaring his shoulders as though preparing for a boxing match, "I'm beginning to resent your tone!"

"Gentlemen! Gentlemen, please!" Sheridan spoke for the first time. "Perhaps this energy could be better used if directed at Lee! My cavalry is ready, and we'd like nothing better than to start smashing things. Say the word."

"Exactly what I had in mind," nodded Grant. "How quickly can you get your men into position to strike the Rebel flank?"

"We can leave at once. Crossing at Jericho Mills we should be able to launch a flanking assault within the hour."

"Do so. Drive their line. Eliminate the overlap so our infantry will have an escape route available, should one be needed."

"It won't. Eleven thousand of these new repeating rifles will have those graybacks scrambling all over each other to get back to their trenches."

"That's what I like to hear!" Grant flashed a broad grin as he chomped down on a freshly lit cigar, "Get to it! Make sure I'm kept informed."

"On my way." Little Phil was out of the tent in the space of a heartbeat.

"Feel better?" Grant glanced at Meade.

"I'll feel better when I know he's pulled it off."

"There aren't many the equal of Phil Sheridan. He'll pull it off."

Grant returned his attention to the map, "Let's see what else we can do to ruin Bobby Lee's morning."

"We don't have a surplus in the way of options."

117

"We have Hancock."

"What?"

"I said, we have Hancock."

"I heard that, General. Just what do you have in mind?"

"Lee could not possibly have mounted this attack without first stripping his lines of their defenders. A substantial number, I'll wager. I'm willing to bet he took them from the trenches opposite Hancock."

"So?"

"So, we counterattack from the left, strike him where he must now be weakest. I want Hancock to hurl his full strength at Lee's right. If nothing else, he'll force Lee to break off the action on our right in order to stave off Hancock."

"General Grant," argued Meade. "I feel compelled to urge caution. If the day goes badly, Hancock's corps could be all that stands between us and total annihilation."

"Your warning is duly noted, George, but I'm damn sick and tired of hearing you whine about Robert E. Lee. Before this day is over he'll rue the day he ever heard of Ulysses Grant. Mark my words!" He stormed out of the tent and shouted for a dispatch rider. A heavy-set man atop a strong-looking bay quickly presented himself.

"General?" he saluted smartly.

Grant had just finished scribbling orders on a piece of headquarters stationary, "Take this at once to General Hancock," he ordered. "Tell him he is to storm Lee's right with all his strength at the earliest possible moment!"

"Straight away, General!" The soldier was in the saddle and on his way in a matter of seconds.

"I hope you're right," sighed Meade as he watched the rider disappear from view. "If you're not, we could easily suffer a major disaster."

"Not this time, George. This time we're going to turn the tables on Bobby Lee. Mark my words."

*   *   *   *

All the while, Gordon's gray-clad infantry continued their unprecedented push, sweeping the Federal line, forcing the Federals to retreat on a course parallel to their own fortifications. Federal losses were terrible and it appeared as though the northerners might never be organized to make a determined stand. Prisoners were taken in droves, and the dazed expressions on their beleaguered faces spoke directly to the speed and fury of the Confederate assault.

Through all of this, Gordon remained in the thick of the fray, urging his men on, oblivious to danger. Several times the sleeves of his uniform were pierced by bullets, but his person escaped harm. With every passing minute his strength grew as Hill's corps passed across the open ground to join in the assault.

"Get back to General Lee!" he cried to a courier with utter joy in his voice. "Tell him the operation thus far has exceeded our expectations! Tell him we have more prisoners than we can handle! Ask him if we might accelerate the pace at which A. P. Hill's corps is joining the attack!"

"Yessuh!"

The fellow wheeled his mount around and spurred him into a full gallop. Within minutes he had crossed the no-mans land between the two armies and quickly reached the base of the knoll from which Lee was observing the progress of the battle.

"What news, good man?" called Lee as he returned the soldier's salute.

"They're on the run, General!" The rider's enthusiasm could easily be seen on his face, and in his voice Lee observed unbounded excitement.

"Splendid!" replied the commander with a boyish grin of his own.

"They're givin' up in droves, Marse Robert! Whole regiments!" The boy let fly his cap and turning his young face skyward he loosed a wild Rebel Yell.

Lee could not help but smile at this display of exuberance, but at the same time he could not lose sight of the business at hand, "We must retain our composure, young man," he lectured. "Victory is not yet at hand. Have I heard the extent of your message?"

"Message? Oh . . . no, suh," the young man blushed slightly and came to attention in the saddle, "General Gordon says we have more prisoners than we can handle. He was wonderin' if you might speed up the reinforcements from General Hill." Lee glanced toward A. P. Hill, "Ambrose?"

"I'll see to it immediately," nodded Hill.

"Very good."

Lee then fixed his eyes upon the messenger, "Return at once to General Gordon. Convey my compliments and congratulations for his initial success, but impress upon him the need for redoubled efforts. He must press the enemy with no respite! Those people must not be allowed the time to form a stable line of defense."

"I understand, General."

"Off with you then."

Lee and Hill watched silently as the rider disappeared in the distance. For several minutes there was only the roar of battle to occupy their attention, but after a short time, General Hill intruded upon the thoughts of his commander.

"General Gordon is proving himself one very fine officer," he noted.

"He most certainly is," agreed Lee.

"I think there could well be a touch of Stonewall in him."

The corners of Lee's mouth turned upwards in a faint smile at this statement. In truth, he had been thinking the same thing. For just a moment his eyes met those of his veteran lieutenant, "Perhaps," he said calmly. "In any event," he added after clearing his throat. "I think we should move ourselves to a position where we can better monitor this affair."

"I know just the place. Not far from the spot where my corps connects with Anderson's."

"Lead the way," smiled the Confederate commander, but

this utterance had scarcely passed his lips when he stiffened slightly, his face contorting as a new tremor of pain rippled through his entrails. "Gwathmey!" he called weakly.

"Here, General!" The physician moved at once to his side.

"Have you more of that disgusting concoction prepared? I believe my stomach is sending me a message in no uncertain terms."

"We've got plenty." The doctor reached quickly for his saddlebags.

*　　　*　　　*　　　*

General Hancock was on the ramparts of his own trenches studying the enemy fortifications when Grant's courier finally located him. He had been awakened by the distant sound of battle and had rushed at once to the front. From his position on the opposite wing he could see nothing of the fighting itself, aside from the thick pall of smoke which drifted across the field. Nonetheless, he was a veteran and it didn't take him long to realize what was taking place.

"Wright's been hit on the flank," he remarked to a staff officer. "Judging from the noise and the smoke, the Rebs seem to be rolling him up at a frightening pace."

"Any orders?"

"Get everything ready to move. I imagine Grant will pull us back across the river to march to their aid, though I seriously doubt if we could arrive in time to be of any help."

"Very good, sir. I'll see to it at once."

"Just have everything ready. We can't move till we receive orders, but when the time comes, speed will be vital."

"Yes, sir."

More than an hour had passed after that conversation before the courier found Hancock.

"General!" he cried. "Orders from headquarters." The soldier reached quickly into his tunic and produced the paper on which Grant had outlined his instructions.

121

"At last!" growled the general as he snatched the paper from the rider's hands. Quickly he scanned his orders. "He wants us to attack?" he gasped incredulously. "Surely there must be some sort of mistake! He knows how strong the Rebel position is!"

"No mistake, sir," said the dispatch rider. "General Grant believes that Lee must have stripped this wing in order to deliver his attack upon General Wright."

"I can read!" railed Hancock. "Return at once to headquarters! Inform General Grant that I shall do my duty!"

"Yessir!" With a swift salute the fellow turned away.

Hancock turned to his staff officer. "I want to see all three of my division commanders at corps headquarters in ten minutes!" he snapped. "Get artillery back into position and have them open fire at once upon the enemy lines."

"As you wish, sir."

Despite Hancock's designated time frame, nearly twenty minutes passed before the three divisional commanders had all assembled at his headquarters tent.

"That's about the size of it," said Hancock, concluding his final instructions. "Apparently General Grant feels the best way to counter this situation is to force Lee to abort his offensive by threatening this wing of his army. If Grant is correct, the Rebels have stripped that wing to make their attack. If that's the case, we have every reason to expect success."

"And if Grant is mistaken?" ventured one.

Hancock made no verbal reply, but the expression on his face spoke volumes.

Another of his divisional commanders was not so reluctant to speak: "If Grant is wrong in his assumptions we'll have a repetition of the last charge we made at Spotsylvania."

"Very possibly," said Hancock in a voice barely above a whisper.

For several minutes little was said. Each man retreated into the solace of his own thoughts. Before long, however, the first of Hancock's batteries opened fire, beginning the barrage which would preface the assault on Lee's works.

"Gentlemen," said Hancock. "I think it fair to say we all have our misgivings about the attack we've been ordered to make. Still . . . we're all soldiers and bound by oath to do our duty. To quote another soldier in another time, 'Our's is not to reason why . . .'"

"Our's is but to do and die," another completed the phrase.

"Return to your men and prepare them for the charge," instructed Hancock. "Whatever you do, don't let the troops sense any feelings of gloom from yourselves. Be of good cheer and pray that Grant has guessed correctly. God be with us."

*   *   *   *

In the opposing trenches, the Confederate General Ewell had suddenly become a very busy man. Lee had already warned him of the possibility of an attack, and he braced his command for just such an event. Moreover, though his strength had been slightly depleted to create Gordon's strike force, he still had the bulk of his riflemen securely in position. More to the point, all of his artillery was on hand, the same guns which had decimated the last Union thrust along the base of the salient at Spotsylvania. Every man in his position knew what was coming the moment Hancock's artillery began to spew fire and shot. They stood to arms and waited for the inevitable wave of blue to burst forth across the open plain. Confidence was not a problem. They expected to shatter Hancock's thrust just as they had done in Spotsylvania.

This same level of confidence could not be found among Hancock's infantry as they prepared to launch themselves upon the field. They shared the feeling which was prevalent among the Union troops; a belief that they were being outgeneraled, mishandled from the top, that their lives were being squandered to no good end. Many complained openly.

Others merely sat in passive silence, staring across at the enemy lines, contemplating the probability of doom.

A certain Captain Edwards of a New York regiment encountered this negative atmosphere as he organized his troops for the coming effort. His orders were received in a mood which at best could be described as sullen compliance.

"Have they gone mad at headquarters?" shouted one private.

"That'll be enough of that!" snarled Edwards.

"After Spotsylvania how could they order another frontal assault against those lines?"

"You open your mouth one more time and I'll have you shot for insubordination!"

"Hold your tongue, Al," urged another. "You're better off taking your chances against the Rebs. A firing squad won't miss."

Al glared angrily at his captain for several moments, but he listened to his friend's advice and said no more.

Many of the troops in Hancock's trenches were green draftees, men who had only been in the army for several weeks and were hurriedly pressed into action to replace the appalling losses suffered by Grant in the Wilderness and at Spotsylvania. Describing these fellows as nervous would be understating the facts. The rising level of anxiety among these new draftees was a significant factor in the growing mood of despair which swept Hancock's position as surely as Gordon was sweeping Wright's.

Minutes before the attack was to begin, Hancock's troops began writing their names, units and hometowns on pieces of cloth or paper, whatever might be on hand. This information was invariably followed by the message: "Killed at Ox Ford, May 25th, 1864."

If Hancock had been looking for an omen to reveal the fate of his attack, he would easily have found it on the backs of his soldiers where they had pinned their crudely fashioned name tags.

"Whose idea was this?" demanded Edwards, addressing

himself to a sergeant.

"Don't know, Captain," came the reply. "Somebody over in C company I think. It seems to have caught on rather quickly."

"Like a brush fire. Didn't anyone try to stop them?"

"No, sir. To be honest with you, it didn't seem like all that bad an idea. At least we'll be able to identify our dead when the Rebs are through with us."

"That's just the damn point, Sergeant! Shouldn't we be thinking in terms of what we're going to do to them?"

"Ideally," admitted the sergeant, "But in all candor, Captain, few of us expect to even reach their trenches." There was a sadness in his eyes bordering on despair.

Captain Edwards knew it would be fruitless to pursue the discussion any further, "Pass the order to stand ready, Sergeant. We jump off in five minutes."

"Yessir," nodded the sergeant, who turned away to do the officer's bidding.

Ewell's Confederate artillery men waited patiently, savoring the opportunity to decimate Hancock's infantry as they had done at Spotsylvania. Not a single shell had they expended in response to the Union barrage. Ammunition was not plentiful, and they were determined to save every round for the Federal infantry. To many, the wait seemed interminable, but their wait was soon to end.

Hancock's infantry would have been content to listen to their own artillery all the day long, but their wait was also drawing to a close. The guns fell silent and the thick pall of smoke they had created began to dissipate.

"Move out!" The dreaded order echoed in their ears.

Out of the trenches they climbed. Despite their trepidation they did not abandon their training and discipline. In a matter of moments they had formed by units and started across the field. Their battle flags and regimental banners were unfurled and snapped proudly in the morning breeze. To the rapid tap of drums they stepped up their pace. They let loose their deep-chested war cry, but it was instantly drowned beneath the roar of Rebel artillery. Bodies and parts thereof were blown skyward. Great gaps began to appear in the ranks of Hancock's brave soldiers, but on they charged.

Ewell's gunners plied their trade with deadly proficiency. The events of May in the spring of '64 had certainly given them ample practice.

"Switch to cannister!" came the inevitable order.

Compliance was swift. The impact of this change was even quicker. Hundreds fell. The field was littered with blue-clad dead and dying.

Ewell's riflemen added the weight of their weapons on the heels of the first volley of canister. The effect was instantaneous and truly terrible to behold. The first ranks of attackers were shattered, and those following saw no point in pressing the issue.

"Hit the dirt! Go to ground!"

Down they went, most of them hugging the earth as though lying in the embrace of their most ardent lovers. Officers tried vainly to reestablish the attack, but their men would have none of it. Every time the order to advance was issued, most of the troops simply raised their weapons and fired in the general direction of the Rebels. For all practical purposes the attack was over. Twenty minutes after their jump off not a single Union soldier had come anywhere close to Ewell's trenches. Thousands had fallen dead or wounded. The rest remained prostrate on the ground itself.

Hancock had gone to the front to monitor his soldiers' progress, but what he found was cause for thorough dismay. He lowered his glasses in silence and turned away from the grisly scene. "It's no good," he admitted, "Get a bugler up there to sound recall," he muttered as he slammed his open hand against a length of timber, ". . . And get our troops out of there before they're all killed!" His eyes peered about until they located one of his more reliable staff officers. "Dispatch a rider to Grant," he ordered. "Tell him he made the wrong assumption. Ewell's out there in strength. Tell him we've been repulsed and our losses are heavy. Advise him I will withdraw to my trenches to await further instructions."

"Very well, General."

"God help us now," muttered Hancock as the shrill blare of bugles sang out over the battlefield.

On the opposite side of the battlefield Phil Sheridan was preparing to announce his presence in spectacular fashion. With eleven thousand troopers, the sum total of Grant's mounted strength, he had crossed the North Anna at Jericho Mills and had maneuvered into position to launch himself into Gordon's left, or so he thought. In point of fact, by the time Sheridan had reached his jump-off point, Gordon had driven Wright back upon Warren. As the panicky remnants of one Union corps worked to assimilate themselves with the troops of a second, Gordon shuffled units to maintain the oblique character of his own line — more or less pinning the Federals to the general vicinity of their own trenches — continuing to deny them any outlet in the direction of Jericho Mills. When Sheridan came within sight of the battle he found himself slightly to the rear of Gordon's left. The New Jersey officer grinned openly as he savored his prospects. "They don't know we're here!" he boasted. "In a few minutes they'll be sandwiched between ourselves and our infantry. Get ready, boys! We're about to turn the tables on Bobby Lee!"

Unfortunately for General Sheridan, indeed for the United States itself, his assessment of the situation was something less than accurate. To begin with he was convinced that the element of surprise would be his. This was a mistake. Wade Hampton saw to that. The Confederate cavalry commander had suspected all along that Grant would try something of the sort if things became desperate. His scouts had monitored Sheridan's progress almost from the time the Federals crossed the river. As soon as Sheridan's intended jump-off position became obvious, Hampton dispatched a rider to Gordon.

Another factor which played a pivotal role in the subsequent series of events was Gordon's line itself. He had overlapped the opposing infantry by a considerate distance. Nearly four thousand of his own infantry had no enemy to their front. They could easily swing about and bring their muskets to bear on the Union cavalry without fear of a threat to their backs by Federal infantry.

Add to this the weight of captured Union artillery which Gordon's gunners were using with considerable success, and you have all the ingredients for a Union disaster.

Sheridan was counting on the new repeating rifles to be a deciding factor. This too was a mistake. These weapons were an advantage, to be sure, but they were most effective when fired from a stationary position. Their impact was questionable at best when fired from the back of a horse charging at a full gallop or fast trot. Therefore, cavalry charges, even those of substantial numbers, were of questionable value when delivered against the firepower of massed infantry.

Gordon received Hampton's warning only minutes before Sheridan's forces arrived at their chosen place on the field. At the same time two more brigades were arriving from Hill's Corps, some thirty-two hundred men in all. Both brigade commanders reported to Gordon for instructions.

"Where do you want us?" asked one.

"You fellas got here just in time," smiled Gordon with a genuine sigh of relief. "We're about to be hit by Yankee cavalry from those woods over yonder. I want you to establish a line of battle there, about fifty yards behind us. I'll shift most of the artillery to your support."

"Straight away, General," came the reply, and both officers immediately set about complying with Gordon's instructions.

Gordon pulled a small piece of paper from his breast pocket and hastily scribbled another set of orders, "Corporal!"

He called to a dispatch rider waiting nearby.

"Sir?"

"Take this to General Hoke. Tell him to shift every man from the point of contact with the Federals to the end of our line. They are to turn around and direct their fire at enemy cavalry as soon as they commence their charge."

"Yessir!"

"Altogether we should have about seven-thousand muskets with which to greet Mr. Sheridan," he noted calmly, speaking to no one in particular. By this time his strength had grown to twenty-thousand, even when subtracting the casualties sustained thus far in the operation. "We'll still have plenty of men to continue the sweep," he observed with no small degree of satisfaction.

Meanwhile, Seth Reilly and his men took control of the most recent Federal position to fall. Scores of dazed prisoners had to be gathered and escorted to the rear. Union dead were scattered over the ground. This latest phase of the attack snuffed out the extreme right of the enemy line, leaving the remnants of Stonewall's brigade with no one to face. Cody Wilder was the first to take advantage of this temporary lull in fighting. He approached the body of a young northerner, gauged the size of the dead man's feet, and set about removing his boots.

"What the hell you doin, boy?" bellowed Ox. "We ain't got time for no shoppin' spree!"

"Aw c'mon, Ox!" protested the boy as he pulled off a boot. "He shore don't need 'em anymore! Look what I'm wearing! I may as well be barefoot!"

"Okay, young-un. Just be quick about it. There's a war goin on."

"That's hard not to notice," grinned Wilder.

"Cody! Hey Cody!" Whitt Simmon's voice sang out. "I just found you one dandy of a rifle!"

"What's that?" Cody glanced up as he laced his new boots.

"A Whitworth! I was hopin we'd run across one! Check it out, look through the scope. This baby is the most accurate rifle in the field. Go ahead and take it. It's yours. I got it off a dead Yankee. Here's the ammo pouch to go with it."

Wilder finished with his new pair of boots and took hold

of the rifle. With the expertise of a marksman he clasped it in both hands testing its weight and balance.

"That scope makes it accurate up to a half-mile," explained Simmons.

"She's a beauty!" praised the boy, as though he were describing a young woman.

"Use it well," urged the corporal as he grasped the lad's shoulder.

Just then he spied Lieutenant Reilly who had been conferring with an officer from Hoke's brigade.

"Face about!" he called. "Get into position over there! We're setting up a line about thirty yards away! Move quickly boys!"

"What's up, Professor?" wondered Ox.

"Yankee cavalry! They'll be coming out of those woods any minute now! Gordon wants us to arrange a suitable welcome."

"Whatever you say, Lieutenant!"

Quickly they moved toward the rear, their own tiny unit all but swallowed by Hoke's brigade. For several moments there was a flurry of activity as the riflemen established themselves in two ranks and dozens of captured artillery pieces were wheeled into place.

"Load and stand ready!" came the order.

With his new boots and the newly acquired rifle, Cody Wilder took up his position in the line, Ox to his right, Simmons to his left.

Meanwhile, Wade Hampton was also preparing to make a move. His four thousand gray-clad troopers were in the woods ready to pounce upon Sheridan's right as soon as the Federal cavalryman exposed himself, Hampton had twelve horse-drawn guns which he placed near the edge of the woods where they might rake the Union right.

By this time, Sheridan too was ready. His eleven thousand riders were massed near the edge of the trees ready to spring their unexpected charge on a hopefully unprepared enemy. In his own mind he expected to emerge a hero; the savior of Mr. Lincoln's Army of the Potomac. From the woods they burst into the open, shouting the Union war cry, flags and banners waving proudly as their well-fed horses bore them toward the rear of Gordon's flank.

"Here they come!" shouted Reilly. "Take aim!"

Cody Wilder was more than happy to obey that order. He leveled the Whitworth toward the oncoming cavalry and using the scope he scanned the wave of riders for the optimum target. Almost immediately, he sighted what appeared to be an officer, a bandy-legged fellow who seemed much too small for his horse.

"No matter how big he is," thought the boy. "There's a gold bar on each of his shoulders."

Without waiting for the order to fire he drew a bead on the officer's chest, took a slow deep breath, and gently squeezed the trigger.

Phil Sheridan felt the bullet strike the left side of his chest and tear through muscle and bone just above his heart. He cried out once before toppling forward across the neck of his horse and tumbling to the ground. His right foot was caught in the stirrup. He was dragged over the ground for nearly a hundred feet before breaking free, but he found no safety. Hundreds of blue-clad troopers were right behind him and they could no more stop than he could fly. Some were able to swerve and avoid their fallen commander. Most couldn't. His body was pummelled by dozens of hooves in a matter of seconds. The exact moment that death relieved Phil Sheridan of his agony is not known. Perhaps he was dead before he ever hit the ground. He may never have felt any of the hooves which pulverized his bones like so many pretzels. Only one thing can be held certain. History records the death of General Phil Sheridan at the Battle of Ox Ford, May 25th, 1864.

"What in the Hell are you doin, boy?" barked Ox. "This ain't no damn squirrel shoot! You're a soldier now! You fire when you get the order to fire! Not when you damn well please!"

A SOUTHERN YARN

"I got him!" Young Wilder was jubilant. "I got me an officer! A Yankee officer! I saw him fall!"

Their conversation was cut somewhat short by the long awaited order, "Fire!"

The response was instantaneous. Thirty pieces of captured artillery shredded the first ranks of oncoming horsemen. Nearly seven thousand Enfield muskets effectively decimated the survivors.

From the woods, Hampton's horse-drawn batteries added their weight to the affair with horrible impact. His four thousand troopers stood nearby, ready to swoop out of the woods into the flank of their enemy.

Bereft of their commander and stunned by the tremendous firepower which had destroyed the leading elements of their charge, the Federal horsemen slowed momentarily, many of them dazed and confused. Some considered the prospect of bidding a hasty withdrawal, but their officers would hear none of it. Too much was at stake. Wright and Warren were in danger of total collapse. Only the cavalry stood between the Army of the Potomac and total disaster.

"Onward!" cried the officers. "Charge! Break the line! Forward!"

With zeal born of desperation the Union troopers reorganized and pressed their valiant charge with renewed vigor.

No one would ever question the valor displayed by Sheridan's troopers that day, though one might have a question or two about the judgment of the men who sent them to certain destruction. They seemed oblivious to peril as they hurled themselves toward the waiting Rebel riflemen.

Gordon's gunners and riflemen weren't about to budge. They methodically reloaded and continued to pour lead and shot into the Federals with murderous frenzy, felling hundreds with every volley.

In the woods to the right of this action Wade Hampton's horsemen were literally chomping at the bit. "Hey General!" yelled one. "When do we get into it?"

A major spared Hampton any reply. "Keep your shirt

on, boy!"

"Not just yet," muttered the general. "But it won't be long."

A handful of Sheridan's riders actually breached Gordon's hastily formed lines. But these were few and far between. They had no support to speak of, and though they inflicted a few casualties, they were all killed or captured in short order. Aside from these, not a single trooper made it closer than fifty yards from the Confederate position. The fire was simply too terrible to endure. Despairing of victory, humbled beyond words, and feeling suddenly all too mortal, Sheridan's riders turned tail and ran.

On the last day at Spotsylvania, Lee's infantry had shown mercy, silencing their guns when the enemy broke off their attack. Not so in this situation. At Spotsylvania there was no thought of destroying Grant's army. The Rebels were content to hold him off, knowing they'd face him another day. This was not the case at Ox Ford. The battle which was raging ever close to the slopes of the North Anna river was beginning to shape up as the "Cannae" Lee had long desired. Gordon's men were determined to accomplish this aim, even if it meant shooting men who were fleeing the fight. As a result, Sheridan's survivors found the way out almost as murderous as the way in.

Moreover, as they were soon to find out, retreat offered very little in the way of safety. They were about to be welcomed by Wade Hampton, and the Carolinian apparently had forgotten all those notions about "southern hospitality".

"Boys!" he cried to the men who awaited his order to charge, "Those fellers killed Jeb Stuart! I don't reckon I need to say any more! Remember Stuart!" He drew his saber and spurred his horse out of the woods.

"Remember Stuart!" The cry was echoed up and down the ranks as four thousand mounted rebels stormed out of the shelter of the woods and raced to intercept the fleeing Federals. Yellow Tavern and the death of Jeb Stuart were still very much on the minds of Hampton and his men. To

133

say they were burning for revenge would be something of an understatement. What they lacked in actual firepower they certainly made up for in zeal. In a matter of seconds the two opposing forces met in a fierce head-on collision. From that point rifles were of little use. The final outcome would be decided by sabers and pistols.

The result was never in doubt. The remnants of Sheridan's troops were decidedly beaten before they were hit by Hampton's riders. The thought of standing and fighting never really entered their minds. Escape and survival had become the foremost priorities. Sabers clashed for several minutes and a substantial number of saddles were emptied before the Federals were able to break it off and flee. They raced for Jericho Mills, and Hampton's rebels were right on their heels in hot pursuit. Hundreds of the Northerners were made prisoner before they could make good their escape.

Once contact was broken the pursuit itself became a one-sided affair. Union cavalry could boast of well-fed sturdy horses, decidedly stronger than those of their Southern counterparts. They easily outdistanced Hampton's troops, reaching Jericho Mills in plenty of time to make a safe crossing. By the time Hampton reached the Mill he found the south bank deserted. Even the infantry who had been assigned to secure the crossing were gone. Moreover, Sheridan's survivors were digging themselves in along the North bank. Hampton toyed with the idea of crossing the river to continue his attack, but he quickly thought better of it.

"Get word back to Lee," he ordered. "Tell him we scattered the Yankee cavalry and inflicted heavy casualties on them. Let him know they've retreated to a position on the north bank of the river. They're dug in really well and it probably would cost us dearly if we tried to dislodge them."

"Very well, General."

"Tell him we decimated their cavalry. We've captured thousands of horses and the battlefield should yield a lot of those repeating rifles the Yanks have been using."

"I'll let him know."

"Get going. If he has any instructions we'll be waiting opposite the Mill."

By this time the mood of John Gordon had elevated to a point perilously close to ecstacy. He had to consciously restrain himself lest his elation cloud his normally good sense of judgment. He had just watched Sheridan's cavalry cut to ribbons in less than a half an hour. This was certainly reason to celebrate in and of itself, but bigger game waited on the horizon. He would not allow himself or his men time to pause and rejoice. There would be plenty of time for celebration after the battle had been waged to its hoped for conclusion.

"Swing about!" he cried, directing his infantry to turn their attentions northward once again. "Press 'em!" he shouted fiercely, "Sweep those trenches! Sweep 'em!"

A half-hour passed, and a telling thirty minutes it was. The last vestiges of Wright's position in the Union line fell to Confederate hands. His corps had been utterly mauled and for all practical purposes it ceased to exist as a viable combat unit. He and his survivors blended into Warren's corps which was hastily redeploying in a frantic effort to stem the tide of Gordon's headlong rush for the North Anna.

Robert E. Lee was in transit when the various couriers located him. Not all of the news was good. From Anderson's corps, the men who held the bluffs overlooking Ox Ford itself, came word of a sobering nature.

"General Lee!" cried the rider as he pulled his mount abruptly to a halt. "General Anderson has been wounded."

"What say you?" A shiver of fear raced up his spine as he digested the fellow's words. At last he was close to victory, not just a bloody repulse of the northern invaders, but total victory. He did not need for anything to go wrong at so critical a moment.

"It's General Anderson, sir! He was standing near the front trying to gauge the effect of our artillery. A Union shell exploded close by. I'm afraid he's been seriously wounded."

"Where is he?" Lee struggled to retain his composure,

not wanting to believe what he had been told.

"The surgeons are working on him, General. They describe his condition as critical."

"Very well," sighed Lee. "Return at once to the hospital tent and convey my concerns to the general. Tell him I will come as soon as time and circumstances permit."

"Very good, sir."

As the rider turned away, Lee addressed himself to A. P. Hill. "General," he said, "I know that you have not been well of late, but I'm afraid I must add to your responsibilities."

"You have only to speak," nodded Hill.

"I believe your entire corps has crossed over to join with General Gordon. Am I correct?"

"You are indeed."

"Ride at once to General Anderson's headquarters and assume temporary command of his corps."

"Very well."

"Dispatch three more brigades from Anderson's troops to support Gordon. Concentrate the remainder near the bluffs over the ford, especially the artillery! We must stop those people from escaping across the river!"

"We'll stop 'em!" saluted Hill, who then spurred his mount in the direction of Ox Ford.

As A. P. Hill disappeared from view more riders arrived with messages from General's Ewell, Gordon and Hampton. Lee suddenly found himself inundated with good news from his lieutenants.

"What word, General?" posed Taylor after allowing Lee time to peruse the various written messages.

"Good news," said Lee calmly. "It seems as though a kind providence has smiled upon our arms this day. General Hancock's assault against Ewell has been soundly repulsed. The Federals gave it up after sustaining heavy losses. The heavy activity we heard coming from the left was Union cavalry attempting a thrust in strength against Gordon's exposed flank. This effort was also foiled and again the enemy took grievous losses. General Hampton seems to think only a third of the Federals escaped across the river at Jericho Mill. We've taken a rich prize in prisoners, animals and weaponry. General Grant had two punches to throw, my friend. He's thrown them both and has only bloody fists to show for it. I almost hesitate to say this, but I believe we may be on the verge of a victory more total than I ever imagined."

"What next?" wondered Taylor.

"Next? We press it, dear Colonel. We press it to whatever conclusion awaits. Come, let us ride to Ox Ford. From the bluffs we can monitor the final phases of the battle and prepare a follow-up strategy."

"General!" Gwathmey interrupted just as they were about to ride. "I think for the sake of insurance you should down another dose." He offered Lee a small tin cup about half-full with the strange looking concoction which quelled the fire in the General's entrails.

The expression on Lee's face spoke of the reluctance he felt and the apprehension with which he regarded Gwathmey's miracle brew. Still, he was in no position to argue with the results, so he braced himself, took the cup in hand and downed its contents in one gulp.

"There!" he gasped, handing the cup back to his physician. "I trust I'll have no further need of that concoction for at least the next hour."

"Most likely," said the doctor. "Now all you have to do is avoid Yankee bullets. Are you sure about going to the ford?"

"Yes. It's important that I see every detail of this battle and not let victory slip through my fingers through some unforeseen circumstance."

"As you wish. Lead the way. I'll be right behind you."

They and their entourage had ridden but a few moments when they spied a patrol of Confederate cavalry racing toward them.

"Hold up," ordered Lee. "Let's see what this is all about."

As the horsemen drew closer, Lee could see a body

draped over one of the mounts, and a northern prisoner atop another. The riders approached and halted about twenty feet from Traveller. Several of them dismounted and carefully removed the dead man from the horse. They laid him prone on his back beneath Lee's questioning gaze.

Lee glanced down at the body, grimacing slightly at the sight of its mangled features. The fellow was small, barely exceeding five feet in height and slight of build. Having been trampled by countless hooves, the man's face was no longer recognizable, but on the shoulders of his uniform were the bars of a general.

"Who is this?" asked the Confederate commander.

"Phil Sheridan," replied the lieutenant who led the patrol.

"Sheridan? This is General Sheridan?"

"It's him all right."

"How can you be sure? He's not the only Federal cavalry officer."

"This Yankee captain here identified him."

Lee shifted his gaze in the direction of the prisoner, "Is this true?" he demanded calmly.

"Yessir," nodded the Federal trooper, "I saw him fall. He was hit by a single shot which was fired several seconds before your infantry delivered its first volley. You've killed Phil Sheridan."

Lee glanced down at the body of General Sheridan. It almost seemed too small, too frail, it certainly did not match Sheridan's fierce, aggressive reputation. Lee turned to Venable who waited close by.

"Over the years thousands of men have died because of my orders," he mused. "Every one of them has taken a little of my own life with him. But this one . . ." he hesitated a moment, shaking his head slightly. "This one is different. God forgive me, Venable, but I must confess to some small degree of satisfaction at the death of this man."

"Understandable," noted Venable, "he killed Stuart, and Jeb meant a lot to us."

"True," agreed Lee. "But there's more to it. I've seen the way he made war on civilians, and I've read in the press about how he loves to smash things. He smashes people's homes and farms, their very lives."

"His days are over."

"So they are. More to the point, we've deprived General Grant of a most valuable officer. Lieutenant, take this body to my headquarters. We'll arrange to have it shipped north for burial."

"Yessir," saluted the lieutenant.

To the west a sudden surge in the level and volume of the fire indicated another push was underway in Gordon's sector.

"Come, gentlemen," said Lee. "I believe our men are reaching a decisive point. I want to be able to see what transpires."

*   *   *   *

As Lee and his party were riding toward the ford, Grant's headquarters became the scene of heightened activity. Dispatch riders were arriving from everywhere. To ease his own nerves Grant had taken to a stump where he sat quietly whittling on the remains of an oak branch, puffing nervously on his cigar.

The first rider was a cavalryman, a young fellow who rode in from the direction of Jericho Mills. A wide bandage was wrapped completely around his forehead, and a thin trickle of blood oozed from beneath it to fall across his cheeks. His uniform was torn and filthy. All things considered he did not have the demeanor of one who bears glad tidings. He rode in at a gallop, jerking the animal to a halt and sliding hastily from the saddle. He was obviously dizzy and unsure of his own footing. Two men moved to support him.

"Grant!" he gasped. "I must see General Grant!"

"Over yonder," said one of the infantrymen. "C'mon,

we'll give you a hand."

Seconds later he was standing before Grant, who chose not to rise from his stump. General Meade stood to one side, arms folded across his burly chest.

"You have a report for me?" posed Grant.

"Yessir!" The boy saluted, nearly losing his balance in the process.

"Let's hear it."

The rider gulped nervously, glancing at the two soldiers who supported him on either side. "Disaster!" he blurted out the word at last. "We were cut to ribbons! General Sheridan's dead. We've got less than four thousand men left, and they're dug into defensive positions along the north bank. We were able to stop the Rebels from pursuing us across the river."

The branch dropped from Grant's hand, but he did retain hold of the knife. "What did you say about Sheridan?" his voice was little more than a whisper.

"He's been killed, sir. The Rebs took him in the first volley. It was awful, General. They tore us to pieces!"

"Sheridan's dead? He's really dead?"

"Yes, sir! I said that. General, we need doctors up at the mill. There's a lot of wounded men up there."

"I'll see to it," interrupted Meade, seeing that Grant was not responding. "You men get this boy to the hospital tents and tell the surgeons to get some assistance up to the Mill."

"Yes, sir!" replied one.

Meade moved around to face Grant, but he found his commander staring straight ahead as if in a trance. He started to speak, but the sound of approaching hooves drew his attention to a second rider, this one approaching from the east. Meade braced himself for another round of bad news.

Hancock's messenger was not wounded, nor did he have the panic-stricken demeanor of the cavalryman who preceded him. Unfortunately the contents of his message were every bit as bad as the previous dispatch.

"General," he began, "We attacked the Rebel position in

full strength just as you instructed. Our assault failed. Our exact losses are still being tallied, but they will probably exceed six thousand. The enemy did not strip his lines as you had hoped. General Hancock requests information about the affair on the opposite wing and awaits further instructions."

Meades' temper was slowly rising to a breaking point, but Grant remained silent, still seated on the stump, still staring with vacant eyes, his mouth hanging open as if in a stupor.

"General, did you hear what this man said?" pressed Meade.

Grant shifted his eyes slightly, staring now at Meade, but still he said nothing.

Frustrated, Meade turned to the courier, "Fetch another horse and stand by," he ordered. "We'll have a return message shortly."

The soldier nodded and turned away.

Meade approached Grant and stooped low, staring at him eye to eye. "General," he whispered. "You must get a grip on yourself. There's a crisis afoot! By God, this army needs you!"

Grant spoke for the first time in several minutes. "Sheridan's dead. The attack failed. Hancock failed. What happened, George? How could this be happening?"

Before Meade could reply, someone called out loudly, announcing the arrival of yet a third courier. As were the others, he was mounted. His horse was still dripping wet, not so much from sweat — he had just swum across the North Anna.

"I have a message from General Warren!" he cried as he reined in and dismounted.

"I'll take it." grumbled Meade, who glanced at Grant before rising to his feet and stepping quickly to the rider's side.

The man reached inside his tunic and withdrew a piece of paper which had been folded several times. Without comment he handed the letter to Meade.

Meade unfolded it, instantly recognizing Warren's handwriting. The letter had been very hastily written. One could almost touch the raw fear which seemed to radiate from every line. Meade read it to himself first, his expression revealing the dismay which was taking an ever firmer grip on his emotions. Finishing it, he looked up, then his eyes shot directly at Ulysses Grant.

"Perhaps I should read this aloud," he declared hotly, not caring who was listening. "It's from General Warren!" He stepped closer to Grant, waving the letter in his face. "General Wright's corps has been virtually destroyed! The Confederate attack is gaining in momentum and strength. He informs us of two things we already know: Sheridan and Hancock both failed in their objectives. He says his position is rapidly becoming untenable and he quite literally is begging for help!" Meade stepped away in obvious frustration, hurling the crumpled dispatch to the ground at Grant's feet and crying, "Goddammit, do something!"

For the briefest of moments, everyone there was frozen in silence.

"Well?" Meade demanded of Grant as his face flushed in angry crimson. "Have you nothing to say? No orders? No grand design?"

"General, please . . ." A nearby staff officer tried to intervene, tried to urge caution, but Meade would not hear of it.

"Never mind!" He dismissed the officer's objections with a wave of his hand. "Did I not tell you?" he fumed at Grant. "Did I not warn you? Every move you've made along this confounded river has been a mistake!" he raged. "This army now faces a catastrophe the magnitude of which defies any attempt at description! Do you hear me, General Grant? Do you know what's happening here? Yesterday the Army of the Potomac was the finest in the world! Today it has been led into utter oblivion! You have much to answer for, Ulysses Grant!"

Grant said nothing in reply. To those who witnessed this sad affair, it appeared as though he recoiled with every sentence from Meade's mouth, each accusation sending him deeper into shock.

"General!" shouted Meade. "Are you going to act or not?"

Grant remained seated and said nothing.

"Then, by God, I will!" huffed Meade. "Orderly!"

"Sir?"

"General Grant appears not to be himself at the moment. Assist him to the hospital and send for his personal physician! I'll be assuming temporary command."

"Very good, sir!" The fellow saluted and turned around to do as he had been bid.

"Where's Hancock's dispatch rider?" demanded Meade.

"Here, sir!"

"Get back to your headquarters at once. Advise General Hancock to withdraw immediately to the north bank of the river and prepare for a retreat toward the Rappahannock!"

"Straight away!" came the reply.

Meade sought out another courier. "Get up to Jericho Mill," he ordered. "Find out who's in charge and tell him to leave a small rear guard and withdraw. Whatever is left of our cavalry will be responsible for escorting the wagon trains! Go then to the trains themselves and get 'em moving north!"

"Yessir!"

Meade swung about and found a staff officer whom he quickly pulled aside. "Get down to Burnside," he instructed, "tell him he must hold his ground opposite the ford at all costs. We cannot allow Lee to cross at this juncture!"

"I understand, General."

"Have him provide all the support he can for Wright and Warren. Those two will soon be trying to cross the river."

"I'll tell him."

Meade stomped off in the direction of his tent, but he found himself face to face with Ely Parker, one of Grant's most trusted confidantes.

"Do you realize what you're doing?" demanded Parker.

"I know full well what I'm doing. I'm trying to save

143

what's left of this army from the destruction Lee has in mind!"

"You're usurping your authority! You have no right to assume command over General Grant!"

"Says who? I have every right. More to the point, I have the responsibility! Are you trying to tell me Grant is fit to command in his present state of mind? Are you blind?"

"He's in a state of shock, but he'll snap out of it!"

"Exactly! And we haven't the luxury of time to relax while he recovers. This army faces the prospect of annihilation! I intend to prevent that."

"By ordering retreat?"

"Very perceptive of you, Colonel!"

"You intend to abandon Wright and Warren?"

"I intend to do the best possible job of covering their retreat, but I will not squander any more lives on the south bank of that Goddamn river! Now if you'll excuse me, Colonel Parker, I have work to do!"

*   *   *   *

By this time less than a mile separated Gordon's troops from the river itself. Here, he decided to make one swift bold thrust to the water's edge, one move which in effect would shut the door for any possible escape by the Federals in the direction of Jericho Mills. To accomplish this he chose Hoke's brigade along with that of Breckinridge and a brigade of Louisiana troops who styled themselves "Lee's Tigers." As the main body of his force continued to push relentlessly down the Federal lines, he pulled the three commanders aside and gave them short, precise verbal instructions.

"Do you understand?" he asked upon his conclusion. "Make an end run around our left. Bolt straight for the river. Establish yourselves in strong defensive positions. Brace yourselves because when the Yankees run out of room to back up, they'll be coming your way, and they'll be there in strength."

"We'll be waiting," replied Breckinridge, the author of the Confederate victory at New Market in the Shenandoah Valley.

"Good! Don't let any of 'em break through! Off with you, and move fast!"

Within minutes all three brigades were in motion, and facing virtually no resistance they carried out a lightning strike straight to the shores of the North Anna, digging in with their left flank not fifty yards from the water itself. In effect, the door was now shut on Wright and Warren.

Those who fought under Gordon now numbered more than thirty thousand, the bulk of whom were pushing straight down the Union lines. To describe these men as an irresistible force would be to vastly understate the case. No one could stand before them. They swept aside every attempt by the Federals to form and hold a line of defense. Even those attempts which were moderately successful were quickly overlapped and forced to retire less they be cut off from their comrades.

Two very opposite emotions were hard at work on the battlefield of Ox Ford: elation and despair. One factor was a driving force in the surge of either emotion, the North Anna River itself. Gordon's infantry, elated by their early victory, were now giddy with the prospect of total triumph. They were not merely repelling the enemy as they had done in the Wilderness and Spotsylvania, they were on the verge of destroying half of Grant's army, and they knew it. Moreover, every step closer to the river brought the Federals that much closer to extinction.

Conversely, those who toiled beneath the leadership of Generals Wright and Warren were on the verge of utter despair. Those who fought at all did so only to survive. Their morale couldn't have been in worse condition. They had been thoroughly out-generaled and now were being out-fought as well. They too were extremely conscious of the river which would soon be at their backs.

Warren had a decision to make. His men held that sector

of the line closest to the river. They were under artillery fire from Anderson's men across the way and faced the possibility of an assault from that quarter. Warren basically had four options: leave them in place; pull them out to support the troops who were vainly trying to stem Gordon's tide; pull them out to establish a corridor in the direction of Jericho Mill; or order them to abandon the line and swim the river to the relative safety of the north bank. The last option might save several thousand lives, but it would surely doom the rest. After a somewhat hasty consideration of the problem — time would not allow a prolonged strategical analysis — he chose a combination of two options. He pulled about half the men from this sector of the line and ordered them west to secure a corridor toward the Mill crossing.

The idea had merit to be sure, but its execution was somewhat tardy. By the time his troops reached the point at which a corridor could be drawn, Gordon's strike force of three brigades was already entrenching. A brief battle ensued and nearly eight hundred of Warren's troop fell dead or wounded before they withdrew. The door was closed. It would not again be reopened.

Word of this failure soon swept through the ranks. Coming as it did on the heels of Sheridan's failure and Hancock's aborted attempt to storm Ewell's line, this loss proved to be the proverbial straw which broke the camel's back. Less than a half-mile remained to the river. Those Federals on the south bank realized at last they were trapped. They succumbed to despair. Panic raced through them like wildfire. Their semi-orderly retreat descended rapidly into a complete rout. Now only one thing mattered. Get to the river. Get across. By the thousands they fled. Some were willing to put up a fight, but they were far too few in number and were quickly overwhelmed. Weapons were abandoned by the thousands. Some northern gunners spiked their pieces before they fled, others didn't bother in their haste to reach the river.

As the Federals fled, Gordon's men nipped joyfully at

their heels. Prisoners were scooped up by the hundreds. Some entire regiments were taken en masse. Abandoned guns were turned about and directed at the fleeing enemy.

Perhaps the supreme compliment to Gordon would address his ability to keep his troops organized and channeled exactly as he wanted. Sometimes in so lopsided an affair it is easy for the victor to become every bit as confused as the vanquished. No so at Ox Ford. Ecstatic though they were, Gordon's men kept their heads. They maintained the integrity of their units and followed Gordon's instructions to the letter.

Gordon himself relentlessly pursued the instructions of his commander, Robert E. Lee. The enemy was to be herded toward the ford. This required a coordinated effort, a push from the south, a nudge from the west, and so on. Gordon himself seemed to be everywhere at once. He barked orders, shouted instructions and exhorted his charges to even greater efforts.

Robert E. Lee reached his observation post on the bluffs over Ox Ford in time to see Federal resistance collapse. Using his glass, he watched a sea of blue flowing frantically for the river. His own reaction was immediate. He had no intention of allowing this part of Grant's army to escape.

"Venable!" he called. "Tell General Hill to direct his batteries on the river's edge and the ford itself. Have him open fire as soon as those people attempt to cross."

"Very well, General!"

Near the base of these same bluffs, Gordon too saw that the opportunity to stop any successful crossing was now at hand. Between his own artillery and that which had been captured he could muster nearly a hundred guns. Muster them he did.

"Maximum range!" he ordered. "Go for the river and the shore line! Stop them from crossing!"

What followed proved to be one of the more grisly episodes of the Civil War. Thousands of panic-stricken blue coats threw themselves into the water in a desperate bid to escape. Some tried the ford. Others shied away from the Rebel guns on the bluffs and attempted to swim. Some made it. Most didn't. The concentrated fire of so much massed artillery turned the North Anna into a churning cauldron of death and pain. Above the roar of guns could be heard the terrible screams of men in agony. Yet even more refugees chose to chance the river, wading through the dead and dying, ignoring the pleas of drowning men, only to be cut down themselves. It was a scene of horror no man could ever forget.

*　　　*　　　*　　　*

Among those who would always remember that day was General George Meade, the victor of Gettysburg. He arrived on a hill overlooking the river just in time to watch the final phase of the slaughter take place. A thick pall of smoke covered the region, but through it he could see the river choked with blue-clad soldiers, many off them floating lifelessly in the currents.

"Dear God!" he groaned aloud as tears filled his eyes, "Dear God in Heaven! How could we have come to this?"

Suddenly it was over. Those who were still trapped on the south bank simply gave up. First in small groups, then by the hundreds they threw down their weapons. In a matter of minutes the remainder of two and one-third corps of infantry had surrendered themselves to Gordon's infantry. At 12:17 p.m. the last shot was fired. The battle of Ox Ford was over. The once splendid Army of the Potomac lay in ruins.

Meade was not in a position to linger on the shores of the North Anna. Nor could he afford to squander more lives by leaving any rear guard along the river. He had no choice but to depart and to do so quickly.

"Any word from Hancock?" he asked of an aide nearby.

"He's across," came the abrupt reply.

"Get word to him. Tell him it's over. Wright and Warren were lost. Have him start north at once. Advise Burnside to do the same. Lee's going to have his hands full with all those prisoners. We should have a few hours headstart on him. I'll conduct a Council of War tonight when we're all together again. We must take stock of our losses and figure out what to do next."

"Yes, sir. General?"

"What is it, Captain?"

"Who will tell President Lincoln?"

"I suppose that unhappy task falls on my shoulders as well. I'll take care of it later. Come, let's get this army the hell out of here!"

*　　*　　*　　*

If gloom was the mood which prevailed among Meade's survivors, jubilation was certainly the order of the day on the opposite side of the river. Many of Lee's veterans wept out of sheer joy. From one end of the position to the other celebration ran rampant.

The southern commander acted quickly to get matters under control. Though grounds for a celebration certainly existed, he allowed them to continue only a short while before acting to restore calm. Too much work had to be done. Thousands of prisoners required processing for shipment to the rear. The battlefield held a bountiful treasure of weapons and ammunition, but time was needed to gather it up. Moreover, he was of no mind to rest on his laurels while Grant escaped with the remainder of his army. He was quick to send congratulations to Gordon for his outstanding success, but at the same time he instructed the Georgian to keep his men at work, to gather the booty and to expedite the disposition of the prisoners.

An hour after the close of fighting, the field was still alive with activity. Lee had dispatched a message to Richmond informing President Davis and Secretary Seddon of the day's results, and was preparing to visit Ewell's section of the line when he spied another patrol approaching with more prisoners. Moments later he was talking to General Wright and General Warren, the two Union corps commanders who had fallen prisoner in the last moments of the battle when all resistance collapsed. Both men appeared exhausted and utterly shocked by their experience. Their uniforms were filthy, Wright himself had suffered a minor flesh wound to the left forearm, and the sleeve of his tunic was heavily stained in blood.

"Are you all right, General?" asked Lee.

"I've seen better days," sighed Wright, shaking his head in resignation.

"Has the wound been tended?"

"Not as of yet."

"I shall have my personal physician administer to it at once," Lee gestured toward Gwathmey.

"That's very kind of you," said Wright.

"I understand how you must feel," noted Lee. "I'm afraid you're probably facing a period of incarceration, but I'll do whatever's in my power to make it more tolerable."

"Thank you, General," replied Warren. "Though I must admit, the thought of captivity in a southern prison holds little charm for me."

"I am truly sorry," said Lee. "These are the fortunes of war. If you'll excuse me gentlemen, I have a great deal of work to do."

"General!" beckoned Wright as Lee turned to depart.

The Confederate stopped and looked back over his shoulder.

"It was a brilliant move, General Lee . . . brilliant."

"Thank you," replied Lee as a thin smile crept across his face. "But I believe the credit must go to General Gordon."

"Extend our compliments," said Warren wryly.

Truth be known, much of the afternoon was lost to the Army of Northern Virginia, but by late afternoon the battlefield had been largely cleared. The prisoners had been broken into small groups and spread out in quickly assembled makeshift camps well south of the North Anna. All of the abandoned equipment and animals had been gathered and logged. Finally, Lee's surgeons were literally overwhelmed by thousands of wounded — most of them Federal. Ordinarily this would have put a severe strain on the Confederates' medical supplies and personnel, but the capture of many northern doctors, along with their supplies intact, served to ease this burden, much to the relief of the wounded themselves.

Though exact totals were not yet available, the final tally of losses at Ox Ford showed a huge disparity, reflecting the lopsided nature of the whole affair. Lee's total casualties barely exceeded twelve thousand. Grant's by contrast, were appalling — twenty-four thousand killed and wounded, and most of the latter were among the nearly twenty-eight thousand prisoners. Of the numbers Grant brought to the banks of the North Anna, two-thirds were not around to take part in the subsequent retreat.

Lee himself had retired to his headquarters. He had just downed another dose of Gwathmey's remedy and was studying his maps, preparing his own follow-up strategy, when a courier arrived and was shown in.

"General Lee?" The voice was that of a young staff officer from Richmond, a baby-faced fellow in his early twenties wearing an impeccable uniform. In all probability he had never seen a shot fired in anger.

"Yes, young man." Lee fixed him with something of a stern gaze.

"I've come by horseback from Richmond, sir. I have a message from the President."

"May I hear it?"

"Yes, sir, of course. President Davis wishes to convey his congratulations on your brilliant victory, General, along with the heartfelt gratitude of the nation."

For just a moment, Lee experienced a dizzy sensation and grabbed the table for support.

"General?" A tinge of alarm could be heard in the lieutenant's voice, "Are you ill? Shall I summon a doctor?"

"No . . . that won't be necessary. You must excuse me, lieutenant. I haven't been well of late. I think I prefer to sit down." He lowered himself into the straight-back wooden chair. "You must tell the President that I thank him for his warm thoughts."

"I think you'll have that opportunity yourself, General. The President and Secretary Seddon are enroute from the capital by carriage."

"I see," nodded the General. "I'm afraid the President will have to join us on the march."

"Sir?"

"I intend to pursue the Federals as soon as practicable. I hope to be on the march by late evening."

"What shall I tell the President?"

"Tell him I shall enjoy meeting him whenever he catches up to us — caution him to take care. General Grant has been defeated, but this doesn't preclude the possibility of isolated Federal cavalry patrols in the area."

"He's travelling with a substantial mounted escort, sir."

"I should hope so. Please return to him and tell him I look forward to our meeting. We have much to discuss."

"Very well, General. Are you sure I can't summon a doctor?"

"He has his hands full at the moment. Our hospitals are overflowing with the wounded of both sides. I'll be fine, Lieutenant. Kindly take my message to the President."

"Yes, sir." He saluted and turned away.

He had been gone perhaps ten minutes when Lee summoned Taylor.

The Colonel stepped into the tent and saluted, "You called for me, General?"

"Yes," nodded Lee. "I'm not feeling particularly well. I think perhaps the strain of today's events have caught up with me. In any event, I'm going to lie down and try to rest for an hour or two. I want you to have Generals Hill, Ewell, Hampton and Gordon here for a Council of War in two hours. Understood?"

"Perfectly," nodded Taylor.

"Very good. In the meantime I don't want to be disturbed except in the case of an emergency."

"Of course, General. I'll see to it. Shall I call for Gwathmey?"

"No. He's far too busy with the wounded. I think a little rest will suffice."

"As you wish, sir. I'll summon your officers."

Taylor departed and Lee moved from the chair to his cot where he stretched out and quickly succumbed to his need for sleep.

Two hours later the General was awakened by a gentle nudge from his chief of staff. Lee opened one eye, tentatively at first, then quickly swung his legs over the side and sat upright.

"What time is it?" He asked as he tried to orient himself to his surroundings.

"Four-thirty in the afternoon, General. The men you sent for are all here. If you'd like to freshen up there's a pitcher of fresh water next to the basin on your table."

"Thank you, Walter," said Lee. "Give me five minutes, then send my officers in."

"Of course, General. Are you feeling any better?"

"Somewhat," sighed Lee. "This illness has sapped much of my strength, but I feel better now than I did earlier."

"Good. I'll keep them outside for five minutes," he turned to leave.

"Walter, have we heard anything more from the enemy?"

"The most recent news has them in full retreat. They have a three hour head start, but they don't seem to be making good progress. Apparently there is substantial confusion still rampant among their troops."

"Good. Let's hope it stays that way."

Lee rose to his feet and stepped gingerly to the side of the tent. Steadying himself with one hand, he used the other to pour water into the porcelain basin on the table.

As Lee was preparing to meet with his lieutenants, the city of Richmond was experiencing pandemonium. News of Lee's brilliant, decisive victory on the North Anna had spread to every corner of the capital. Church bells began ringing at once. Robert E. Lee had just saved the capital from a Union thrust for the second time in two years. Celebrations broke out all over the city, and though there may have been a distinct shortage of food and drink, there was certainly plenty of dancing in the streets. In fact, President Jefferson Davis found it almost impossible to leave the city, so crowded were the thoroughfares.

The same could not be said of Washington, D. C. The first word of Grant's disaster reached the United States capital about 3 o'clock in the afternoon. General Halleck, the army chief of staff, was alone in his study, deeply engrossed in a book when there came a knock upon his door.

"Come in."

The door opened and a young officer stepped inside and said: "A telegram has just arrived from General Meade, sir." He presented it to Halleck.

"Ah!" said the old general with a broad smile. "The Army of the Potomac! Grant must have made a move." He opened the thin envelope, adjusted his bifocals and held the telegram close to his oil lamp.

The message itself was surprisingly brief, considering the impact of its contents. There were only a few lines, and Halleck was able to scan these rather quickly.

"Dear God," he whispered softly, turning his head away.

"Sir?"

"A moment . . . please!" Halleck returned to the telegram, reading it completely through a second then a third time just to be sure.

"This can't be possible!" he exclaimed, much louder than he would have preferred.

"General?" stammered the young lieutenant.

"Are you sure this message is accurate?"

"Yes, sir! I was there myself! It's authentic, I'd stake my life on that!"

"You may soon be staking your life . . . much sooner than you might imagine!"

"General? Is something wrong? What news did the message bring?"

"Disas . . ." Halleck stopped before he completed the utterance of the word. "Never mind. I want you to have my carriage brought around at once."

"Yes sir. Shall I tell the driver your destination?"

"You'll do well to learn how to mind your own business," huffed Halleck.

Ten minutes later, the general stepped out of his home in full dress uniform. He walked briskly to the waiting carriage, nodded to the attendant who opened the door, then glanced up at the driver. "Take me at once to the White House," he ordered.

As Halleck had been, Abraham Lincoln was in his study. He had been reading the latest newspapers from New York, Philadelphia, and Washington when he heard the knock on his door. The door was opened by a servant who proceeded to invite General Halleck inside. Lincoln looked up and realized something wasn't right. Halleck looked ill, his face drawn and frighteningly devoid of color.

"Why, General Halleck!" he greeted. "Forgive me for saying this, but you don't look at all well. Perhaps you've been pushing yourself too hard. I think a rest might be in order. Don't you agree?"

"Mr. President," sighed Halleck in a tone of stoic resignation. "I'm afraid I have news of a very grievous nature. I think you may wish to remain seated while I relay it."

"What's happened?" demanded Lincoln, some of the color draining from his own face.

"This isn't going to be easy . . ." hedged Halleck.

"General, please, there are certain situations in which I am not fond of suspense. This is one of them. Obviously you have bad news. Kindly get on with it. Dragging it out won't make things any easier."

"Yes, Mr. President. The Army of the Potomac . . ." His voice broke and he had to pause to clear his throat. "The Army of the Potomac has just sustained a disaster of unheard of magnitude."

"Disaster? What sort of disaster?" The alarm in Lincoln's voice was apparent in every syllable he uttered. Though he had confidence in Grant, the last three weeks had raised more than a few questions in his mind. The battles in the Wilderness at Spotsylvania had resulted in thirty-five thousand casualties, horrible losses with precious little to show in return. And now this talk of calamity. "Come, General, explain. And do be quick about it."

"I don't know how to explain, Mr. President. I don't know what went wrong. I know the two armies were facing one another on the North Anna River. You knew this as well. However, neither of us has really been privy to the details of that confrontation. Apparently, Lee was able to divide Grant's army and isolate one wing by itself. That wing was destroyed. I've just received a telegram from General Meade. He doesn't paint a very pretty picture. Sheridan is dead. The cavalry is in shambles. Wright and Warren have either been captured or killed, along with their entire commands. Hancock and Burnside have been roughly handled and the whole army, what's left of it, is in retreat."

"I can't believe this!" Lincoln buried his face momentarily in both hands. "The finest army in the world!" he muttered.

"Meade's taken temporary command. It seems General Grant has gone into a state of shock."

"I shouldn't wonder!" spat Lincoln. "I may be heading in that direction myself!" He rose and began to pace to and fro across the study. "What happened, Halleck? I can't understand this at all! Lee was beaten! Every dispatch we received said that the Rebels were on the verge of total collapse! Am I wrong?"

"No, Mr. President. The communications we received have all been very optimistic. Apparently too much so."

"Apparently! Now what, Halleck? Answer me that!"

"I'm afraid you find me somewhat at a loss for suggestions, Mr. President. I'm still rather stunned myself. I have no idea how this could have happened."

"Do we have any exact figures on casualties?"

"No, sir. But two entire corps were lost as well as the bulk of their cavalry."

"Dear God! Dear God!" groaned Lincoln. "The retreat! Where is Meade leading them?"

"In the direction of Fredericksburg."

"What is the logistical situation from our end?"

"Ten thousand reinforcements left the city this morning bound by rail for Fredericksburg. Baldy Smith left the Bermuda Hundred by ship with fifteen thousand men. He should be arriving soon at Port Royal."

"Then we can make up some of Grant's losses very quickly?"

"So it would seem."

"The question is, what do we do next?"

"I'm still at a loss, Mr. President."

"Apparently General Grant is in a similar state of mind, a luxury which I myself cannot afford. What if Lee chooses to follow this victory up with a thrust toward Washington?"

"I have no information on the condition of his army, Mr. President. Surely he must have taken substantial losses. I seriously doubt if he can muster a serious threat to the capital."

"Dare I chance that, Halleck? I think not. I want you to order Hunter to retreat out of the Shenandoah Valley as far north as Winchester. There he is to adopt a defensive posture in case Lee attempts to use the valley again as a conduit into the north."

"Very well, Mr. President," Halleck nodded solemnly.

"Get word to Baldy Smith and advise him to move at once to join with the Army of the Potomac. Send a reply to Meade. Tell him I need more information and I need it fast!"

"As you wish, Mr. President."

*   *   *   *

"Gentlemen," Lee addressed himself to the council of his highest ranking officers, "Let me first congratulate you for a tremendous effort this morning. The bravery and initiative of yourselves and your men may well have turned the tide of this war. The Confederacy is deeply in your debt. So much for congratulations. Now we must prepare for the greater struggle which still lies ahead. The Army of the Potomac has been badly crippled and as we speak it is in full retreat. Nevertheless, it is still a potent fighting force and it would not behoove us to to underestimate its capabilities. I want that army, gentlemen. I don't want it to escape under any circumstances. If we can destroy Grant, Washington City will be ours. The war could be won. That is our next objective."

He turned to Wade Hampton, "Your scouts have been active?"

"Yes, General."

"In what direction is the enemy retreating?"

"At present Fredericksburg seems to be their destination."

"There's certain logic to that, but I've been considering the possibility that Fredericksburg is a ruse."

"Sir?" Hill arched his bushy eyebrows.

"We've received information from our agents operating in the Bermuda Hundred. Fifteen thousand infantry left by ship under the command of Baldy Smith. They are heading for Port Royal on the Rappahannock, which by the way, is now Grant's supply base, or at least it's been so intended.

"Do you think Grant may turn toward Port Royal?"

"Possibly, and if he does we must turn him. Gentlemen, understand this. If we can prevent Grant from crossing the

159

Rappahannock we can force his surrender. We cannot let him reach Fredericksburg ahead of us, nor can we let him get to Port Royal first. If he does, he'll simply escape down-river by ship."

"How do you propose to stop the reinforcements which he's been slated to receive?" asked Ewell.

"More to the point," interjected Gordon, "How do you plan on stopping the Federals from reaching the Rappahannock? They already have at least three hours lead on us."

"I realize that, General," deferred Lee. "Success will depend on our willingness to push ourselves. General Hampton, you are to take the bulk of our cavalry and ride completely around Grant's army. I specifically want you to strike at any resupply efforts from Fredericksburg itself. More particularly you are to interpose yourself between Grant and Fredericksburg. He will be forced to either stop and give battle or turn away."

"And if he stops?"

"I intend to be right behind him."

"Count on us."

"Should you have the opportunity to strike at his trains anywhere along the way, avail yourself."

"Happily," smiled Hampton.

"Now," said Lee, "As for the infantry. General Gordon, you've done a superb job this day. I intend to recommend you for promotion to permanent corps commander."

"Why . . . thank you, General. I really don't know what to say."

"Say nothing. Continue to fight as you did today. For the time being you are to retain control of the troops you have. Your men bore the brunt of today's action. They may rest in place until nine o'clock tonight."

"Yessir, they'll be happy to hear that!"

"General Ewell, when Jackson had your corps, his men were nicknamed "The Foot Cavalry." Do you remember?"

"Of course," nodded Ewell.

"I want you to revive that spirit. Get on the march immediately. Move parallel to Grant, and stay several miles to his east."

"Yes, General. My destination?"

"Port Royal. Get past Grant, then interpose yourself in the same fashion as Hampton on the other side. Grant will have the same two choices, and the rest of us won't be far away."

"And if we bump into Baldy Smith?"

"You are free to use your own discretion. Obviously it would behoove us to limit Grant's reinforcements to the greatest possible degree."

"Understood."

"Bear this in mind, however. Grant may receive substantial reinforcements, but we mustn't let that fact deter us from our ultimate goal; keeping him below the Rappahannock. If we can maneuver him to a place along that river below Fredericksburg with his back to the water, we'll have him. He won't escape us."

"What then?" ventured Gordon, "Washington City?"

"Let's not look too far ahead," continued Lee. "For now we have Grant. We also have an opportunity to destroy him and his army. Let's make sure he doesn't escape. General Hill, you are to remain in charge of Anderson's corps for the moment. You will depart at once and remain in the wake of Grant's army. You should be able to move faster than the Federals, but don't close with them. I want you in a position to make a decisive move if Grant pauses to lash out either at Hampton or Ewell."

"Understood," nodded Hill.

"General Gordon. While your men are resting, get them organized. Choose ten thousand to keep with you, the rest are to follow General Hill."

"Yes, General. Where am I going?"

"You're to follow in Hampton's footsteps, but don't stop until you've reached the Rappahannock below Fredericksburg. Have your engineers bridge the river in the quickest fashion. Get across. Establish yourself on the north bank.

Then wait. I intend to herd those people to the banks of the river. You'll be informed of the exact location as that knowledge becomes available. Once you know where Grant will be adjust your own position so you are exactly opposite him. The Federals will then find themselves trapped south of the Rappahannock."

"And cut off from any source of assistance," noted Ewell.

"Precisely," nodded Lee. "Grant will have three choices. Surrender, attack to break out, or hold out until the food and other supplies are gone."

"Are you precluding the possibility of a substantial relief effort from Washington?"

"Not at all, but if the scenario we desire comes to pass, we will have the upper hand along with the freedom of mobility needed to check any attempt to relieve Grant. Moreover, if Grant is trapped, we'll be able to play on Mr. Lincoln's traditional fears for the safety of Washington. He'll be able to raise another army, of that have no doubt, but if he suspects the possibility of a threat to the Federal capital, he'll keep that army close at hand."

As he concluded his instructions, the group lapsed into silence. Every man was lost in his own thoughts, contemplating his assignment, wondering what the next few days would hold in store for them.

"Do each of you understand what's expected of you?" pressed Lee.

His question was answered by simple nods of the head or grunted assents.

"Very well," he continued, "You are all dismissed. Generals Hill, Hampton and Ewell, you are to leave immediately. General Gordon, prepare for a 9 p.m. departure. In the meantime, I shall desire a complete inventory of weaponry and supplies captured today."

"You'll have it," replied Gordon.

"Good. Gentlemen, Providence has smiled upon us today. Let us all pray that God continues to look favorably on our undertaking. Bless all of you and good luck!"

*　　*　　*　　*

An hour had passed since the advent of darkness and the Army of the Potomac was still settling into its night camp. Since breaking contact with Lee's army, they had been able to put only fifteen miles between themselves and the North Anna River. Those who remained with the Army of the Potomac were exhausted, somewhat battered, and all too demoralized. After assuring himself that Lee wasn't close at hand, Meade had ordered a halt to the march so his beleaguered troops could concentrate their numbers and obtain some badly needed rest. Meade himself was in his own tent drafting a detailed report to his President when he noticed a shadow at the tent flap. He glanced up to see Colonel Parker.

"What can I do for you?" he asked impatiently. "Make it fast. As you can see, I'm rather busy at the moment."

"Then I'll be brief," replied the colonel with a smug smile. "General Grant has recovered from the state of shock he experienced earlier. He has reassumed command of the army, and he'd like very much to see you in his headquarters at your earliest convenience."

Meade sat upright and dropped his pen on the table. Several moments passed before he was able to fully absorb Parker's words. "I see," he finally replied. "Kindly inform the general that I'm very pleased at his recovery and that I shall be along shortly."

"How shortly?" pressed Parker.

"Within thirty minutes."

"Very good. I'll let him know."

"You do that."

There was a definite expression of disgust on Meade's face as he watched Parker disappear into the darkness. The general's shoulders slumped in resignation as he turned around to dress himself for the meeting with Grant.

Meade fully expected a reprimand, an anticipation which was responsible for his high level of anxiety upon entering Grant's tent. He soon found his fears to be groundless.

"I want to apologize for this morning," said Grant. "That's never happened to me before. The doctor says I slipped into a state of shock. I guess it was the news of Sheridan's death."

"You don't owe me any apology," said Meade, somewhat confused at Grant's conciliatory tone.

"I also want to thank you for taking control of the army. If it hadn't been for you, Lee may have bagged the whole lot of us."

"I merely did my duty."

"You did it well. Now let's put our heads together and figure out how to regroup."

"Regroup?"

"To get even, and in the process get this war over and done with."

"General Grant," ventured Meade, "At the moment this army is in no shape to be getting even with anybody. I haven't totaled all the exact figures yet, but very likely we have fewer than forty thousand men left, perhaps as few as thirty-five thousand. Lee's soldiers did their work all too well."

"We've been hurt," agreed Grant. "I'd be the last person to argue that. However, we may be down, but don't be counting us out yet. We have twenty-five thousand troops enroute to us from two different sources. Once they've linked up with us we'll be able to face Lee on an equal basis."

"We've outnumbered him nearly two to one since the campaign started," countered Meade. "Our superior numbers don't seem to make a difference."

"Let's not get into this again, George. I prefer to look ahead, not backwards. Has President Lincoln been informed?"

"I assume so. I sent the wire to Halleck."

"Good. That's what I would have done. Have you done anything about reorganization?"

"Not yet. We really haven't got that much to reorganize. Hancock's corps lost abut six thousand men, but the survivors are intact and he's in charge. Colonel Custer seems to be the ranking cavalry officer and General Burnside is still in charge of his corps, what's left of it."

"That sounds fine to me. I don't know this man, Custer very well. What kind of officer is he?"

"Bold, brash, sometimes impetuous. He's the best we have at the moment."

"Okay. We march again at first light, but we're no longer heading for Fredericksburg."

"Sir?"

"As of tomorrow we're marching northeast for Port Royal. Baldy Smith should be arriving there tomorrow. I think we should link up with him first. His men are all veterans and they'll put us over fifty thousand again in one fell swoop."

"General . . ." Meade hesitated, not wanting to arouse wrath on the part of Grant, "If we shift to Port Royal we'll be moving toward the wider regions of the Rappahannock!"

"Your point being?"

"It would be very difficult to retreat across it if we were forced into that choice."

"I have no intention of retreating north of the Rappahannock."

"You had no intention of pulling back from the North Anna. My only point, sir, is that we shouldn't preclude any of our options."

"I appreciate your concern, but rest assured, we can handle Bobby Lee."

"Can we? He's been handling us up to this point."

"For starters we need to slow him down. I want General Hancock to leave a rear guard to harass the rebels starting tomorrow morning. Three thousand men should do the trick. Also, I want the trains to set out ahead of everybody else. Have Custer provide a thousand troops as escort."

"Yes, sir." Meade acquiesced quietly, knowing the futility of further argument.

*   *   *   *

A SOUTHERN YARN

Lee too had halted for the night. He was travelling by carriage with A. P. Hill's command which went into camp about five miles south of Grant's army. Hill's men could rest through the night, unlike Hampton's troops and those of Gordon and Ewell, all of whom would be on the move throughout the hours of darkness. Lee himself was just getting ready to retire for the evening when he heard the sounds of a commotion just outside. Throngs of curious graybacks were gathering around a carriage. The President of the Confederacy, Jefferson Davis, had just arrived. Lee stepped outside to greet the chief executive and his party.

"Good evening, Mr. President," said Lee. "I was just beginning to worry. I thought you would have joined us hours ago."

"Greetings, General," Davis stepped over to him with his right hand extended. "We would have joined you much earlier, but we stopped at Ox Ford to see for ourselves. Please accept my sincerest congratulations. It was a tremendous victory, General. Tremendous! I had to pinch myself to be sure it wasn't a dream!"

"Thank you, Mr. President," returned Lee. "It was indeed a fortunate turn of events. General Gordon and his men certainly deserve the credit. They did the fighting." He turned his eyes away and nodded at the Secretary of War, who approached just behind Davis. "Mr. Seddon," said Lee. "I'm very pleased to see you as well."

"General," smiled Seddon, "The people in Richmond are beside themselves with joy. Your victory at Ox Ford has them dancing in the streets."

"As I said," noted Lee. "The credit belongs to General Gordon and the men he leads. In any event, although I appreciate all this adulation, there is still a war going on and much work for us to do, Mr. Secretary. We took tens of thousands of prisoners this morning. I'm afraid they're presenting us all with something of a logistical problem. Are you prepared to handle it?"

166

"I have people working on it now. The Federal prisoners will be divided into a number of small groups and shipped by rail to different locations across the South. It will take time of course, but I think we can adequately house the prisoners."

"Good. Maybe you should plan ahead from this day forward. I intend to send you lots of prisoners before this campaign draws to a close."

"You'll get no argument from me," quipped Seddon. "You round 'em up, I'll take it from there."

"Just what do you have in mind?" asked Davis.

"Do I detect a note of apprehension in your voice, Mr. President?" posed Lee.

"Perhaps. You won a great victory today, General. Our language hasn't enough superlatives to describe it, but it will be wasted if we follow it with another Gettysburg."

"I understand your reservations," nodded Lee. "Yet I hope you'll hear me out on this matter."

"Certainly," nodded Davis, not wishing to offend the one man who could turn the dream of Southern independence into a reality.

"Would you gentlemen step into my tent?" beckoned Lee. "We can talk more freely in there."

The three of them were soon seated around a table on which lay a map of Virginia. Colonel Taylor was also present, though he remained standing to one side.

"What exactly do you have in mind?" pressed Davis.

"Grant lost the bulk of his army today, but much of these losses can be made good in a matter of days unless we act quickly."

"Specifically?"

"First, we must prevent reinforcements from reaching the Army of the Potomac. To that end I have General Ewell on the march toward Port Royal. It is my hope that he will intercept and give battle to Baldy Smith before that officer can link up with Grant."

"Go on."

"General Hampton has taken the cavalry on a swing to the west. He has been instructed to interpose himself between Grant and his source of supply at Fredericksburg."

"I see no problem so far. Your strategy appears sound," commented Davis.

"I intend to prevent Grant from crossing the Rappahannock," continued Lee. "My intention is to maneuver him to the river somewhere between Fredericksburg and Port Royal, and to trap him on the south bank. We will attempt to destroy whatever remains of the Army of the Potomac."

"If it can be done, you are certainly the man to do it," smiled Davis with an approving nod.

"If we are successful, Mr. President, my desire is to strike northward as quickly as possible."

Davis' expression changed instantly to one of obvious concern. "General, a word of caution. Twice you've attempted to invade the North. Twice you've been turned back. Another setback on the scale of Gettysburg could deal a shattering blow to our hopes."

"One moment, Mr. President," Seddon intervened. "I believe General Lee is speaking of contingency plans here. All of this would hinge on the destruction of Grant. Am I right?" He turned to Lee.

"Exactly," nodded the General, stiffening slightly as a twinge of pain meandered through his stomach. "If we can destroy the Army of the Potomac, there would be no obstacle to an invasion of the North."

"Invade the North? To what end? You and I both know how little the Confederacy has in the way of resources. We could not long sustain you in the field if you were to invade the North."

"I understand that, Mr. President, though I would argue certain points. At Ox Ford we captured vast quantities of arms and munitions, and if we can force Grant's surrender we'll obtain even more. In any event, sir, I do indeed agree with your basic premise. If we are to invade the North it must be with a specific mission in mind. Moreover, this mission would have to be accomplished in a short amount of time."

"I assume you have a particular mission in mind?" quizzed Davis.

"I do."

"Then kindly skip the suspense, General. Do share your ideas with us."

"Very well," sighed Lee, taking a deep breath. "I propose to capture Washington City."

"Wh . . .?" Davis' voice stuck in his throat. He paused, covered his mouth with one hand and cleared his throat. "Washington, D.C.?" he pondered. "You're thinking about trying to capture the Federal capital?"

"If we can force the surrender of Ulysses Grant, that possibility will present itself."

"General, if my intelligence is accurate . . ." Davis paused, his eyes searching about as if he could find his desired words drifting across the tent. Finally, after a brief support-seeking glance in Seddon's direction, he shifted his attention back to Lee. "General," he repeated, "you are talking about the capture of the world's most fortified city."

"I realize that, Mr. President," replied Lee with a nod.

"You can't be serious."

"I most definitely am," countered the gray-haired commander, "But my hopes for success rest on two factors."

"They are?"

"Grant's eventual destruction and your complete support."

"I see."

Davis sat back and crossed his arms over his chest. "Putting aside for a moment any discussion of Grant's demise, what exactly do you expect from me?"

"Simply put," said Lee. "More men."

"You might as well be asking for a train load of gold."

"I'm not ignorant of that fact. No one is more familiar with our manpower situation than I."

"Then you know we're drafting fifteen year old boys and

169

fifty year old men."

"Children and grandfathers."

"Do you see where we have a choice?"

"No. Our backs are against the proverbial wall, which to me makes the capture of Washington City that much more imperative."

"How so?"

"Our overall strategy has been to fight a defensive war. With certain obvious exceptions it has served us well to this point, but I maintain that it will not result in Southern independence. In essence, the United States has locked us into a war of attrition. We cannot win such a war. You know this as well as I. If we are to prevail in this struggle, we must take the offensive, at least to the limit of our resources. We must capture the Federal capital. Such a feat would bring us European recognition and would probably force the United States to seek a negotiated peace."

"Your logic is hard to argue with, General," sighed Davis as he rose to his feet and began pacing about the tent. "I'm not saying I'm against the idea," he continued, "Yet I must face certain realities. You speak of taking the offensive to the very limit of our resources. I submit, General, such a limit would be reached all too quickly. You want more men? Where am I to find them? Look across the Confederacy. Other than in Virginia its hard to find grounds for optimism. Texas is cut-off from the rest. Louisiana is occupied. Thomas controls Tennessee. Sherman has his eyes on Atlanta. Many of our ports have fallen to the enemy, the others are effectively blockaded. All of my generals constantly repeat the same request: more men. Quite frankly, I'm at a loss. I don't know where to find any more men. What am I to do? Should I draft twelve year olds?"

"No, Mr. President. God forbid we ever resort to such a move."

"What then?"

"I have long advocated the idea of freeing slaves, tying that freedom to service in the army."

"I know. We've finally come to your point of view. We have plans to do just that, but many of us question the zeal with which such soldiers might pursue their tasks."

"Time will answer that question," sighed Lee, shifting in his seat to accommodate still another spasm of stomach pain.

"Colonel," he turned to Taylor. "There's a pitcher of Gwathmey's concoction on the nightstand by my cot. Would you be good enough to pour a dose?"

"Certainly, General," nodded Taylor.

Downing a mug of the remedy with a stoic expression, Lee turned again to President Davis. "Mr. President, I know what pressure you must feel. I think I can appreciate the frustration you must experience every time an officer like myself requests more men. Nonetheless, I must press my argument. My request goes beyond the others. I'm not asking for help to simply delay the inevitable. If I can destroy Grant, and if I can be reinforced, I sincerely believe Washington City can be captured. I hope that you will give this request every possible consideration."

"Is that helping?" Davis gestured toward the empty mug.

"Considerably. It has not cured me by any means, but it effectively controls the symptoms of my illness. Dr. Gwathmey says only rest and a proper diet will dispel the malady which brought this on."

"Rest and good food," chuckled Davis. "Rare and precious commodities for a man in your position."

"I'll rest in due course, Mr. President. Providence blessed us with a tremendous victory this morning. That victory, in turn, has presented us with a terrific opportunity. We would be ill-advised to squander it."

"I know, General . . . I know."

"Georgia and the Carolinas have substantial militias. Perhaps you could persuade them to donate some of their strength to the common cause."

"Perhaps," nodded Davis. "Yet bear in mind I cannot force their compliance. Such is the nature of our Confederacy. If a state wishes to contribute troops from its militia, it

171

will. If not . . . well . . . what more can I say?"

"You'll consider my ideas?"

"Consider them? Of course. You said your plans hinged on two factors. The first being General Grant. If you can complete the destruction of the Army of the Potomac, then we'll talk of your ambitious plans in detail. Agreed?"

"Fair enough," nodded Lee.

"Then we'll take our leave, General. Perhaps you'll be able to snatch some of that rest Gwathmey insists you need."

"Hopefully," smiled Lee.

"Consider it a presidential directive, General. As soon as we take our leave, you are to retire to that cot and get some sleep."

"Happily," returned Lee.

"I trust you'll keep us informed about the tactical situation as it unfolds?"

"You may count on it, Mr. President."

"Very good." Davis gestured to Seddon who rose at once to his feet. "God bless you, Bobby Lee. Sleep well."

"Thank you, Mr. President. I believe I will."

By noon of the next day the tactical situation showed several new developments, most of them of a positive nature from the Confederate point of view. Not surprisingly, the first word came from Hampton. His troopers had outpaced Grant's army during the night and had raided and captured two small wagon trains destined for the Army of the Potomac. The result was another bountiful haul from the Federal stocks: weapons, medical stores and ample quantities of rations.

"Our thanks to Mr. Lincoln!" laughed many of Hampton's riders as they stuffed their saddlebags.

After dispatching the trains in Lee's direction with a strong escort, Hampton ordered his men to stand by in a position directly between Grant and Fredericksburg. To Lee this news couldn't have been better.

The tactical situation to the northeast was much the same. Ewell's corps, marching all through the night, had drawn even with Grant and was quick to push ahead of him. Ewell was following a line of march parallel to Grant's and roughly seven miles to his east. In Ewell's dispatch to Lee he reported his position as being well south of Port Royal, and that his scouts thus far had seen no sign of Baldy Smith. However, several scouting reports indicated a shift on the part of Grant, who now seemed destined for Port Royal itself.

As for Grant, it was not until shortly after midday that his own scouts reported the presence of a Rebel corps to his right and Rebel cavalry to his left. He was somewhat peeved that the graybacks had been able to move so fast, but there was little he could do to pick up his own pace. The wounded and the wagon trains held up progress considerably and neither of these could be left behind. But what was Lee up to? Obviously he had divided his army again, but to what end? Grant assumed that Lee was duplicating the strategy which he himself had employed on the march south from Spotsylvania. Grant had planned to dangle Hancocks's corps out by itself as bait, hoping Lee would lunge after the isolated unit, thereby exposing himself to a devastating strike in the open field by the rest of the Union army. Was Lee doing the same thing? Was Ewell out there as bait for still another trap? Grant wasn't entirely sure, but on one score he had already made up his mind. His immediate goal was Port Royal. As May drew to a close, this quaint little Rappahannock harbor town seemed to hold the key to Grant's fortunes. If Ewell was in the way, so be it. Grant would simply sweep him out of the way. He quickly reviewed his plans. Hancock's rearguard, twenty-five hundred men in all, would soon initiate hostilities with the main body of Lee's army. If they could slow Lee down, there might be time to achieve Ewell's destruction. Having pondered the situation and after issuing formal instructions, Grant sat back to rest and await the next set of developments.

These weren't long in coming. By 3 p.m. he received word from Washington. Ten thousand men were enroute to Fredericksburg and would link up with Grant regardless of his position. Even better, Baldy Smith had unloaded his fifteen thousand bayonets in Port Royal and was already enroute to join him. From Grant's point of view, things were finally beginning to look up. At least he could count on additional strength, and he would soon be in a position to overwhelm Ewell. Also came word from the south. Hancock's rearguard had engaged the lead elements of Lee's army, Hill's command, forcing Little Powell to suspend his march and deploy for battle.

The rearguard was of brigade strength and they put up a spirited fight. However, within roughly an hour, Lee was able to surmise this as only a rearguard and that a full-scale confrontation was not imminent. He knew he could not afford any lengthy delay, especially with Ewell off by himself hoping for swift support. Accordingly, he resolved to bypass the rearguard altogether. One thousand men were ordered to envelop and contain the Federal force, but not to attack them. If the Federals chose to leave, they would have to fight their way out, and their prospects for success would be questionable at best. Meanwhile, the rest of the Army of Northern Virginia would be closing in on Grant.

For Dick Ewell, the day could hardly have been termed uneventful. He was no Stonewall Jackson, but the men he led were Stonewall's veterans. It was not the first time they had been dangled as bait to snare a Union army. In August of 1862, their forced marched through the Shenandoah Valley precipitated the Second Battle of Manassas. In point of fact, Jackson's corps withstood repeated assaults by the main body of the Union army under Pope before Lee arrived on the scene with relief. Jackson was gone, but his spirit lived on in the hearts of his men. They knew what Lee expected of them and they were more than willing to give it.

By late afternoon, Ewell had marched within twelve miles of Port Royal. Here he was forced into a decision. Scouting reports were arriving from all directions. First he learned that Baldy Smith was marching south out of Port Royal. At about the same time, he received reports of a change in the direction of Grant's march. "Well boys," he said to his assembled staff. "Looks like we might be in for a long evening. You'd best get ready."

"Who do we hit first?"

"Let's go ahead and take a crack at Baldy. I don't imagine he's expecting it."

"Then what?"

"Then we dig in and wait for Grant. We'd best pray Lee isn't too far behind him."

By this time, they had gained the road which ran from northeast to southwest, connecting Port Royal to Bowling Green. The road itself was a curious affair, narrow and winding, macadamized in some places, mere dirt in most others. The scouts reported a shallow ridge about a mile and a half above the point where Ewell reached the pike.

"If we march fast we can reach the ridge before the Yankees coming out of Port Royal," reported the scout. "Looks like a fine spot to raise a little ruckus."

"Very good. Lets keep moving. Just a little farther, boys!" he intoned, "Another mile, just another mile!"

Foot-sore and bone-weary they were, but they still felt the exhilaration brought on by the previous day's lopsided victory. Moreover, to the man they realized how great an opportunity they had. With very little in the way of grumbling, they took to the road and started toward the ridge.

Having summoned reserves of energy and determination, Ewell's veterans reached the designated ridge in little more than a quarter-hour. All three divisions were deployed in a line of battle which ran perpendicular to the road itself, effectively blocking any passage. Ewell was in a precarious position, and he knew this better than anybody. His corps faced the very real possibility of being isolated, facing sizable Union forces, front and rear. Accordingly, he resolved not to take the offense. He ordered his men to dig in along the crest of the ridge and to build fortifications which could be useful in both directions. In essence he was sending one message to the Federals: "Come and get me."

A SOUTHERN YARN

In terms of strength, Ewell was in far better shape than his adversaries may have imagined. In numbers he stood equal to the blue force advancing from Port Royal. In the way of firepower, however, he was far superior to Baldy Smith and not too inferior to Grant's entire army. The reason? Ox Ford. Much of the captured artillery had been assigned to Ewell, doubling the number of guns normally allotted to his corps. His artillery commander had already demonstrated a significant ability to make effective use of these guns; first at Spotsylvania and again at Ox Ford. In both instances, his gunners successfully broke up determined Union assaults. A surge of confidence welled up in Ewell's breast as he watched his gunners deploy their pieces, hub to hub all along the line.

*　　　*　　　*　　　*

That very morning Baldy Smith received word of the disaster at Ox Ford. The telegram was waiting for him when he left his ship at the dock in Port Royal. The message was from Halleck, and its content was blunt and to the point: Grant had taken horrible losses and was retiring toward Fredericksburg. It had become imperative to reinforce Grant at the earliest possible moment. He was ordered to get his men off their ships and on the road to Bowling Green. This he did, putting them immediately on the march, sending several patrols of cavalry out ahead to scout the terrain. Several miles had been put behind them when the first of these riders returned with news. The rebels had apparently anticipated his arrival and were marching to intercept him. Estimates of Rebel strength ranged up to a corps. As Smith digested this news a number of possibilities entered his mind. This Rebel corps stood between himself and Grant, that much was obvious. If the two could join forces these Rebels could easily be eliminated. Such a turn of events would go a long way toward neutralizing the failures of the last few weeks. There was only one problem of any consequence: Smith didn't know where to find Grant. He knew only that Grant was retreating toward Fredericksburg. He had not yet received any word of the shift in Grant's direction of march. He therefore dispatched cavalry to locate Grant while he himself continued south toward a face-off with General Ewell.

*　　　*　　　*　　　*

At about this time, Gordon with ten thousand men had caught up with Hampton's cavalry. Together they advanced several miles closer to Fredericksburg without encountering any significant opposition. Small mounted units were dispatched to the east with orders to comb the countryside until Grant was located, and in this fashion they learned of the shift in the direction of the Federal march.

"What should we do?" asked Gordon. "Do we conform to this shift or do we follow Lee's original instructions?"

"I think the answer's pretty clear," said Hampton. "Lee expected this and he's got Ewell and Hill to concentrate on Grant. I think we should both comply with his instructions. You'd best press ahead and get yourself across the Rappahannock. If nothing else you'll give Lincoln something to worry about."

"And you?"

"Exactly what I was told to do. Stay between Grant and Fredericksburg. Interfere with any resupply efforts."

"All right," sighed Gordon. "I'm on my way."

"Good luck," nodded Hampton.

"You too," came the reply.

As Gordon resumed his drive for the Rappahannock, and Hampton positioned his cavalry to interfere with Federal communications, Ewell's men completed their defensive preparations and sat back to await the enemy. Ewell himself completed a tactical report which he quickly dispatched to Lee by way of a rider. Following this, he too resigned himself to the inevitable wait.

The ridge itself was not particularly steep nor excessively

high. However, it offered a commanding view of the surrounding countryside — much of which belonged to Wheatley Farm, a tobacco and corn operation of several hundred acres. The Wheatley family wasted no time abandoning their home. They gathered a few precious possessions together and ventured to the home of a neighbor nearly two miles away from the soldiers who were about to convert their peaceful farm into a bloody battleground. Fortunately, from their point of view, the house itself was situated off to one side and might be spared any bombardment.

It was very nearly half past three in the afternoon when the lead elements of Baldy Smith's column approached Wheatley Farm. At once, they spied the Confederate position atop the ridge. The way south was blocked.

Baldy Smith was not one to shy away from a challenge. He had come to Virginia to kill Rebels. If Rebels held the ridge, then he would immediately concentrate on their destruction. Pulses began to pound and many a Federal throat tightened in anticipation of the approaching battle. The blare of bugles and the rattle of drums could be heard over the thunder of horse's hooves as caisson after caisson rolled into position. In all Smith had forty guns with which to hammer the Confederate line. Having fully deployed his troops he signaled his gunners to open fire.

For thirty-five minutes the bombardment continued with no let-up. More than a thousand rounds of shot blasted Ewell's hastily constructed earthworks. However impressive it may have seemed on the surface, the barrage had little effective impact on the defenders of Wheatley's ridge. A lot of landscape was rearranged. Some of the newly erected ramparts were splintered. A lot of smoke was generated, but very few casualites were inflicted and not one of Ewell's fifty guns was damaged.

Satisfied that he had sufficiently softened the Rebel line, Smith made ready to storm it. The artillery fell silent and the infantry moved forward. He had decided to commit six thousand to the first attack, massing them near the center of the line, concentrating their strength to achieve one major breakthrough. If a hole could be punched through the Rebel position, another three thousand men were ready to pour through it and sweep the enemy from the ridge. Everything was ready, and the time had come to put the plan into action. Accordingly, Smith issued his orders and his infantry began to move across the half-mile of open grassland which separated themselves from the graybacks.

Ewell wasted no time in responding. All fifty of his guns were trained on the mass of blue which surged forward toward the ridge. They opened fire immediately, the gunners plying their skills with deadly precision. Huge gaps were torn in the enemy ranks as hundreds fell victim to Southern guns.

Still they pressed forward, all of them convinced that they had a historic opportunity to deal Lee a crushing blow. There came another volley, then a third.

"How many guns do they have up there?" raged Smith in obvious frustration. Never had he seen such a display of firepower on the part of a Southern army.

"Too damn many!" growled a veteran staff officer. "We'll never take that ridge by storm, General. We should break it off."

"Not yet," argued Smith, preferring to give the effort more time.

Then came the musket fire. From every point on the ridge Confederate riflemen poured lead into the already decimated ranks of the attacking force. So intense was the Rebel response no one could stand before it. Only a pathetic few actually reached the crest of the ridge and these were either cut down or captured before they could do any real harm. In the face of such determined and well-orchestrated resistance, Smith's assault literally evaporated. Two-thirds of the six thousand man force were killed, wounded or captured. The remaining third bid a hasty retreat to their own lines. The guns fell silent and both commanders contemplated their next move.

"Only a strong flanking move will drive them from that

ridge," argued Smith after he had hastily summoned his officers.

"Maybe so," said a brigadier. "But in the meantime we're losing both time and men. Remember our orders, General. We are supposed to link up with Grant at the earliest possible moment. He needs every man we have, and right now I'd wager there's three or four thousand of them dead or wounded between here and the crest of that ridge."

"General," came another opinion. "Our scouts indicate no substantial Rebel forces behind that ridge. We could go around it. Simply bypass it and reach Grant."

"There could be an entire corps of Rebels up there!" fumed Smith.

"If so, they're isolated. Let's just leave them there. If Grant so desires, we can return with the entire army and crush them. Right now, with our present resources, we lack the strength to take that piece of real estate."

Smith mulled these thoughts over in his mind for several moments before coming to a decision. "Very well," he sighed. "We'll go around. I want one brigade to demonstrate against their right flank. The unit will screen the rest of us as we slip past. The sooner we find Grant, the sooner we can exact a little vengeance against the Rebs on that hill."

The screening movement proved effective, if for no other reason than the questions it raised in Ewell's mind. He had anchored both flanks and could readily shift defenders if the need were to arise. However, could they resist a flank attack in force? The appearance of a full brigade on his right left him wondering. It forced him to continue thinking in a defensive mode. As the Rebels prepared to receive a second attack, Smith slipped away and resumed his southern march.

Ewell now faced still another choice, but information he had received from his scouts helped him decide. Should he pursue or stand pat? According to the most recent information Grant was heading toward Port Royal and the vanguard of his army was within six miles of Wheatley Farm. Ewell seriously doubted his own ability to chase down Baldy Smith and bring him to battle before Grant could reach the field. Moreover, reasoned Ewell, Grant would be unlikely to resist the opportunity to destroy an isolated corps of Confedrate infantry. Better would it be for Stonewall's men to remain exactly where they were.

"Swing them guns around, boys!" he shouted to the artillerymen. "We'll have company from the other side before much longer."

"You think we'll have to face the whole Yankee army?" asked one sergeant.

"Could be," nodded Ewell.

"We did it before," said one veteran gunner who sported a thick, heavy, gray beard. "The second time around at Manassas."

"Then we'll do it again," insisted the sergeant.

"That's the spirit!" grinned Ewell. "Grant's about six miles behind us. Lee's less than ten miles behind him. All we have to do is hold on for a spell. Get busy, boys! Let's fortify the southern approach to this ridge!"

Well to the west of Wheatley Farm, General Wade Hampton was about to go into action himself. His scouts reported a long wagon train enroute from Fredericksburg to resupply and reinforce Grant. Ten thousand green recruits were making the last leg of a march to join the Army of the Potomac. This left Stuart's successor with a couple of options. He could pick the place and force a decisive battle. However, his troopers would be somewhat outnumbered and such a choice might expose them to the degree of casualties suffered by his Union counterpart at Ox Ford. A second option involved a series of hit-and-run raids against the wagons all along their route of travel — a route which became more lengthy every hour due to the eastward shift of Grant's own line of march. To Hampton this made more sense. In this fashion he could at least prevent some of the resupply efforts expected by Grant.

"Mount up, boys!" he shouted somewhat gleefully, "We've got a party to attend."

Hampton had also benefited from the bountiful harvest in munitions taken by Lee at Ox Ford. His horse artillery boasted of twenty guns with copious supplies of ammunition to keep them working.

His choice certainly turned out to be the better one. In a series of closely coordinated raids he succeeded in destroying some fifty wagons and capturing an almost equal number. Five hundred of the mounted Federal escort were felled or captured. Nearly two thousand of the brand new infantry were cut off from the main body and captured. All this was achieved at a cost of only four hundred men, killed or wounded. Eventually, however, the enemy drew too close to the main body of Grant's army and Hampton was forced to break off contact, retiring in the direction of Fredericksburg.

As for Grant, the arrival of Baldy Smith provided a much needed shot in the arm to uplift his sagging fortunes. True, Smith showed up with slightly less than eleven thousand men, substantially fewer than the fifteen thousand who accompanied him to Port Royal. Yet, eleven thousand were far better than nothing at all. Grant was happy to welcome them with open arms. Moreover, he learned of the opportunity to crush an isolated corps of Confederates and he ordered Meade to proceed in that direction at once.

Among the commands of Burnside and Hancock were numerous veterans; men who still held vivid memories of the debacle at Second Manassas. As they marched toward Wheatley Farm they made it a point to remind their officers of their concerns. They, in turn, voiced these reservations up the chain of command until Grant himself was aware of the possibilities.

Not that Grant was ever unaware. He knew Ewell was being dangled as bait. He opted to go after the bait, gambling that he could hold Lee at bay long enough to destroy Ewell. At best this was a long gamble.

Robert E. Lee was travelling by carriage near the rear of Hill's command. He was not well enough to ride Traveller for any length of time, but he was not so uncomfortable that he needed to travel prone in the back of an ambulance. All along the way, he was in receipt of information on the enemy's movements, as well as any clashes which were taking place. He learned of Hampton's hit-and-run approach against the supply train from Fredericksburg. He also knew of the initial battle at Wheatley Farm and that Ewell would soon be facing all of Grant's strength; a force which would exceed forty-seven thousand men with the addition of Baldy Smith. He ordered his scouts to make a thorough reconnaissance of the region surrounding Wheatley Farm. Having issued these instructions he expected and ultimately received a detailed topographical map of the area on which to base his strategy for the next confrontation.

Moreover, the Army of Northern Virginia had to deal with numerous efforts to thwart its pursuit. Several rearguards were left behind by the Federals. The units were small, and in the final analysis not overly effective. Lee's technique was to simply bypass them wherever possible — always to the east.

It was nearly dark when the first units of the Army of the Potomac neared the outer fringes of Wheatley Farm, too late to initiate any hostilities of consequence. Grant swore vehemently at the prospect of losing such an opportunity, knowing full well that Lee would be up before the next day dawned. Consequently he ordered a hasty ill-prepared attempt against Ewell's left flank. Three thousand men were ordered to storm the Rebel position, but they fared no better than Smith's troops earlier that afternoon. Nine hundred of them were killed or wounded in the assault, all to no avail. They gained no foothold on the ridge, and were forced to retire or face annihilation.

"Now what?" posed Meade.

"We deploy for battle," said Grant calmly. "I want all of our artillery to concentrate on that ridge. Don't let the Rebels get any sleep. Have the gunners find the right range and keep up the bombardment through the night."

"That could pose a problem, General," said Meade. "For the first time in memory we experience a shortage in ammunition."

"There's a supply train coming from Fredericksburg."

"I know, and we've been receiving reports all day. They've been hit several times by Rebel cavalry. Losses and damages thus far have been considerable."

"How serious is the shortage?"

"We can fight for a spell, but an all-night bombardment wouldn't be wise, especially with Lee coming up on our rear."

"A point well taken," sighed Grant in a tone which reflected resignation and frustration more than anything else. "Can we afford to fire three to six guns at periodic intervals?"

"I imagine so."

"Make the arrangements, then get back to me. If Lee's coming we should arrange a suitable reception."

"Splendid idea," smiled Meade. "A measure of revenge for Ox Ford might make us all feel immeasurably better."

As darkness descended on the Central Tidewater of Virginia, Grant and Meade forged strategy with which to greet Lee the following morning. The topography maps of the immediate vicinity provided little in the way of encouragement.

"If these scouting reports are accurate, Ewell's sitting on the best defensive terrain for several miles in any direction," noted Grant, cupping his chin with one hand.

"Not surprising," replied Meade. "Perhaps this isn't the best ground on which to face Lee. Our troops have been resting in position since we arrived here. They can march at a moment's notice. We could move ten miles farther, to the northeast. There's some higher ground as you approach the Rappahannock. From there we could easily secure an open line of supply to Port Royal. It would be an ideal situation from which to regain the initiative."

"Leave?" Grant arched his eyebrows and stared rather intently at Meade. "March another ten miles north?"

"Can't you see the advantages?"

"I'd have to give up Ewell."

"I guess you have to weigh the costs and benefits of such a move."

"I want Ewell."

"General . . ."

"No! Wait just a moment and listen. Baldy Smith thinks there are ten to fifteen thousand Rebels on that hill. If we take them we will have dealt an irreparable blow to Robert E. Lee."

"This is not good ground," insisted Meade.

"Damn the ground!" snarled Grant. "I'm not going to retreat another ten miles merely for the sake of finding a mole hill on which to hide! In any event, it doesn't make sense! Lee has divided his army. Should I step aside and let the two forces reunite? That is not sound military tactics. I intend to keep my own army intact and in between Lee and Ewell."

Meade knew it would be useless to argue any further, "As you wish," he sighed.

The argument aside, Meade and Grant sat down to design a defensive strategy with which to receive Lee on the morrow.

The task of driving Ewell from the ridge fell to Hancock, marking the third time in as many weeks that Hancock's corps was assigned the job of taking a position from Stonewall Jackson's old troops. They had tried on the last day at Spotsylvania and again at Ox Ford. Neither time had their efforts met with any substantial success. In both incidents their losses were considerable. Hancock's troops were deployed primarily against Ewell's left flank, the eastern section of his line. Hancock placed the bulk of his numbers against the flank itself, but he still had enough strength to concentrate against Ewell's front and rear.

The remainder of Grant's army began to dig in a long, arc-like formation just below Hancock. Their attentions were directed in the southeasterly direction. Baldy Smith held the right, Burnside the left. In the center, Meade was in control, commanding little more than a corps. This was not a demotion. It was merely the most practical fashion to deal with the shortage of general officers which was now making its presence felt in the Army of the Potomac.

Throughout the long night, the wagon train from Fredericksburg reached the army a few units at a time. Grant decided to hold on to all of these troops, including the escort. In this way he added another ten thousand rifles to his numbers. Well before dawn of the next morning Grant was able to field a total of fifty-five thousand men. He knew Lee would barely be able to match this number, and this knowledge only served to fuel the expectations of himself and those he led.

Ewell was hardly in a position to ignore the obvious. The Federals were going to try to sweep him from the ridge by way of his left flank. He responded by beefing up defenses in that side of the line. Twenty of his guns were put into place and another thousand muskets were shifted to positions along the left flank. This done, Ewell could do little more but wait for the coming of dawn.

That same night, Gordon slept on the south bank of the Rappahannock. Most of his men got a decent night's sleep as well, all save the corps of engineers. All through the night they labored by torchlight on a pontoon bridge with which to span the river. It was Gordon's intention to take up positions on the north bank well before noon of the following day.

Gordon was sleeping like a baby that night, but the same could not be said of his commander. R. E. Lee slept fitfully, if at all. It wasn't so much the stomach malady. The illness was on the decline and there was still a potent quantity of Gwathmey's remedy to mask its symptoms. It was concern for the next day which denied sleep to the Confederate general. His post-Ox Ford strategy was bold at the very least, and with it came great risk. The army was divided, more so than it ever had been, even at Chancellorsville. The reports he was receiving indicated that Grant had benefited from major reinforcements during the day, though not as many as the Federal commander had hoped for. Moreover, Ewell now faced all of Grant's strength alone. Speed was of the essence now. There was no thought of stopping for the night. They must reach this place called Wheatley Farm by daybreak and be in a position to confront the Federals who would be assailing Ewell.

Some were already drawing parallels to the Second Battle of Manassas. The comparisons held some validity, but Lee knew better than to be seduced by past victories. For one thing, there was a substantial difference between the two situations. At the Second Battle of Manassas, the Union commander, General Pope, was taken completely by surprise when Longstreet launched his assault against the flank on the Union left. Lee knew the element of surprise would not be available to him at Wheatley Farm. Grant was monitoring the course and pace of his pursuit. How then should he respond? Suddenly Lee found himself missing the men whom he trusted most: Longstreet, in Richmond recuperating from wounds taken in the Wilderness; Stuart and Jackson both dead. It was from Longstreet's tactical philosophy that Lee found the solution. The man he affectionately called "My Old Warhorse" believed that defense should be the order of the day. He maintained that the best approach to modern warfare was defensive. Dig in, fortify yourself, let the enemy attack you.

When he turned his attention to the map of the region he saw his answer. According to the scouting reports Grant was facing Ewell with roughly a corps of infantry. All the rest of his army was in position to blunt any rescue attempt on the part of the Confederates. He would have to be coaxed out of position. To drive him out in one full scale battle would probably prove costly. He would have to persuade Grant to take the offensive or go after him piecemeal. After a short period of reflection Lee made his decision. He would continue marching through the night, past Grant's dug-in forces. Once north of Wheatley Farm he would swing about and down toward Ewell. He planned to confront only those forces who would be assailing Ewell. His express purpose was to establish a continual line with Ewell on the extreme right. This position would stand essentially perpendicular to the Army of the Potomac, a situation which would place Grant's left in extreme peril. What the ultimate results might be, only time would tell, but on paper the plan appeared sound.

With some two hours remaining before dawn, the Army of Northern Virginia moved into position astride the ridge on Wheatley's farm. The long march from Ox Ford had been exhausting but uneventful. No attempt was made by Grant to interfere with Lee's movements during the night, though Union cavalry did monitor his progress and the direction of his march. By morning Lee was firmly dug in with Ewell on his right and his back to Port Royal.

Morning also brought the advent of hostilities along the ridge. Hancock opened up with a thunderous barrage. Using every one of his guns he hammered Ewell's position mercilessly for a solid hour. Lee held silent all of that time. Finally the guns fell silent and Hancock hurled his troops forward. Straight up the far left of the ridge they charged; straight into the teeth of Ewell's guns.

The first wave was shattered, its survivors thrown back along the second. Still they pressed forward, cresting the ridge, reaching the first line of fortifications. With the aid of a small looking glass Hancock was able to detect hand to hand fighting along Ewell's perimeter. At once he ordered the next wave to start forward.

Here Lee intervened. Using the long range artillery captured at Ox Ford he pounded the face of the ridge, leaving attackers stunned, many of them stumbling about in a daze. The delay this action caused gave Ewell enough time to rally his defenders and finally hurl back a surprisingly determined enemy. Losses on both sides were considerable.

Having assisted in the repulse, Lee then turned his attentions to the offense. All along the line he unleashed his artillery, splitting the air itself with the thundering crescendo of cannons. On the tail end of this barrage he ordered an infantry assault in brigade strength.

It was designed to be a probing action more so than anything else, a test of Grant's defenses. This effort was only a partial success in that information was gleaned. From a more practical standpoint, however, the attack failed. No grayback penetrated to within bayonet range of the enemy. Grant was ready for them.

Following this probe against the Union left was a lull of approximately two hours. The Federals used this time to shift their lines to correspond with Lee's position. The Confederates used it to mass their strength for another try against the northern line. The roar of Rebel guns signaled the end of the lull and when the barrage died down, two divisions of Hill's infantry rushed forward. They were concentrated against the position of Grant's line which shielded Hancock. Their goal? Eliminate the shield and provide a definite link between Ewell and the rest of the Southern army. Both sides knew how crucial the results of this fighting would be, leading to a protracted display of carnage in which both sides lost heavily. For the longest time it appeared the Union line might hold, but Lee would not be denied. A third division was committed to the effort and Lee himself arrived at the front on horseback. Doffing his hat, the Confederate general exhorted his men to greater efforts, praising their courage and strength. The impact of his presence was immediate. These fresh troops hurled themselves into the fray with a fury seldom seen in modern warfare, finally breaking the back of the Union resistance. This sector of the Federal line collapsed, its surviving defenders retreating in disarray.

Wheatly Farm, however, was no Ox Ford. The Cannae along the North Anna River would not be repeated in the southern approach to Port Royal. The northern retreat did not disintegrate into a rout. Beleaguered and bloodied though they were, Grant's soldiers reorganized themselves and quickly formed a second line from which to resist any further advances by the Rebels. Lee had managed to establish his link with Ewell, much to the relief of the latter, but he could do no more without exposing his men to even more peril. Reluctantly Lee called off the attack and ordered his troops to dig in.

The opposing lines were well within range of each other and the battle continued to rage back and forth throughout the afternoon. Among the Rebels in the forward positions were Seth Reilly and the dwindling group of survivors from the Stonewall Jackson brigade. They numbered a mere sixteen, but what they lacked in number they certainly made up for in enthusiasm. Cody Wilder wielded the Whitworth with uncanny skill. So effective was he that most of the riflemen in the opposing trenches refused to raise their heads over the ramparts to return the Rebel fire.

Reilly aimed his musket, pulled the trigger, and quickly ducked back down to safety. It was late afternoon by this time, and Reilly was bone-tired. He slumped wearily against the earthen wall of the trench and rested his freshly loaded musket across his lap. One could scarcely discern the color of his face through the smoke and grime.

"Got him!" Cody's boyish voice sang out over the din of battle. The lad quickly scooted down next to his lieutenant. "Hear that, Perfessor?" he grinned. "I got me another one!"

"You're one helluva shot, boy," returned Reilly. "I'll definitely give you that. Take a break. Keep your head down for a few minutes. Let some of them Yankees enjoy a few more moments of life."

"Sho nuff!" chuckled Wilder, wiping sweat from his face with the sleeve of his tunic. "How long you figure we'll keep this up?" he wondered aloud.

"No tellin'," said Reilly. "This'll end up being a battle of wills, a test to see which of us blinks first."

"I don't plan on blinkin', Perfessor."

"Professor," corrected Reilly for the umpteenth time.

"Right."

"I don't think Lee plans on blinking either. This could

end up being a long afternoon."

Just then the water boy showed up. Suspended from his shoulders were two wooden pails, each with several ladles. He stopped and called "Water!" At once he was surrounded by a small horde of ravenously thirsty soldiers who drank greedily.

"Easy, fellas!" urged the water boy. "Save some for the next section of line!"

"Sorry about that," chortled Ox as he downed his third ladle of water. "I've got a bigger gullet to fill."

"All right you guys!" ordered Reilly. "Back on the line! Be quick!"

"You must be gettin' old, Professor!" grinned Ox. "You got no sense of humor anymore!"

"Never mind that!" returned Reilly as bullets whined overhead. "Get back into action!"

So the day went.

*   *   *   *

By sundown the fighting had waned, with neither side able to secure any true advantage. To the Army of the Potomac, however, a draw was essentially a setback if not an outright defeat. They had marched to Wheatley Farm with the express purpose of annihilating Ewell. In this they failed. Grant had hoped to cripple Lee as the latter arrived on the field. Here again his efforts proved fruitless. Moreover, Lee had managed to interpose himself between Grant and Port Royal, a move which put definite limitations on Grant's options at battle's end.

When darkness finally forced a halt to the fighting Grant summoned Meade for a brief conference. Meade arrived at Grant's tent looking somewhat dazed and ruffled. He wasn't used to spending so much time in the actual heat of battle.

"You look terrible," said Grant as he watched Meade enter and take a seat.

"I've felt better," admitted Meade.

191

"I suppose it's safe to say the day didn't turn out quite the way we planned it."

"Safe," agreed Meade. "However, by the same token, it hasn't worked all that well for the Rebs. We've achieved another standoff."

"I'm afraid even the standoff will work to their advantage," moaned Grant. "We've expended a great deal of ammunition today. The supply train from Fredericksburg provided only partial compensation. I'm afraid we're facing some very real logistical problems."

"Not surprising," grunted Meade. "What do we do now?"

"I guess I'm looking for advice."

"Could we go through another day like this?"

"If we did it would bankrupt us so far as ammunition is concerned."

"Nothing more coming from Fredericksburg?"

"Not for the time being. Apparently the Rebs have got Wade Hampton standing in force between us and Fredericksburg. Shipments have been suspended until that threat can be neutralized."

"Can it?"

"Not with our present strength."

"Then we have no choice but to withdraw."

"That's a choice I'm reluctant to make," muttered Grant.

"Nonetheless, we'd be wise to leave this place, forget about Port Royal and march west. Upon reaching Fredericksburg we can refill our coffers and swing about to deal with Lee."

"That appears to be our only choice," sighed Grant, his tone heavy with resignation.

"Then we should leave tonight, and do so with all possible stealth."

"Agreed," nodded Grant. "We'll march sometime after midnight. Choose one brigade to function as a rearguard."

"I hate to sacrifice so large a number."

"So do I, George, but if we don't we may imperil the

whole army."

"I know," sighed Meade. "I'll choose one of Burnside's brigades."

"Very well. I'll prepare a report for the President and get some sleep. Wake me about half past eleven."

Meade nodded wearily and left the tent, leaving Grant alone to ponder his options.

The range of options remaining to Grant was not broad enough to keep the Federal commander up too late. He had lost seventy-five hundred men that day, a small number in comparison to his totals in the Wilderness, at Spotsylvania or at Ox Ford. Small though they may have seemed, these losses were crucial. They effectively neutralized the reinforcements who had come in with the wagon train. What was he to do? Grant faced a problem to which he was altogether unaccustomed. He was very much on the defensive and, as he was now coming to realize, fighting for his very existence.

What was he to do? Very likely, he could not expect reinforcements from Washington for at least another week. Could he send for Hunter, or at least part of his command? That option didn't hold much promise. Very likely, Hunter would not be able to arrive from the Shenandoah Valley in time to do any good. Besides, Lincoln wouldn't tolerate any substantial weakening of Federal strength in the Shenandoah Valley. To do so might invite yet another Rebel sortie into Pennsylvania. What of Butler? The so-called beast of New Orleans still commanded a sizeable force in the Bermuda Hundred. Could they make a difference?

"Not any time soon," muttered Grant. Finally, he realized the truth. In terms of options he had one: to reach Fredericksburg before Lee could force him into battle again.

After penning a short dispatch to President Lincoln he retired to his cot for three hours of desperately needed sleep.

*   *   *   *

The next morning when Reilly and his troops prepared

to renew the battle they found no enemy to engage.

"They pulled out," said the lieutenant. "Looks like we won."

The word raced like wildfire through the Confederate position. The Yanks were gone!

Orders from Lee weren't long in coming. Get after them! He was sure of only one thing, Grant would make for Fredericksburg. He had no other solution for his supply problems which were becoming more acute by the day.

The rearguard left by Meade experienced only moderate success, slowing the graybacks down by an hour and a half. Most were killed or captured, but a small number were able to escape and ultimately rejoined their comrades.

The pursuit was on! Unfortunately for Grant, Lee had one undeniable advantage. His name was Wade Hampton and he was waiting in Grant's line of march. The Southern cavalry commander had six thousand troopers with him. Their orders were to dismount and fight as infantry, to stall Grant's retreat just long enough to allow Lee to catch up. He was only too happy to oblige.

The wheels in R. E. Lee's mind were turning all the while. His strategy remained the same, to herd the Federals to the banks of the Rappahannock somewhere below the town of Fredericksburg. To accomplish this he could not allow Grant any opening to the south. Accordingly, he ordered two divisions to swing south at double time and to pass Grant no matter how much effort was needed. Lee had suffered over six thousand casualties at Wheatley Farm, his losses uncomfortably close to those of his opponent. Yet Hampton was waiting to the west with his six thousand. The numerical advantage would belong to Lee, and with two divisions marching to cut Grant off from a southern escape route, he felt confident that his strategy would bear fruit.

By mid-afternoon the Army of Northern Virginia still hadn't caught up to Grant, but the signs of a hastily planned retreat were all too numerous. Abandoned wagons, stray animals, discarded gear and weapons were strewn everywhere in the wake of Grant's army. Stragglers began appearing. Only a few at first, but then in ever increasing numbers.

Sometime after three o'clock contact was made between the lead elements of Lee's army and the rear of Grant's. Lee called for a halt at once, not to attack but to rest and be ready for the next push.

"I'm about damn tired of walkin'!" groaned Cody Wilder as he collapsed prone on the ground. "When this is over I ain't walkin' no more. I'm gonna get me a horse and ride everywhere I go."

"Good idea," approved Whitt Simmons.

"Hey, Corporal!" summoned Wilder. "When do you think this will all end?"

"Hard to say, young-un," replied Simmons. "Seems to me like it's been goin' on forever."

"Do you think if we bag that fella Grant the war will be over?"

"Too hard to say," repeated Simmons. "It's possible. It's just too hard to say right now."

"Time's up!" called Reilly. "Up on your feet! Let's keep moving!"

*　　*　　*　　*

In Washington President Lincoln found himself facing a variety of strategic concerns. He had received the latest dispatch from Grant, a report which sought to put the affair at Wheatley Farm in the best possible light. Lincoln, however, had long since learned the art of seeing through smoke screens. He summoned Halleck and greeted this general with something of a long face.

"There's been another battle between Grant and Lee," he said calmly.

"I've already heard. A place called Wheatley Farm, just south of Port Royal."

"It appears we lost again."

"I got the impression they fought to a standstill."

A SOUTHERN YARN

"The report seemed heavily coated with sugar, General. In the final analysis the result was the same. It was Grant who was forced to yield the field of battle. Lee stopped him from reaching Port Royal, now he must seek his salvation in the direction of Fredericksburg."

For several moments Halleck said nothing and a weighted silence hung over the room. "Grant's a very capable officer, Mr. President. You yourself said that you liked him, that he gave you victories, unlike many of our other commanders."

"Perhaps I spoke too soon. His list of victories is impressive, to be sure, but against what caliber of opposition? Is he the equal of Lee? The Wilderness, Spotsylvania, Ox Ford and now Wheatley Farm. Four major battles and still nothing which can be claimed a legitimate victory. Ox Ford of itself could prove the undoing of this Federal Union. Two months ago he marched south at the head of the finest army in the world. Only a ghost of that army remains, and this ghost is wandering aimlessly in tatters about Central Virginia. What am I to do, Halleck?"

"He needs reinforcements. Substantial reinforcements."

"He's just added twenty-five thousand men to his numbers. Did they make any difference? Apparently not."

"One moment, Mr. President," interrupted Halleck. "Am I to misunderstand you? Do you plan on withholding support?"

"Should I throw good money after bad? Should I present General Grant with another one hundred thousand lives to squander? Look what he's done, Halleck! He's sustained the most hideous casualties of the war! After the Wilderness he was quoted as saying he would fight it out on that line all summer long if necessary. Look at the result! Lee has manhandled him at every turn!"

"Mr. President, you didn't answer my question."

"Two months ago I was convinced we were seeing the beginning of the end. That was apparently a delusion. Now I find myself in a position where once again I have to think

196

in terms of the defense of this city. If Grant fails to elude or stop the Rebels, we'll have nothing to stand between Lee and Washington. I cannot allow this city to fall."

"Are you going to abandon those men?"

"I will not allow this city to fall. The consequences would be enormous."

"Then you'll send no more reinforcements?"

"That's correct, Halleck. Hereafter you are to concentrate our strength in the Alexandria region."

"Very well, Mr. President. What of Grant?"

"To my knowledge he still commands nearly fifty thousand men. For the time being he must rely on his own abilities. Supplies I'll continue to send as long as I can reasonably expect them to make it through. Reinforcements I'll not send, at least until Grant can demonstrate that he has retaken the initiative."

"This will not sit well with General Grant," mused Halleck.

"The last month hasn't sat particularly well with me, General. Unless someone has suspended our Constitution without my knowledge, I am still Commander-in-Chief of our armed forces! Accordingly, I have determined not to reinforce Grant until he proves himself capable."

"Are you looking for a victory, Mr. President? How can you handcuff Grant and expect him to produce a victory?"

"I'm not handcuffing him, Halleck!" A flash of anger burst from Lincoln's deep set eyes. "And at this stage of the game I'm not looking for a victory per se. I'd be content to see him slip away from Lee's grasp and gain the north bank of the Rappahannock. Then and only then will I reinforce the Army of the Potomac. Until then my first priority is the security of this city."

"I see," muttered Halleck.

"Kindly convey my feeling to General Grant."

"Very well, Mr. President," Halleck sighed heavily and departed with a noticeable droop in his shoulders.

*   *   *   *

A SOUTHERN YARN

R. E. Lee had just finished studying the most recent scouting reports when Generals Ewell and A. P. Hill arrived at his tent. "Good afternoon, gentlemen," he lifted his eyes momentarily. "Please come in."

When they had comfortably seated themselves Lee pushed the paperwork aside and began to explain his strategy for the next confrontation. "I believe General Grant now realizes his best chance of redemption lies to the north of the Rappahannock," he said calmly. "He'll avoid us unless we can force a showdown."

"That shouldn't be a problem," interjected Hill.

"Agreed," nodded his commander. "The only question centers on the place, and I think I may have the answer. His present line of march seems to be edging south, but the two divisions we dispatched earlier will be capable of nudging him north once again. As things now appear, I believe he would like to swing around Fredericksburg in order to cross the Rapidan and the Rappahannock above the town. Once across he'll have access to the supplies stockpiling in Fredericksburg, and he'll have all of Northern Virginia in which to maneuver."

"What about Gordon?" wondered Ewell.

"He's already north of the river," replied Lee, "But let's not get ahead of ourselves. We must first focus on the problem at hand. Grant must not be allowed to move anywhere to the west of Fredericksburg. I think I may have found just the place to contain his march and force him to divert sharply northward. "Here," he said as he tapped a spot on his map, "A little village called Four Mile Fork, directly south of the town itself. I've already sent word to Hampton. His cavalry should be there within the next hour, putting them almost directly in Grant's path. If the Federals decide to make a fight of it we'll be on top of them from the outset. If not, they'll have but one unobstructed path of escape. This way . . ." he traced a line along the map itself. "To the northeast, a line of march which will take him directly to the Rappahannock. The river at this point ranges up to a third of a mile in width and cannot be forded at this time of year. If all goes well we could have him pinned against the Rappahannock by tomorrow's sunset."

"I think we can do it," nodded Hill with a devilish smile on his face.

"God willing," concurred Lee. "Your men must be ready for action at a moment's notice. Keep them sharp. Do you understand?"

"Perfectly, General," said Ewell. "This may be the least of our problems. The men sense an early demise for General Grant and company. They're eagerly anticipating one final showdown."

"They'll soon have it. Come, Gentlemen, it's time we resumed out pursuit."

*   *   *   *

Just as the sun was edging toward the western horizon, the lead elements of Grant's dwindling army brushed against Confederate forces, namely two divisions which had been earlier dispatched by Lee to outpace the Federals. The action itself was inconclusive, but in the dim of twilight Grant could not make an accurate assessment as to the strength of his opposition. Accordingly he avoided further contact, skirting the Rebel forces and shifting his line of march just slightly to the north.

They had progressed but a few miles when the clatter of musket fire forced them to halt. Lines of battle were quickly formed and skirmishers were ordered forward to determine the size of the Rebel force. They were met by a tremendous barrage of artillery and carbine fire, retiring at once to the relative safety of their lines.

General George Meade took the dispatch from the courier's hand, glanced over it and quickly turned it over to Grant. "Little information was gleaned from that effort," he said calmly. "We weren't able to discover their strength. We did find out they're using those new repeating carbines of ours and they're backed by a huge number of cannons."

"The bounty from Ox Ford," mused Grant.

"Apparently."

"What the Rebels lack in numbers they make up for with extra hardware."

"Our hardware at that."

"No point in dwelling on that particular issue," grumbled Grant. "The point is we've got Rebels dug into our front and we may not have the numbers necessary to push them aside."

"I think pushing them aside is out of the question. We can't be sure how many of them are out there, and we know that Lee is close on our heels. If we stay here we may end up trapped in a hammer-anvil situation. I believe that's to be avoided at all costs."

As frustrated as he was over his recent run of failures, Grant still couldn't argue with Meade's logic. "I agree," he sighed.

"How are we to respond to this new set of circumstances?"

"You tell me," muttered Grant.

"It's too dark to initiate hostilities," argued Meade. Lee's right behind us and we've got Rebel infantry screening our left flank. We've been marching all day and the men are exhausted. I think we'd be wise to dig in here. If Lee chooses to attack in the morning, let him find us strongly fortified. Perhaps we can deal him a crippling blow on the morrow from a defensive posture."

"Possibly," concurred Grant. "And if Lee chooses not to attack tomorrow?"

"We still have one avenue of escape open to us, north into Fredericksburg itself, or east of the town if we so choose."

"Our field of choices is rapidly dwindling, General," said Grant. "I received a dispatch from Washington earlier this afternoon."

"And?" probed Meade.

"It seems the President has become anxious for the safety of the capital."

"Nothing new in that. He's always been concerned about Washington City."

"Halleck tells me Lincoln has decided to withhold any more replacements until we make the north bank of the Rappahannock."

"I see," mused Meade.

"We must shake Bobby Lee from our tail."

"Obviously. The question is . . . how?"

"I want this army on the march again an hour before dawn," huffed Grant.

"Very well. Our destination?"

"Fredericksburg itself. Unless we're forced to give battle we should reach the town by noon. Send a dispatch to the garrison commander. Advise him to prepare his evacuation at once. The hospitals should be attended to first. All the wounded and the medical personnel are to be shipped out before sunrise. All the rest of the stores and soldiers are to be ready to join our column when we pass through the town."

"As you wish, sir."

There was a note of sadness in Meade's voice as he acknowledged Grant's instructions. Where was the indomitable conqueror who boasted that he would never retreat? "Anything else?" he pressed.

"That's it. You'd best get some rest, George. Tomorrow promises to be a long day."

*   *   *   *

At the headquarters of Robert E. Lee a similar scene unfolded, though the mood was decidedly more positive.

"Hampton did a fine job of stopping him today," said the gray commander, addressing himself to Hill and Ewell. "I don't think Grant will try him again in the morning. I think he may still be blind as to our strength and our intentions."

"Very possibly," agreed Hill. "His action today reflects hesitation, possibly even confusion."

"He'll try for Fredericksburg," predicted Ewell.

"My thoughts exactly," nodded Lee, "and I want him to find it in Confederate hands."

"General?" posed Hill.

"Send riders at once. Have Heth and Wilcox take Hampton's place. Instruct Hampton to strike Fredericksburg with all his strength. Tell him I would like to see the town recaptured before dawn if at all possible."

"That's a tall order," noted Ewell.

"Only because of the time element," argued Lee. "He'll find it defended only by garrison troops and rear echelon personnel."

Staff officers quickly prepared the necesssary orders and within minutes riders were racing to deliver them.

Wade Hampton was asleep on the ground when Lee's courier arrived, and was not a little surprised by the order to storm Fredericksburg. Once he was fully awake, however, a sly smile began to creep across his face, and he began to appreciate the opportunity to wreak a little havoc in the style of his deceased predecessor, Jeb Stuart.

"Do we take the guns?" asked one staff officer as preparations for the ride began.

"Only a few," replied Hampton. "We'll be travelling light for this particular mission and our relief will need a lot of artillery if Grant decides to come this way again."

Just a few minutes before 4 a.m. the infantry began to arrive. Hampton's men quickly took to their mounts. Numbering close to five thousand they broke up into three columns, stole quietly west for a mile or two, then struck north for the town of Fredericksburg.

Lee's prediction as to the defensive capabilities of Fredericksburg proved uncannily accurate. Moreover, Hampton's thrust was entirely unanticipated. He struck the Union forces in the midst of their evacuation and quickly threw them into complete disarray. In terms of organized resistance there was very little, and this evaporated almost at the outset. Three trains of federal wounded had already been sent north before the attack started. A fourth got underway just as Hampton struck the perimeter of the town. Aside from these, precious few escaped. Sunrise found the Stars and Bars flying defiantly from the highest church steeple. Leaving a small number of troopers to guard his many prisoners, Hampton moved just to the south of the town and dug in to await Grant.

The latter was already on the march, hoping to steal a couple of hours on old man Lee. Leaving their campfires blazing in the pre-dawn darkness, Grant's men filed quietly into their columns and started north.

Lee was ready for this move. Rebel scouts were scattered here and there along the Federal line of march. Once they were able to verify a mass movement by the Army of the Potomac, the southerners immediately took up the chase.

What followed could hardly be styled a pursuit in the classic sense. In point of fact the two armies were engaged in a running battle from the outset. Sporadic gunfire could be heard well before sunrise, and by the time day had dawned the volume of sheer noise approached that of a full scale battle.

Here, Grant found himself at an extreme disadvantage. He was hampered by his wagon trains, but he could ill afford to abandon them. Accordingly, he had no choice but to fight. Still refusing to be brought to bay he chose to leave rearguards in his wake. As morning waned he found himself forced to leave ever-larger units behind, desperately hoping they might buy him some time.

Whatever hopes he may have entertained of escape through Fredericksburg were cruelly dashed by the return of a badly shot up scouting party.

"What happened?" demanded Grant, angrily chomping on his cigar.

"The Rebs have Fredericksburg, General," reported the

captain who had led this particular patrol. "There's a bunch of them dug in just below the town."

"In what strength?" snarled Grant, cursing beneath his breath.

"Several thousand and they're using our carbines."

In obvious frustration, Grant hurled his cigar butt to the ground and turned to Parker standing nearby.

"You know something, Ely?" he fumed. "For the first time I'm beginning to wonder whose side God's really on!"

"What now?" demanded Meade impatiently.

"We need to put ourselves north of that Goddamn river!" raged Grant. "Keep the army moving! Skirt the town to the east, then we'll swing west for the nearest ford!"

"Good!" nodded Meade approvingly, still nursing a faint hope that they might escape annihilation.

*   *   *   *

"We've done it!" exclaimed Lee, swinging a clenched fist in a rare show of emotion. He had just learned of Grant's move to the east of the town, and he was understandably elated. "He cannot cross the river below Fredericksburg unless he builds a bridge, and for such a task he has no time! He's going to try to follow the south bank upriver until he locates a suitable crossing."

"Gentlemen!" he smiled momentarily, as he savored the possibilities, "I believe we may be close to checkmate!"

"What's our next move?" asked Venable.

"We divide in two. General Hill will take half the army and march straight through the town. He will cut off Grant's route of escape. Ewell will take the rest of the army and continue nipping at Grant's heels. Hampton will keep the cavalry in a position to support either wing, should it become necessary."

"What do you think he'll do?" pressed Taylor.

"He may give battle or he might withdraw downriver to try and end run. I hope he chooses the second option. If so, we'll shadow him for a few miles, then drive him into the river itself!"

Seth Reilly and his men were part of Ewell's command and found themselves chasing Federals all day long. One rearguard after another confronted the pursuing Rebels but the result was always the same. Some fought to the last man. Others gave it their best shot, then calmly surrendered.

"We should stop takin' prisoners!" fumed Cody Wilder as he ushered several despondent Yankees toward the rear at bayonet point. "It takes too much time!"

"Just imagine yourself in their shoes!" countered Reilly. "Turn those fellas over to the provost people and get your tail back into action! Be quick!"

"You got it, Professor!"

"Hey! You said it right!"

"You see? I'm learnin'!"

"It's about damn time!" grinned Reilly. "Get on with you!"

A short time later they came across a small group of Union stragglers huddled together near a broken down wagon. There were eight of them in all, most of them engaged in the task of lifting the wagon high enough to allow their comrades to replace the shattered wheel. Reilly and his men had just covered two hundred yards of ground in which they had not seen a Federal. They had spied the white canvas of the wagon before seeing any of the northern soldiers, and as a result they crept quietly forward until they were literally on top of their hapless victims. Reilly waited until everyone was in position before making his move.

"Give it up, Yanks!" he shouted suddenly. "We've got you covered!"

Down came the wagon. The Federals appeared confused, uncertain about what to do next. One of them came to the wrong conclusion. He reached for his musket, but a bullet from Reilly's revolver felled him 'ere the butt of his musket left the ground. His comrades quickly raised their hands. For them the war was over.

As Reilly prepared his prisoners for transport to the rear, Whitt Simmons climbed into the wagon and began to rummage around.

"Hey, look at this!" he cried, sticking his head out of the back flap.

"What is it?" called Ox, raising his musket as though a threat were about to materialize.

"Coffee!" Whitt flashed a broad grin. "Must be five hundred pounds of it here! God! Does this ever smell good!"

"Grab a couple of bags!" said Reilly. "Let's keep moving!"

Before too much longer they had rejoined the main thrust against Grant's rear, driving the Federals toward the Rappahannock.

No sooner had the lead elements of the Army of the Potomac rounded the northeast corner of Fredericksburg than they spotted A. P. Hill's infantry deployed in a long line of battle. The Rebels were already digging entrenchments in anticipation of a Federal punch.

"If we break through we're home free," noted Grant.

"Our chances aren't especially good," muttered Meade. "We're looking at the anvil. The hammer's breathing down our necks."

"You really know how to rain on someone's parade, George."

"Be that as it may, we'll never break that line before Lee breaks us. We should dig in, General, and we should do it fast."

"As much as I hate to admit it," sighed Grant, "You may be right. Give the orders. We may as well give the Rebs a reception they won't soon forget."

Thus went the remainder of the afternoon. The Army of the Potomac dug in along a line shaped somewhat like a boomerang. The Army of Northern Virginia faced this position in two distinct lines roughly perpendicular to one another. If Grant was hoping to receive a full scale assault against his position, he was soon disappointed. Lee had no intention of squandering his soldiers in such a fashion. The advantage was his. Time was now on his side. There was no need to rush headlong into a wall of lead. He would simply wait the Federals out leaving them one avenue of escape southeast along the banks of the Rappahannock. The two armies exchanged artillery and musket duels through the rest of the day, but neither ventured beyond the relative safety of their trenches.

By this time, Lee had established communications with Gordon who was camped on the north bank about ten miles below the scene of the fighting. Using signal flags Rebel soldiers on the south bank conveyed Lee's instructions to Gordon. Simply put, the hero of Ox Ford was to break up camp and march up river, staying out of sight and remaining mobile until Grant's final position would be fixed. Whereupon Gordon would dig in along the river opposite Grant, add his weight to the siege which would be underway, and effectively block any attempt by the Federals to escape across the river.

That night Grant summoned his major officers for a Council of War. After everyone had been seated he rose to his feet and began speaking.

"Gentlemen," he took the cigar from his mouth, "I think we should use this opportunity to take stock of our situation and make plans for the immediate future."

"From where I'm sitting the immediate future looks awfully dim," remarked Hancock bitterly.

"Let's not get carried away," cautioned Grant. "Things may not look promising at the moment, but that could change at any time. We should not be giving into despair. General Meade, what about our present strength?"

"The last couple of days haven't been overly kind," replied Meade. "Desertions, stragglers, or casualties have all taken their toll. I calculate we've got slightly less than forty thousand men remaining to us."

"I see," mused Grant softly. "Mr. Parker, have you obtained the information I requested earlier?"

"Yes, General, and the news isn't good."

"Let's hear it."

"I assume the Rebels captured everything in Fredericksburg. Whether they did or not is a moot point. The bottom line is this: We don't have it. With our remaining stock of munitions we can probably fight for ten or twelve days, depending on the pace. After that, we'll be throwing rocks at 'em."

"Food?"

"Most of the food wagons made it. We won't run out for another three weeks."

"We don't have another three weeks," grumbled Hancock.

"Enough of that!" snapped Grant.

"All due respect, General!" fumed Hancock. "Do you really think Lee's going to sit back and let us run out of supplies?"

"He may! In any event, I don't plan on leaving that type of decision to him. We will decide our best moves, which is precisely the purpose of this meeting!"

"Very well," relented Hancock, who by now was convinced their situation was hopeless.

"For starters, there's one factor which you all need to be aware of. Washington has decided against sending us reinforcements until we can elude Lee and reach the north bank of the river. We're on our own."

"General," Ambrose Burnside interrupted. "Perhaps we can loot stores from the enemy."

"Not likely," Grant shook his head slowly. "Lee will be guarding all those places heavily."

"Just what do you have in mind?" asked Meade.

"Lee has yet to close two possible avenues of escape: the river itself and the south bank."

"The river is too wide here," interjected Hancock. "There are no fords nearby. We would have to bridge it. Do you think Lee will stand idly by while we cross the Rappahannock under his nose?"

"A point well taken," nodded Grant. "As desperately as I'd like to put this army on the other side of the river, I'm not quite ready to make an attempt of that sort. My first preference is to take the downriver option."

"He'll be waiting for us. Mark my words," commented Meade.

"Perhaps, but do you see another choice?"

"The river here is only sixty or seventy yards across. The further downriver we march, the wider and deeper it becomes."

"What's your point?"

"Just this," noted Meade. "If you envision having to cross that river, we should do it here. This place offers our best chance, though I admit it's only a slim chance."

"You may be right," said Grant. "But I prefer the second option. If we can slip away from here and get a few hours on Lee we could reach Port Royal ahead of him. From there we could withdraw unmolested by ship."

"That's a long shot at best," remarked Hancock.

"You're not afraid, are you?" posed Grant. "Surely not you!"

"Afraid? Hardly! I'm just making a realistic appraisal of our chances."

"All right!" huffed Grant. "A long shot it is! Does anyone have a better idea? Lincoln wants us to prove our mettle. What better way to prove it? As far as I'm concerned the issue is settled. We try for Port Royal! We'll slip out of here tomorrow night just after midnight. In the meantime, instruct your troops to stay alert and hold fast!"

*   *   *   *

As Grant and his officers argued their future, a similar council was underway at Lee's headquarters. From this meeting, a strategy emerged; one which was based entirely on Grant's movements. If the Federals remained in place, so would the Confederates. If they attempted to bridge the Rappahannock, Gordon would be alerted and the army would attack with all its strength. If Grant tried to sneak downriver, Ewell would move with him outpacing him and ultimately blocking this route as well. Gordon and Hill would soon arrive and the final seige would be underway. Lee and his officers slept well that night, content to wait for Grant's next move.

Night had long since fallen and the men of both armies busied themselves with preparations for the next day's action. It was uncommonly warm that night, considering it was still early in June. The air was unpleasantly heavy, thick with moisture. Insects abounded, adding their weight to the discomfort on both sides of the line. Though Seth Reilly and his men were bone-weary, rest was a luxury they could not enjoy. The advent of darkness found them creeping cautiously forward to man a position on the picket line. Only fourteen of them remained — fourteen out of the entire Stonewall Brigade. Reilly himself reflected on this sad statistic as he crouched low in the underbrush peering out into the darkness. Sweat literally poured from his body, soaking his tattered gray uniform.

"Why in hell does it have to be so damn humid!" he complained softly, his voice heard to no one but himself. He pulled a soiled kerchief from the pocket of his tunic and wiped the sweat from his forehead and face. Stuffing the newly dampened cloth back into this pocket he continued forward until he spied a fairly large tree which could easily afford him cover against the enemy lines. He crept to its base, pulling himself up to sit up against the smooth bark.

"Good enough," he muttered as he laid his musket across his lap. "Let's hope the Yanks are in a peaceful mood tonight."

To his left and right the rest of his command moved into position one by one. Cody Wilder managed to locate himself behind the same poplar as his lieutenant.

"Just like a lost puppy," thought Reilly as he nodded a welcome in Wilder's direction.

"Hey, Professor!" An unmistakable baritone pierced the night. A voice that could only have belonged to Ox. "What in the hell did we do to deserve picket duty?"

"Luck of the draw, I guess," returned Reilly. "No sense complainin'! Let's cut the chatter and keep our eyes peeled. Bobby Lee doesn't want our guests to leave without saying good-bye."

"Whatever you say, Professor, but from where I'm sittin' it doesn't look like the Yanks are plannin' on goin' anywhere a'tall."

"Can it, Ox!" This time it was Corporal Simmons who spoke. "You remember Sharpsburg?"

"Who could forget that one? Why'd you ask?"

"Because I reckon the Yanks were sayin' the same thing about us the night after the battle."

Ox thought about it for a moment, his mind going back to that night in September of 1862 when Lee fooled McClellan into thinking the Army of Northern Virginia was going nowhere. The Union commander awoke to a rude surprise the next morning.

"I see your point!" he chuckled softly and turned his eyes on the enemy camps, searching for any signs of mass movement.

An hour passed . . . then two. All was quiet, save for the constant din of nocturnal insects and the oft-heard cry of a whippoorwill. Reilly had grown rather sleepy and was actually dozing off when he heard a voice calling out from the direction of the Federal camps.

"Hey, Reb!" came the cry. "You out there?"

Reilly came awake at once, stiffening against the tree, pulling his musket into a ready position. "You know it, Yank!" he called back.

"You fellas enjoyin' the night?"

"Reckon I'd enjoy it a whole lot more if I was home in bed!"

"Boy, do I know that feelin'!" chuckled the Yankee. "Listen!" he continued. "Might any of you be hankerin' for a cup of fresh coffee?"

Reilly thought about it for a second and decided he really didn't have the heart to tell the man about the spoils taken from a broken down wagon earlier that day. "Coffee sounds good!" he replied. "What do you have in mind?"

"Wouldn't mind some chewin' tobacco!"

"We could probably find a little!" called Reilly. "How about meetin' us in the middle in . . . say . . . ten minutes?"

"Lookin' forward to it!"

Reilly turned back and glanced over at Ox. "You want to go?"

"Sure!"

"Whitt?"

"Love to go, Professor."

"How about you, Cody?"

"Are you serious?" gasped Wilder. "You're goin' out there to drink coffee with Yankees?"

"Yep. It's one of the fringe benefits of picket duty. Every now and then we call an informal truce and swap stuff with a few of their boys."

"With Yankees?"

"They're people too, kid. They ain't all that much different than us. Are you goin' or not?"

"I don't know, Professor. I guess I will. If you think it's okay."

"It'll be fine. Trust me. Ox, do you have any food stashed in your bedroll?"

"Yessuh. Some bacon and a few biscuits."

"Bring it along, and don't forget your skillet."

"Right."

Moments later the four of them were moving out into the open, watched closely by their comrades as they disappeared into the darkness. They walked about forty yards before finding a suitable place to sit and talk. It was a small copse of very large oak trees and it made them almost feel as though they were reclining in a gazebo of some sort. They made themselves comfortable and waited. Moments later several figures emerged from the darkness, five of them, no, six in all.

"Howdy, Reb," said the one in the lead.

"Come on in!" greeted Reilly. "Have a seat in the parlor!"

"Thanks! Is this what they call southern hospitality?"

"Sure 'nuff! Ox, go ahead and light the fire. You fellas hungry?"

"Wouldn't mind a bite to eat."

"We'll have some bacon in the skillet in a few minutes," said Reilly as tiny fingers of flame began to lick and curl around the small stack of branches and twigs which Ox and Cody gathered.

Within minutes, the little campfire was casting a pale glow about the copse, providing a fair amount of illumination for the truce gathering. Those in blue and those in gray circled the fire and set themselves on the ground. One might have expected the two groups to sit opposite one another, but this didn't prove to be the case. They intermingled freely, save Cody, who remained close to Reilly and couldn't seem to shake the look of suspicion from his face.

The leader of the Federal bunch was a sergeant, a tall, lean man with a slight stoop to his shoulders and a clean shaven face.

"Where y'all from?" posed Reilly as the aroma of fresh bacon drifted lazily past their nostrils.

"Minnesota," replied the sergeant, as he gestured to his comrade with the coffee and the pot. "Place called Duluth."

"Minnesota?" Cody leaned toward Reilly. "Where's that?"

"Out west a spell, then way up north right next to Canada — and don't tell me you don't know where Canada is."

"Okay," nodded the boy, even though he really couldn't picture a location for Canada.

"So where's that famous Virginia tobacco we've been hearing so much about?" The sergeant flashed a friendly grin.

"Right here," smiled Reilly, pulling a pouch of tobacco from his pocket. "Got a little chew here, and some stuff to smoke. Any of you got pipes?"

Three of them did.

As the night wore on the tension in the air gradually eased. Conversation became more lively, even Cody began to warm up to their northern visitors. They shared the bacon and coffee, tobacco and a few cold biscuits. They took to spinning yarns and swapping tales. Time and again bursts of laughter rang out from their copse of ancient oaks.

It is said all good things must come to an end. So it came to be with the truce between the survivors of the Stonewall Brigade and several Yankees from a badly battered Minnesota regiment. Dawn wasn't far away. The time had come for both groups to return to their lines. They doused the fire and rose to their feet. There was a definite note of sadness in the air as they clasped hands and said their good-byes.

"You know something?" asked Reilly as he shook the sergeant's hand. "I don't think I got your name."

"My friends call me Fritz, Fritz Olaf."

"Good to meet ya. My name's Seth. Seth Reilly." He released the sergeant's hand and started toward his own lines but after a few steps he stopped and turned. "Hey, Fritz!" he called, "I hope you make it!"

"You too!" grinned Olaf with a wave of his hand. Then he was gone.

A short while later, Reilly and his party had rejoined the others and were preparing to catch a few minutes of sleep before sunrise brought the renewal of hostilities. Reilly looked down at the boy seated next to him behind the same tree they had shared at the beginning of the night. "Sure seems strange don't it?" he mumbled softly.

"What's that?" Cody quickly opened his eyes.

"Us and those Yanks? All night long you'd have thought we were long lost friends. As soon as the sun comes up, we'll be tryin' to kill each other again. Doesn't make a whole lot of sense sometimes."

Cody mulled this over in his mind for several minutes before making a reply. "You're right, Professor," he said at last. "Except for one small thing. This is our land, and I don't think any of us ever invited those folks to come here and take it from us. We never invaded Minnesota, wherever the hell that is."

A sad smile crept across Reilly's face. "You got a point, boy," he said. "And in a little while we'll be shootin' at each other again."

"I don't see how they can expect us to fight," protested Wilder. "I'm so sleepy I can't even keep my eyes open."

"I don't think there'll be much action today," mused Reilly. "I think Lee's got Grant locked into a waiting game."

"Good. They can wait and I'll sleep."

Reilly's prediction proved to be accurate. Daylight came, but the two armies remained in place. Aside from an occasional long range artillery duel and sporadic sniper fire, the day was largely uneventful.

Robert E. Lee was content to let things ride on that particular day. He knew Grant would not long resist the temptation to bolt downriver, and he assumed the Federal chieftain was using this time to rest troops for the march. This was fine with him. Rest worked both ways. Lee himself chose to remain in his headquarters — the home of a Mr. David Holsinger in the town of Fredericksburg itself. Here he was able to eat one reasonably decent meal and to sleep undisturbed in a real bed for nearly eight hours.

Toward late afternoon, a courier arrived at the Holsinger home with a telegram from Richmond. It carried news of a supply train which would arrive in Fredericksburg well before dark. A large quantity of ammunition was on board along with two thousand soldiers; men who had recovered from earlier wounds and were ready to resume their duties. Among this group was none other than Peter Longstreet, one of Lee's most distinguished lieutenants, the hero of Chickamauga.

"Splendid!" remarked Lee with a broad smile. "Welcome news indeed! This is a train I must meet."

Meet it he did. When General Longstreet stepped from his car, Lee was right there to greet him. "My Old Warhorse!" greeted Lee as he offered his hand. "Welcome back! God knows how much we've missed you!"

"Good afternoon, General." Longstreet spoke in a somewhat forced tone. "It feels good to be back with the Army of Northern Virginia. Much like coming home. Hopefully this time around I'll be treated to a longer stint."

"Let's certainly hope so," returned Lee, as the two started walking toward a waiting carriage. Though he was very pleased at the return of Longstreet, his joy was somewhat tempered by the General's appearance. Longstreet's wounded arm was still in a sling. He had obviously lost a lot of weight and the pallor on his face suggested that he might not be fully recovered from the wounds he suffered in the Wilderness. When the two of them were seated in the carriage, Lee voiced his concerns.

"Peter," he said, "As happy as I am to see you, I must be frank. Might you be rushing your recovery just a bit? You look as though you could use another week or two in the hospital."

"True," said Longstreet. "I'm nowhere near one-hundred percent, but I can no longer wax idle in Richmond. Another week in that hospital and I may well part with my sanity. Besides, at the rate you're winning victories, the war might easily end before I'm fully recovered. If what I read in the papers is accurate, you were seriously ill at Ox Ford. That didn't stop you from leading this army. In any event, I wanted to rejoin you in time to close out Grant."

"My Old Warhorse!" chuckled Lee. "Indomitable to the core. You may have arrived just in time. I think we'll be able to write the final chapter on Ulysses Grant within the next several days. Do you want to resume command of your corps? Or would you prefer to rest a day or two before becoming active?"

"No more rest. I've had my fill of inactivity. Give me work; then you will find the key to my full recovery."

"Work you want? Work you shall have."

For the remainder of the ride, Lee briefed his lieutenant on the tactical situation, concluding with his desire to coax Grant downriver, then slam the door shut.

"I believe the strategy is sound," nodded Longstreet as the briefing concluded. "Yet I do have some concerns. You've deliberately left Grant an open door through which to escape."

"Correction," interjected Lee. "I've left him with the impression he has an open door. Ewell is poised to march at the tap of a drum."

"I understand, but what if Grant is able to slip away undetected? What if he gets a three-hour start on us? He could reach Port Royal and I imagine the Federal navy would be only too happy to pick him up and transport him to a place of his choosing."

"I understand your concerns," replied Lee. "But I think it's a risk worth taking. We've outmarched them consistently since the Wilderness. I have the utmost confidence we can do it again. For us to force a surrender now would require jumping into a full scale battle. It would do us little good to eliminate Grant if we cripple ourselves in the process. I prefer to catch him strung out on a line of march, preferably another mile or two downstream where the river broadens enough to make it virtually impossible to bridge."

"Still the same," argued Longstreet. "Would it not be wiser to err on the side of caution? If we are positive Grant will attempt to escape downriver, why not preempt his move? Why not throw someone in his path to insure he will only get so far?"

"I suppose such a move wouldn't hurt," admitted Lee.

"From Wheatley Farm, you drove them into the waiting rifles of Wade Hampton. Why not repeat the process, this time in the opposite direction?"

"Good idea," smiled Lee. "I had intended to rest

Hampton's cavalry, but I don't suppose they'll mind one more brief ride. Ah, Peter! This army surely has missed you!"

Longstreet wasn't the only soldier to be welcomed back to the army that day. Among those who detrained at Fredericksburg was Jonas Willem, the young lad who very nearly lost his leg at Spotsylvania. After receiving directions from the provost people, he set out to find Seth Reilly and the other survivors of his unit. It took him nearly an hour to locate his friends but at last he found them.

"Hey, Professor!" he called when he spotted Seth Reilly. "Remember me?"

"Jonas!" gasped Reilly in surprise. "You old polecat! What's the matter? The belles in Richmond more than you can handle?"

"Used 'em all up!" laughed Willem. "Got bored and figured I'd come back and give you guys a hand!"

"Hell, boy!" laughed Ox. "You look a sight better than when I carried you out of that salient! How's the leg?"

"Doc says I'm gonna walk with a limp from here on out, but at least I still have two legs to walk on! Are you getting bigger, Ox? Or am I just imagining things?"

"Been eatin' food! The Yankees left us a whole lot of food at Ox Ford!"

"And he ate most of it!" joked Simmons.

"Who's this?" Willem gestured in Cody's direction.

"Our newest addition," explained Reilly. "He joined up right after you got hurt. Name's Cody Wilder."

"How do, lad," Jones nodded at the boy. "Dear Lord, I thought you guys were robbin' the cradle when you took me in! He ain't even got any peach fuzz on his face! How old are you, boy?"

"Never mind," said Whitt. "You oughta see him shoot a rifle! He can shoot the eyes out of a squirrel at a hundred yards!"

"Really?"

"No doubt about it," agreed the lieutenant.

"No one believes me," interjected Evan Peterson. "But I

swear it was him what killed Sheridan at Ox Ford. There ain't no question in my mind!"

"Could well be," nodded Reilly. "He's got the eye and a steady hand. He was usin' a Whitworth. Might have been Cody. Who knows?"

"And you!" Jonas grasped Reilly on both arms. "They went and made you an officer!"

"Yep," Reilly grinned sheepishly.

"They should've done that a year ago!"

"No big deal!" said Reilly. "I'm the same ol' me."

*   *   *   *

The mood in the Union camp was anything but upbeat. Stoic resignation is the term which best describes the demeanor of Grant's officers as they went about their preparations for the downriver clash. George Meade was rapidly sinking into a morass of pessimism, but he did his noble best to conceal this emotion. Morale was already a serious problem among the rank and file. No point in compounding it with demoralized generals. He and Grant had argued strenuously over their prospects for success once the downriver retreat began. Grant refused to even consider it a retreat and he was convinced they would pull it off. Meade believed otherwise. He knew Lee was too smart to leave open an avenue for escape. The old fox was doing it for a reason. Grant had disagreed vehemently. He reasoned that Lee must be just as badly hurt as the Army of the Potomac and that he didn't have the strength to confront the Federals from every angle. Meade knew how useless it was to argue the point. Time alone would prove one of them right.

Night fell. Several bands on both sides of the lines began to fill the air with music. One could easily discern who had the upper hand by listening to the types of songs either side was offering. Amidst all this, Wade Hampton quietly slipped out of Fredericksburg heading south at the head of a column of four thousand riders. His mission? To slam the final door shut on the Army of the Potomac. The column moved south for nearly five miles before swinging east in a broad arc which brought them ultimately to the south bank of the Rappahannock River, directly in Grant's rear. It was just after midnight when they arrived at their chosen destination. They dismounted immediately and began digging in. As their spades were flying, the Army of the Potomac was already heading in their direction.

Grant took every precaution to insure a successful getaway. Every campfire on the Union side remained burning and a detachment of cavalry remained behind to keep them burning. One band stayed in place to add to the deception with music. All of this went for naught.

If nothing else, Robert E. Lee was prepared. He had scouts in position all along Grant's anticipated line of march. As soon as the first Federal brigade marched off, Lee was informed. His orders to Ewell were quick and to the point: Leave at once, parallel the enemy, pitch in to him as soon as he bumps into Hampton. He even went so far as to emulate Grant's deception, keeping his fires burning, the bands playing. All this to convince Grant his ruse was successful.

General Hancock's corps of infantry, what remained of it, comprised the vanguard of the Union thrust. Behind him came Meade with Baldy Smith bringing up the rear.

The return of Longstreet brought about a quick reorganization of Lee's troops. The constant marching and fighting since Ox Ford had scattered much of Longstreet's corps. Some of his troops marched with Hill. Others were with Gordon across the river. Lee drew some from Hill and some from Ewell, giving Longstreet roughly seven thousand men for the coming fury. Longstreet departed on Ewell's heels with A. P. Hill right behind him. By 1:00 a.m. both armies were on the march except for those few who had been left behind to keep up appearances. The days of the Army of the Potomac were numbered.

It was very nearly 3:00 a.m. when the lead elements of Hancock's corps bumped into Wade Hampton. They were greeted by a volley of carbine fire so intense nothing could stand before it. Dazed and bewildered, Hancock's troops stumbled about blindly while their officers tried to rally them and form them into some sort of cohesive formation. This was not to be. Before they could reform, they were struck from the right by Ewell's corps. The one-legged general had managed to get his artillery into position hub-to-hub at the perfect moment. His cannons roared, spewing smoke, flame and deadly canister into the Union ranks. By the pale light of the moon, his infantry poured musket fire into a thoroughly bedazzled enemy.

Within minutes, the issue was decided. The Army of the Potomac was very close to disintegrating. Its soldiers fled headlong in the only direction still open — the Rappahannock River. The chase was on.

Fortunately for Grant, the darkness ultimately proved to be an ally. Otherwise his entire army might well have been gobbled up in one fell swoop. As it was, Hancock's corps was decimated, completely overrun. Hancock, himself, was taken prisoner. The rest of the army was routed, but managed to stave off total defeat at the very last minute. Two of Grant's vital wagon trains were captured, destroyed or simply lost in the confusion which followed the opening volley.

From all of his commanders, Lee received word of victory. The enemy had been driven very nearly into the river itself. However, to the man his officers requested a cessation at hostilities until daybreak. The darkness was hindering their efforts and resulting in needless casualties among their own ranks. Lee was only too happy to agree to their request. After all, the door had been shut. Grant was now firmly trapped with his back against the Rappahannock. For the Army of the Potomac, the end was very near.

Dawn found the Federal troops dug into a single line roughly in the shape of a semi-circle; both ends anchored by the river itself. Only twenty-nine thousand men remained to Grant.

Not long after sunrise, Lee received an unwilling guest

at his headquarters. It was the Union corps commander, General Hancock. He had not been wounded, but his physical appearance certainly provided evidence of the severity of the ordeal he had just experienced.

"General Hancock!" greeted Lee. "It's good to see you weren't hurt! May I offer you some coffee?"

"I think I could stand a cup," grimaced Hancock.

"This isn't the fare we normally drink," said Lee. "We captured it from you all yesterday."

"Along with the heart of my corps. You played your hand very well, General."

"Thank you. A biscuit?"

"Please," nodded Hancock. "I guess for me the war is over."

"So it would seem."

"Grant should give it up. There's no point in prolonging this contest. You've clearly won."

"Somehow I doubt if General Grant shares your assessment of this situation."

"Probably not, yet something tells me you'll convince him before too much longer."

"I intend to make every effort," noted Lee.

"Can you arrange for word of my capture to be sent to my family?"

"I'll see to it."

"Thank you, General." Hancock saluted his captor and was led away by his guards.

Lee quickly finished his sparse breakfast and sent couriers to summon his major officers for a brief Council of War. When they had all gathered, he put the question to them.

"Gentlemen, our opponents have been brought to bay. As I see the situation, General Grant is hopelessly trapped. Gordon is now in position on the opposite side of the river. The scouts tell me the river is nearly eighty yards wide and there are no usable fords in the general vicinity. In other words, we have him right where we want him. The question is, what should we do next?"

"Smash 'em!" exclaimed A. P. Hill at once. "I don't think we should hesitate a minute! Let's just storm in there and finish it!"

"I disagree," interjected Longstreet in the strongest possible tone. Grant has had time to entrench all along the line. I think to attack would prove very costly."

"General Ewell?"

"I think I must side with Longstreet. If the Federals are trapped we don't really need to storm in. Time becomes our ally."

"Wade?"

"Hard to say," mused Hampton. "I can see arguments for both points of view. Part of me shouts out to get this thing over with. Part of me recoils at the casualties we'd understandably take."

"Thank you," nodded Lee. "I'm afraid I must side with Generals Longstreet and Ewell. We have to look past this situation. We must now start thinking about longer term goals and objectives. If we attack Grant now, I am sure of the result. We will win. The question comes down to cost. How badly can he hurt us? I think we would lose anywhere from ten to fifteen thousand men. They are men the Confederacy simply cannot replace, men we will need if we are to transfer this war out of Virginia. The best course of action is to lay siege to those people until they have no choice but surrender. That is what I intend to do."

"Do we sit on our heels?" prodded Hill. "Or do we make life uncomfortable for them?"

"The latter of course," said Lee. "But not right away. I'm going to send a note across to General Grant. I believe it's only fair to give him an opportunity to surrender before we open fire. Return to your commands. Wait until I give the word before you initiate hostilities."

After they had all departed, Lee procured quill and paper from Colonel Taylor and sat down to write a brief letter to General Grant. In it, he noted circumstances had led the Army of the Potomac to an untenable situation. He expressed his desire to avoid responsibility for the further effusion of blood and offered Grant the opportunity to discuss terms of surrender. The message was delivered under a white flag about 9:30 a.m.

Ulysses Grant read the note through twice and put it aside with a weary sigh.

"Can I read it?" asked Meade.

"Go ahead."

Meade perused through it quickly, then looked over at Grant. "He seems to think our situation is hopeless."

"Do you?"

"I don't know. It's tense. No question about that."

"Do you think I should surrender?"

"Not yet."

"Me, neither. I don't think he wants to attack us, and if he gives us a few days anything could happen. Lincoln might have a change of heart and send us help. We might even figure out a way to cross this river. There's a thought. Let's put the engineers to work. They should be able to build a pontoon bridge in sections. All we'll have to do is tie the sections together and race across. Good! Let me have some paper!

In no time, he was seated at his table penning a reply to Lee's letter. In it he noted that he did not share Lee's appraisal of the current situation and he saw no need to discuss terms for surrender. By 10:30 a.m., this note was in Lee's hands.

By 11:00 a.m., Lee was receiving reports of unusual activity among the Federals. Apparently they were felling a large number of trees, many of them near the edge of the river itself.

"More fortifications?"

"Not likely," replied Lee. "I have the feeling General Grant is up to something. He may be contemplating the construction of a bridge."

"A bridge, sir?"

"It's not out of the question. Get word to Gordon across

the river. Have him refrain from any activity against the Federals at least for the time being. Tell everyone else to open fire. Make sure you inform Gordon about the possibility of a bridge. If those people attempt to assemble such a device on the water itself, it will be up to Gordon to destroy it."

"Very well, sir."

"Inform our officers that for a change we have plenty of ammunition for the artillery. Tell them to use it."

Within ten minutes the early summer calm was shattered by thunderous volleys of Rebel cannon fire. The Federal batteries returned this fire, but only for a short time. Grant was faced with a definite shortage of munitions, and was forced to operate within that constraint.

By early evening, with still an hour of daylight remaining, Grant's engineers finished their bridge. Twelve sections had been constructed, each of them twenty feet long. Into the water they went, hastily linked together in a single line parallel to the shore. With only minutes of daylight remaining, the Federals made their move. The lower end of the bridge was secured to the shoreline. Several men with poles stood by on the upper end of the bridge. All eyes were upon them as they pushed off from the shore, nudging the top end of the bridge out into the river's current. Slowly it drifted out away from the south bank. If the engineers were correct in their calculations, the top end would strike the north bank, or come reasonably close, just as the base described a ninety degree angle with the south bank. So it was planned.

Unfortunately for Grant, he still did not know of Gordon's presence on the opposite shore. However, he was about to become aware of these Rebels in no uncertain terms. Gordon himself was rather coy in the way he handled the affair. With ten thousand rifles and nearly sixty pieces of artillery to back him up, he could easily afford to be coy.

Gradually, the bridge neared the north bank. Confederate artillery on the south bank spotted it and began to open fire, but with no success. Closer it came.

Then Gordon struck. A company of riflemen opened

fire, killing or wounding all the polemen in a matter of seconds. On the heels of this volley came the artillery, all sixty cannons blazing. The newly constructed bridge on which Grant was resting all his hopes was swiftly reduced to free floating sections and scorched fragments. The spirits of the Federal soldiers sank like a lead weight as they watched the remnants of their intended solution drift lazily down the Rappahannock.

Now Gordon's ten thousand swung into action against Grant himself, deploying near the very edge of the river and opening up with a steady level of musket and cannon fire; all of it directed at the narrow strip of land in which the Army of the Potomac was hopelessly trapped. All through the night, the barrage continued, not only from Gordon but from Hill, Longstreet and Ewell as well. Not until a mere hour of darkness remained did the guns fall mercifully silent. Lee dispatched the order to all of his commanders. "Cease firing, let us wait and see what the new day brings."

Dawn brought with it a strange sight. A thick rolling mist carpeted the ground and hid the river from view. In the Union position scarcely a tree was left standing. Everywhere the trunks and boughs of fallen trees jutted grotesquely from the thick fog. Grant's survivors were dazed, literally shocked into numbness, but they dug in behind the vast wreckage of wood, determined to make their final stand as costly as possible for their opponents in butternut. There were some, few in number, who saw the pre-dawn fog as an opportunity. Quietly, they slipped fallen logs into the river and attempted their escape. Though the Rebels had taken precautions down river to prevent such an exodus, it is certain that some of those Federal deserters successfully eluded detection and made good their escape. How many got away in this fashion will never be known.

As the sun continued its slow ascent in the eastern sky, Robert E. Lee contemplated his next move. "No attack," he said at last. "We will continue as we did yesterday."

On the opposite side of the line, Grant too faced a decision. His own headquarter's tent lay in ruins. His personal wagon had been shattered by one of the thousands of cannon balls hurled into his position. He sat atop a fallen tree surveying the wreckage which had once been the finest army in the world. As he did in the Wilderness, he took to himself a stick and began to ease the stress by whittling.

It was Meade who made the rounds among the troops that morning, and it was a gloomy assessment he presented to General Grant. "We have fewer than twenty-five thousand effectives left," he reported calmly. "Enough rations to sustain them from two to four days. Fifty-four pieces of usable artillery, but ammunition grows scarce."

"How do you rate our chances?" mouthed Grant, taking his attention momentarily from the stick.

"Are you looking for an honest answer, General?"

"Preferably."

"We have no chance, sir. He's beaten us."

"I see," sighed Grant wearily.

"We could make a final stand, maybe even take a bunch of them down with us, but nothing we do will alter the final result. This army is finished."

Grant said nothing and for several minutes an awkward silence hung between the two men. Grant returned to the task of whittling, gouging large chips of wood from the branch in his hand. At last he stopped and with eyes filled with sadness, he looked directly at Meade.

"Then I guess there's nothing left for me to do, except to go and see General Lee." He groaned, "I think I would prefer to die a thousand deaths."

Meade made no reply, averting Grant's eyes, glancing away as a thick lump began to rise in his throat.

"I imagine the Rebels will soon resume their barrage," noted Grant softly.

"In all likelihood," concurred Meade.

"If I'm going to do this, I should do it soon."

"Agreed."

"Would you find a volunteer to ride out with a flag of

truce? I will write General Lee a quick note and request a meeting."

"Very well."

True to his word, Grant penned a brief note, saying only that he had reconsidered his present situation and wished to meet with Lee to discuss terms of a possible surrender.

It was just after nine in the morning. The heat of the sun had long since dissipated the fog. Lee's gunners were making ready to open fire. His infantry was poised in the trenches, ready to add their weight to the upcoming barrage. Grant's soldiers remained in place, waiting for the first volley with a growing sense of dread and despair. Suddenly, a horse and rider appeared from the Union side. The cavalryman quickly unfurled a white flag attached to his saber, then moved cautiously out into the open.

"Hold your fire!" ordered a Confederate colonel just to the right of Seth Reilly and his men. "Truce rider!"

Everyone stared intently at the northerner; all of them wondering what this latest development might portend.

"Are they givin' it up?" wondered Cody aloud.

"Could be," nodded Reilly. "Could very well be."

The Federal trooper dug his heels into the flank of his mount and approached the Rebel line at a canter. His course led him directly to Lieutenant Seth Reilly and those who remained of the Stonewall Brigade. The rider saluted smartly as he reined to a halt.

Reilly returned the salute, but said nothing, not wanting to upstage the colonel who moved quickly to his side.

"State your business," said the officer somewhat abruptly.

"I bear a message for General Lee from General Grant."

"You may deliver it to me."

"I have orders to deliver it to no one but General Lee. I'm sorry, Colonel."

"I see." A terse smile appeared on the colonel's face. "Lieutenant?"

"Sir?" Reilly stood to attention.

"Kindly escort this gentleman to Lee's headquarters. If you need a mount, you may take mine."

"Yessir," nodded Reilly, gesturing to Cody to fetch the colonel's horse. Once mounted he nodded at the northerner. "If you'll follow me . . ." He beckoned.

Ten minutes later they reached Lee's headquarters. Soldiers and attendants scurried here and there, staring curiously at the soldier in blue who still carried his truce flag.

Hearing the commotion, Lee rose to his feet, setting aside the letter he was writing to his wife, and stepped out of the tent. The first man he saw was Reilly.

"Why, good morning, Lieutenant," he beamed. "It seems the fates have crossed our paths again."

"Good morning, General," Reilly saluted his commander.

"I see you've brought a guest."

"Yessir, a messenger. He carries a letter to you from General Grant, with orders to deliver it to you only."

"I see," mused Lee. "Well, let's have it."

The rider reached inside this tunic and withdrew a small envelope which he handed down to Lee.

"Are you to wait for a reply?" asked the gray commander.

"Those were my instructions."

"Very well. If you'll excuse me, I'd prefer to study this in the privacy of my tent. Please dismount and rest your horse; I shan't be long."

Inside the tent, Lee seated himself and placed the letter on the table. He found that his hands were on the verge of trembling as he contemplated the contents of that envelope.

Both Taylor and Venable were at his side.

"It must be an offer to surrender," said Colonel Taylor.

Lee adjusted his glasses and proceeded to read through the note.

"Well?" asked Venable, his impatience becoming obvious.

"Just as you said," Lee glanced at Taylor. "He wants to

meet to discuss the possibility of surrender."

"Excellent!" exclaimed Venable. "It's over!"

"What sort of terms do you plan to offer?" posed Taylor.

"Actually, I haven't given it much thought," admitted Lee.

"Will you meet with him?"

"Of course," huffed Lee. "An opportunity of this sort doesn't come along every day. Colonel Taylor, be good enough to locate a suitable place for our meeting, preferably a house, I think. Mr. Venable, stand-by while I write a reply."

"Yessir! With the utmost pleasure!"

Several minutes later Venable emerged from the tent and stepped over to Grant's courier. Trying to remain calm, he handed the rider another envelope; this one containing Lee's reply. "General Lee asks that you all return to the same point on our line. Lieutenant Reilly here has been appointed as your escort. We'll find a place to hold this meeting. Reilly will bring you whenever you're ready."

"Very well," agreed the rider.

He and Reilly remounted and started back toward the front. When they reached the lines, Reilly reined in while the Federal trooper continued to his own army.

"What's the scoop, Professor?" asked Whitt.

"Looks like the Yankees might be ready to give it up," came the reply. "Looks like I've got to hold on to the colonel's horse for a while longer. Marse Lee wants me to deliver Grant to him."

"Deliver him?" asked Cody.

"Escort him . . . might be a better way to put it."

"Where to?"

"I don't know yet. They'll find a place and let us know."

Back at Grant's headquarters, gloom appeared to be the order of the day. The general himself laconically prepared for the brief journey to the other side of the line.

"Are you going alone?" asked Meade as he fidgeted nervously.

"No," replied Grant. "Parker will ride with me."

"Is there anything I can do?"

"Just wait, George. You'll be in charge 'til I get back."

"Very well."

"Not that there's much left to be in charge of," mused Grant absently.

At half past ten, two riders appeared in front of the Union entrenchments. Another white flag was unfurled and the two started toward the Confederate lines reaching them in a matter of moments. Once again, Reilly was waiting.

"Lieutenant Seth Reilly of the Stonewall Brigade, sir," announced Reilly, sitting his mount at attention and saluting the enemy commander.

"At ease, Lieutenant," said Grant as he removed the cigar from his mouth. "Did you say you were with the Stonewall Brigade? I thought we bagged the lot of you at Spotsylvania?"

"You got most of us, General. But there were a few of us who managed to slip away."

"So it seems," smiled Grant. "Well, Lieutenant," the smile faded, "I wouldn't mind staying here and chatting with you for a spell, but I believe someone's waiting for me."

"I know, General. I've been assigned to escort you."

"I see. Just where are we going?"

"A man by the name of Shaner has a farm up river about a mile and a half from here."

"Very well. Lead on. We'll be right behind you."

Robert E. Lee and his staff had already gathered at the Shaner Farm to await the arrival of General Grant. The home itself was of stone construction, rising two stories above the rolling farmland which sustained it. A broad veranda enclosed the front and both sides of the house. On that particular day, the twenty-first of June, 1864, his porch became the gathering place for a host of Confederate officers. Lee was there along with his headquarters staff, all of his corps commanders, numerous divisional commanders and a substantial number of lesser officers, all of them eager to catch a glimpse of the legendary "Unconditional Surrender" Grant. Every man there knew he was about to witness the making of history, and was eager to be a part of it.

No one was more aware of their feelings than Lee himself, and their obvious enthusiasm quickly became a source of concern to the General. He stepped out onto the spacious porch and cleared his throat loudly to get the attention of his officers. Silence was quick to ensue.

"Gentlemen," intoned Lee, "I can't help but notice a certain level of enthusiasm among your numbers, understandable, of course."

This comment was greeted by smiles and chuckles all around.

"It occurs to me that such exuberance might lead some of you to temptation. We may indeed make history today; all of us are witnesses to it. Some of us might be tempted to take home a reminder . . . a souvenir, if you will. Let me remind you that we are guests of the Shaner family. This is their home. We will, of course, respect their privacy and property. Everything which is here now had better be here when we leave. Have I made myself clear?"

Each man among them nodded his assent. None even considered the possibility of doing otherwise.

"Thank you, gentlemen. Now, if you'll excuse me, I believe I'll step inside and sit for a spell."

Not long after Lee's admonition to his officers, Seth Reilly arrived at the dirt lane which led to Shaner's home. He paused at the entrance, checking the various landmarks against those in his directions. Certain he had found the right place, he turned in his saddle and spoke to General Grant.

"I reckon this is the right place, sir. There's a home at the end of this lane. General Lee is waiting for you there."

"Very well, Lieutenant," nodded Grant. "You may continue. We'll be right behind you."

"Yessir." Reilly nudged his horse's flanks and the animal started forward.

Though noon was yet an hour away, the day was showing every promise of becoming uncomfortably hot. Reilly was grateful for the cool shade offered by the stately maple trees which flanked either side of the quarter-mile lane. On the ground connecting each tree were well tended flower beds of brightly blooming pink azaleas and rhododendrons. Lovely they were, but the sight of them spawned a spasm of homesickness in Reilly's heart.

"Almost as if there were no war," thought Reilly, as images of home and his own wife's flower gardens filled his mind.

Minutes later, the lane ended and the three horsemen pulled to a halt in front of the Shaner home. Three enlisted men came forward to take charge of the horses. Reilly was the first to dismount, coming to attention at once, saluting the officers on the porch and stepping quickly aside.

All eyes were on Grant who had yet to discard his cigar. One by one, Lee's officers joined in a salute to Grant who returned their courtesy before tossing the cigar butt unceremoniously to the ground. With a weary sigh, he dismounted. He glanced quickly at Parker, searching perhaps for reassurance. When he turned back to the porch, he spied Lee who had descended to await him. Long ago, during the Mexican War, Grant had met Lee and he had no trouble recognizing the Confederate commander.

However, it was not Lee but Longstreet, his arm still in a sling, who stepped forward to greet the Union General. The two had been friends long before the onset of the Civil War.

"Good morning," said Longstreet with a warm Georgian smile. "It's been a long time."

"So it has." Grant returned the smile and offered his hand. "I heard about your wound, but it appears you're mending well."

"Can't complain," replied Longstreet as he shook Grant's hand. "Come on, I'll introduce you to Bobby Lee."

"After the last several weeks, I feel I know him very well; though perhaps it could be argued he knows me a good deal better."

Introductions were then made, and the two commanders shook hands. Lee did his best to make Grant comfortable in a situation which was obviously awkward for the Union officer. Grant made mention of meeting the older man many years before during the Mexican conflict, and Lee at least gave the appearance of remembering the occasion. The men stepped inside followed only by Colonel Taylor. Everyone else remained on the porch, though several could be seen peering through the windows.

Once inside, the officers moved to a small round table in the parlor. Here they were seated and prepared themselves for the negotiations to follow. For the longest time, nothing was said. Neither Grant nor Lee spoke and an uneasy silence prevailed. It was Taylor who finally got the ball rolling.

"If you'll pardon my saying so, gentlemen," he offered, "I believe the two of you have something to discuss. Perhaps you should get started."

Another minute of stillness crept by, but at last Grant began to loosen up. He cleared his throat and seemed unable or unwilling to look Lee in the eye, but he finally did speak.

"You seem to have me in an untenable situation," he noted calmly.

"One could easily draw that conclusion," concurred Lee, doing his best to spare Grant's feelings, knowing how he himself would feel in the same situation.

"I believe my options have dwindled considerably," continued Grant.

Lee said nothing, but nodded his agreement.

"I suppose I must now ask under what terms you would consider accepting the surrender of my army."

"I understand," said Lee. "Before this morning, I truly hadn't given the matter a great deal of thought."

"And now?" pressed Grant.

"I've thought of nothing else for the past two hours, but I've found it difficult to reach a definite conclusion."

"I see." Grant's shoulders dropped noticeably.

"You see, General," continued Lee, "Our respective situations are remarkably different. If our roles were reversed, if I was trapped and asking you for terms, you could readily afford to be generous. The loss of the Army of Northern Virginia would be the death knell of the Confederacy. Were I to surrender, the war would be over . . . plain and simple."

"No argument there," nodded Grant.

"Not so in your case. Your surrender to me would reflect merely the loss of the Army of the Potomac, a critical loss to be sure, but it won't necessarily bring about the war's end. President Lincoln will have to scramble, but he'll surely assemble another army.

"Undoubtedly," agreed Grant.

"Can you appreciate the position this puts me in?"

"I understand, General." The tone of Grant's voice was heavy with resignation.

"I would dearly love to be able to parole you and all your men so that we could all go home. I want this thing to be over, General Grant. There's been far too much suffering . . . too much death."

Grant said nothing.

"Unfortunately when you and I conclude our business today, this terrible war will continue, and it is still my responsibility to defend our homeland. I'm afraid this leaves me in something of a quandary. It is not my desire to insult you with a demand for an unconditional surrender, but unfortunately, I'm not in a position to offer terms which anyone would consider generous."

For several moments, there was quiet as Grant pondered his options. It didn't take long for him to realize that the options simply weren't there. Another day of constant shelling from all sides would undoubtedly reduce the remnants of his army to a few fragments. There really was no alternative but to surrender on any terms which Lee chose to offer. Despair was all too evident on his face as he lifted his eyes to meet those of his southern counterpart. "Name your terms, General," he said softly. "I'm hardly in a position to argue the matter. For us to continue the battle at this point would result only in useless slaughter."

"Very well," nodded Lee. "All of your remaining weapons are to be surrendered in working order. This applies to the remainder of your ammunition and medical supplies as well. Have your troops stack their weapons and come forward in brigade size units. All officers of "general" rank will be sent to Richmond. I will use whatever influence I have to arrange confinement by house rather than prison camp."

"That's very kind of you," said Grant.

"I can't guarantee anything. Conditions are hard in the South right now; food is scarce and public feeling against the Union is running high."

"I understand," sighed Grant. "I just want you to know we appreciate any effort on your part to ease the conditions of our confinement."

"I'll do what I can."

"Thank you."

"Have you any other questions?"

"No . . . not at this time."

"Very well. Colonel Taylor here will formalize the terms in writing. I would like the actual surrender to begin at three o'clock this afternoon, no later."

"As you wish."

The actual writing of the surrender document took over thirty minutes, primarily because Taylor had to make a second copy so both generals would have one. While Taylor wrote, Lee and Grant passed the time in idle conversation — chatting about their respective wartime experiences. Lee did his best to ease the other man's obvious discomfort, but despite his efforts, the wait seemed interminable to Ulysses Grant.

At last all was ready. Taylor presented each general with a copy of the surrender document and a writing instrument. Both officers perused the paper, insuring themselves of its accuracy, then each signed, traded papers, then signed again.

With Grant's second signature, the Army of the Potomac officially passed into history.

Grant pushed himself back from the table and rose slowly to his feet. Without raising his eyes, he unclasped the sword which hung at his side and handed it across the table.

Lee took it and laid it gently across the table.

"General," he offered, "I give you my solemn word. When this war is over, no matter what the outcome, you shall have this back."

"Thank you, General." Grant could scarcely speak for the lump which clogged his throat. "That means a great deal to me."

Lee offered his hand, "Good luck to you, sir."

"And you, sir." Grant took Lee's hand and grasped it tightly.

With that he stepped back, saluted Lee, then turned and walked out of the house.

Lee's officers immediately came to attention and saluted the Union commander who returned their courtesy without breaking stride. He descended the stairs from the porch, spied Parker and called for his horse. Moments later, he, Parker and Lieutenant Reilly were on their way back to the front lines, a ride which Grant was to recall in later years as "the longest of my life."

As Lee watched the trio disappear in the distance, he turned to Captain Venable at his side.

"Ride at once to Fredericksburg, Captain. Send a wire to Richmond. Kindly inform the President and the Secretary at War of today's events. Tell them also that I am requesting a meeting with them at the earliest possible moment to discuss our strategy for the next phase of the war."

"Very good, General." Venable saluted and started away to find his horse.

"Gentlemen," Lee raised his voice and addressed himself to his officers gathered about him on the porch. "The Army of the Potomac has just been formally surrendered. We will start receiving prisoners by 3 p.m." He tried to continue but was immediately cut short by a wild chorus of cheers and Rebel Yells.

"Gentlemen, please!" Lee's voice rose above the din. "I share your joy, make no mistake about it! However, the war is not over and we have much remaining to do!"

This statement returned relative calm to the group.

"Of future plans we will talk later," continued Lee. "In the meantime, I wish you to return to your troops. Inform them of the surrender, but stress this order from me: There is to be no celebration in the presence of soon-to-be prisoners. I have no wish to humiliate these people. There's no need for us to add insult to injury. Tell your men to maintain some sense of decorum until the prisoners have been sorted and dispatched to the south. Am I clear?"

Every man replied in the affirmative.

"Good. God has indeed blessed us this day, my friends. I would prefer that our behavior continues to meet His good graces. Before you depart, let me take this opportunity to thank you all and congratulate you on jobs well done. No finer group of soldiers did any commander ever lead. God bless you all."

"Three cheers for Robert E. Lee!" cried A. P. Hill, who had resisted the urge for about as long as he could contain himself.

The chorus of cheers which followed were the only celebration allowed the Army of Northern Virginia that day in the early summer of 1864. When those officers returned to their troops they followed Lee's wishes to the letter.

all out!" Reilly barked the order to his troops. "Fifteen minute break; take advantage of it!"

"Just like the old days," grinned Ox as he plopped his bulky frame onto the ground. "Remember Stonewall? He used to make us lie flat on our backs during these breaks."

"I remember," mused Whitt as he methodically rubbed the soreness from his feet. "I particularly remember looking over at you and thinking you resembled a beached whale when you were lying prone; come to think of it, you still do. How can you still be so damn huge when there's so little food to be had?"

"Just lucky, I guess," sighed Ox as he lay backwards and stared contentedly at the bright blue sky above.

"It's 'cause he eats anything!" quipped Jonas. "Ah seen him eat a sassafras plant once, leaves, roots and all!"

"It was damn good, too!" retorted Ox.

"You guys are supposed to be restin'," interjected Reilly.

"Professor?" Cody jumped into the conversation. "Are we close yet? We must be gettin' close; I smell water, I'm sure of it."

"Well, at least your nose works, boy. You should be smellin' water; the Potomac River is just beyond that rise over yonder. I reckon no more than a half-mile."

"Hot damn!" chortled Jonas. "Another hour or so and we'll be in Maryland! Can you believe it?"

"Sounds fine to me!" exclaimed Cody. "I hear tell there ain't no scarcities up in Maryland. They got more food than they know what to do with."

"I heard that!" This from Ox.

"Will you guys pipe down?" barked Reilly. "All of you better damn sight remember Lee's orders when we cross that river! No looting! Civilian property is to be respected at all times!"

"We're awful damn hungry, Professor!" said Ox.

"You're always hungry, Ox. How much you consume never seems to matter. If you weren't so damn big I'd swear you had a worm! Just remember the orders! All of you!"

Following the surrender of Grant on the shores of the Rappahannock, Robert E. Lee had little trouble convincing President Davis that the capture of Washington, D. C. was feasible. Yet nearly a week passed before his own army started north. The delay itself was unavoidable. Time was needed to process the many prisoners taken when Grant surrendered and to incorporate the newly captured ammunition.

Whatever else might be said of the delay, it can certainly be argued that Lee put it to good use. His final victory over Grant spawned a flurry of celebrating all across the South. Hope of ultimate independence spurred many a man to join or rejoin the army. Convalescing wounded left their hospital beds ahead of schedule to return to their regiments. When Lee finally started forward from the Rappahannock, he did so with seventy-five thousand men. Four hundred guns he had at his disposal along with a copious supply of ammunition. The only drawback was the lack of food, but Lee was hoping to find a solution in Maryland.

Before leaving for the North, he completely reorganized his army into four smaller corps of infantry as opposed to the three with which he normally operated. The corps commanders themselves were as follows: Longstreet, Ewell, Hill and Gordon. Hampton remained in charge of the cavalry with five thousand troopers behind him. Having completed the re-shuffling of his army, Lee started north for the third time in the war.

There was a marked difference in purpose in the summer of 1864. In 1862 and '63 Lee was attempting to promote European recognition, or at the very least carry the war to northern soil. Now he had but one purpose: to capture

Washington, D. C. and put an end to the most terrible war the world had ever seen. With this goal foremost in mind the soldiers of the Army of Northern Virginia reached the shores of the Potomac River, near White's Ferry on the second of July.

Though Grant was no longer a factor, the situation in the South remained critical. The Confederacy was divided along several lines. Texas was cut off. New Orleans and Vicksburg occupied. Tennessee and Kentucky were in Union hands and Sherman crept ever closer to Atlanta. Butler remained in the Bermuda Hundred with a potent force and most critical of all, the Union Blockade continued to tighten its virtual stranglehold with every passing week. In the face of all this, only one entity was capable of insuring the possibility of Southern independence: The Army of Northern Virginia.

Accordingly, President Davis and Secretary of War Seddon agreed to mobilize whatever resources and manpower which could still be found in the exhausted Southland, and to funnel it north to "Lee's Miserables."

*   *   *   *

When the first elements of the army started across the Potomac, General Peter Longstreet was not among them. On his own initiative, he slipped away from the army and journeyed to nearby Leesburg. Here he planned to meet with the legendary partisan commander, John Singleton Mosby, who had obtained the rank of colonel in the Confederate Army. Longstreet had an idea in mind, a plan he would entrust to no one but Mosby. Their meeting took place in the morning of July 2, 1864 at a small tavern opposite the Courthouse in Leesburg. Longstreet arrived first and waited nearly thirty minutes before Mosby was able to join him.

"Greetings, Colonel," said Longstreet as Mosby entered.

"General, I'm sorry about this, I did try to get here on time." Mosby began brushing several layers of dust from his tunic.

"No need to apologize. I understand. In any event, I didn't give you much notice. Come in and have a beer — I'm buying."

"Sounds good to me," grinned Mosby.

After they had each downed hefty mugs of beer and engaged in several minutes of small talk, Mosby steered the conversation toward business.

"General, your note said something about a mission. What exactly do you have in mind?"

"Do you know the purpose of our invasion?"

"I assume Lee intends to carry the war into the North one more time."

"That and much more. We're going straight for Washington. Lee hopes to capture the Federal capital."

"Whew!" Mosby whistled through his teeth. "A lofty aspiration to be sure, but does he know what he's up against? You're talking about one of the most fortified cities in the world!"

"True," admitted Longstreet. "Yet all this time the Federals have been building defenses against a possible thrust directly from the south. The bulk of the city's defenses are actually on the south bank of the Potomac in the region of Alexandria, or along the opposite bank facing south. We're ignoring them. Lee plans to strike from the north. As impossible as it may seem, I believe we'll pull it off. I think Washington will fall."

"If anyone can do it, Lee can."

"That seems to be the general consensus. However, there are certain contingency factors the General may not have considered."

"Such as?"

"The city will probably fall, but the members of the Federal government will attempt to escape."

"Most likely," agreed Mosby. "But I don't see how this can be prevented. There are a lot of ways out of Washington."

"Granted. Some of them will undoubtedly elude us. That's where you come in."

"I figured as much. What do you have in mind?"

"As you said, there are a lot of ways out of Washington. One of them is the Potomac River. I believe at least some of the Federal dignitaries may opt for that avenue. I think they'll take ship and sail downriver."

"Wait just a minute, General," protested Mosby, "my men are rangers. We've trained ourselves to fight from horseback. We are best at the hit and run, whatever else we may be, we're not sailors. We've never fought on a river. We're certainly no match for Yankee warships!"

"Just hold your horses, Colonel," smiled Longstreet. "I'm not transferring you to the navy. I've got something else in mind."

"All right. I'm listening."

"Ox Ford and Grant's recent surrender provided us with a bounty of new weapons — particularly artillery. Lee has reorganized our infantry into four separate groups. Each corps now has one hundred guns. You'll find seventy-five of them waiting for you in Manassas."

"What?" Mosby's jaw dropped.

"Fifty from my corps, twenty-five from Gordon. A thousand infantry are there as well. I might add that we gave you the best of the Yankee guns."

"You're giving me a thousand men and seventy-five guns?"

"Yep."

"Does Lee know?"

"Not yet."

"Just what am I supposed to do with them?"

Longstreet gestured to one of his staff officers who quickly produced a navigational chart of the Potomac River. He unfolded it on the table and pointed to a bend in the river midway between Alexandria and Woodbridge.

"Right here," he said. "The river is only a half mile wide. Get there as quickly as possible. Establish yourselves on the south bank. It's possible that Lincoln has summoned all the Federal troops on the Maryland side to Washington to bolster its defense. If so, move some of the guns to that side to set up a cross fire."

"Then what?"

"Wait. I'll have a courier-relay system set up from our position to yours. When Washington falls, or appears about to fall, you'll be one of the first to know."

"And?" pressed Mosby.

"You must try to stop any Yankee ship which tries to escape from Washington."

"What if it's an ironclad? We can't stand up to an ironclad."

"I've had my agents working on that problem. If their information is correct, there are no ironclads near Washington. The nearest are undergoing repairs in Baltimore. If anyone tries to escape by water, they'll be in a wooden ship."

"Will they be warships?"

"Most likely, but your firepower will match theirs and you will not be vulnerable to sinking."

"Will they be powered by sail or steam?" Mosby was definitely becoming interested.

"Both. When the action starts, you will have to move fast."

"I'm beginning to like this idea!" Mosby flashed a hearty grin.

"I thought you might. Have you any other questions?"

"Nope, assuming I can take this map with me."

"Be my guest," nodded Longstreet. "How large a force have you now?"

"Only a hundred men. They're waiting for me east of here near a village called Ashburn."

"Good! Leave at once for Manassas. Speed is of the essence. Once Lee is across the Potomac he will strike immediately for Washington. You won't have a lot of time."

"We'll be there. Count on it."

"I am."

*   *   *   *

In Washington, D. C., there was a definite sense of panic in the air. Hundreds of residents had already packed their belongings and evacuated themselves from the city. Thousands more were contemplating a similar course of action. Civilians and soldiers clogged the streets. In short, the capital of the United States was a city gripped in fear.

Lincoln himself had not succumbed to the temptation to run. He remained in the White House and continued his preparation for the defense of his nation's capital. As Mosby and Longstreet were conversing in Leesburg, Lincoln and Halleck were meeting in the Oval Office.

"What are the latest reports?" asked Lincoln calmly.

"Lee is apparently crossing the Potomac as we speak."

"Where?"

"White's Ferry."

"Any information as to his intentions?"

"I should think it's obvious, Mr. President. He's not going to Pennsylvania this time."

"You think he'll try for Washington?"

"He'd be a fool not to."

"I see. Any word from Thomas or Sherman?"

"Rebel cavalry has been very active in Tennessee and Georgia. Nearly every major railroad bridge in that region has been destroyed. It could be several weeks before any help arrives from that quarter."

"Can we hold them at bay for that long?"

"I don't know. I've been able to concentrate nearly sixty thousand men here in Washington. More than a third of them are on the Virginia side of the Potomac."

"Bring them back to this side. They'll do us no good in Alexandria."

"Very well, Mr. President."

"Sixty thousand is a healthy number, Halleck. We could

245

hold for months if need be."

"Possibly, Mr. President, but I have my doubts. The men I speak of are not any army. They've been gathered from all over this area, but the bulk of them have no combat experience. They're garrison troops. There are only a handful of seasoned officers available. No one has taken charge as yet."

"Then you must take charge, Halleck."

"Me, sir?"

"There's no one else."

"Mr. President, there just isn't any time. Lee will be knocking on our gates within a day, two at best."

"And we will be waiting for him. If these men aren't seasoned, we'll not risk calamity by sending them to fight the Rebels in the open field. We'll fight from prepared defensive positions. You must see to it, Halleck, and there is precious little time."

"I'll do what I can, Mr. President."

"I know you will. God bless you, good sir."

"Thank you, Mr. President." Halleck saluted and left the office, desperately trying to quell the sensation of utter helplessness which threatened to overwhelm him.

With Halleck gone, Lincoln returned to his desk, seating himself behind it. With elbows resting on the desk top he buried his face in his hands as if deep in thought. He didn't have long to ponder whatever was going through his mind. He had but a few moments to himself before there came a knock on his door. He looked up quickly, blinking his sad deep-set eyes to regain their focus.

"Come in," he beckoned.

The door opened and Secretary Seward entered quietly, shutting the door behind him.

"Please sit down."

"Thank you, Mr. President." Seward took a seat on the opposite side of the desk.

"Have you been to see them?" asked Lincoln.

"Yessir."

"What did they say?"

"I have complete assurances from the English and French ambassadors. Neither country will recognize the Confederacy as long as slavery persists in the South."

"Regardless of the military outcome?"

"That is correct, Mr. President. Even if we lose the war, God forbid, the Confederacy will be a pariah among nations. No one will recognize them unless the British and French act first, and they will not act as long as the Rebels cling to their peculiar institution."

"Well, Mr. Seward," Lincoln managed a weak smile. "This constitutes the only good news to reach my ears in some time. If Lee takes Washington, it could truly be a fruitless victory."

"I knew you'd be relieved to hear it, Mr. President, and now I think we should discuss contingency plans."

"Such as?"

"Evacuating the Federal government from this city."

"Like rats leaping from a sinking ship."

"Use whatever analogy you like, Mr. President. Can we allow the Rebels to bag us all? Who will run the country? Who will press the war?"

"Do you really expect me to leave? What kind of example would I be setting for our countrymen?"

"Damn what anyone thinks, Mr. Lincoln!" Seward's temper flared for a moment. "The country needs a leader; someone to rally them in this our most desperate hour! Who better than you!"

"Now, now, Seward!" smiled Lincoln. "We mustn't lose control of ourselves. Especially now. This crisis calls for cool heads."

"Pardon my saying so, Mr. President, but the temperature of our heads will be of little consequence to the country if we are all taken prisoner! The city can always be retaken! The Union must have a government!"

"The Union has a government, Mr. Seward. That will not change. We are all merely officials in the final analysis. If we are captured, new officials will be chosen to fill the vacancies. The Union will go on."

"We can't just sit here and wait for capture, Mr. President! That's impossible! Our escape will go a long way toward insuring the continuity of government in this nation! We owe it to the Union not to be captured!"

"Very well, Mr. Seward!" Lincoln raised one hand to calm the other man. "Assuming the city will fall — an event which may or may not happen — what do you have in mind?"

"We have two options, one overland, one by water."

"Do continue."

"I believe the overland route to be the most risky. Rebel cavalry has already been reported in the town of Damascus. They're moving fast to seal the exits although a number of our congressmen have already fled toward Baltimore."

"Have they now?" Lincoln arched his eyebrows.

"I'm afraid so, and more are just waiting for you to say the word."

"My earlier analogy about the sinking ship is beginning to seem more appropriate."

"Mr. President, the government must go on."

"So it must. What about the rails? Is it still safe to take a train out of here?"

"Only to the Northeast. We are receiving reports of sabotage by Rebel sympathizers. That route is available, but probably not later than tomorrow afternoon.

"Very well. You may inform the members of Congress and my Cabinet that if they choose to leave, they have my permission. Advise them to do so before the Rebels can close the escape routes. I suppose you might want to inform the members of the Supreme Court as well."

"I'll see to it, Mr. President." Seward appeared visibly relieved. "I'll instruct everyone to rendezvous in Baltimore. We can continue the war from there."

"You do that."

"What about you, Mr. President? Will you be leaving with us?"

"I've made my intentions clear, Seward. I'll not leave the

city until I'm sure this city is about to fall, or is in the process of falling."

"I thought as much."

"I'm in no mood to argue the point, Seward."

"And I'll offer no argument. I've already made arrangements for you. There are three steamships docked at the wharves near Fourteenth Street. They'll be waiting to carry you and the other holdouts downriver to the Chesapeake then up to Baltimore. One of them, The *Oneida*, sports forty guns."

"I feel safer already," quipped Lincoln. "I suppose it's fortunate the Rebels have nothing in the way of a navy."

"Of the three possible escape options, I believe water to be the safest."

"Thank you, Seward. Pay no attention to my mood. I do appreciate your foresight."

"You're welcome, Mr. President."

"Is there a train leaving tonight?"

"Yes, sir."

"Do you plan to be on it?"

"I had entertained hopes of that nature."

"Do so, and be good enough to take my family with you."

"I will, Mr. President."

"Thank you, Seward. You'd best be off. Time doesn't seem to be on our side."

"God bless you, Mr. President."

"I'm sure He will, Seward."

*　　　*　　　*　　　*

As Abraham Lincoln continued to contemplate an increasingly bleak future, the last regiments of the Army of Northern Virginia crossed unopposed into Maryland. Elements of Hampton's cavalry were dispatched at once to attack and secure the summit of nearby Sugarloaf Mountain. No better observation post could be found for fifty miles in any direction. The rest of the army started east, passing through

Darnestown and Poolesville. Curious civilians watched from their homes or gathered near the roads to gawk at the motley assortment of soldiers who comprised Lee's invincible army.

The vanguard of the column, Ewell's corps, had reached a point some five miles east of Poolesville when the order came to halt for a forty-minute break, time enough for the rear of the column to close in a little. Seth Reilly and his troops spotted a farmhouse about two hundred yards from the road. At first they resisted the temptation to move in that direction, contenting themselves with the copious supply of wild blackberries growing alongside the road. However, they soon picked the bushes clean and began to cast hungry eyes in the direction of the house, itself.

"How about it Professor?" posed Whitt.

"You know what Lee said. We're to leave civilians alone."

"He didn't say we couldn't visit 'em," argued Ox. "We're not a bunch of renegades, Professor. We won't do 'em no harm."

"I'm starvin', Professor." This last from Cody.

"Okay, okay!" relented Reilly. "We'll go pay our respects. Whitt, Jonas, Cody, Ox and myself. The rest of you guys stay put. If they give us anything to eat, we'll bring some back to ya."

After winding their way through a field of waist-high corn, the little group of Confederate soldiers found themselves in the front yard of the Allison family. They marvelled how perfect, how untouched by war everything appeared. The barn sported a recent coat of paint. Chickens scurried everywhere. In a fenced paddock behind the house, several cows grazed contentedly.

"It's been years since I've seen anything this nice," observed Whitt.

"Yep," agreed Reilly. "These folks don't know how lucky they are."

Just then the front door opened and a burly man in his fifties stepped out onto the porch. "What can I do for you fellas?" he asked.

Almost out of instinct, Reilly came to attention. "Good afternoon, sir, my name is Lieutenant Seth Reilly and I'm with the Army of Northern Virginia."

"I'm Caleb Allison," returned the farmer. "This is my home."

"And a fine home it is, sir," added Reilly.

"How can I help you?"

Reilly still wasn't sure whether they were being received as friends or enemies, Maryland being one of those states characterized by divided loyalties. "I guess you would say we're awful damn hungry," he said tentatively.

"Starvin'," corrected Cody very quickly.

"I see." A faint hint of a smile appeared on Allison's face.

"This seems to be a prosperous household," said Reilly. "Would you consider sharing some of your food with us?"

"I think we could spare a little," nodded Allison. "Are there more of you?"

"Well, sir, the whole army is passing through the general vicinity."

"I don't think I could feed your whole army, Lieutenant," chuckled Allison.

"I left ten men out there on the road."

"So be it. You're all welcome, come on inside."

"Jonas!" Reilly turned to Willem. "Go get 'em!"

"This'll take longer than forty minutes, Professor!"

"Don't worry about it! We'll catch up! Just go get 'em!"

Once inside they passed through a large comfortably furnished living room into a substantial kitchen in the rear of the house. Allison's wife, a portly, handsome woman in her late forties was just pulling a loaf of fresh, hot bread out of the oven.

"Mary Ann!" called Allison. "We've got guests!"

The woman turned and her eyes opened wide at the sight of the Rebel soldiers. "Rest easy, woman!" soothed Allison. "They mean us no harm. These men fought with Tom."

Reilly shot an inquisitive look in Allison's direction.

"Our son, Tom," explained the older man. "He was with

the First Maryland, the Rebel version. He was killed in the spring of '62 at Front Royal. He fought under Stonewall Jackson."

"That a fact? Well then, it's a small world."

"Did you know him?" Allison's eyes searched Reilly's for an answer.

"No, sir, but we were there. You're looking at what's left of the Stonewall Brigade.

"Really? You were there? Do you know anything of the First Maryland?"

"They fought like tigers!" boasted Ox. "Right now, they're on the march with Gordon!"

For the next hour and a half, Stonewall's remnants ate ravenously and there seemed no end to the food. Allison's wife, his daughter and the young widow of his son kept the food coming in ample quantities. Freshly baked ham and chicken were piled high on oblong platters; green beans and potatoes cooked with bacon were served, not to mention the hot bread with freshly churned butter and gobs of sweet honey. To wash it all down there were pitchers of cold, freshly-drawn well water or chilled milk. All in all, it was a feast such as the Virginians hadn't seen in an eternity.

While they ate, they talked, swapping war stories for the most part.

"Do you really think you can capture Washington?" wondered Caleb Allison.

"No question," replied Reilly. "I truly believe no power on earth could stop us now."

"I hope so," said Mrs. Allison. "If for no other reason than to put an end to this Godforsaken war!"

In the midst of all that was plentiful, Reilly wondered how she could say that, especially when he thought of all the wretched misery and suffering he had seen in Virginia. Then he remembered that she had lost her only son: "Like so many others," he thought.

"Tell me," she continued. "How could you ever stoop to taking a boy like this?" She gestured in Cody's direction.

"He just sorta walked in and joined us."

"He's just a boy!" she argued.

"His Pa was killed at Manassas," said Ox. "Yanks killed his ma and burned out their farm. What else is he supposed to do."

"He's just so young!" She shook her head and walked away. "So terribly young!"

Cody just shrugged his shoulders, his mouth so full he could scarcely chew.

After warm good-byes, the Rebel soldiers departed with full stomachs. Their bellies weren't the only things to be stuffed. The Allison's insisted on their taking all the bread, ham and chicken their haversacks could carry. Reilly's men were hardly of a mind to argue with them.

By nightfall, the army was camped just west of Rockville where Jeb Stuart had seized a Federal wagon train the year before. The next morning they resumed their march only to be met by a brave but futile effort southeast of Rockville. A force of Federal infantry some ten thousand strong had marched south from Frederick the night before and attempted to block the Rebel thrust against their capital. Lee brushed them off with no more effort than a man swatting at gnats on a warm evening in July. A quarter of their number was killed or captured. The remainder fled south to incorporate themselves into Washington's last ring of defenses.

The Fourth of July found the Army of Northern Virginia marching into the little town of Silver Spring, Maryland right on the northwest boundary of Washington, D. C. Here the Southerners encountered the first bona fide resistance from Union troops in well-fortified positions. Lee decided not to make any serious attempt to breech those defenses before the advent of darkness. Instead, he dispatched his cavalry in an arc around the city to glean every bit of information to be had, and to cause whatever mischief they might see fit to cause. That night there was no independence day celebration in the capital of the United States.

Hampton's efforts were profitable in several ways, the

first being information. They learned that ten train-loads of officials and baggage had departed Washington for Baltimore in the previous two days — a procession they were able to put an end to by destroying every line of track coming out of the city. However, they encountered no sizeable resistance to their sweep. Here and there they spied an isolated Federal cavalry detachment, but they were all driven off. They learned that the bulk of the Union forces in the area were in defensive positions in the city itself. The rest were gravitating toward Baltimore, which was rapidly taking on the appearance of a new Federal capital. By the morning of the fifth, Washington was completely cut off. Every exit was sealed. Its only link with the outside world was the Potomac River.

Having held a brief Council of War on the night of the fourth, Lee was ready to strike on the morning of the fifth. He learned that his enemy had nearly seventy thousand men to defend the city, but they were strung out in a series of forts and breastworks around most of the capital's perimeter, making for a thin line at best. Halleck had no choice in this matter. Not knowing exactly where the Rebel blow would land, he had to man every foot of his line.

Lee decided to divide his army in two. Longstreet and Gordon marched north out of Silver Spring, then west to the Old Georgetown Road which they followed back toward the District itself. Hill and Ewell remained with Lee in Silver Spring. As a result of the maneuver, the fifth of July passed with no serious action. Hampton's cavalry continued to prowl along the Union perimeter, probing here and there, offering one feint after another for Halleck to ponder.

As for the final strategy itself, this had clearly been determined. The object was the capture of Washington, not the elimination of Halleck's hastily assembled army. Accordingly, wherever possible, the Rebels would bypass Federal fortifications and drive straight for the heart of the city. If Halleck was still of a mind to make a fight of it after the capital was in Southern hands, Lee would oblige him one fort at a time. The plan of attack was fairly basic: a massive artillery barrage to soften the Federal defenses followed by an infantry assault. Once a breakthrough was achieved, the Confederates would make straight for the downtown section of Washington. The barrage itself was scheduled to get underway by 5 a.m. the next day.

There was an air of pure excitement sweeping through the Rebel camps that night. The bands played merry songs, and the men sang along in the most boisterous fashion. They sensed victory close at hand. One more tangle with the Yankees was all they needed. For the first time in countless months, the bellies of Lee's soldiers were full. Their strength — mentally and physically — was at a peak. Lee felt so good about his prospects that he found himself guarding against overconfidence.

At 5:15 a.m. on the morning of the sixth, the first volley of artillery roared out from the Confederate lines. One hundred fifty guns went into action, filling the air with the thunderous crash of cannons. They continued firing in prearranged sequence, thirty guns per volley, one after another so that scarcely a second would pass without the terrible roar of Lee's guns echoing across the air currents.

Not ten minutes later, Longstreet and Gordon wheeled their guns into position and opened fire on the opposing fortifications at the circle on the northern end of a dirt road known as Wisconsin Avenue. Their efforts, as those of Hill and Ewell to the east, were devastatingly effective. For three straight hours, the onslaught continued without so much as a hint of a letup. Most of the targeted Union fortifications were reduced to piles of rubble. The Federal defenders, many of whom were seeing their first real action of the war, were numbed by the experience. Their casualties were heavy, but the real impact was the effect these losses had on those who were not hurt. As a fighting force, their abilities would be negligible at best.

Shortly after 8:00 a.m., the guns fell silent. Long lines of Confederate infantry were poised in their jumping-off position for the lunge they hoped would trigger the collapse of Washington. Sweaty palms and fingers clutched muskets as these men fixed bayonets. As before any attack, the anxiety level mounted while they waited for the fateful order to charge. Seth Reilly moved calmly among his men, soothing their nerves, offering words of encouragement and praise.

"Listen boys," he urged, "most of the Yanks over there have never fired a musket in anger. They're green and right about now, they must be feeling a wee-bit shell shocked. Hit 'em hard and fast! I want to hear that rebel yell from every one of you! Scream like banshees! We've only got a hundred fifty yards to cover and we can do it fast!"

Then came the signal. As soon as the order came to charge the Federals, a colonel stood up exposing himself to enemy fire. He drew his sword and held it high. "Give 'em hell, boys!" he shouted with a wild cry.

From countless thousands of throats the Rebel Yell echoed skyward. Over the breastworks came the boys clad in gray and butternut, their bayonets gleaming in the early morning sun, their battle flags snapping smartly in the breeze. If anyone could have been close enough at that moment to read the expressions on their faces and in their eyes, they would have drawn but one conclusion: These soldiers were fiercely determined. They would not be denied. Like a tidal wave, they rushed across open ground into the face of the enemy.

The enemy, in this case, was still recoiling from the morning's relentless bombardment. They were numb. Many of them were experiencing their first taste of combat, and they weren't finding it particularly palatable. They had four batteries in position, and from these spewed two volleys of canister and grapeshot. The jittery Federal riflemen delivered one volley of musket fire, then found themselves face to face with Rebel bayonets. At that moment, for all practical purposes, the battle was over. The Union line broke in panic, scattering for the rear and whatever safety could be found.

Whooping and hollering like a herd of wild cattle, the victorious Southerners swooped over the Federal ramparts and at once found themselves in hot pursuit of a fleeing enemy. Washington's first line of defense had been breached, and through this gap poured the Army of Northern Virginia. Over the Old Georgetown Road, Gordon's infantry met with similar success, ushering a second thrust toward the center of the city. The final capture of the Federal capital was but hours away.

*   *   *   *

Abraham Lincoln paced nervously back and forth across the Oval Office in the White House, listening intently to the distant rolling thunder of gunfire from the north and northwest. "I should be up there myself," he muttered to himself. In truth, it had been his intention to ride to Fort Stephens to observe the fighting, but Halleck stayed his hand.

"Mr. President," he argued, "I must insist that you remain here. For you to journey to the front line now would be to invite certain capture! If this were a mere raiding party, or a diversion of some sort, I might think otherwise, but such is not the case! That is Robert E. Lee knocking on our gates, Mr. President, and he has the entire Army of Northern Virginia at his back! If Grant couldn't stop him, I seriously doubt that I will be able to! Please stay here, sir! And do be ready to take ship at a moment's notice!"

"I guess he's right," thought Lincoln. Just then he heard a noise, the rustle of a woman's clothes to be exact. He turned to find his wife, Mary, standing in the doorway. She was unable to mask the overwhelming expression of sadness which clouded her features.

"I have everything packed and loaded in the carriage," she whispered softly.

"I wish you had taken the train to Baltimore with the children," he observed.

"I'll not leave you," came the instant reply.

"I know and believe me, though I fear for your safety, I'm deeply grateful you chose to stay."

A SOUTHERN YARN

"We'll see this through together, as we have done everything else."

"Perhaps we may not have to leave," said Lincoln, in a tone which was most unconvincing, even to himself. "It sounds as though our boys are putting up a pretty good fight out there."

"Perhaps," she smiled for just a moment.

Any thoughts either of them were entertaining in that direction were soon to be cruelly dashed. Not five minutes after Mrs. Lincoln's appearance in the doorway, there came a second visitor, a young cavalry officer to be precise. Mrs. Lincoln gasped at the sight of the young man, for he had very obviously been wounded. Numerous splotches of blood stained his tunic, and a wide bandage had been wrapped several times about his head.

"Mr. President!" he saluted, but found himself wavering as though about to faint. Rather than standing to attention, he leaned heavily against the doorpost for support. "We're licked, sir!" he panted. "They've broken through in two places! One group is heading into Georgetown, the other's coming straight down the 7th St. Pike! You must leave, sir! And quickly!"

The Lincolns exchanged glances. "Get help for this young man." ordered the President. "I'll fetch the rest of my things from upstairs and we'll be out of here! I hope Captain McRoberts had the foresight to keep steam up!"

*   *   *   *

Meanwhile downriver from the capital, at a place just north of Woodbridge, Colonel John Singleton Mosby was laying his final plans.

"Looks like Longstreet was right about the river," he mused, stroking his chin and staring northward. "I reckon she's about a half mile wide through this stretch."

"Where do you want the guns?" asked an artillery officer who had only recently been marching with Longstreet.

"Forty of them here along these bluffs, and I want them surrounded by earthen walls. Your men better get busy."

"Very good, Colonel, and the others?"

"I'll put my men to work cutting trees. We'll build a few rafts in no time flat. I want the rest of the guns on the Maryland side. If a Yankee ship shows up we'll catch 'em in a cross fire."

"Good idea, Colonel. With this much firepower, they'll have a hard time getting anything through here."

"Unless the Yanks got themselves an ironclad we don't know about, in which case, we'll be spittin' against the wind."

The officer responded with a mere shrug of his shoulders and a half-smile.

"Let's get to it," said Mosby.

With so many backs and arms bent to a single task, the work went surprisingly fast. Within the hour, forty guns were dug into the bluff overlooking the river. A bank of earth was piled in front of and around the guns to provide protection from enemy shells. Five lengthy rafts had been constructed, loaded and poled across the Potomac to the sandy beaches on the Maryland side. The guns were then dragged up the steep banks overlooking the river and put into position just as their counterparts on the southern side. As the last spadeful of dirt was tapped into place, the distant sound of battle drifting downriver reached the ears of Mosby's new command.

"Sounds like they're locked into it," said one man, a farmer from Arcola, Virginia, who rode with Mosby.

"Sounds that way," agreed the Gray Ghost. "If any of those Yanks are plannin' on passin' through here, we'll probably see 'em before too much longer. Where's Major Henrickson?"

"Here, sir!" came the reply.

"I'm goin' back over to the Maryland side. You'll be in charge here. If a ship shows up, open fire at your own discretion."

"As you wish, Colonel!"

"Good! Well let's hope somebody shows up, otherwise we sure did a hell of a lot of work for nothin'!"

"They'll be along," said Henrickson. "I feel it in my bones."

"I hope your bones know what they're talkin' about," grinned Mosby with a wave of his hat as he stepped aboard the raft.

Back in Washington, the end was drawing irrevocably nearer for those who toiled in the defense of their capital. Lee's infantry bore straight through the thickly wooded northern hills of the city toward the heart of the Union capital. As the Rebels descended a hill overlooking U Street, on the outskirts of the downtown area of the city, they spied a hastily drawn line of defense. The equivalent of three regiments of infantry had taken down trees and thrown up barricades in the hope of at least retarding the advance of Ewell's infantry.

"Boys!" Seth Reilly called to his troops. "As soon as we scatter those fellows, we'll be on our way to the White House! Another hour and we'll be having lunch with Mr. Lincoln!"

A wild hurrah greeted these words and the men made ready to charge. Artillery was brought forward, twenty pieces in all. They were lined hub to hub and before long, they had reduced much of the Union breastworks to piles of rubble and woodchips.

"Let's go get 'em!" cried Reilly as he and two thousand other graybacks burst forward with a yell. They were within twenty yards of the barricade when they received an effective volley of musket fire from the Federals. Among those on the receiving end was a flag-bearer to the left of the Stonewall Brigade. The young fellow clutched futilely at the gushing wound in his throat as he fell dying to the ground.

As for the Stars and Bars he carried, they never touched the earth. Cody Wilder saw to that. Darting to his left he snatched up the faded torn battle flag scant seconds after it left the dying man's fingers. This was a critical moment. The Union volley had been deadly, felling many a good man. In

260

that moment the attackers wavered, as if pondering the possibility of calling the whole thing off, retreating so as to reorganize. Cody would have none of that.

"Follow me!" His boyish voice sang out above everything else. "I'm going to the White House!" He charged to the forefront, waving the Rebel banner for all to see.

Those around him were shamed that they had even considered the possibility of a retreat. They stormed after him, reached the Yankee breastworks right on his heels. Cody gained the top first, standing alone, striking a defiant pose. With one hand he held the flag high overhead. In his other was the Whitworth which he leveled in the direction of the first Union officer to come in view. He pulled the trigger and started to descend the far side of the wall when suddenly he stiffened. The rifle dropped from his hand first, then the flag, which Jonas quickly retrieved. Young Wilder clutched at his chest for a brief second, then collapsed backwards into the arms of Seth Reilly.

Reilly picked the boy up in both arms, standing there dumbfounded for a moment as hundreds of Ewell's infantry stormed over the barricades in pursuit of fleeing Federals. The lieutenant carried Cody back to the road, laying him down, cradling his head in his arms much as a mother might comfort her child. He glanced over at the hole in the right side of Cody's chest and knew immediately the wound would be fatal.

The other members of the brigade gathered around the limp form of the boy they had come to hold so dear. Whitt was there, as were Ox and Jonas, with the rest standing just to the side.

"Hold on, Cody!" urged Ox. "We'll get help for ya."

Cody's eyes were open, but they were fast taking on the glassy appearance which signals the approach of death. He turned his head slightly and stared up at Reilly's face.

"Did I do good, Professor?" he mumbled in a voice which was barely audible.

A thick lump clogged Reilly's throat and his eyes brimmed

with tears as he looked down at the lad. In his mind, he was holding the dying body of one of his own sons, and this thought drove terror to the very marrow of his bones.

"You did fine, boy," he nearly choked on the words. "You did just fine."

Cody opened his mouth to speak again. "I knew we'd . . ." He never finished whatever he wanted to say. His head rolled lifelessly to one side as a thin trail of blood oozed from the corner of his mouth and dribbled down his hairless chin.

"Dear God," whispered Ox, as the big man struggled to control his own emotions.

For Reilly, there was no more thought of struggle so far as emotions were concerned. During the long course of the war, he had seen thousands of men die, and he thought he had become hardened to it. Not so. He held the lifeless boy tightly in his arms and broke down completely, his back racked by deep, choking sobs.

Whitt reached down and gently closed Cody's eyes. With one hand he clasped Reilly's shoulder, "I'll take care of the boys, Seth," he said calmly. Then he stood, motioned to the others and led them over the barricade, leaving Reilly alone with his grief, still cradling the dead boy. Within minutes, all was quiet, save for the moans of the wounded lying where they had fallen on both sides of the barricade.

At the wharf just to the side of Fourteenth Street, pandemonium was breaking out. Lincoln had boarded the *Oneida*, as had most of the Congressmen, secretaries and cabinet members who had chosen not to leave Washington by train when they had the opportunity. However, a huge throng of civilians had gathered at the dock, all of them clamoring for permission to come aboard. At the President's request, all three ships lowered their planks to allow at least some of these people the chance to escape the Rebel onslaught. This proved to be a mistake. Panic seized the people as they pushed and shoved to fight their way aboard. Women and children were shunted aside. Men fought with one another for access to those planks. More than a score were pushed or punched into the river. Many of these drowned. Pistols appeared. Shots were fired. The panic grew more intense with each minute. Finally, the captain of the *Oneida* decided to cast off while there was still time. It was so ordered, but the crowd of civilians wouldn't leave the planks. In the end, Union sailors had to fire their muskets into their own countrymen so the plank could be drawn and the vessels could get underway.

Ten minutes later, General Dick Ewell of the Confederate army stood on the very same dock. His troops occupied the White House and the Capitol building. Looking downriver, he could barely see the stacks of three Union steamers disappearing in the distance.

"Looks like some folks don't appreciate good company," he grinned.

In Silver Spring, Robert E. Lee mounted Traveller and prepared to ride with his staff into the city which his army had just captured. Once in the saddle, he turned to Colonel Taylor.

"Did you make sure that my orders were sent to all commanders down to the regimental level?"

"Of course, General."

"Were they as explicit as I asked? No civilians are to be harassed in any way. No property is to be damaged or looted. Foreign embassies and their personnel are absolutely off limits."

"I wrote them just as you said," sighed Taylor.

"Good," nodded Lee, somewhat reassured.

"But, General," pressed Taylor. "There are some questions from some of our officers."

"In reference to?"

"The Negroes, sir. Apparently there are a lot of them in and around Washington. Doubtless many are fugitive slaves."

"I thought my orders were rather explicit in that regard. The war isn't over, and we certainly have more important things to worry about than chasing Negroes. We did not come here to serve as a fugitive slave posse, Colonel. There will be time enough later to discuss the Negro question. In the meantime, they are to be left alone! Did you make that clear in my orders?"

"Perfectly, General. I'm just relaying the questions which were raised."

"This is one situation in which there is no room for questions, Colonel. The whole world is watching us. Let us be worthy of that honor."

They formed into a column and started down the 7th St. Pike at a brisk pace.

*   *   *   *

At Halleck's headquarters, the Chief of Staff of the Union armies had other worries. He knew the line had been twice breached and the city was rapidly passing to Confederate control. But his army, if it could properly be termed an army, had not been destroyed. The Federals has sustained fewer than ten thousand casualties in the battle, leaving sixty thousand men still available for future operations, provided they could avoid capture. In this regard, Halleck acted quickly. In point of fact, he had acted before the battle even started. Each of his commanders had been instructed to hold as long as possible, but if it became obvious that the city was falling, they were to abandon their lines and march north into Montgomery and east into Prince Georges Counties. The ultimate goal was to rendezvous all these displaced soldiers somewhere in Howard County, a farming region just to the north of Montgomery and Prince Georges Counties, and just to the west of Baltimore. If this was accomplished, Halleck could turn his attentions into molding these men into a cohesive fighting force.

Truth be told, confusion is the term which most aptly describes the fall of Washington. Lee's twin forks pierced the Federal defenses and drove straight into the heart of the capital, leaving most of Halleck's befuddled defenders to fend for themselves. They wasted no time in leaving, though not all of them were able to effect a successful escape. Within thirty-six hours after the capture of the White House, Halleck was able to gather some fifty thousand men in the rolling hills of Howard County. He quickly styled them the Army of Central Maryland and began plans to continue the war.

*   *   *   *

About a half-hour after Lee entered the city of Washington, he and his party started down the long hill which bottomed out at the barricade where young Cody Wilder gave his life. By this time, all was quiet. A few civilians were on hand giving aid and comfort to the wounded. But for those, the area was deserted. Lee reached the base of the hill and spied a soldier up ahead, an officer who was sitting on the ground holding the limp body of an infantryman. The General rode to within several feet of the pair and reined Traveller to a halt. Immediately, he recognized the man whom he first met in the salient at Spotsylvania. In the fellow's arms was a boy who couldn't have been more than twelve or thirteen years of age. The boy was dead. Lee could readily see where the bullet had pierced his right lung. This was the gray commander's most victorious moment. All of his enemies had been vanquished. The Union capital was his. Yet despite all this triumph, as he looked down up on the frail, lifeless face of Cody Wilder, Lee could feel nothing but overwhelming sadness.

Seth Reilly was still lost in his world of grief, and hadn't even noticed the approach of his commander and the other riders. But as he sat there, he finally became aware of a shadow, and then of horses snorting and stamping their hooves. He glanced up into the face of Robert E. Lee.

"Once again our paths have crossed," said the General.

Reilly stared at him for the longest time without making a reply, and when at last he spoke, it was to say only this: "End this thing, General For God's sake, end this thing!"

265

"I will, son," Lee nodded solemnly. "I swear it. Is there anything I can do here? May I send someone for the boy?"

Reilly only shook his head and held Cody even closer to him, rocking him gently as if trying to ease him to sleep.

Taylor coaxed his horse up next to Lee. "General," he spoke softly. "There's nothing we can do here, and your presence is sorely needed at the Capitol itself."

Lee nodded gravely, and with one parting glance at Reilly and the boy he signalled for his party to press on.

*   *   *   *

On board the *Oneida*, Lincoln left his quarters and made his way across the crowded deck to the side of Captain McRoberts.

"Good afternoon, Mr. President."

"Captain," Lincoln nodded in reply.

"A beautiful day for a river cruise, sir, though I wish the circumstances were different. It's hard to enjoy the scenery when it's clouded by so much despair."

"True," agreed Lincoln. "Captain, I want you to know how much I appreciate your waiting as long as you did. There are a lot of important people on these ships. It would be very difficult to run the government without them."

"I understand, Mr. President, though I must confess to a number of misgivings. We may have tarried too long. All three of these ships are badly overloaded. They aren't handling particularly well and we certainly haven't been able to generate much headway. I can only hope this is going to be an uneventful voyage. If we are called upon to fight, there could be real problems."

"I don't foresee any problems, Captain. The Confederate Navy is virtually non-existent, especially in these waters. How soon will we make Baltimore?"

"Depends on our speed, sir. No later than tomorrow morning by sunrise I think, possibly earlier."

"Good. I need to meet with my military experts to plan

the recapture of Washington."

*   *   *   *

Downriver, Mosby was alerted to the return of a patrol he had dispatched earlier into the Maryland countryside. He immediately addressed himself to the sergeant who had led the patrol.

"Did you find them?" he demanded.

"Yes, suh. Two of 'em, just like you asked."

"Well done!" beamed Mosby. "See that little skiff over there? Use it. Take a couple of men and row yourself to the other side. Take one of the flags and tell Major Henrickson to run it up in place of ours."

"Suh?"

"You have a problem, Sergeant?"

"You want our boys to run up a Yankee flag?"

"That's right. What better way to lure Yankee ships into our trap? Do you think they'll try to steam through if they see all this fire-power and the Stars and Bars on both banks?"

"I guess not," grinned the sergeant.

"Get over there and get back quick. We may have company before too much longer."

Mosby's words proved to be all too accurate. No sooner had Henrickson switched flags than three wispy columns of smoke were spotted upriver.

"You're not going to have enough time to row back across," said Henrickson. "Just stay put. Gunners! Load your pieces and stand ready!"

Every man moved to his battle station, including a large number who were there to serve as sharpshooters rather than as gun crews. Now it was only a matter of waiting to see what the river was bringing their way.

*   *   *   *

On board the *Oneida* the mood of despair hadn't eased

267

too much. But for the sound of the ship's engines, silence prevailed. Few people had anything to say. Most were lost in their own thoughts. In truth, many were still drifting in a state of shocked disbelief at the capture of their capital. Their three ships plodded along sluggishly at a speed of little more than five knots. Around a bend, they came and here they first spotted the gun emplacements still a mile away.

"They seem to be ours," said Captain McRoberts. "Yet I don't remember them being there when we came upriver several weeks back."

Lincoln took the glass and quickly studied the positions on either side of the river. "Halleck ordered them here when he made the arrangements for us to evacuate downriver," he observed as he lowered the glass.

"Possibly," hedged McRoberts. "But I'm not sure. I think we'd better prepare for trouble. Mr. President, you and the first lady should stay below in your quarters at least until we pass."

"Very well, Captain," nodded Lincoln. "I'll certainly defer to your judgment."

"Ensign!" McRoberts called to an aid. "Signal the *Emerson* and *Duluth* to take up positions on either side of us and to remain there until we pass those gun positions up ahead."

"Very good, Captain!" The fellow saluted smartly.

"All hands to battle stations! Ready the guns!" bellowed McRoberts. "I want all the steam this bucket can muster!"

The problem was, he already had all the speed the *Oneida* could generate, given the present conditions and the extra mob of refugees on board.

On all three ships, there was a flurry of activity as civilians scurried to get below or seek some kind of cover while sailors jumped to their battle stations. Trap or no trap, McRoberts was determined to steam straight through the teeth of it.

*   *   *   *

Major Henrickson lowered his glass and turned to a

nearby lieutenant, "Here they come," he remarked calmly, "three wooden warships," he paused and surveyed his line bristling with heavy guns. "I bet we sink every one of 'em, mark my words! Stand ready to switch back to our flag at my command!"

On came the tiny flotilla, three abreast, steaming straight into the Rebel trap. They were only a half-mile away, then a quarter . . . two hundred yards, the Rebel gunners could almost hear the water bouncing off their bows. Then they were squarely into the passage, well within the range of the Rebel shore batteries.

"Strike those colors!" shouted Henrickson. "Raise ours! Open fire and shoot straight, boys! Shoot straight!"

Down came the Stars and Stripes, up flew the Stars and Bars. The first volley thundered away, and at such close range it would have been difficult to miss.

The *Duluth* was nearest to the south bank of the river, and she received the full brunt of that first volley. The effect was deadly.

Metal and wooden fragments shot through the air, killing or wounding many of those on deck. One mast was shorn in two, crashing back to lean against a second. Several spars broke away and crashed headlong to the deck. Holes were blown into the stricken ship just above the waterline. Crippled, but undeterred, the *Duluth* maintained her speed, and her position as a shield for the *Oneida*.

She managed to deliver a volley of her own, destroying one Rebel gun and inflicting several casualties on Henrickson's troops. By this time, the Southerners had reloaded for the second volley.

"Let 'em have it!" cried Henrickson with a wave of his sword.

Once again the guns roared. This time the effect was instantaneous, and all too deadly. One shell penetrated an existing hole in the *Duluth's* side, slamming into her powder magazine. The resulting explosion was heard for miles. The ship disappeared in a huge ball of fire, and for several long moments the sky rained bits and pieces of wood, sail, rope, metal and flesh. As spectacles go, this one was grim indeed.

On the opposite end of the flotilla, the *Emerson* fared somewhat better, though it was not her destiny to escape. She exchanged two quick volleys with Mosby's batteries on the north bank before a fateful shot deprived her of her rudder.

"Stop the engines!" cried her master, but for the *Emerson* it was too late. The captain could only watch as his ship careened sharply to starboard, barely missing the *Oneida's* stern as she crossed her wake, steaming straight into the southern bank of the Potomac, where she buried her keel deep in the loose mud and sediment. Her crew and passengers, literally staring down the barrels of several hundred Rebel muskets, had little choice but a hasty surrender.

Leaving only the *Oneida* herself, and she it was who carried the most important passenger of all. Captain McRoberts had her at a full head of steam, but with the loss of both his "shields", he knew his chances were slim. From both sides of the ship, his gunners fought valiantly, taking out several pieces of artillery on either shore of the river. Still, for all her courage, the *Oneida* was a doomed vessel.

From both banks, the Rebels worked at a feverish pace, sending hundreds of shells searing across the river toward their final target. The roar was deafening, magnified even more by the Potomac itself. Thick palls of bluish-gray smoke shrouded the beaches, making visibility a murky proposition at best.

At last the Confederate gunners found the range of their target, first Henrickson, followed quickly by Mosby. If someone had been counting, he would have tabulated no fewer than thirty individual hits in the space of a mere sixty seconds. Two shells opened holes in her starboard side at the waterline, not far from her stern. Another shell blasted her in the stern itself, critically damaging the propeller shaft. At once, she began to lose headway. For the *Oneida*, things would only get worse. On deck chaos reigned. Half of the guns were out of action. A good many of her crew were dead or wounded, including Captain McRoberts, who lay dying at the very edge of the poop deck.

The situation was little better down below. Several fires burned out of control. Dead and wounded, civilian and military alike, littered the narrow companionways. Sailors and passengers fought one another for access to a porthole and fresh air. Panic now had a chokehold on the *Oneida's* jugular. Sailors could not hear their orders above the wail of terror stricken government officials. Another round of shells struck the doomed vessel, hastening her trip to the bottom of the Potomac. She began to list to starboard and everyone knew she was finished.

*   *   *   *

"Abandon ship! Abandon ship!" This was an order everyone heard, and though it came from a lowly petty officer, no one was of a mind to question his authority. Only five lifeboats remained undamaged. These were quickly lowered. Sailors and civilians alike scurried over her sides, jumping or diving into the cool, deep waters of the Potomac. Just below the main deck, several sailors worked desperately to clear a passage to the nearest available hatch. Their task was all the more urgent when one considers the main beneficiary of their labors: The President of the United States. With their bare hands, they shifted fallen timbers and cleared away deck planking, much of which was still scorching hot. Gradually, they created a path through a mountain of torn and twisted debris, but time was fast working against them. Smoke from numerous fires clogged the companionway so breathing soon became well nigh impossible. Below their feet they could feel the water rising up through the *Oneida's* lowest decks. Finally they pushed away the last obstacle, and the foremost among them reached the ladder which led up through an open hatch. He pushed the sides of the ladder with both hands and peered up into the face of an officer.

271

A SOUTHERN YARN

"Do you have the President?" demanded the face at the top of the ladder.

"We do, sir!"

"Send him up first! Quickly, men! We've only a minute or two!"

Abraham Lincoln appeared seconds later, with his wife close at hand.

"Hurry, Mr. President!" cried the officer as he thrust an arm down through the hatch.

"You must help Mrs. Lincoln first!" shouted the Chief Executive, whose face could barely be seen through the thickening smoke.

"Aye, sir!"

"Send her up!"

Seconds later, the officer grabbed hold of Mrs. Lincoln's arm and drew her swiftly through the hatch. She was coughing violently, almost unable to stand as she choked and gasped, trying to expel a considerable amount of smoke from her lungs.

Behind her came the President himself, climbing the ladder under his own power, turning once he left the hatch so that he might assist the sailors who were still below.

"Mr. President!" cried the officer. "We're sinking, sir! You must get overboard!"

"Not yet!" argued Lincoln. "We must get these men to safety!"

"Mr. Lincoln, please!" pleaded the sailor.

"Help me!" ordered Lincoln as he reached below to grab hold of an unconscious crewman.

When the last of these men had been extricated, Lincoln took hold of his wife and walking calmly to the edge of the dying ship.

"Come, Mrs. Lincoln," he beckoned in the most soothing tone he could muster. "I believe the Rebels have invited us to take a swim in the Potomac."

"Mr. President," A petty officer quickly presented himself to Lincoln. "Can you swim, sir?"

"Well enough. So can the Missus."

"Make for that lifeboat, Sir! Yonder . . . ten yards or so!"

"We'll make it!" Lincoln nodded. He and his wife exchanged one last glance, clasped one another's hands and leapt overboard, splashing loudly into the churning waters of the river. Moments later they surfaced and began swimming toward the lifeboat. Lincoln had no problem but the first lady was burdened by her cumbersome dress and many petticoats. She began to struggle, and the President returned quickly to her side, calling for the lifeboat to come to their assistance, a signal which elicited a swift response from the crew of the boat. Moments later, they were safely aboard. As they were seated in the boat, Lincoln was quick to notice the absence of other civilians. Other than the Lincolns themselves, the boat's complement consisted entirely of sailors, twelve in all, expert rowers to the man.

"Make for the Maryland shore!" ordered the ensign who was in charge. "Downriver from those Rebel guns!"

Propelled by sure deep strokes, the boat jumped across the choppy water heading for Maryland.

*   *   *   *

On the Virginia bank, Henrickson's gunners had reloaded for yet another salvo, but they hesitated looking to their commander for the first word.

Henrickson gazed out at the last remaining Union ship. Her stern had nearly disappeared below the surface, and her final demise was only moments away. "She's had enough!" he shouted. "Let's get out there and gather up those survivors!"

On the opposite bank, John Singleton Mosby was studying the scene through his field glasses. There was nothing left of the *Duluth* but a cloud of steam rising from the spot where she exploded. The *Emerson* and her crew and passengers were now in Henrickson's hands. He shifted the glass in time to watch the last seconds of the *Oneida's* existence.

273

A SOUTHERN YARN

When she sank, he shifted the glass back and forth, noticing the bulk of her survivors struggling to reach the Virginia shore and the waiting arms of Henrickson's troops. Shifting the focus of his gaze slightly downriver, he spied five lifeboats moving away from the scene of the battle. They were heading for the Maryland side, but it appeared obvious that they might attempt an escape downriver.

"Do you see those boats?" He glanced back toward one of his officers.

"Yessuh."

"Drop a few rounds in front of them, see if we can't persuade 'em to change their minds without having to kill anybody else."

"Very well, suh."

"Oh . . . Lieutenant, move ten of these guns downriver another hundred yards in case they don't change their minds."

"We have neither horses nor caissons, Colonel."

"We have our backs, sir. Do as I say."

"Yessuh!"

Moments later a half-dozen guns boomed in anger, landing their projectiles in a neat little pattern not twenty yards from the bow of the lead boat. The northerners paid no attention.

"Again!" barked Mosby as he watched ten of the guns being rolled back toward the dirt road which paralleled the river. "I'm going with those guns!" he told the lieutenant. "Keep firing, but don't try to hit anyone. Leave that to us!"

By this time, Henrickson had seen the danger from his vantage on the Virginia shore. He, too, sent several guns into action against the fleeing lifeboats, which were now spreading out so as not to offer a single concentrated target.

Ten minutes of warning shots found the lifeboats passing beyond Henrickson's range, and nearing the extent of Mosby's first position. It also found ten of Mosby's guns and the "Gray Ghost" himself, sitting up on a bluff in a position to strike with impunity at the fleeing flotilla.

"A few more warning shots, Colonel?" asked one of his gunners.

Mosby pondered this question for several moments, his eyes darting toward the western horizon where the sun had just set, bathing the river in the pale glow of dusk.

"Nope," he replied. "No more time. Pick one out and sink it. We'll see if the rest of 'em get the message."

"Gotcha," grinned the gunner.

Two salvoes roared away before they found the range. With the third volley, the Rebels scored one direct hit on the boat just ahead of Lincoln's. The vessel itself broke apart. Six of its occupants were either killed outright or drowned. The others were pulled aboard the remaining four boats. Several of these men had suffered serious fragment wounds and they bled profusely.

"Enough!" cried Lincoln in despair as he cradled the head of a wounded man. "They'll kill us all! We cannot escape those guns! Make directly for shore! Do you hear me? That is a direct order from your Commander-in-Chief! Row directly to those guns. Someone must have a white handkerchief! Wave it! Wave it!"

The boats changed course at once, moving directly toward Mosby's ten guns.

"They've given up!" Mosby let loose a whoop. "We've got 'em!" He raised his glass to study the people in the boats, but in the dim twilight, there was little he could determine. "Bunch of civies out there," he observed. "Let's get down to the beach and wrap 'em up!"

One by one the boats reached shore and their occupants became prisoners of the Confederacy. Lincoln's was the last boat to beach, and the President himself was the first one out.

Mosby was there on the beach, casually supervising the disposition of the prisoners. Thus far he had seen no one he might recognize, and at first he could not recognize the tall, hatless man who waded toward him in the near darkness.

"You," he pointed toward Lincoln. "Over there with the others." As Lincoln turned, Mosby caught a glimpse of his profile and at that very instant recognition took place. "Dear God!" he whispered so that only he could hear. "We've just captured the President of the United States!" Mosby stepped into Lincoln's path, staring up into the man's face just to be sure of his conclusion. There was no doubt about it. The "Gray Ghost" came to attention at once and smartly saluted his enemy, "Mr. President," he said. "I'm afraid I must inform you that you are now a prisoner of the Confederate States of America."

"So it would seem," replied Lincoln grimly. "And who, pray tell, might you be?"

"Mosby, sir, Colonel John Singleton Mosby."

"Ah, yes!" Lincoln nodded and for a second a smile appeared on his face. "If you'll permit my saying so, you have been a thorn in our side for longer than I care to remember."

"Why, thank you, Mr. President," Mosby flashed a mischievous grin. "It was ever my intention."

"Of that I have no doubt. Now may I remind you, sir, we have wounded among our number. They require immediate medical attention. Are you in a position to provide it?"

"On this side of the river, we are not. We have medical personnel with our main force on the Virginia shore."

Suddenly, the full impact of whom he had captured threatened to overwhelm Mosby. His imagination went momentarily out of control conjuring up images of Union cavalry charging down to the beach to rescue their President. He began to bark orders, informing his lieutenant to take half their party back upriver with all the prisoners save the Lincolns.

"Get everyone and everything loaded on the rafts and back to the Virginia side," he continued.

"In the dark, sir?"

"Of course in the dark! You idiot! Now move!"

The other half of his party, along with President and Mrs. Lincoln, as well as the more severely wounded of the Federal sailors were loaded into three of the lifeboats and started immediately across the Potomac. Mosby sat directly opposite the Federal Chief Executive in the boat. Abraham Lincoln began his journey into captivity.

The news of Lee's capture of Washington and the subsequent apprehension of President Lincoln swept through the South like wildfire. Every telegraph wire in the land hummed through the night carrying the details of this tremendous victory to every corner of the land. In every town and city church bells rang unceasingly, lending their music to the jubilant celebration which erupted throughout the Confederacy. The result of all this was a strong belief that the long, terrible war was finally ending, and that a final Southern victory was near at hand.

This feeling was shared in the halls and chambers of the Southern Capital, though here, the elation was quickly tempered by a healthy dose of realism. The war was not over. Lee held Washington, true, but could he hold it indefinitely? Halleck had managed to gather some sixty thousand men in the hills of central Maryland and was in a position to strike if he so desired. The Union blockade continued to strangle the South and was actually growing stronger with the passage of time. Much of the Confederacy still suffered beneath Union occupation, and the indomitable Sherman was pressing Johnston in Georgia.

To help balance this, Richmond would soon receive a number of very important guests. Among these were the President of the United States, four members of his cabinet, two justices of the Supreme Court (not to mention a substantial number of lower court judges), seventeen members of the House of Representatives, and nine senators. This says nothing of the many bureaucratic officials who found themselves in southern hands following Lee's swift stroke against the Union capital. In short, within twenty-four hours of the Confederate victory in Washington, the Federal government of the United States was in utter disarray, facing a long period of virtual paralysis.

As for Robert E. Lee himself, he shared the jubilation which his victory generated, but his buoyant mood was short-lived. Within hours after taking a tour of Lincoln's White House, Lee had arranged to visit the British embassy, fully hoping that he would emerge with a guarantee of British recognition for the Confederacy. This was not to be. After an hour with the ambassador, Lee left the embassy with a somber expression on his face.

Venable was waiting with the horses outside, and was quick to detect the change in his commander's mood.

"I take it things didn't go the way you'd hoped," he observed as he handed the General Traveller's reins.

"A valid assumption," replied Lee curtly as he took the reins and mounted his horse.

After mounting his own animal, Venable turned again to Lee. "Will they recognize us?" he demanded.

"There will be no diplomatic recognition forthcoming, either from Britain or France." Lee nudged Traveller's flanks and started away.

"Why not?" queried Venable as he caught up to Lee. "Didn't we just capture the capital of the United States and send its President running for his life?"

"It makes no difference."

"That doesn't make sense. Why won't they recognize us?"

Lee pulled his horse to a halt and with sad eyes he stared directly into Venable's face.

"In a word, my friend — slavery. As long as we cling to the institution of slavery, no one will recognize us. We'll find ourselves an outlaw nation, isolated from the rest of the world."

He started forward again, lapsing at once into silence.

Venable said nothing, but one thought crossed repeatedly through his mind: "Will it all be for nothing?"

The next day was a busy one at the Headquarters of the Army of Northern Virginia, which Lee had chosen to locate in the village of Silver Spring, Maryland. There was a constant coming and going of scouts, couriers, reporters (from both sides), photographers and government officials. Word arrived from Mosby via Longstreet informing Lee of the capture of Abraham Lincoln and numerous members of the Union government. Coming on the heels of the British refusal, this information had a very positive impact on Lee's outlook. Perhaps the victory would not be fruitless after all.

That same afternoon Seth Reilly waited for the return of Jesse Saunders, a boyhood friend who rode with Hampton's cavalry. Reilly had asked the trooper to locate a suitable place in the vicinity of Silver Spring where the body of Cody Wilder could be laid to rest.

His parting instructions were: "I want it to be in a place where he can rest peacefully for a long time, a place which won't be disturbed for a hundred years or more."

Just after 2:00 p.m., Saunders returned to Ewell's encampment and located Reilly.

"I think I found what you've got in mind," he said as he wiped a layer of sweat from his forehead.

"Whereabouts?" Reilly looked up at the rider, but had to shade his eyes against the afternoon sun.

"About a mile south of here there's a road which cuts off to the east. I think it's called Piney Branch Road. Follow it for about two miles. It'll drop into a little hollow with a good size stream flowing through. The locals call it Sligo Creek. I marked a spot with a pile of stones about a hundred yards up from the road. It's real nice, Seth, lots of trees, plenty of small game around. I think the boy would approve if he had a say-so."

"Thank you, Jesse," nodded Reilly. "I owe you one."

"Don't mention it. You want me to round you fellas up some horses?"

"That's okay. Lord only knows we're used to walkin'."

It took them just over an hour and a half to make the hike down to Sligo Creek and the grave site. It was a typical July afternoon, which is to say it was hot and unbearably humid beneath a cloudless, hazy sky. By the time they reached the burial spot, all the men were soaked in their own sweat. Before digging Cody's grave, they took time to refresh themselves in the fresh, clean water of the creek itself.

"Jesse was right," noted Ox as he splashed cold water in his face. "The boy would have like this place."

"I suppose," said Reilly, his demeanor taking on a sullen tone.

"All right, fellas, let's go to it. Two men digging at a time. We'll work fifteen minute shifts. We're digging this one six feet down. Cody deserves better that the shallow graves most of us end up with."

For the next two hours there was little talking among the men. They worked quietly, and the only noise was that of spades slicing into dirt. At last they finished, and with little fanfare, they lowered the shroud covered body of their young comrade into the ground. Then, taking turns with the shovels, they filled in the grave, burying still another soldier of the famed Stonewall Brigade.

When the last spadeful of earth had been patted into place, they piled stones from the creek across the grave and erected a small wooden cross with the following inscription: "Here lies Cody Wilder, a soldier of the South who gave his life on July 5, 1864."

Lieutenant Reilly delivered a brief but touching eulogy, and they said farewell to young Wilder.

They had covered perhaps a quarter of the return march when they spied a rider in Confederate uniform approaching from the west. Within another minute, the trooper pulled up and saluted their lieutenant.

"Are you Reilly?" he asked.

"Sure 'nuff," nodded Reilly.

"Thought so. They told me I'd find you fellas out here someplace. I've a message for you from Lee's headquarters."

He reached into his tunic and pulled forth a small brown envelope, handing it to Reilly in the same motion.

"See you boys," he flashed a grin, saluted and wheeled

his horse around.

"What's it say, Professor?" wondered Jonas.

"Easy does it," returned Reilly. "Let me get it open."

"Who's it from? Is it from Marse Robert?"

"Who else would send the Professor a message from headquarters!" laughed Ox.

Reilly opened the envelope and withdrew the message, seeing at once that it was from Lee himself.

"It's from the General," he acknowledged.

"I knew it!" grinned Jonas. "What's he say?"

"Wants to see me at headquarters tonight. Doesn't say why. Reckon we'd best get crackin, boys!"

"Double time!" barked Whitt as they resumed their march.

It was very nearly nine o'clock before Reilly was able to present himself at Lee's tent. The General had just finished an interview with a northern journalist — a writer for Harper's magazine. This fellow bid a respectful goodnight and made his exit, whereupon Reilly was ushered in.

"Ah, Lieutenant!" Lee rose from the small wooden chair behind the little table which served as his desk in the field. "I do believe you're a sight for weary eyes," Lee crossed the tent and shook Reilly's hand.

"Why . . . thank you, General. Though I must confess ignorance as to why."

"Sit down and I'll explain." Lee gestured toward a chair, waiting for Reilly to be seated before he himself sat down on the cot. Before saying anything more, the General removed his wire-framed spectacles and rubbed his eyes with one hand.

"Did you see the fellow who just left?" he asked.

"Yessir. Looked like a writer of some sort."

"Indeed," nodded Lee. "A journalist for a northern magazine. I've been besieged by people like him since the day began. I can't recall too may spare minutes since this morning. It's been difficult to run the Army today, I can tell you that for a fact."

"If you'd rather me come back tomorrow, General . . ."

"No. That won't be necessary, Lieutenant. Quite frankly, you're one of the few people I really wanted to see today."

"Very well, sir, though I still don't know why you wished to see me."

"The boy . . . the boy you were holding when I came upon you yesterday. How old was he?"

"None of us ever knew for sure. We figure he might've been thirteen."

Lee cast his eyes toward the floor of the tent. "So young," he muttered.

"His name was Cody Wilder."

"Have you written to inform his parents?"

"He was an orphan."

"I see," Lee sat upright and took a deep breath. "I've seen a lot of death, Lieutenant," he sighed. "Over these last two years, I've seen tens of thousands of men die, knowing all the while they were losing their lives because of orders I gave."

"That's a burden I don't envy you, General."

"It's a burden every officer must accept, Lieutenant. The difference between yours and mine is a matter of degree. Sad to say, I've learned to accept the guilt which goes hand in hand with the responsibility of command. I believe I may have surrendered some of my humanity in the process, but I suppose that is the price which must be paid.

In any event, I've digressed. What I wanted to tell you is how deeply I was touched by what I saw yesterday."

"All of us were kind of attached to the boy, General."

"And I didn't even know him, but seeing him dead in your arms hurt, Lieutenant, hurt deeply. You told me to end this thing, and I swore I would. That is why I summoned you."

"Is it over, sir?" Reilly's senses became quickly alert.

"No . . . no, not yet. In point of fact, you and I may already have done everything possible to end it on terms satisfactory to our country. Unfortunately, our efforts may not be enough."

"I'm not sure I follow you, sir."

"It may be that nothing we do on the battlefield will bring an end to this."

"Why not, General? It's a war, isn't it?"

"And a more tragic affair there never was," nodded Lee with a weary sigh. "Yesterday after the fighting ended, I paid a visit to the British Embassy."

"And?" pressed Reilly.

"The ambassador was very complimentary of our efforts, but very succinct on another matter . . . one of perhaps more vital concern."

"Which is to say?"

"Many of our hopes rest on the obtaining of diplomatic recognition from Great Britain. I'm afraid it won't be forthcoming."

"I don't understand, General," Reilly shook his head in disgust. "In the last sixty days we've utterly destroyed the Union's best Army and captured its capital. Does that not deserve the recognition of our fellow nations?"

"To our way of thinking, yes. To the British there is another issue to consider."

"That is?"

"In a word . . . slavery. I have it on good authority no nation in Europe will recognize us as long as slavery exists, even if we were to march unopposed through the North — which, by the way, is well beyond our humble abilities at this point in time — we would still be considered an outcast among the nations."

"Just what are our prospects, General?" Reilly's shoulders slumped noticeably.

"Despite everthing we have just achieved, the best we may be able to hope for is a protracted stalemate."

"Then it will never end."

"I don't know, son. I just don't know."

"General," Reilly searched Lee's eyes as if they held an answer. "I did not put on this uniform to preserve slavery."

285

"Nor did I."

"I joined to protect my home from hostile invaders."

"I think that describes most of us," nodded Lee.

"Southern independence has become a goal I cherish, sir, but in all frankness, slavery is something I don't give a damn about one way or the other. I've never owned a slave, nor do I have the slightest inclination to do so. None of my ancestors have ever owned a slave. None of my men have ever owned a slave. To us, this war is not about slavery!"

"I know that, Lieutenant. The British are looking at this situation from a different perspective."

"Never mind the British, sir! What about our own politicians?"

Lee could only shrug his shoulders, "This whole thing should not be in their hands," he sighed. "I will say this, Lieutenant, yesterday I made a promise to you and to that boy who died in your arms. I haven't forgotten it, and I'll do everything in my power to keep it."

"I know you will, sir. To be honest I think I have more faith in you than in any man or institution on earth."

"Now, now, Lieutenant," Lee smiled self-consciously and glanced away. "It's to an all-powerful and all-loving Providence that we all owe our faith."

"I haven't lost my faith in Him, General. Believe me."

"There is one more matter I'd like to discuss with you." He paused a moment, put on his glasses, adjusted them and proceeded to search the top of his table, which was strewn with paperwork.

"Ah! Here it is!" he smiled as he lifted a large envelope from beneath a stack of papers. "It seems to me you deserve a furlough, Lieutenant, both you and the rest of Stonewall's Brigade."

"That would be fine, sir! Just fine indeed!"

"It's a sixty day furlough." noted Lee as he handed the orders to Reilly.

"Sixty days?" gasped Reilly. "Are you serious, General?"

"Perfectly. There is one hitch, however. As you read

286

through the orders, you'll notice I dated it two weeks hence. I apologize for that, but I do feel it's necessary to keep everyone here for a while longer. General Halleck was able to escape Washington along with most of his garrison. He's gathering a substantial force around him in central Maryland, about twenty-five miles north of our position. I don't think he'll attack, but I do want to be sure of his intentions before I start sending people home."

"I understand perfectly, General! Dear Lord, the boys are going to love this! Thank you, sir! I don't know what else to say!"

"Nothing else is necessary," smiled Lee as he escorted Reilly out into the warm, July night air. "A goodnight to you, Lieutenant."

"And you, sir." Reilly came to attention, saluted, and started back to his camp.

Robert E. Lee's prediction concerning the possibility of a protracted stalemate proved to be accurate on all fronts, save one. In Maryland, Halleck did nothing. In Tennessee, Thomas remained quiet. In the Bermuda Hundred, Butler would not budge. In Georgia, however, the same could not be said. Sherman was convinced he could take Atlanta, and to that end he continued to push Johnston across Georgia. On the seventeenth of July, impatient with Johnston's inability to cope with Sherman, President Davis replaced him with John Bell Hood, a questionable choice at best. Hood fared little better and the fall of Atlanta loomed as a distinct possibility.

On all other fronts, the two sides were locked in a stalemate. From the Union point of view, the lack of activity could be traced to the problem of unified command. The Union ship of state was adrift, with neither a captain nor navigator to set her course. Lincoln was a prisoner, as were Secretary of War, Stanton; Secretary of the Navy, Gideon Welles; the Attorney General, Edward Bates; and the Postmaster, Montgomery Blair. The Vice President, Hannibal Hamlin, had escaped to Baltimore, along with the Secretary of the

A SOUTHERN YARN

Treasury, Simon P. Chase; Secretary of State, William H. Seward; and the Secretary of the Interior, John Usher. From Balitmore, they moved to New York City wherein they established a temporary capital, pending the recapture of Washington.

Unfortunately, though they could call New York a capital, their makeshift government could barely function. Vice President Hamlin was asked to assume the powers of the Presidency during Lincoln's absence. He flatly refused, citing the lack of constitutional authorization for such a step. No one else was willing to step forward, and the government lapsed into stagnation.

Acting on his own initiative, Seward opened a line of communication with Richmond, hoping to arrange some sort of prisoner transfer which would include Lincoln.

Lacking any single authority to give them direction, the Union field commanders were left to their own devices. Aside from Sherman, most of them chose to do nothing.

As for Lincoln, he had become a quasi-permanent resident of the Confederate White House in Richmond. No less a facility would do for the incarceration of the President of the United States. On several occasions, he was approached about negotiations, but nothing of a serious nature ever took place.

For the South, the euphoric mood of June and early July began to fade as the year approached August and Sherman approached Atlanta. Many people were beginning to despair of an outright victory over the North, this despite the fact they held the Union capital and its President. Pressure began to mount for some sort of negotiated settlement.

On the tenth of August, 1864, Jefferson Davis acceded to the popular desire for talks. To this end, he summoned Robert E. Lee from Maryland to serve as a technical advisor during negotiations. He planned to start with Lincoln himself.

Lincoln received Davis' message concerning another possible meeting and decided to accept it — albeit reluctantly.

The passing of time had actually served to elevate his mood, raising it from the pits of virtual despair in which he wallowed right after his capture to a place somewhere in the middle of the spectrum. Though he had been denied any information about the war for several weeks, he still had a fair idea of where things stood. The Rebels held Washington, but he doubted their ability to move at will through the North. In this his calculations were correct. The Union blockade could only grow stronger, increasing its stranglehold on the South. Sherman was in Georgia; heading hopefully toward Atlanta. Kentucky and Tennessee, along with much of Louisiana, Alabama and Mississippi were being occupied by Union troops. Texas and Arkansas were both cut off from the rest of the Confederacy.

"Indeed," thought Lincoln. "If the Rebels want to bargain, I'll be happy to oblige them, and I intend to do so from a position of strength, prisoner or no."

Lee arrived in Richmond on the twelfth of August, and found the capital alive with activity. Everywhere he went people swarmed around him, eager to hear stories of his battles against Grant and his capture of Washington. Finally, he was able to reach the Davis residence and some degree of privacy. When he entered Davis' study, he found the President standing by an open window, enjoying the cooling effects of a gentle breeze coming off the James to waft softly through his curtains.

"Good afternoon, Mr. President," he said calmly.

Davis turned at once, appearing startled for a moment, but quickly shedding that look.

"Ah, General! So very good to see you!" He crossed the room to shake Lee's hand. "Your presence during these discussions will be immensely valuable to our cause."

"I don't see how, Mr. President," demurred Lee. "I am but a mere soldier. The political world is not one in which I feel particularly comfortable."

"I understand, sir," nodded Davis. "Yet, these talks will center on several issues, many of them of a military nature."

A SOUTHERN YARN

"Whatever service I may offer is yours."

"Excellent! Please relax and rest from your journey. We will meet with Mr. Lincoln tomorrow morning."

"Very well," replied Lee. "By the way, where is President Lincoln?"

"On the very top floor. He and his wife share one of our rooms — under guard of course."

"Of course," smiled Lee as he bid goodbye to the President and turned to leave so as to spend the rest of the day and night with his own family.

The thirteenth brought a mixed bag of news from Georgia. General Hood had yet to demonstrate an ability to stop Sherman, but his dispatches were full of promise. Davis resolved to put the best possible face on the matter and sent for Lincoln. At half-past nine in the morning, Lee arrived, accompanied only by Colonel Taylor. They gathered about a large, round mahogany table in the President's study. Here began the negotiations which would ultimately bring about an end to America's Civil War.

President Davis was first to speak. "President Lincoln, I am of the opinion we've wasted enough time," he declared firmly. "This fratricidal war must end, and the power to end it rests in our hands. Shall we attempt it?"

"You give me too much credit, President Davis. As you know all too well, I am but a humble prisoner, hardly in a position to negotiate a just peace."

"On the contrary," argued Davis. "Despite your status as a captive, you are still the President of the United States. The Federal Constitution is rather silent about dealing with such an unusual situation. No one has the legal authority to replace you. Vice President Hamlin refuses to even consider it. For better or worse, you are still President of the United States. No one but you can negotiate a treaty with us."

"Perhaps, but to write such a treaty would simply be an exercise in futility. It would never receive the necessary two-thirds majority in the Senate. I believe you are wasting your time, Mr. Davis."

"I think not," retorted the Confederate leader. "For starters, we hold several of those senators prisoner like yourself. Others were killed trying to flee Washington. The United States Senate is not the obstacle you may think it is. Moreover, you have it within your power to bypass that body altogether."

"Oh?" Lincoln arched one of his bushy eyebrows.

"Let's not be coy, Mr. President. If you sign an executive order, it has the force of law and it needs no congressional approval."

"I see you've done your homework," mused Lincoln.

"Not much was needed. As you may recall, I once served in the United States government."

"Of course," Lincoln nodded glumly.

"Moreover, you will note the absence of any formal declaration of war against the Confederate States of America."

"Such a declaration would acknowledge the existence of your Confederacy," countered Lincoln. "It has always been our position that you don't exist — legally . . . as a nation."

"I understand your reasoning," nodded Davis, pausing to sip water from a glass. "Yet the fact remains: no formal state of war exists between us. That leaves the power to end the fighting in the hands of two men, you and me. Do we accept the responsibility which has been thrust upon us, or do we continue to stand idly by while our countrymen kill one another?"

"Put to me on such terms, I can hardly see where I have much choice in the matter."

"I'd hoped you would see it that way," said Davis calmly. "Shall we talk?"

Talk they did. All that day and the next. In fact, their discussions continued until August passed from the calendar and September was upon them. Their efforts bore no fruit. The war seemed no closer to an end.

As for military operations, stalemate was the order of the day everywhere except Georgia, and here the news was all bad for the South. Sherman continued on the offensive and the defense of Atlanta was fast disintegrating. On the third of September, Davis' worst fears were realized. The fair city of Atlanta fell to the Union invaders. Feigning illness, Davis cancelled the talks scheduled for the fourth, using this time to devise yet another strategy for dealing with the pugnacious Sherman.

It was only logical that he consult with General Lee; and by way of showing how much he valued the Commander's opinion, it was Davis who made the brief cross-town trip to Lee's home, rather than the General calling on the President.

"Hood has failed us completely," complained Davis as he seated himself in the parlour with a cup of coffee. "Truth be known, I'm at my wit's end. Who in Georgia can stop Sherman?"

"There are numerous qualified officers in the Army of Tennessee," replied Lee. "Yet I am not overly familiar with any of them, and would therefore be loathe to make recommendations from among their number."

"What am I to do?" pressed Davis. "We cannot give Sherman free reign to roam at will through our heartland!"

"What of Longstreet?" pressed Lee.

"Longstreet?"

"He's from Georgia. A fact which would not go unnoticed among the soldiers in Hood's Army. Hood himself can be reassigned to me. I will place him at the head of a division, a level of command more suited to his talents."

"The idea has possibilities," mused Davis, cupping his chin with one hand.

"You will recall Chickamauga, Mr. President," continued Lee. "It was Longstreet who engineered our victory there. If he had been placed in charge of the Army of Tennessee immediately after Chickamauga, Sherman would not have reached Atlanta, much less taken it."

"Hindsight, General. Moreover, Longstreet failed miserably at Knoxville not long after Chickamauga."

"He was given an impossible task to accomplish with far too few men," argued Lee.

"Perhaps."

"Mr. President, I am not one to inject myself into personality conflicts, but I believe General Bragg bore some degree of animosity toward Peter Longstreet, and I feel General Bragg should shoulder at least some of the responsibility for Knoxville. Longstreet would be perfect for the command of our forces in Georgia. He carries my very highest recommendation."

"All right," Davis relented with a sigh. "I'll send for Hood. You may inform General Longstreet of his promotion and transfer. I should like to see him on a train south within twenty-four hours."

"Very good, Mr. President. I'll cable Silver Spring at once. Rest assured you'll not regret this decision."

*   *   *   *

As Lee and Davis were concluding their discussion, Abraham Lincoln was pacing to and fro across his room, very much like a caged lion. He paused near a window overlooking a street below. He yawned and stretched his lanky frame, his fingers very nearly touching the ceiling overhead. Glancing outside the window, his eyes caught sight of a large crowd of people gathering on a street corner close by. The object of their attention appeared to be a young boy who was hawking newspapers. His curiosity aroused, Lincoln directed his attention toward the crowd, and was soon awarded for his patience.

"Extra," cried the boy. "Read about it here! Atlanta falls to Sherman! Read all about it! Get your paper right here!"

Lincoln stood back from the window momentarily stunned. Had he heard correctly? If so, Atlanta was now in Union hands. A smile crept slowly across his face. "So . . ." he mused softly. "Tecumseh is still on the move. Good news . . . good news indeed!"

Two days passed before Davis could bring himself to initiate another round of talks with Lincoln. No doubt he regretted this move within moments of the opening words, "It appears you are no longer holding all the cards," Lincoln was quick to take the verbal offensive.

"How's that?" Davis struggled to control the sinking feeling in his stomach.

"No need to be coy, Mr. Davis," smiled Lincoln. "I am aware of the recent events in Georgia. I know Sherman has taken Atlanta."

"How . . .?"

A puzzled, painful expression appeared on Davis' face.

"The paperboy out on the corner," chuckled Lincoln. "He's a very good salesman, but you really should have taken the precaution to make sure I heard nothing of what he had to say."

Davis sat down at the table, his shoulders slumping noticeably, "I suppose too much freedom of the press is not such a good thing after all."

"That might be described as one of the weaknesses of your Confederacy," agreed Lincoln.

"Still," retorted Davis as he straightened his posture. "Individual freedom remains a cornerstone of this Confederacy's foundation."

"How do you reconcile that statement with the institution of slavery?"

"How did the United States make the same claims for the last seventy years?"

"A valid point," nodded Lincoln, "And one to which we might return at a later date."

The Federal President suddenly found himself buoyed by a newly reborn confidence. "As for now, I believe you came to talk of peace, but with Sherman's recent success I can't say I'm inclined to cooperate. I prefer to take a wait and see approach."

Davis was frustrated, to say the least, but he did his level best to mask his emotions, "Very well," he sighed. "I suppose I would be of a like mind if I were in your shoes. However, let me point out one thing. The loss of Atlanta can be traced to inferior leadership on the part of Generals' Johnston and Hood. I've already taken steps to alleviate that problem. Hood has been relieved of his command. General Longstreet now commands the Army of Tennessee."

"A wise choice," smiled Lincoln. "Though it remains to be seen whether he will prove a match for Sherman. Do keep me posted."

There is little one could describe as significant in Willoughby, Georgia, a tiny hamlet some twenty miles to the southeast of Atlanta. Its population barely exceeded seventy souls, and the war had already claimed a fair number of these. On the 18th of September, 1864, the Civil War came home to this isolated farming region, blazing the name of Willoughby into the pages of history forever. Here, William Tecumseh Sherman squared off against Peter Longstreet, fully expecting to drive him from the field as he had Johnston and Hood so often. It was not to be. Once again, Lee's "Old Warhorse" proved his uncanny ability to hold a position. After a fierce, day-long battle, Sherman recoiled sharply, the unfamiliar taste of defeat lingering in his mouth. Nearby, ten thousand of his proud soldiers lay dead or wounded on the field of battle. The Union thrust toward southern Georgia was stopped cold. After weighing his options, Sherman chose the only realistic alternative. His army limped back into Atlanta to lick its wounds and ponder the future.

To describe Jefferson Davis as overjoyed by this latest turn of events would be to understate the case. Moreover, he moved swiftly to capitalize on Longstreet's victory to spark the stalled negotiations with his Federal counterpart. Several newspapers were obtained, not only from southern cities, but also from Baltimore, Philadelphia, Chicago, New York and Boston, all to assure Lincoln of the validity of Longstreet's triumph over Sherman. Since it took time for his agents in the North to obtain and deliver newspapers, September was nearly over before he could confront Lincoln with solid evidence. A crestfallen Lincoln could only sigh in frustration as the truth became apparent.

A SOUTHERN YARN

"A good deal of time has passed since the encounter at Willoughby," observed Lincoln. "For all I know Sherman may already have resumed the offensive."

"I'm afraid not," returned Davis. "He hasn't budged from Atlanta and his cavalry is finding it increasingly difficult to maintain his line of supply back into Tennessee. In all honesty, the situation has developed into a stalemate just as it has on every other front. Now, Sir, may I suggest to you that we can either allow it to continue like this ad infinitum, or accept the responsibility which rests on both our shoulders and put an end to this fratricidal madness."

"I have a responsibility to save the Union," huffed Lincoln.

"We are not destroying your Union, Mr. President. We have merely removed ourselves from it. The United States will endure, indeed it will probably continue to grow, but it will do so without us. You and I have the power to bring peace to our respective nations. Should we turn our backs on peace, we will one day find ourselves having to justify our decisions before God. I am willing to talk, Mr. President. If we make the effort, perhaps we'll find common ground."

"Talk, Mr. Davis? or dictate?"

"I believe I said TALK, Sir, and by that I meant negotiate."

"Which implies a give and take, a willingness to be flexible."

"On both our parts."

"Very well," sighed Lincoln. "We'll talk, but not today. I think we should each draw up a list of . . . shall we say desires? My vision of a peace as opposed to yours. From such a starting point perhaps we may one day arrive at this common ground you spoke of."

"Excellent!" beamed Davis. "I'll have writing materials sent to you at once! We can exchange our views tomorrow over lunch."

"Agreed," nodded Lincoln, "Though I think your smile may vanish when you see what I envision from all this."

"Probably," shrugged Davis. "No one said it would be easy, but at least we'll be taking the long-awaited first step."

Davis could scarcely contain his excitement over the possibility of serious talks with the leader of the United States. Nevertheless, when the appointed time arrived, he presented himself to Lincoln as the very picture of composure. The two men sat opposite one another at a small round table. A somewhat sparse lunch of cheese and bread was served, but neither man paid much attention to the food.

"May I see your proposals first?" queried Lincoln.

"Certainly," Davis nodded, eager to be underway.

He handed Lincoln a small packet of papers which the latter opened and laid out on the table.

Here Lincoln paused, perhaps for dramatic effect. After laying out the proposals, he reached into a vest pocket for his reading glasses. These were an older pair of inferior design and prescription, but the Union Chief Executive would have to make do. His good glasses were at the bottom of the Potomac. Deliberately taking his time, Lincoln pulled a tattered handkerchief from his inside coat pocket and proceeded to wipe each lens with meticulous care.

Finally, Davis could stand it no longer.

"Excuse me."

Lincoln stopped what he was doing and looked over at Davis.

"Should this pace continue they'll be serving us supper before we exchange our first word."

"So?" replied Lincoln with a curt smile. "Time seems to be the one thing I have plenty of."

"Then perhaps you'd be good enough to allow me the same opportunity with your own proposals."

"Not just yet," Lincoln demurred. "All of this shall be done in its proper sequence. Let's discuss these first."

"Fine! Stop wiping those confounded glasses and read!"

Lincoln's smile was barely noticeable, but it was definitely an indication of satisfaction. His opponent was obviously rattled — a good sign. He finished cleaning the glasses, put his handkerchief away and picked up page one.

A full twenty minutes passed before he finished reading, by which time Davis had just about reached the limits of his patience.

"Interesting." mused Lincoln, dropping the last page and pushing himself away from the table, scraping the legs of his chair against the wooden floor as loudly as possible.

"You want us to recognize the legality of secession per se, then acknowledge not only the secession of the members of the Confederate states, but also of Kentucky and Missouri?"

"Correct," nodded Davis. "Both of these states are represented in our Congress."

"A fact which is of little matter to me!" huffed Lincoln. "Both states are primarily in our control! And what is this about Maryland?"

"Maryland is a state with a strong southern tradition. Her people should have the option to either stay or remain in your Union!"

"Out of the question! Shall we lift Washington, D. C. into the air and deposit it in Pennsylvania? Should the capital of the United States be located inside the Confederacy?"

"A logistical problem of little importance to me!" retorted Davis. "My concern lies with the people of Maryland!"

"Regardless of your so-called concerns, Maryland will have no choice in the matter! Of that you can rest well assured!"

Davis could find no reply to this and so he struggled to retain what was left of his own composure. One thing became apparent. No constructive dialogue would take place in so acrimonious an atmosphere. The entire discussion would have to be toned down lest the opportunity be lost.

"You asked for proposals," he said in a surprisingly calm manner. "You have them. All of this is open to negotiation, such is the purpose of our meeting. Shouting will accomplish little, if anything. You haven't even commented on my other suggestions."

"You're referring to the bilateral talks for the purpose

of demilitarizing our borders?"

"And for re-establishing commercial ties."

"The idea holds its share of promise," submitted Lincoln.

"Why don't be both refrain from further argument until I've had a chance to read over your ideas?"

"Very well," agreed Lincoln, picking up his own packet and handing it across.

Davis took it, removed the papers and balanced them in his hand.

"Weighty material," he remarked.

"Just read it," said Lincoln in a voice which resembled something of a growl.

Fully intending to take every bit as much time as Lincoln had, Davis began to study the first page. His intentions were immediately forgotten.

"Impossible!" he railed. "Absolutely out of the question! Do you think we've come this far just to free the slaves at your request? Nonsense!"

"It's either that or the war goes on. I cannot go home empty-handed!"

"Then you'll be here for a good while!"

"You want independence. I can grant it, but not without something in return! The people of the North must not think they shed so much blood for nothing! Freedom for the southern slaves will at least give this effort some meaning."

"Not from our point of view!"

Lincoln shrugged, "Do as you will, but I will not sign any agreement which leaves the Union nothing but dead sons to mourn."

The two men glanced angrily at one another for several minutes in stone silence.

Davis, realizing there was little to be gained by continuing on this note, spoke next.

"I propose we adjourn for today. Each of us needs more time to study these ideas. Perhaps we can schedule another round on the morrow."

"I don't see why not. I haven't anyplace else to go. There

don't seem to be any pressing engagements on my schedule for tomorrow."

"Very well. Around noon?"

"I'll be waiting."

Feeling thoroughly depressed, Davis sent messages to the homes of Robert E. Lee and Judah Benjamin, the Secretary of State; requesting a meeting that same evening. Both men agreed and since Lincoln was being held at the Confederate White House, they decided to gather at the Lee residence.

Not long after dusk, President Davis and Secretary Benjamin arrived at Lee's home within minutes of each other. The General, himself, greeted them and escorted them to a rectangular table in the dining room. A plate of sweetcakes had been prepared and a pitcher of cold water was there to help wash them down. After all three men had seated themselves, General Lee gestured toward the cakes.

"Would you like a bite to eat, Mr. President? I apologize for the simplicity of our fare, Sir. Unfortunately, it's all we have at the moment."

"No apology is needed, General. My own pantries aren't exactly overflowing. I hope you won't mind if I pass right now. I'm really not in the mood to eat anything."

Lee nodded and glanced in Benjamin's direction.

The secretary plucked three cakes from the plate and poured himself a glass of water.

"Mr. President," Lee spoke again. "You don't seem to be in the best of humor."

"I suppose not," agreed Davis. "Quite frankly, I'm feeling rather demoralized at the present time."

"I assume this mood you're in is a result of today's encounter with Lincoln?" Benjamin spoke for the first time.

"Exactly," sighed Davis wearily.

"In other words," continued the Secretary of State, "the first round of negotiations didn't get off to a rousing start."

"On the contrary, it was far too rousing. As soon as we exchanged proposals, it degenerated into a shouting match."

"Unfortunate," said Lee.

"Would you prefer to have us involved?" wondered Benjamin.

"Yes and no. I want the negotiations themselves to be a face to face encounter between myself and Lincoln, yet I find myself in need of assistance. The proposals I advanced need to be reworked. More importantly, his ideas must be evaluated and responded to. This is why I asked to meet with the two of you."

"I'm at your disposal," Benjamin was first to reply.

"As am I," added Lee. "But, let me mention, as I have on previous occasions, I am but a soldier. This game of politics is not one in which I feel particularly competent."

"Well," smiled Davis. "You might want to get used to the idea of politics. The present level of your popularity in the South establishes you as the front runner for my job when all this is over."

"Assuming we achieve our independence," Benjamin remarked softly.

"Exactly," concurred Davis. "And to that end, shall we begin by restructuring my original proposals?"

This didn't take long, as few modifications were really needed in this regard. The three men decided to yield on the issue of Missouri and Maryland. These states could remain in the Union despite their southern character. On the matter of Kentucky, they decided to stand firm. Kentucky's secession would have to be recognized. One item did they add to the list of southern demands. The region known to the North as West Virginia would be returned to the Confederacy, becoming once again part of Virginia itself. This would establish the Potomac and Ohio Rivers as borders between the two nations.

"That wasn't so difficult," sighed Benjamin as he poured himself about a third of a glass of warm water.

"Revamping our ideas wasn't the challenge which worried me," said Davis. "Responding to Lincoln's will not be so easy."

"Then let's hear them," insisted Lee. "There's little to be

301

gained by wasting time wringing our hands."

"Very well. President Lincoln will agree to our independence, but only if the slaves are freed. He will not be party to our agreement otherwise. As he put it, he cannot return to the North empty-handed. He must have something to show his countrymen to prove they didn't sacrifice so much for no gain whatsoever."

"The eternal sticking point," noted Benjamin.

"So it seems," sighed Davis. "Yet, how do we respond? He knows we have the upper hand militarily, but this doesn't faze him in the slightest."

"Because this upper hand you speak of is an illusion." argued Lee. "The present stalemate does nothing but buy us time. We are still blockaded. The bulk of our country suffers beneath Union occupation. If we allow this affair to continue as a war of attrition, we will ultimately lose."

"We have their capital! We've captured the most important people of their government!" Davis' anger began to flash once again.

"Also an illusion!" countered Lee forcefully. "The capital is merely a city. Most of their government escaped and is now in New York. As for Lincoln and our other high-level prisoners, let me remind you, Mr. President; this is an election year in the United States. In a matter of months, the Union will have a new president, and we could be facing warfare on an even more terrible scale!"

Davis said nothing, but the expression on his face said a great deal.

Here Benjamin interrupted, "Prolonged war is not a prospect we should seriously entertain, Mr. President. Eventually we will lose."

"I'm not altogether ignorant of that possibility."

"Then concessions on our part are certainly warranted," pressed Lee.

"Are you suggesting we agree to abolish slavery?"

"I'm saying we have little in the way of a choice! Even if we were to win a war of attrition, our independence would

302

gain us little. We would be a pariah among nations! No European country will recognize us. What future would we be leaving our children?"

"I hear you, General!" huffed Davis. "I just don't see how it can be done!"

"In some ways it's already underway," observed Benjamin.

"Explain." Davis shot an angry glance in the direction of his Secretary of State.

"As General Lee clearly noted, most of the Confederacy is in Union hands. We really have no control over the future of slavery in those regions."

"True," Davis agreed.

"Moreover, we are currently in the process of recruiting black men into the army — with the possibility of freedom as their reward."

"Also true."

"Then I suggest we continue this process to its logical conclusion."

"Very easy to say," Davis replied sardonically. "How do you suggest we go about this? I am a slave owner. Perhaps you could convince me, but who would convince all the others? Do you want to see the Confederacy fragmented?"

"The Confederacy is already fragmented," said Lee. "The United States Army has done a thorough job in that regard."

"Mr. President," Benjamin took a deep breath as he prepared to make a point. "Where is your plantation?"

"Mississippi, as you well know."

"Could you go there now? Leave today, spend several weeks relaxing at home?"

"Of course not! The Federals seized it sometime ago!"

"And your slaves?"

"I suppose they've been freed. I imagine some may have taken ranks with the Yankees."

"Exactly — and the same could be said for thousands of slave owners across the South. Tell me, what would you say to compensation?"

"What are you getting at?"

"Compensation! How would you like to be paid for all the slaves you no longer have?"

Davis leaned closer to Benjamin, his curiousity definitely aroused, "What exactly do you have in mind?"

"Though it may ultimately prove an illusion, we currently hold the upper hand in the military arena. I suggest we use it to bring this war to a swift and certain conclusion on terms favorable to our primary cause — namely the independence of this Confederacy. The South has suffered terrible damage at the hands of northern invaders, we are certainly due some sort of war reparations, don't you think?"

"I do indeed!" A smile began to form on Davis' face.

"Reparations in the form of gold and Federal currency. Perhaps, even an investment in Confederate bonds."

"I'm beginning to like this idea."

"I don't think we should settle for anything less than three times the market value of every slave in the Confederacy. The government will keep one-third of this in the treasury, which hopefully will stabilize the value of our own currency and curb inflation."

"And the rest?"

"It will be distributed to the slave owners as compensation for their freed slaves — at double the market value."

"What if certain slave owners don't go along with the idea?"

"I've given a great deal of thought to this, Mr. President. The constitution of the Confederacy, like that of the United States, provides the government with the power of eminent domain."

"Yes, but historically the power has been used to take private land in order to build public roads. I don't see how it applies to slavery."

"To be precise, Mr. President, the power of eminent domain gives the government the right to appropriate private property for public use. The philosophy behind this concept is that in some situations, the public good outweighs any private interest. Slaves are considered property, are they not?"

"Obviously."

"Is not the survival and independence of this nation of vital importance? The ultimate public good?"

"One could certainly advance such an argument."

"Then exercise the power of eminent domain, Mr. President."

"I can assure you the complete support of the Army, Mr. President," added Lee.

"We can work out the logistical details later, Mr. President. Essentially, each slave owner will receive double the market value for his slaves. The slaves will be freed upon receipt of that money."

"I think it might work," nodded Davis, feeling very satisfied with the results of their conversation.

"It might indeed," said General Lee approvingly.

"But I'm not without my reservations," Davis voiced an expression of doubt. "What happens to the slaves? The former slaves. Once freed, what becomes of them? If they end up wandering in gangs of vagabonds, there will be chaos!"

"That's the beauty of this idea, Mr. President. Ending the war in this fashion, on our terms, allows us to develop a program for easing the slaves into freedom. The money paid to us by the North will stabilize our economy overnight. Freed slaves will require jobs, will they not? The jobs are certainly available. Most of the South needs to be rebuilt. Moreover, those who will be in the position of employers will have the money to pay salaries. Again, let me caution you to consider the alternatives. If the Federals win, we'll be at their mercy. A number of the more radical Republicans in the United States Congress are proposing ideas which will be disastrous in the long run."

"I know. I've read some of their commentaries in the Federal Press. They pretend to be friends to the black man. They speak of creating a tropical paradise here in the South where former slaves will rule the former slave owners. Their true motive is to keep the Negroes in the South. They fear a massive influx of former slaves into their cities."

"Precisely," agreed Benjamin. "If we follow my suggestion, slavery will end, but we will be in control of the postslavery era."

"To preserve slavery in everything but name?"

"No, though some will interpret it in such a fashion. Freedom comes with responsibilities. Education will be important for the freed slaves, along with jobs, or land on which to farm. I imagine some of them will leave and migrate to the North. Others will drift into our own cities, but many will stay where they have lived their entire lives."

"Ironic, isn't it?" voiced Davis. "We're going to win this miserable war, but in the process we'll be sparking a huge upheaval in our way of life."

"An upheaval which is inevitable, Mr. President. No matter who wins. If the Yankees win we'll be treated as conquered people. Our lands will be occupied. The southern states will be reduced to the status of colonies. At least this way we remain in control of our own destinies."

"There will be nothing easy about this," contemplated Lee. "The Negroes, even when freed, will find themselves on the bottom rung of society's ladder. They will not be content to languish there forever. They will want political equality, and I foresee a time when they will organize and fight for it."

"No doubt," agreed Benjamin. "I think that's a situation future generations will have to solve. We are all products of our time. You, General, are a soldier. The President and I are politicians, perhaps hoping to be remembered as statesmen. None of us are engineers of society. We can't pretend to know all the answers to the various problems we are about to face. All we can do is establish the framework for these Confederate States, to survive intact. Our descendants will have to do the rest. Who knows? It may take another hundred years or more to solve the racial situation to everyone's satisfaction."

"A hundred years at the very least," concurred Davis. "But, as Secretary Benjamin pointed out, this Confederacy will emerge intact, and from the outset that has been our prime objective.

Gentlemen, I thank you. We've accomplished a great deal this night. In the morning I shall present these proposals to President Lincoln. I have a good feeling about this . . . a very good feeling."

The instincts of Jefferson Davis turned out to be something of an omen, and a good one at that. Abraham Lincoln studied the amended Confederate propositions and agreed to them. The two men signed a tentative truce agreement that very night, though another week passed before a more formalized, detailed agreement could be hammered out. The sticking points here were the exact amount of money which was to change hands and the method of payment.

On the 25th of September, the terms of the truce were released to the Southern Press. As expected there was a loud protest from the most ardent of the slaveholders, but it was quite literally drowned out by the spontaneous burst of joy and relief from the majority of the southern population.

On the 27th of September, 1864, Abraham Lincoln was escorted to Washington, D. C. along with all other Federal officials who had been taken captive upon the fall of that fair city. Lincoln proved to be a man of his word. On the 5th of October, he released the terms of the executive agreement he had signed with the Confederate States of America. Slavery was ending. The secession of the Confederate States was recognized. The long and horrible war between the states was at an end.

Though the war was officially ending, the people of the South resisted the urge to celebrate. There were still far too many blue uniforms to be seen on southern lands. On the 21st of October, the last of these Federal soldiers crossed the Ohio River. When word of this final departure reached President Davis in Richmond, he took pen to paper. A thousand thoughts raced frantically through his head as his shaking hand attempted to write. The blockade was gone. Already scores of heavily laden ships were making their way toward the ports of the Confederacy. New Orleans was free, as were Vicksburg and Atlanta, Memphis and Knoxville. Pausing to steady his hand, Davis took several deep breaths, then returned to the executive proclamation taking shape on the desk before him. At last he finished, and though it seemed hours in writing, the document was scarcely three paragraphs in length, plain and simple. The impact of its words would not be lost on the people of the South. History would record it as the proclamation of Southern Independence, and the 21st of October became the official Independence Day of the Confederacy, a national holiday of thanksgiving.

Davis rose from his seat and stepped out of his office, handing the Proclamation to a waiting courier.

"I want criers reading this in every city, town and village of the Confederacy," he announced firmly.

"Very well, Mr. President."

This done, Davis walked out onto the wide veranda of his Richmond home. Two soldiers awaited by the flagpole some twenty yards away, the Stars and Bars folded neatly in the arms of one. All of this had been prearranged by Davis for maximum symbolic effect.

"Raise the colors," came the Presidential order.

The banner unfurled slowly as it made its way to the top of the pole. Mother nature made her own contribution at this point with the appearance of a stiff breeze. Very quickly the flag was flying proudly, high in the air, its colors gleaming in the early afternoon sun.

By this time, a substantial crowd of people had gathered to witness the event, and for them Davis had these words: "Friends! Countrymen! Today, for the first time, our flag has been raised over a free and sovereign country. On this day, the Confederacy is taking her rightful place in the community of this planet's nations! Give thanks, fellow citizens! God has truly smiled upon us!"

EPILOGUE

Two days following the Proclamation, the Army of Northern Virginia reduced its rolls to a quarter of their wartime strength. Seth Reilly and his command were in Gordon's corps at the time, camped astride a series of hills just west of Culpeper, a position which afforded them a magnificent view of the Blue Ridge Mountains. By mid-morning of the day, Reilly and his men had been mustered out of the service. Reilly gathered them for a final farewell before they scattered in the directions of their respective homes. They couldn't have asked for a more beautiful day to say good-bye. The air was crisp, clean and cool, delighting their nostrils with the varied scents of autumn. The sky itself was a deep breathtaking shade of blue. Off to the west, so close one could almost touch them, rose the peaks and knolls of the Blue Ridge, their foliage ablaze in the colors of fall. Reilly would long remember that scene: his men gathered before a silhouette of yellow, scarlet and orange, which stood tall against a stunning sky.

"Well, fellas," he paused to clear the lump fast forming in his throat. "I guess this is it."

"You goin' back to that school, Professor?" this from Jonas.

"I reckon. If they'll have me."

"They'd be crazy not to." volunteered Ox.

"Thanks," smiled Reilly. "Now for the hard part," he sighed, taking yet another deep gulp of air to calm his emotions. "I must say goodbye to a bunch of guys who've been my family for the last three and a half years."

"Don't be gettin' all sentimental on us," quipped Corporal Simmons. "You're liable to make us cry."

"You're right," agreed Reilly, his voice on the edge of breaking. "In any event, we'll see each other again. All of you have my address, and I have each of yours. Stay in touch. Jonas, you'd best learn to write, boy. I want to hear from you."

"I'll do my best, Professor. I'll never forget you. I promise you that much."

"Good," Reilly flashed the lad a quick grin. "See that you don't."

Several moments passed in silence as they waited for their lieutenant to gather his thoughts.

"You all have helped make history," he declared at last. "You fought against overwhelming, seemingly insurmountable odds. You never lost heart. You never despaired, even when matters were at their darkest. What you have accomplished will amaze generations yet unborn. Take pride in yourselves. For your country, you won independence. For yourselves, you've earned the respect of the entire world."

"You shore do have a pretty way of sayin' things, Professor."

"Then hear this. Our job has only just begun. Most of the South lies in ruins. It will take a lifetime to rebuild what this war has destroyed. Remember who you are and what you're capable of doing. Dive into it, dear friends, and God bless each and every one of you! Off with you now! The future awaits."

One by one they filed pass Reilly. Some shook his hand; others wouldn't be content with anything less than a vigorous bear hug. Whitt Simmons was last in line.

"Words fail me," said the corporal.

"Your farm's only a couple of days from Williamsburg," replied Reilly. "We'll be seein' a good bit of each other. Count on it."

"I am." Whitt gave Reilly a hug, stepped back, saluted and started for home.

*   *   *   *

Travelling by rail, carriage and foot, Reilly found himself approaching his modest home on the outskirts of Williamsburg some forty-eight hours after bidding farewell to his soldiers. He hardly reached the front porch when he heard a boyish voice cry out from inside.

"It's Pa!"

Out they came, both boys and their mother, literally stumbling over themselves to be first to embrace the returning warrior.

There they stood, the two boys hugging their father's torso, Irene Reilly's arms wrapped tightly about her husband's neck, and the lieutenant wishing he had two more sets of arms. This time there was no holding back the tears.

Irene pulled back and gazed at her husband through tear-filled eyes. "I almost can't believe this!" she sobbed. "Is this really you? Are you really home?"

"You best be believin' it! This is not a ghost you're holdin' onto, and I can't wait to taste a hot, home-cooked meal!"

Reilly was wrestling with a host of new emotions. As always, the sight and touch of Irene left his knees feeling like jelly. As for his boys . . . God, how they had grown!

"Is it really true?" she wondered aloud. "Are the Yankees gone for good? Are we really free?"

Reilly pulled her close again, and his eyes darted down the lane some fifty yards to the home of a former slave family. An elderly black man, Amos Murphy by name, stood on the porch, one arm about the shoulder of his wife. His two grandchildren were clinging to his knees. The two men exchanged glances, and in their eyes one could easily read the questions they held concerning the future.

"It's true, darlin'," whispered Reilly. "I reckon we're all free."

PRODUCTION NOTES FOR THIS BOOK

The text of this book was set in Baskerville, a transitional typeface designed by John Baskerville in the eighteenth century. This type embodies the charm of the older type styles which predated it, and the exactness of the modern types, of which is was the precursor. Its openness and readability make it particularly popular as a book face.

The typesetting and job coordination was done by Willard Press, Inc., Manassas, Virginia; BookCrafters, Inc. of Fredericksburg, Virginia, did the printing and bindery, with the text run on the Cameron press, the four color cover done by offset lithography. The color separations for the cover illustration was done by Sun Crown, Inc., Washington, D.C.

The typography, hand lettering of cover and chapter initials, cover design and illustration have been done by Nancy J. Willard-Chang, with the cover concept by the author, R. W. Richards.